Dinosaurs and Prime Numbers

by TOM MORAN

First Edition: December, 2012

Cover illustration by BOB

www.bobmoran.co.uk

For Jemma

THIS IS A WORK OF FICTION.

Walton Cumberfield expresses subjective views about a variety of well known people, places and products. These views are purely an eccentricity of the character and are not shared or endorsed by the author. Any references to real people, living or dead, are purely fictitious and not intended to be taken literally or seriously.

PROLOGUE

What is your earliest memory? I can remember as far back as 1981, when I was four years old and we were living in Peterborough. I cannot recall a great deal about this time, you understand, but one event will always stick out in my mind...

I was sitting out in my sandpit, entertaining myself as best I could with an old garden bucket and the family pooper-scooper, when a most peculiar thing happened. A man jumped out of the bushes, strode across the lawn towards me, looked me furiously in the eye and shouted; "You're an idiot!"

Now, I have to admit that being only four years of age I could not readily construct a coherent argument against this criticism. In fact, as it happened, I just sat there in the sand and listened intently as he continued his verbal assault...

"You're an idiot, and everyone thinks you're an idiot and you'll always be an idiot and I hate you! You'll never amount to anything! You bloody berk!"

I remember thinking that this diatribe was largely unwarranted, but before I could question his reasoning, he turned away from me and shoved something into his mouth. Two seconds later, he disappeared in front of my very eyes.

At the time, it was the most extraordinary thing that I had ever seen. Of course, this is no longer the case. For that, dear friends, was just the beginning...

ONE

A COLD DAY IN HELLESDON

It was February again. I remember waking up much earlier than I had expected to – a surprising happenstance considering the fact that I had stayed up until three o'clock the night before drinking sherry and writing poetry (it was a Monday, after all). I pulled my feet up to my chest and shivered against the icy chill of the morning. The winter had set in good and hard that year, and my boiler was broken (again) because I had refused to pay a professional repairman and tried to fix the fault myself using PVA and Lego®.

Suddenly the door to my spare room slammed shut with a slumber-defying bang, and the sound of heavy footsteps rumbled inelegantly through the landing and down the stairs. You see, at the time I had taken in a lodger named Roger to help out with the rent and undertake a percentage of the hoovering duties. I selected him because he struck me as someone who was sensible, tidy, quiet and a good subject for poetry. Alas, I have only written one poem about Roger so far, but I am jolly pleased with it:

Roger is my lodger,
He's a tough old codger,
He's very nice, and smells of spice,
With a face like a Jammie Dodger.

I am particularly proud of my use of a simile in the last line, which makes an apt, yet somewhat unsympathetic reference to Roger's shiny red nose. I have since been informed that this is the result of damaged blood vessels caused by the alcohol addiction that also ended his marriage and cost him his job with Investacorp LTD.

I should also point out that he does not smell of spice, but I used some artistic licence here. He gave the poem 7/10.

I wrapped the duvet underneath me to form a nice little cocoon, and managed to sleep for perhaps another hour or so, during which time I had a very peculiar dream about a hooded man who chased me around Shepherd's Bush with a sword made out of breakfast.

And then my dog was barking.

And then my dog wasn't barking.

And then I woke up.

Let me tell you about my dog. He was five-years old at the time; a Nova Scotia Duck Tolling Retriever by the name of Keith Matthews. If I'm being honest (and I often am), I don't think I've ever had a more perfect companion - excepting, of course, the occasional occurrence of secret dog trumps, his late-night barking competitions with next door's alsatian, and his tendency to eat the vast majority of my post.

For a moment I wondered if Keith Matthews really was barking downstairs, or if it was just part of the dream. Then I wondered, as I wonder most mornings, why nobody had invented a way to record dreams onto a DVD and watch them back over breakfast. Perhaps, I would often hypothesise, the content of said dreams would only make partial sense to a fully conscious mind – but at least it would be more interesting than 'The Wright Stuff'.

I got out of bed and pulled on my favourite pair of trouserpants and thermal socks. *It's darn cold today*, I thought to myself. Then, for some reason, I had an overwhelming compulsion to share this thought with the rest of the world by making it my status on The Facebook:

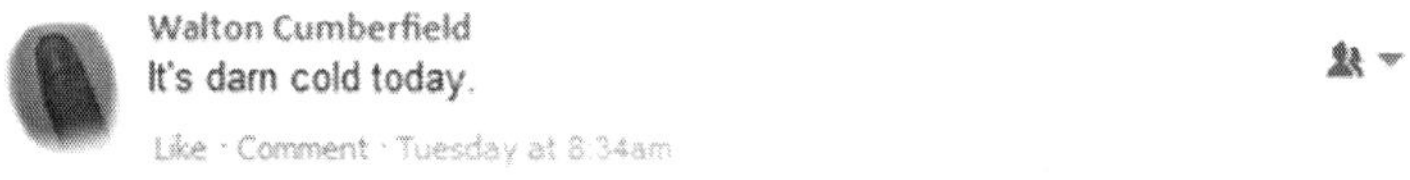

I love The Facebook. At the time in question I had somewhere around 36 'friends' and four pending requests. One of these requests was from my Great Auntie Boris who I wasn't sure about connecting with as she is obsessed with the healing power of crystals. Another was Kevin Donahue who I think went to the same school as me, although I can't be sure. The third candidate for my online attention was *CardCentre*™ who had included an enthusiastic message with their friend request but lost credibility for being more of an online retail business than a person. The final prospective e-companion was a man named "Gus Lovecroft" whose name and face I did not recognise, and I suspected may be a 'predator'.

Outside the wind was howling like a dying poodle, and I watched through my window as the morning papers flew about in the street like a journalistic blizzard. The frost had dusted the cars like icing sugar, which reminded me of the time that I was run over by a Skoda Felicia. I had walked out in front of the car with misplaced nonchalance, assuming, rather foolishly, that I would be unharmed – the TV advert having led me to believe that Skoda Felicias are made out of cake. They are not. I spent nine days in the hospital and met a nurse named Mildred, who did not want to be my girlfriend. This did not matter, of course, as I already had an on-again, off-again relationship with my postwoman, whose name was Melanie Bogg.

I picked up the sparkly scarlet envelope on my dressing table. Valentine's Day was coming up, and I wanted to make it an extra special one that year. I had decided to invite Melanie to Bannatyne's Health Club in Lowestoft because she was always saying that she wanted to lose weight, and because I thought it would make a good subject for poetry. I opened the card and re-read the message I had authored the evening before:

My dearest Mel,
I think you're swell,
Tu es une trés bonne mademoiselle.
This Valentine's,
I hope you're fine,
To come with me to Bannatyne's
(the health club in Lowestoft)

Dynamite, I thought. I was particularly proud of this poem as it included some French (for added romance) and had a good metre. Roger had insisted that the last line should be removed from the poem as it detracted from the rhythm of the rest of the piece – but I explained to him that it was an important line as it gave the words a realistic context (i.e. explained what I was getting at). Then he told me that he didn't really care and asked me not to wake him up to offer constructive criticism if I wasn't going to listen to it. Roger is of course not a writer, but an employee of Apollo's Flame and Grill who often wears a chicken costume and hands out leaflets about grilled meat. It's sad really, when you think that he used to be a Senior Marketing Planning Manager on £60k a year. He seems happy enough though, and as I keep reminding him, at least he's still in advertising...

Before getting on with my day I had taken to educating myself by reading at least two entries from *The Guinness Book of Records 2008* – an exciting book which Roger had bestowed upon me as a thoughtful gift a few weeks before. On that particular morning I learnt all about Geoff, the man with the world's largest collection of naval lint (not sure what this is – some kind of maritime military chocolate?) and Fjeza, a Taiwanese lady with the world's smallest face.

Soon after this I was skipping merrily down the stairs, invigorated by the promise of the new day and considerably more optimistic than usual about my romantic endeavours. I set the Valentine's card down on the sideboard with a view to posting it on my way to work that afternoon. I wouldn't need to address it of course, or even attach a stamp – one of the many benefits of wooing a member of the postal service.

Suddenly there was a knock on the door. My heart did a back flip as I considered the possibility that Melanie was on the other side with a parcel for me. Sometimes I would send myself an oversized parcel so that she would have to knock on the door in order to deliver it. Alas, it wasn't Melanie at all. It was Lizo from Newsround again, offering to sell me some spoons.

"Bloody Nora!" I exclaimed. "For the last time, Lizo from Newsround, I don't want to buy any of your blasted spoons!"

Lizo from Newsround pulled open his jacket and showcased his wares with bumptious aplomb.

"Just a little one?" he said. "For old time's sake..."

I frowned and shook my head. I really didn't need any spoons. I had seven.

"Come on, Walt," he said, leaning vivaciously on the doorframe. "You know how it is... We've all got to make a living somehow."

"This isn't a living!" I said. "You can't be a door-to-door spoon salesman. That isn't a thing! Nobody does that!"

He fixed me with an intensely arrogant stare. "Exactly. And that's why I have the monopoly on the market."

"It's not a market!" I yelled. "Nobody wants to buy your stupid spoons."

He raised one eyebrow. "But you did, once."

"No I didn't!" I exclaimed. "Why do you keep saying that? I have never bought a spoon from you!"

"You did," he insisted. "Last month, you bought five spoons and a ladle." He took out some kind of inventory written on the back of a choc-ice wrapper.

"No I didn't!" I yelled. "Now, go away!"

I'm sorry to say that I slammed the door in his face. I am a fairly tall man, but I have a relatively short temper, and Lizo was pushing his luck (yet again). I watched him through the frosted glass until he left, which was a full seven minutes later.

When he had gone I breathed a huge sigh of relief, and was just about to go upstairs for my morning poo when I noticed something awry on the floor by my feet. There were several hunks of paper and bubble wrap, torn to pieces in a mess of sticky saliva and orange hair. So, Melanie had already been.... and Keith Matthews had clearly been up to his old tricks again. *That bloody dog*, I thought. *When will I ever get to handle my post without fishing it out of his stools?*

Hold on a minute... Where is that bloody dog?

I went into the kitchen and looked under the table where he normally sleeps, but found only squeaky toys and torn up old newspaper (The *News of the World*, which I would buy specifically to catch his night-time accidents). *He must be up and about then*, I thought. *But why can't I hear him?* I listened for a moment longer. Nothing. Nothing at all – which was bizarre because usually Keith Matthews would make an awful racket. You see, I had lost him in the woods the previous summer, and when he eventually returned I decided it prudent to attach a small bell to his collar to give an audible indicator of his whereabouts. Despite this, I somehow managed to lose him again in October, so I thought it best to add a couple more bells. Then, when I lost him again the following March, I threw away his collar altogether and replaced it with a tambourine.

It was freezing outside, so all of the windows were closed, and if Roger had accidentally let him out, then Roger would have got him back (as Roger is very good with Keith Matthews, except on Wednesdays). Suddenly on that seemingly unremarkable February morning, I found myself with a new mystery to solve. Now, although I was quite obviously overwhelmed with concern for the wellbeing of my canine companion, I have to admit that I did feel a small buzz of excitement at the same time. I hadn't done any detective work since Roger lost his purple tank top back in November – and that case had only lasted 20 minutes since it turned out to be in the tumble drier, under some large pants. This case, on the other hand, was already proving to be a bit of a head-scratcher, and I am a rather big fan of head-scratchers.

I poured myself a steaming mug of hot blackcurrant squash and lit my pipe to make me feel like Sherlock Holmes (who famously drinks hot blackcurrant squash). Keith Matthews had gone – that much was clear. All of the windows and doors were closed and yet somehow he had managed to get out...

Perhaps someone had broken in and taken him? No – there were no signs of forced entry, and any burglar worth his salt would have noticed the blue Sylvac Pottery "bunny" on the worktop which is easily worth twice as much as Keith Matthews.

Maybe it was "take your dog to work day" at Apollo's and Roger had taken him without asking permission? No – Roger would never do that. The very idea was beyond absurd - and besides, they had held a "take your dog to work day" only a few weeks before, so it was unlikely they would hold another one until the following year.

Then I remembered a film I once saw about dinosaurs which I think was called *The Jurassic Theme Park*. Towards the end of the film, some of the nastier orange dinosaurs taught themselves how to open doors. Perhaps, I thought for a moment, Keith Matthews had also figured out how to open doors? He was, after all, a very intelligent dog... No – he wasn't *that* intelligent. And besides, why on earth would he have wanted to go outside on such a bleak winter's morning? I noted that it was so cold in the park across the road that several birds had got stuck to the icy climbing frame (it looked just like that scene from that film called *Psycho Birds*).

I didn't know how he had gotten out – but he definitely wasn't in the house, which meant that he must be somewhere *outside* the house, which meant, in turn, that I would have to leave the house in order to find him. I have to say, I didn't like the thought of that one bit. I have always hated the cold, ever since my cousin Archie shut me in a fridge for nine hours back in 1986. He is dead now, I assume, as he is not on The Facebook.

***

It was snowing outside, as the above illustration shows, so I knew that I would need to dress appropriately.

No time for my morning poo, I thought, making my way to the cupboard under the stairs. *If I'm going to find my dog then there's no time to lose.* I opened up the cupboard and pulled out an old pair of

Wellington boots, a scarf, a thick woolly jumper, and my favourite balaclava (which I am not allowed to wear in Sainsbury's).

"I am just going outside," I said, taking my telescopic walking-pole for extra stability. "I may be some time." There was no one else in the house, of course, but I thought it too good a joke to keep in my head. When I had finished laughing I picked up my Valentine's card, pushed open the front door and strode out into the cold like a heroic explorer.

Across the road, in the park, a Police Community Support Officer was attempting to pry the birds from the climbing frame with a spoon, which I assume he had bought from Lizo (from Newsround), who was sitting on a bench nearby, tucking into a Ginsters. The wind was cutting into my eyes through the hole in my balaclava, and I could already feel myself shaking so hard against the cold that my back muscles were starting to spasm.

Then my phone started to vibrate.

Well, actually it wasn't my phone. You see, I had taken to borrowing Roger's phone, since he had a smart phone and I could use it to update The Facebook while on the move. My phone is smart-casual at best, and cannot connect to interweb with three Gs or whatever it's called. I pulled Roger's phone out of my pocket and looked at the smudged, slightly cracked screen. *Mum Calling.* I pressed the green button and held it to my ear.

"Hello Mum," I said. "How's it going?"

"Roger?" she said. "You sound different."

Of course. It was *Roger's* mum. What a perfect wally I felt – my mother (Raquel Stenington) had been dead for nearly two years to the day. I quickly hung up and updated my status on The Facebook.

I walked into the centre of the park and began to call my dog's name ('Keith Matthews', 'Keith', 'Mr Matthews', 'K to the M-Unit' and any other variation I could think of). This led to a rather awkward exchange with a jogger whose name also happened to be Keith Matthews. He seemed quite annoyed that I had interrupted his morning exercise regime, but did agree to keep an eye out for any stray Nova Scotia Duck Tolling Retrievers wearing tambourine collars. His nipples stood erect against the cold like a couple of tent poles underneath his T shirt. I didn't want to notice them, but I did notice them, and then I couldn't stop noticing them.

Until I noticed somebody else.

A few yards down the path, an elderly man was sat on a bench, staring at me – his mouth gaping open like a disabled haddock. He had a matted, greying beard and his face was covered in flaky skin and blotchy sores. In his hands, on which he wore a pair of old fingerless gloves, he was holding a cup of something steaming, and using said steam to warm his cracked, scaly face. His clothes were baggy, but you could tell that beneath them was a skinny, decaying, wreck of a body. He was just sat there, hunched over, shuddering against the wind. And he was staring – just staring at me!

Then the man began to smile slightly – only slightly mind... *Perhaps he's got wind*, I thought. No – he was smiling at me... He was definitely smiling at me... So I did the polite thing and smiled back. Then he cautiously raised his right hand in the air and began to wave. I didn't want to be rude, so I waved back. The man shrugged. He seemed to want me to go over to him. I didn't want to, of course, as he looked like he probably smelt of old milk.

He shrugged again, and began to beckon me over, shifting himself to make room on the bench beside him. It was at this point that I noticed something moving on the floor behind his coat. I didn't like the situation one bit, but I saw that Lizo from Newsround had clocked me again and was fast approaching from the other direction, no doubt with another spoon-related selling pitch. Would that man ever give up?

I took a deep breath and started towards the man on the bench, fixing my gaze upon him nervously. I knew I needed to keep my wits about me, lest he should suddenly do something unpredictable, like Doctor Fenton (which is another story, for another time).

His coat moved again, and a fluffy, ginger tail popped out from beneath his dirty coat. Did it? Yes, I could have sworn it did... I clenched my fists tightly in readiness – for I knew at once that this was no ordinary man. This man had a fluffy tail. This man was some sort of half-human, half animal hybrid the likes of which I had never...

No – *hold on a minute...*

I stopped. The wind blew the bottom of his coat aside for a brief moment, and revealed that the man did not have a tail at all. In fact, the tail in question belonged to a Nova Scotia Duck Tolling Retriever with a tambourine collar who was curled up under the bench. Something about it seemed familiar...

"Good morning," I said politely, when I reached the old man.

"Morning," he replied, his brow still taught with suspicion.

"That's a nice dog you have there," I said – trying to play it cool. I was 78 percent sure by now that it was *my* dog. "What's his name?"

"Freddy." He said.

"That's a nice name," I lied.

I crouched down to get a closer look at "Freddy", but the man shifted his legs across to obscure my view with the bottom of his coat. He took a sip from his cup, which I could now tell contained some sort of soup – possibly mulligatawny.

Okay, I thought. *No more Mr Nice Walton.*

"What are you doing with my dog?" I asked him, firmly but calmly (but also shaking my fist).

"Your dog?" he spluttered. "No, no, no. This is *my* dog."

"Liar liar, pants on fire!" I shouted, wagging my finger at him. I could tell he was slightly taken aback by my rhetoric skills.

"This is my dog!" he said again. "I've had him for 10 years!"

"Rubbish!" I screamed. "Where did you get that tambourine collar?"

"He was wearing it when I found him, weren't you Freddy?" He moved his legs aside and patted the dog.

"Stop calling him that! His name is Keith Matthews, and you haven't had him for 10 years, because he's only four years old!"

The scruffy man laughed (and dribbled slightly through the gaps in his teeth). "You think this dog's four years old?"

"I don't think. I *know*!" I insisted. "Now give him back."

"This isn't your dog, friend. See for yourself."

He moved his legs apart and gestured for me to look between them. That was the second time in my life that a strange man had done this, and the last time hadn't ended well. I looked at him nervously as he followed up his invitation with a gentle nod to the ground. Slowly, I got down on my hands and knees and reached for my dog.

"Come on, Keith," I whispered reassuringly. "It's time to go home now." The dog looked up at me through tired, cloudy eyes, his mouth surrounded by clumps of downy, grey fur. His head moved slowly, as though the weight of it was too much for his neck to bear, and his mouth hung limply open as he panted and dribbled grotesquely. *What the fudge?* This dog was old. *Very* old. Even the tambourine around his neck was worn and rusty. One thing was at once abundantly clear - this *wasn't* Keith Matthews.

I pulled my hand away, but the dog smelt it and came towards me, limping clumsily with its tongue lolling out of its mouth. Then I could smell the thing. It was carrying with it a putrid stench like nothing I had smelt before. This wasn't Keith Matthews at all. I didn't know this dog, and I certainly didn't want it slobbering all over me and giving me mange (again).

"Okay," I said, trying to push the mutt away as kindly as possible. "Okay, my mistake... Nice to meet you Freddy..."

The old man put his hand on my shoulder. It smelt like fish.

"I'm supposed to give you a message," he said.

"What are you talking about?" I asked, still trying to fend off Freddy as he tried to lick my face like a rude gypsy.

"I was told to give an important message to the man in the balaclava."

"That doesn't make any sense!" I said, gritting my teeth and pushing Freddy back beneath the bench. "Cripes! Will you please tell your dog to stop harassing me? He's dribbling all over my trouserpants!"

I did feel sorry for the poor thing, as it looked at me with a face full of hurt and confusion, but it did really, really smell, and I couldn't put up with it for much longer.

"What *is* this message, anyway?"

"Shed seven," he replied.

I shrugged, still looking at Freddy and keeping him away with my feet. "Shed seven? What the heck does that mean?"

"I think it's a band."

"Yes, I'm aware of that. But what does it mean to me (Walton Cumberfield)?"

"I don't know. I was just told to give you that message."

"Told by who?" I asked, taking off my balaclava so that he could infer the full extent of my annoyance.

As he looked upon me his eyes widened and he started doing his frightened salmon impression again, remaining speechless and considering me for a few seconds.

"By who?" I asked him again.

He shook his head and wiped some dribble from his beardy chin. Then he laughed to himself, as if accepting that he had been the subject of some hilarious lampoon.

"By you," he said, very quietly.

"What did you say?"

"By you," he said again.

"What are you talking about?" I demanded.

Somebody tapped me on the shoulder. It was bloody Lizo from Newsround again...

"Would you like to buy some spoons?" he asked, holding up a selection.

"Not now, Lizo from Newsround!" I screamed. "This really isn't the time!"

"I'll do you a deal: Two for three. No – three for two. Here – I'll give you seven for a sixpence, how's that?"

"No, no, no!"

I knocked the spoons out of Lizo's hands and they fell to the floor with a loud metallic clatter. A few concerned heads turned in our direction as the crusty old man behind me let out a throaty cry of panic.

"Freddy!" he cried. "No, Freddy! Come back!"

I turned to see 'Freddy' hobbling off as fast as his tired old legs could carry him. He had clearly been startled by the commotion with the cutlery, and was now fleeing the scene in that aimless way that animals do, with no regard for his destination, like a crazed lemming. The old man struggled to his feet and attempted to give chase, but all he could muster was a fast-paced limp. I knew he was unlikely to catch up with his companion, and feeling partly responsible for this development, I decided it appropriate to join the pursuit.

"Somebody stop that dog!" I shouted as I thundered across the grass, overtaking Keith Matthews (the jogger) on his umpteenth lap of the park. "Don't let him reach the road!"

Now, if I were a bus driver (and, God-willing, some day I will be), I would constantly be scanning the road ahead for any developing hazards that might require me to adjust my speed or direction; perhaps a car pulling out of a junction without looking, a set of lights about to change to red, or a man chasing a dog across an adjacent park and shouting at the top of his voice in an urgent and desperate tone. It is unfortunate, therefore, that I am not a bus driver. Because, if I were, then perhaps *I* would have been driving the number 47 bus that morning, instead of the inattentive ignoramus who was unwisely assigned to this important duty. Perhaps *I* would have noticed Freddy running out in front of the bus and slammed on the breaks. Perhaps if *I* were a bus driver, then poor old Freddy would still be alive...

Unfortunately for Freddy, I am not a bus driver.

The old man roared in emotional anguish as he drew close enough to see what had happened.

One dead dog, one missing dog... and I still hadn't delivered my Valentine's card or found time for my morning poo.

Bloomin' heck, I thought. *What a stinker of a day this is turning out to be...*

TWO

CHERYL COLE'S PYJAMAS

That afternoon I posted my Valentine's card before phoning around some local animal charities to tell them about Keith Matthews. Unfortunately they all informed me that a dog has to be gone for over 24 hours before you can report it missing. Minutes turned into hours. Hours turned into days. Days turned into weeks. Weeks turned into porcelain statues of George Allagiah, which turned back into weeks and then into days, which eventually turned back into hours again. My perceptions of time had been somewhat corrupted by the traumatic nature of recent events, coupled with the fact that I had let my curiosity get the better of me and ingested two sachets of silica gel to see what would happen. I believe that the ensuing dehydration was causing me to hallucinate. Either that, or I had finally gone "proper bonkers" like my grandfather always suspected I would.

I used an interweb site called eBuy to track down some LPs by the band "Shed 7" and spent many an hour listening to their music with the hope of discerning some sort of clue regarding the crusty old man and his mysterious message. Alas, although they were very enjoyable (well done to you, Shed 7), these sessions did not turn up any results, and I was still very much at a loose end. I was most grateful, therefore, for the welcome distraction of one of my favourite outreach activities...

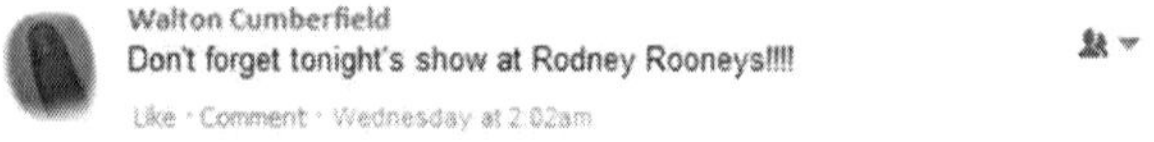

On the second Saturday of every month I would drive down to Rodney Rooney's Retirement Home in Little Melton to entertain the residents with a toy theatre production. I made the theatre out of old cereal boxes and new glue, which my Uncle Boris sourced for me from his job at the horse sanctuary (I imagine they use it to glue on their horseshoes).

My cast were figurines made from pipe cleaners, and they each had celebrity faces stuck to them to give them more "character". I had removed the faces from some back issues of Heat magazine I picked up at auction some three years previous (condition: soiled). I normally specialise in post-war drama about letter-bombs, but on this particular occasion, I was premiering my latest piece entitled *Who's Stolen Cheryl Cole's Pyjamas?* - a white-knuckle action thriller with a controversial plot, compelling characters and a surprise twist ending (she had stolen her own pyjamas, for insurance reasons).

They're going to bloody love it this week, I thought to myself as I carefully lifted the stage into the back of my Vauxhall Corsa. I love old people, you see - so much so in fact that I hope one day to become one myself. They all seem to be very happy over at Mr Rooney's, and lounge around in utter peace and harmony for every hour the day has to offer – except Marjorie of course, who is convinced that the birds are stealing her grass and is terrified of peas.

As usual I was very nervous during the short drive to the home, and had to stop several times to go to the toilet and have a sip of sherry from the decanter in my glove compartment. I have always been a very anxious performer, ever since I played one of the main roles in our school's production of Mark Ravenhill's *Shopping and Fucking* when I was nine. I pulled up the car and sat in silence for a moment, taking a few deep breaths.

Showtime!

Mr Rooney greeted me in his usual manner;

"Not you again! I've told you before – no one's interested in your sodding toy theatre nonsense! Now bugger off or I'm calling the police!"

Mr Rooney had a peculiar sense of humour, which I did not quite understand, but I laughed all the same and began setting up the stage in the Butterfly Room. I sighed a happy sigh and smiled to myself as the pre-performance nerves started to intensify. Some old people were gathering in the entrance, looking on in anticipation of another world-beating piece of theatre. I love performing to the elderly, as they have more life experience than young people, which gives their critical opinions more integrity. Some young people I know tend to view the elderly as stereotypes and always put them in a box (not literally) – but I suspect that they do not understand the quiet dignity with which these wonderful people live out their winter years.

"Hello Walton" said one of them, chewing on a Worther's Original and trumping with unabashed contentment. "What are you up to today?"

(I didn't respond because I was deep in concentration, reattaching Paris Hilton's left leg with a piece of Blu-Tack.)

"Another play is it? Oh yes - well done, well done..."

I afforded him a half-nod as I checked off the props on my list.

When the stage was set I went and collected my audience, wheeling them in (quite literally) from all over the home. Some of them objected, and had to be heavily sedated, but others were comparatively agreeable.

The first performance went off without a hitch, and many applauded at the end. Three people who I had retrieved from the haemorrhoid unit gave me a standing ovation, and one gentleman who had a special room all to himself, applauded and cheered throughout the whole play, and long after it had finished. We all had tea and biscuits (except for Henry Johnson) and before long (around about 6.30pm) everyone was tired and ready for bed.

Everyone, that is, except for me...

I always get tanked up on adrenaline (and sherry) following my toy theatre performances, and was soon out in my car, listening to Blink One Hundred and Eighty Two and kicking back 'old school' with the hazard lights on.

I looked out of my window at the large, white building behind me, and thought for a moment what it would be like to be old. I wondered if they minded wearing slippers all day long and feeling tired by the early evening. I wondered if they minded the stale smell of old carpet in every room, or the slushy food served in tin foil trays. I wondered if any of them missed being able to kick back 'old school' to Blink One Hundred and Eighty Two in the back of their Vauxhall Corsas. I wondered if I would miss that. Then I had another glass of sherry (which was bloody lovely) and pressed eject on the CD player. That particular CD had a scratch on track nine and it was beginning to sound like a broken record (literally).

The radio was tuned to BBC Radio 4, the sound of which immediately filled my little car. I turned it off straight away, as I find it very hard to kick back 'old school' to *The Archers*, despite being one of the show's biggest fans (I have listened to it more than twice). As I fumbled through the CD collection below the passenger seat I was interrupted by a knock on the window.

"What are you still doing here?" shouted Rodney Rooney through the glass. I wound my window down and gave him one of my warmest smiles.

"Hello Rodney," I said. "Did you enjoy my show?"

"No I did not!" he snapped. "It was the worst one yet!"

Rodney had a sort of ironic, faux grumpy, dry wit to him, which I, for one, found hilarious. I laughed for a few minutes and then offered him a sherry.

"What? No, of course I don't want a sherry. Why are you sat in my car park drinking sherry?"

"In celebration of a job well done," I explained proudly.

"Well done?"

"Thank you."

"Well done?" he continued. "What was so bloody well done about that? Some of my residents are still crying!"

I leaned back in my seat and sighed a triumphant sigh. I had intended for the show to be emotionally moving, but had no idea how lasting an impression it would have on my audience.

"Do you think I should send the script to a professional theatre company?" I asked him.

"I think you should get the fuck off my property!" He yelled.

Classic Rodney. I took that as a "yes".

"I'll go over it again a few times before I send it off to places," I thought (out loud).

Rodney slammed his fist on the roof of my car enthusiastically, and shouted, "Get lost!"

What a hoot!

"Do you have any notes yourself?" I asked.

He engaged me with a serious frown. "Any notes?"

"About how to improve the show?"

"How to impr-?" He composed himself, like an automatic symphony. "Well, for starters, its content."

"Interesting," I said, nodding eagerly (I love intellectual conversations). "And what would you say was wrong with the content?"

"It was unsuitable."

"For who(m)?" I asked (I'm never quite sure which is right, so I sometimes pronounce the 'm' very quietly).

"For anyone!" he yelled – really getting into it...

"Really?" I asked, puzzled. "I tried to make it quite broad. It's aimed at all ages."

"It has a decapitation sequence in it!"

He had a point there. I made a note to myself (on The Facebook) to remove the decapitation scene.

"Listen, Cumberfield," he began. "I don't know why you insist on coming here and subjecting my residents to your ridiculous charades, but it's got to stop. Understand?"

A blue Range Rover pulled up behind Mr Rooney.

"I said, do you understand?"

The driver's door opened and a plump chap with a thick black beard hopped out onto the gravel.

"Are you even listening to me?"

He walked around to the other side of the Range Rover and opened the passenger door.

"Cumberfield? I said are you even listening to me?"

He offered his arm to the passenger and assisted a little old woman out of the vehicle. She had wispy white hair and a kind face, which I immediately recognised.

"Mrs Fupplecock!" I exclaimed, climbing out of the car and stumbling slightly (I shouldn't have had so much sherry).

Mrs F leaned forward and squinted in my direction.

"Walton?"

"Hello to you, Mrs Fupplecock!" I shouted. "What the blazes are you doing here at Mr Rooney's?"

I ran over to her as fast as my tipsy little legs would carry me and gave her a hug. I didn't know what to do next, so I panicked and gave her a disposable lighter.

"That's for you," I explained. I *really* shouldn't have had so much sherry...

"Thank you darling," she said, handing the lighter to the younger, bearded man. "This is Nigel. He's my son."

"Hello Nigel," I said, with a friendly grin. "Are you two here to visit friends?"

"No, darling," replied Mrs F with a small laugh. "I'm moving in."

I looked in the back of the Range Rover and saw that it was full of suitcases.

"Why?" I asked. "Why do you need to move here? You have a lovely house."

"Because I need looking after," she said with a sigh. "I'm not as young as I used to be."

"Can't Nigel look after you?"

Nigel shifted uneasily and Mrs F looked at the ground. I realised I had made it awkward, so I ran away and then came back again a few minutes later.

"Would you like some help with your bags?" I asked.

"Oh, that would be helpful. Thank you very much."

I opened the boot and pulled out a couple of leather suitcases.

"Do you work here or something?" asked Nigel, frowning like bit of a dick.

"Sometimes," I replied. "I'm the entertainment manager."

"No he isn't!" shouted Mr Rooney, who had come over (uninvited) to see what all the fuss was about. "Now, what's all this fuss about?"

"Nigel Fupplecock," said Nigel, offering his hand.

"Ah, Mr Fupplecock," said Mr Rooney. "Welcome, welcome… I'm Rodney. Rodney Rooney. I'm the owner. Sorry, is this man bothering you?"

"Oh no, not at all!" said Mrs F. "Walton's an old friend."

*

It's true. I was an old friend. In fact, I first met Mrs Fupplecock at the age of seven and a half, when I was put into a "special group" at school for some of the more gifted children. There was me, Dennis Potts, Sally Scroggins and Oliver Postlethwaite (who sometimes dribbled). Mrs F ran our special club and taught us about all sorts of interesting things like dinosaurs and prime numbers. She was the best teacher I have ever had, or ever will have, and she smelt like honey and crystallised ginger.

A few years after she retired from teaching, her husband (Mr Fupplecock) was sadly killed at Alton Towers by an unfortunate accident on the Squirrel Nutty ride. She didn't really like to talk about it, so this is all the information I have relating to Mr Fupplecock's bizarre and unlikely death. Anyway, the point is that she soon replaced her husband with a beautiful Nova Scotia Duck Tolling Retriever bitch (female dog) named Lucy, who became her most trusted and faithful friend. I would often see Mrs F walking Lucy around the park near to my house, and we would sometimes meet and talk about the kind of things we liked to talk about (like dinosaurs and prime numbers).

Unfortunately for Mrs F, the butcher of fate had yet more bad sausages to hurl in her direction, and a few years later, in that very park, Lucy was set upon by another dog who impregnated her with his unsolicited seed. Of course, when she informed me of this, I phoned the police straight away. They were very concerned at first, but seemed slightly underwhelmed when I mentioned that Lucy was a dog, and lost interest entirely when I mentioned that the perpetrator was also a dog. Then they hung up on me and asked me not to bother them again.

Nine weeks later Lucy gave birth to a litter of seven puppies, which all needed re-homing as quickly as possible, as Mrs F was getting too old to take care of so many animals. Three went to the Chester family up on Oakheath farm, two to the Denslows on South Street, and one to a man named Perks who had a mental brain disease and could only communicate in direct quotations from the film *The Shawshank Redemption.*

I was over for Sunday lunch at the time (it was a Thursday but Mrs F's calendar was faulty and I didn't have the heart to tell her). She was busy carving up the meat when Perks came to the door, so I answered it for her.

"I understand you're a man who knows how to get things," he said.

"I'm sorry?" I replied. "Oh, you must be Mr Perks? Are you here about the dogs?"

"I have to remind myself that some birds aren't meant to be caged," he said, solemnly. "Their feathers are just too bright. And when they fly away, the part of you that knows it was a sin to lock them up does rejoice. But still, the place you live in is that much more drab and empty that they're gone. I guess I just miss my friend."

"Are you crazy?" I asked.

He smiled. "Crazy as a rat in a tin shithouse, is what."

And he showed himself in.

"Where are you from, Mr Perks?" I asked.

"There's a big hayfield up near Buxton. You know where Buxton is?"

"No," I said. "I'm not entirely sure."

"It's got a long rock wall with a big oak tree at the north end. It's like something out of a Robert Frost poem."

I shrugged. He wasn't really making any sense, and I couldn't get an immediate handle on his mental condition, since I have only ever seen *The Shawshank Redemption* once, and it was in Danish with French subtitles.

"Is that Mr Perks about the dogs?" asked Mrs F, calling through from the kitchen.

"I'm not sure," I replied. "He's acting a bit funny."

He turned and scowled at me, and then said: "You're gonna look real funny sucking my dick with no teeth."

I thought that was a bit inappropriate, but I didn't say anything as it wasn't my house.

"Well," I said, "let's see what these puppies make of you, shall we?"

"I doubt they'll kick up any fuss," he said. "Not for an old crook like me."

I showed Mr Perks through to the utility room, where Lucy lay in her bed with the last two puppies. They all looked very happy together, and for a moment I felt bad about having to separate them. Still, this man seemed very nice, and although he did seem to spend an uncomfortable amount of time examining the pups' hindquarters, I was 90 percent sure he would make a good owner.

"We were hoping you'd be able to take them today," I said.

"Let me tell you something my friend," he said, very seriously. "Hope is a dangerous thing. Hope can drive a man insane."

"Yes," I agreed. "That's… true."

I had literally no idea what he was talking about, but nodded and smiled as he continued to study the pups. Then Mrs F came in from the kitchen and asked me to go and watch her potatoes. I was happy to oblige, as Mr Perks was making me feel massively awkward.

"What was his name?" he said as I was leaving.

"I'm sorry?" she asked.

"That tall drink of water with the silver spoon up his ass."

"Oh. That's just my friend Walton," she explained. "He's here for some lunch. We're going to eat soon."

He turned and scowled at her, and then said, "You eat when we say you eat. You shit when we say you shit. You piss when we say you piss. You got that, you maggot dick motherfucker?"

"You poor man," said Mrs F, putting a hand on his shoulder (because she a very kind lady). "I've seen this before. My husband's cousin had the same problem. Am I right in thinking that you can only communicate in direct quotations from the 1994 film *The Shawshank Redemption*?"

A single tear dribbled down Perks' right cheek. "There's not a day goes by I don't feel regret," he said.

Mrs F shook her head sympathetically. She really was a very nice lady.

Anyway, as it turned out, Perks didn't want both of the dogs (although this was almost impossible for him to articulate). I watched from the kitchen as he carried the female out through the hall to the door, followed by Mrs F.

"You take good care of her now," she said. "If you're just taking the one, that'll be 100 pounds."

"Don't you ever mention money to me again, you sorry son of a bitch!" yelled Mr Perks. Then he slammed the front door and left.

What a strange fellow, I thought, as I went back into the utility room to check on Lucy. I knew how upset she would be that yet another of her offspring had been taken away from her, so I shared a dog biscuit with her and patted her on the head for bit while Mrs F finished cooking our Sunday (Thursday) lunch.

The last of the puppies stumbled to its feet and scurried over to me, wagging its little tail. Lucy didn't seem to mind, so I reached out and gently stroked him behind his tiny ears. He attempted to climb onto my knee, but eventually got tired and then did quite a lot of sick all over my favourite pair of trouserpants. I was quite annoyed but also slightly amused. No one had been sick on my trouserpants since lower school assembly in 1989, when the child next to me brought up his breakfast during the morning prayers (I suspected he might be a staunch atheist). I decided in that moment to name said puppy after the child in question. That child's name was Keith Matthews.

I took him home that evening, and I never told him that he was the result of a sexual assault.

*

Seeing Mrs F that day at Rodney Rooney's made me think about poor old Keith again. Where had he gone? Why would he just run off like that? Like a defunct American mint, it didn't make any cents (sense) at all (LOLs).

When I had finished shifting her cases up to her room (number 41) I sat with Mrs F for a while and we had a lovely chat about all sorts of things, like dinosaurs and prime numbers. Then she asked me how Keith Matthews was doing, and I remember that I began to cry a bit. Although they were secret tears, I'm pretty sure that she knew about them, as she took my hand in hers and offered me some words of comfort.

"Oh Walton," she whispered. "I'm sure he's fine. He's probably just a bit of a wanderer, like his father was."

"His father?" I asked.

"He was a stray. Well, sort of... He was found by a homeless man, so I suppose he *does* have an owner."

I sniffed back a few more secret tears and turned to Mrs F with my third most serious expression.

"His father was a stray Nova Scotia Duck Tolling Retriever who was owned by a homeless?"

"A homeless *person*, yes," she said.

"What did he look like?" I asked.

"Well, he looked like a Nova Scotia Duck Tolling Retriever. And he had a tambourine instead of a collar."

I had only known one dog other than Keith Matthews who wore a tambourine collar. Suddenly the penny dropped. But surely… Could it be that 'Freddy' was Keith Matthews' father?

"I thought I told you this, Walt. After all, you gave Keith a tambourine collar of his own. I thought it was a tribute to his parentage."

"I can see why you would think that," I said. "But you never told me about Keith's father. I only gave him a tambourine collar so that I wouldn't lose him so often. Besides, why would I want to pay tribute to a sex offender?"

"Oh Walt, I've told you before – that's not really how it works with animals..."

She took a tube of fruit pastilles out of her purse and offered it to me. I took it with a smile and put it in my pocket, happy in the knowledge that I would eat them later while watching *Coast*.

"I think I've met that dog," I said. "Just a couple of weeks ago."

"Yes," she said. "I've seen him a few times in that park. His owner lives under the bridge on Lower Goat Lane."

I was going to tell her about the number 47 bus, but I thought it would probably just add more grief to what must already have been a difficult day for her. Then Nigel came in and said he was going home (like a dickhead), so I stayed with Mrs F and helped her unpack her things. I introduced her to all of the other residents (except for Henry Johnson) and stayed with her until she was tired and ready to go to sleep.

"It's getting late now love," she said. "I think I'm going to hit the hay."

"Will you be alright?" I asked.

"Oh, I'll be fine," she assured me. "Don't you worry about me. I've lived in worse places."

Then she looked at me very seriously for a moment.

"What is it?" I asked.

"79 Primrose Avenue, Newton Poppleford," she whispered.

"I'm sorry?"

"That's where I lived when I trained to be a teacher. You should remember that."

"Why?" I asked.

"79 Primrose Avenue, Newton Poppleford. It's in Devon."

Suddenly Mrs F was talking in riddles and I worried that she might have a mental brain disease.

"Okay, Mrs F," I said. "I think that's enough excitement for one day…"

"When I was five," she continued, "I had a cat called Mr Nibbles. I used to write stories about him."

I smiled at her. "Oh, Mrs F, you know how I love your stories. But it's getting late now –"

"Tell me about him."

"About who?"

"My cat," she said, as though it were obvious. "Tell me about my cat."

Oh God, I thought. *She really is losing it.*

"Mrs Fupplecock – I don't know anything about your cat."

"Just tell me what I told you."

I was getting very confused, but I thought it best to oblige her, so as not to hurt her feelings.

"When you were five you had a cat named Mr-"

"Not now, darling," she explained. "Another time. Tell me about it... another time."

I got up and put on my coat. She was obviously quite tired and the stress of moving was obviously affecting her senses.

"I'll leave you in peace now Mrs F," I said.

"79 Primrose Avenue," she whispered.

"Goodnight, Mrs Fupplecock."

"Until next time," she said grinning, and closed her eyes as I turned out the light.

Bonkers, I thought. *Completely bonkers.*

*

When I walked into my house that evening I stepped on an envelope that was lying on our hallway floor. At first it made me sad, remembering that Keith Matthews wasn't around to intercept and ingest the thing – but I was conversely heartened by its contents:

Dear Walton,
This Valentine's,
I will be fine
To come with you to Bannatynes
(the health club in Lowestoft).
Love Melanie. x

With all that had taken place in the last couple of days I had almost forgotten about this romantic story thread. I sat on the stairs and read the note again with a big fat grin on my face. I mean, okay... her poem was essentially just an abridged facsimile of my own work with alternative pronouns to shift the narrative meaning to her own point of view, but I sincerely appreciated the sentiment all the same. You have to understand that the prospect of a whole day in the company of Melanie Bogg is not a privilege earned with ease or regularity. Still, it seemed as though my poetry had done the trick this time! Our relationship was well and truly "on again"!

I left the front door open, as I had done the previous night, in case Keith Matthews decided to come home again. Then it was straight to bed for a good night's sleep in preparation for the following day's adventures.

The following day being, of course, February 14th.

And what a day it was going to be!

THREE

HELLESDON HATH NO FURY...

I *hope they have a McDonald's here*, I thought as we drove through the front gates of the health club. *I'm starving.*

Melanie was sat next to me, looking radiant as always; her smooth, elegantly-crossed legs shimmering in her trademark skin-tone tights. It made me wish I'd had time to tidy up the Corsa before picking her up that morning, or at least remove some of the food waste.

We circled the car park for 20 minutes until I decided to park in one of the disabled spaces. *Why do they need to park so close to the club if they're here to do exercise anyway?* I thought to myself. Then I decided that this was good satire, so I put it on The Facebook:

Walton Cumberfield
Why do disabled people need to park so close to a health club?
LMFAO!
Like · Comment · Share · 2 hours ago ·
Lizo from Newsround likes this.

"What are you doing?" asked Melanie, placing her hand on my leg and making me nervous (in a good way).

"I'm updating The Facebook" I replied.

"No, I mean why are you parking here? You can't park here. You need a blue badge."

I opened up the glove compartment and pulled out an envelope from behind the sherry decanter. Inside the envelope was a blue disabled driver's badge.

"We can use my mother's badge," I said.

"I thought your mother was dead," said Melanie.

"Exactly," I said, and positioned it neatly on the dashboard.

Noticing Melanie's hand was still very firmly rested on my left thigh, I wondered if it was best to go into the club, or to wait a bit and see where things went in the car.

"Shall we go in then?" asked Melanie.

"We could do," I said. "Or we could kick back 'old school' for a bit."

"No. Let's go in."

Bugger.

We went into the club and found a nice little café (they didn't have a McDonald's) where I ordered two plates of fish and chips with tartare sauce. Melanie had a ham salad. Someone once told me that you shouldn't go swimming immediately after eating as it gives you the craps, so we decided to go for a brisk walk on the treadmills for a bit (while holding hands for extra romance). We talked about all sorts of things, but mainly reading, as that is a thing that Melanie likes to do. Her favourite book is *To Kill A Mockingbird* by Lee Harper, which I have not read because I am not very interested in hunting. Also, she says that it is about racism, and I do not like racism one bit (unless it is directed at Belgians!).

Melanie became a postwoman because her favourite tele-visual programme was Postman Pat (and his Black and White Cat) back in the eighties. One of our most interesting conversations that day was about how she believed that Pat, although fictional, had raised great awareness for his profession and was possibly the most influential deliveryman of all time. I enjoyed her line of argument, although I did counter it with a stronger case for Father Christmas. In the end we agreed to disagree and settled our differences over some pear 'smoothies' at the juice bar.

"I'm trying to eat more pears," I told her as she slurped her drink.

"Why is that?" she asked (and put her hand on my leg again btw!)

"Last month I planted a pear tree in the back garden."

"That's nice," she said. "What made you do that?"

"It was Roger's idea." I explained. "I told him that I didn't want to do any gardening one Sunday because it was raining, and he told me to grow a pear."

Then Melanie laughed (for some reason) and held my hand for a bit (which was really nice but also slightly embarrassing as my hands were not at their optimum level of moistness).

"I think you look very beautiful today, Melanie," I told her, trying to give her one of my warmest smiles.

"Aw," she said. "You are a smoothie."

I laughed really loudly because Melanie had attempted to make a pun relating my manner to the particular type of drink that we were consuming. I should stress that I did not in any way find this funny – in fact I thought that it was a bit pathetic if I'm honest, but Melanie is a REALLY nice lady and I was definitely falling in love with her at this point in time. I probably would have fallen in love with her already were it not for the "on-again, off-again" nature of our relationship (which made things very confusing on The Facebook).

After our smoothies we went to the spa for some couples relaxation therapy, which I had booked in advance over the interweb. Unfortunately, due to an administrative error (probably due to some sort of interweb virus / fungal infection), we were booked into the wrong slots and could not receive our therapy together. Melanie was lucky enough to get the last private room that was available, while I ended up sharing a Swedish massage session with a Scandinavian man named Gort. Gort was a heavy set, no-nonsense sort of fellow with a perfectly bare chest and muscles that looked as though they were about to burst through his skin. He seemed pleasant enough at first, but my view of him quickly changed when he insisted on making happy sex noises throughout his treatment and repeatedly moaned the name "Dorthe" when his neck was rubbed.

Afterwards, Gort showed me the way to the steam room, where he nonchalantly removed his gown and strode naked into the misty abyss. Not wishing to appear antisocial, I immediately followed my naked Scandinavian friend into the chamber of fog, but not wanting to give him the wrong idea, I decided to keep my pants on. I am generally quite embarrassed about people seeing my willy, as it is slightly below average in size and looks almost exactly like Ian

Hislop.

I pawed the air in front of me as I moved through the steam so as not to walk into a wall, a bench, or Gort's bottom. After several minutes of this, I began to suspect that this might be the largest steam room in the entire world. How could I have been walking for so long and not reached a wall, a bench, or another person? And where the hell had Gort got to? There was just steam - nothing but yards and yards of endless steam…

"Hello?" I shouted.

"Hallo," came a voice (from somewhere).

"Is that you, Gort?" I asked. (It sounded like Gort).

"No, this is Peder. Who is this?"

Peder? That couldn't be right. It definitely sounded like Gort. Also, it seemed quite unlikely that there would be more than one Scandinavian in Lowestoft at any given point in time. No - it was probably one of Gort's little games – after all, he seemed like a bit of a joker.

"I can't find the wall," I said, spluttering as the steam filled several of my lungs.

"It is over here," came Gort's voice from behind me.

I turned on the spot, almost losing my footing on the wet tiles as I did so, and faced the direction of his voice.

"Where are you?"

"I'm here, silly pants!" came the voice again – except that this time it seemed to be coming from my right...

Never mind, I thought. *If I just keep walking I'm bound to find something.* I continued to make my way through the miasma, clawing at the air like a desperate mongoose (who was blinded by fog) until I realised that I had been walking around for nearly nine minutes. Just how big was this steam room?

A wave of nausea hit me like a sack of giraffes and I felt my sweat-drenched skin suffocating me like a very large, tight sock. My chin rested on my chest as I gasped for air, and as I looked down I noticed that I suddenly had four feet for some reason. I remember noting that this was odd, since I distinctly remembered only having <u>two</u> feet before entering the steam room. The heat must have been affecting my senses. Then a man in a cloak came towards me with a breakfast sword, and I knew that I must have passed out.

Seconds turned into minutes. Minutes turned into hours. Hours turned into a sort of half man - half burger creature with a soldier's hat on, which turned back into hours, which turned into minutes (which eventually turned back into hours again) and before I knew it, the best part of the afternoon had passed me by, and I was waking up on the hard tiled floor with a head like a sore bear.

Gort had set the steam room to its maximum temperature before going in, which was obviously the ideal heat for his resilient, Scandinavian, sauna-dwelling physique, but not so ideal for me (Walton Cumberfield). I had not experienced temperatures above 70^{0}C since my boiler malfunctioned, and the extreme heat of the steam had caused me to become so disorientated that I was unable to find the edge of what in the end had turned out to be a relatively small room. As luck would have it, some sensible fellow (Zeus bless that man) came along later in the day and reduced the temperature. Thus I was able to regain consciousness, move clumsily towards the light, and escape my smoggy prison.

As you might expect, this trauma had left my senses in a state of disarray, and as such my memories of the time between waking up and regaining the power of coherent thought are somewhat disjointed. I remember staring into the changing room mirror for quite some time, not altogether sure of what I was seeing. You see, the hours spent in that steam room had rendered my skin very loose and wrinkly, and I now had the appearance of a very large scrotum / Roger Moore. In fact, my skin had become so wrinkly that I could barely recognise myself. At one point I started to wonder just how long I had been trapped in that steam room, since I appeared to have aged at least 50 years. Then I got a bit scared and started looking for my trousers, which I found on the floor by my locker for some reason. Then I got confused, sat down for a bit, and updated The Facebook.

Walton Cumberfield
Goddey89 atgs sopa inbb adh/?dkjhgf878r54 :-)
Like · Comment · Saturday at 5:04pm

The next thing I knew, I was attempting to negotiate the corridors of the health club in search of some assistance, but regularly forgot where I was or what I was doing. I kept thinking that I was going to be sick, but then I wasn't sick. It was horrible. Fortunately by this point I had managed to put on my trouserpants, although for some reason I had decided to wear them as some sort of jumper.

When I reached the canteen I wandered thoughtlessly through the staff entrance and became convinced (for some reason) that I was the new catering manager - a charade which several of the staff actually believed. I spent a short amount of time serving peas to hungry (and confused) customers, while ordering the rest of the staff to make a bacon casserole for somebody called "Auntie Margaret". This carried on until Dan Prescott - the actual catering manager, made a very good case for his identity and was quite rightly reinstated to his official position. I was forced out of the kitchen by all of the staff apart from Sunjin - a nice young man who had believed in me right from the beginning. He got very angry at this point and threw down his apron screaming "if he goes, I go! Damn you! Damn you all to hell!"

I am told that this called into question Sunjin's work ethic on a more general level and he was regrettably asked to seek out alternative employment at the end of that week. I have not seen him since, as he is not on The Facebook.

Of course, the mix-up in the canteen led to the involvement of the club security team, who subsequently gave chase as I fled through the club, still very much in a state of delirium. They cornered me at the main reception, where I evaded capture by hiding in a sunbed for another couple of hours (with a man named Dennis, who may have been a hallucination due to my dehydrated brain). I am pretty sure I wrote a poem to pass the time at this point, but I cannot remember how it went. Since I cannot remember that poem, here is an acrostic poem about the social constraints surrounding the consumption of pizza...

"Pizza" (an acrostic poem, by Walton Cumberfield)

Pepperoni, yum yum yum.
In my tummy tum tum tum.
Zero people go against the
Zeitgeist which most oft' dictates.
A man must eat up every crumb (of pizza).

When I was sure that the security team had definitely gone, I emerged from the sunbed and staggered about for a bit looking for a water dispenser. I don't know how long this search lasted, but I do know that I eventually gave up and ended up taking a seat just outside the disabled loos to catch my breath.

"There you are!" said a portly middle-aged woman in a red blouse. "Come on, Mr Spencer – the others are waiting."

She was talking to me. Why was she talking to me? I smiled politely. I always used to smile politely when strangers spoke to me, in case they were friends with my mother / my mother.

"I've been looking for you," she said as she trotted up behind me.

I wasn't sure at this point whether my name was Mr Spencer or not, but it didn't really matter since my tongue was so dry that any form of verbal protestation had been rendered impossible.

Then I started moving forward. You see, in my confusion I had accidentally sat down in a wheelchair that someone had left outside the disabled loos, and now I was being wheeled back towards reception by this kind lady who appeared to have mistaken me for someone named Mr Spencer.

Reg Spencer, I later learnt, was an 84-year-old man who had recently returned from a three week holiday in La Gomera with his niece. Now, you may be wondering how any woman of sound mind, however portly, could confuse me (Walton Cumberfield) with an 84-year-old man who had recently returned from a three week holiday in La Gomera (with his niece). Well, after spending a whole afternoon unconscious in a steam room and a further two hours hiding in a sunbed, my appearance was in fact exactly like that of an 84-year-old man who had recently returned from a three week holiday in La Gomera. Unfortunately, as I was wheeled away, the real Reg Spencer was still inside the toilet (the room, not the fixture), waiting for one of the other members of support staff to come and assist him.

Anyway, I must have blacked out for a bit shortly after my exchange with the portly assistant, as the next thing I knew, I was standing in the middle of the swimming pool taking part in a water aerobics session for the over seventies.

It was largely underwhelming. Our instructor's name was "Gav" and his tiny shorts and feigned enthusiasm put my teeth on edge. This was evidently not true of the other members of the class, as they had no teeth and seemed to be quite fond of "Gav" and his antics. The exercises were dull, the water was murky, and I'm 98 percent sure that the man standing to my right was passing water during some of the more strenuous routines. Some Valentine's Day this was turning out to be!

Then I remembered Melanie and looked at the clock. It was 7:30, and I had made reservations for dinner at eight with KFC. And what the heck had she been doing on her own all afternoon? She was probably worried sick! Knowing that something had to be done, and fast, I pretended that I had seen Sean Bean through one of the windows at the back of the room, which made everyone far more excited than I had suspected it would. During the madness that ensued I crawled out of the pool and made good my escape. I found my trouserpants in the changing room, put them on (in the usual fashion this time) and went to retrieve the rest of my things from my designated locker. They were all there – my watch, my vest, my green shirt, my purple tank top, my socks, my "sneakers" and my Kit Kat chunky. Everything except my wallet…

"Mr Spencer?" came a voice from around the corner.

They had obviously noticed that I was missing. I thought I was going to be sick, but then I wasn't sick.

"Hello? Mr Spencer?"

I quickly put on the rest of my clothes, picked up an armband and threw it in the opposite direction from the one I intended to travel in (just like in films when they throw things to confuse their pursuers).

"Is that you, Mr Spencer?" came the voice once again. "Did you just throw an armband?"

I ran out the opposite end of the changing room and found

myself in reception again. Picking up a flyer to hide my face from any lingering members of security staff, I sidled up to the front desk and spoke to a woman named Beth.

"Hello, I'm Beth," said Beth. "How can I help?"

"Hello," I said, "I'm Walton Cumberfield, and I've lost my wallet. I think it's been stolen."

"Well, I didn't take it," said Beth, defencively.

"I know that, Beth," I assured her. "Since we've known each other you've never given me any reason to doubt your moral integrity. No – the reason I am telling you about this is that I presume you have a lost property section somewhere back there?"

"We do. But there's not much in there. Just a phone charger and half a can of Pepsi someone left on the side last Wednesday. If you think that your wallet's been stolen, perhaps I should alert the security team."

She picked up the phone.

"No!" I screamed, and everyone looked around. "No - that won't be necessary."

"It's not a problem."

"Really, it's fine." I said. "Please just make an announcement for Melanie Bogg to meet me here in reception."

"Right you are, sir."

I smiled politely and took a seat, carefully making sure that it wasn't a wheelchair, much to the confusion of the people sitting around me. Many of them were giving me funny looks, so I covered my face with the flyer I was holding, and hoped that Melanie would arrive soon. I thought that I was going to be sick, but then I wasn't sick. This had been the worst Valentine's Day since Hilda McIntyre dumped me at the dump back in 1997. In fairness, I probably shouldn't have taken her to the dump on Valentine's Day, but I had a broken hoover that I desperately needed to get rid of, and Hilda had explicitly stated that she didn't mind what we did...

"What do you fancy doing?" I remember asking her.

"I don't know," I remember her answering. "I really don't mind."

"Well, where would you like to go?" I had asked (quite clearly).

"You can choose. I really don't have a preference."

Turns out that Hilda McIntyre was a liar, which is something that I constantly remind her of on The Facebook:

Hilda McIntyre
Just got some brilliant news :-) New job and a new niece!!!!
Like · Comment · 4 hours ago via mobile
Rita Maxwell and 14 others like this.
View all 5 comments
Leslie Norman Awesome! You deserve it hun! ;-) xxxx
3 hours ago via mobile · Like
Walton Cumberfield You are a liar.
2 hours ago · Like

After I had been sat in reception for a couple of minutes, I noticed that some of the people around me were starting to giggle. I then realised that the flyer I was holding was in fact an information leaflet about irritable bowel syndrome. I put it on my lap and tried to look dignified, but this was fairly difficult because I had an itchy bum (which I get sometimes).

"There he is!" shouted someone from across the room.

I turned to see the portly woman pushing an empty wheelchair in my direction. I thought I was going to be sick but then I wasn't sick.

"Come on now, Mr Spencer! You mustn't go wandering off. You're not on holiday any more you know!"

"Would Melanie Bogg please report to reception. Your friend is here. Melanie Bogg to reception."

The other oldies were pouring out of the changing room now, and I realised that I was heading for a pretty sticky situation.

"There's been a misunderstanding," I said.

The portly woman took my hand and gently encouraged me to get out of my seat.

"No, really – I don't need a wheelchair." I insisted.

"So you keep telling me, Mr Spencer. But it's a long walk to the minibus today – some idiot went and parked in the last disabled space."

"Seriously – you need to listen." I spluttered as she pulled me to my feet. "Please – you don't understand."

"Get in the chair, Mr Spencer."

"No, really I –"

"Don't make a scene!"

"Please, my name's not Mr –"

"Get in the chair!" she yelled.

I got in the chair and she rolled her eyes. "There, now that wasn't so hard was it?"

I looked down in submission. "No ma'am."

"Right. Now, you just stay put. I'm going to find Mr Rooney so we can get going."

She waddled out into the car park and left me sitting there like a melon. Where was Melanie? I knew I had to get out of there, but I couldn't leave without her – not on Valentine's Day. Things were very quickly going from bad to worse, and my bottom wouldn't stop itching.

"Excuse me?" somebody said from the other side of the room. "Is this one of yours?"

A nice young lady was walking towards one of the group's supervisors with an old man on her arm. He was very frail, extremely tanned, and walking so slowly that he was practically going backwards. It was Reg Spencer... The real Reg Spencer!

"Somebody's stolen his wheelchair," she explained.

This announcement elicited what can only be described as a hubbub of disapproval among those that were present, so I thought it best to slowly wheel myself towards the exit.

"What the devil's going on here?" shouted Rodney Rooney, bursting into reception like a bull in China. "What are you doing with Mr Spencer?"

"He was in the disabled toilets, and somebody stole his wheelchair," explained the woman.

"Stole his wheelchair? Who the hell would do a thing like that? Somebody call security!"

The portly woman scurried in and stood beside Mr Rooney, followed almost immediately by Melanie, who went straight to the reception desk.

"Hello," she said. "I'm Melanie Bogg. You called for me on the tannoy..."

I could feel my brow getting sweatier and sweatier, and my bottom-itch wasn't letting up either.

"Ah yes," said Beth. "Your friend is here."

She pointed in my direction.

"What's going on?" asked the portly woman.

"Some absolute bloody bastard has stolen Mr Spencer's wheelchair," shouted Mr Rooney.

"Hang on a minute," said the portly woman. "If you're Mr Spencer, then who's…"

She turned and looked at me.

"Who's who?" asked Mr Rooney.

"That man over there who's scratching his bottom," she said.

"I don't know…"

Melanie was already standing in front of me, her face fraught with confusion, her beautiful lips quivering with what I suspected to be genuine rage.

"Walt?" she said, quietly. "What the hell are you doing?"

Mr Rooney peered into my face. His lips were also quivering (but they were not beautiful as he had a couple of fever blisters).

"Cumberfield?" he asked, in disbelief.

I looked at Melanie – then at Mr Rooney. A small team of security staff were quickly assembling behind them. I looked at Melanie again – then at Mr Rooney – then at Beth (for some reason) – then at the portly woman – then at the real Reg Spencer – then back at Melanie. Then I thought that I was going to be sick but then I wasn't sick. Then I looked at Rodney Rooney again. Then I *was* sick. All over his brogues...

*

Melanie didn't say a word until we got onto the bus to go home. We had to take the bus as it turned out that my mother's disabled driver's badge was a fake and my Corsa was clamped. She didn't answer any of my questions, she didn't laugh at any of my jokes, and she certainly didn't put her hand on my leg.

I should have taken her to the dump.

When we passed through Loddon I thought it was about time I set things right, so I asked her what was wrong.

"What's wrong?" she snapped. "What's wrong? I'll tell you what's bloody wrong!"

I was glad she had decided to open up.

"You left me waiting outside those changing rooms all afternoon – just standing there like a lemon."

"The expression is 'like a melon'," I corrected her.

"No it isn't. Why are you such a moron? I've never been so embarrassed in all my life." She twisted the hem of her skirt and shuddered with anger. "What kind of idiot gets lost in a steam room? What kind of idiot hides in a sunbed? What kind of idiot steals somebody else's wheelchair?"

"I didn't steal it," I reminded her. "I sat in it by accident."

"By accident?" Her face was going red. "How could you possibly do something like that by accident? I thought I'd give you another chance today, but you blew it. Once again, you blew it. I can't take it anymore!"

"Oh come on, Melanie," I said. "I know you're upset we missed our reservations, but we can still make it back in time for *Cracker* and I've got some chicken dippers in the freezer."

"I don't understand you. Who do you think you are? Where do you get off embarrassing me like that?"

"I normally get off on Sweet Briar Road," I explained. "Then it's just a short walk around the corner to my place."

"I'm not coming back to your place."

We sat in silence for a bit, and I took out my (Roger's) phone to give myself something to do. Melanie just sat there, fuming like an angry badger.

"I'm sorry you had a rubbish Valentine's Day," I said eventually.

"No," she said, relaxing a little bit. "I didn't. I had a perfectly fine afternoon as a matter of fact. I took a spontaneous climbing lesson with a man named Gort. It was very pleasant."

"You did what?" I exclaimed.

"I very much enjoyed his company," she said. "And we're going out to dinner next Wednesday evening."

That Scandinavian arsehole! Clearly Gort had double-crossed me – and after all we'd been through together...

"You can't go to dinner with him!" I shouted. "He's a double-crossing son of a bastard!"

"Don't talk like that!" said Melanie. "People are looking."

"I don't care if they're looking. You can't go out with him - he's too big for you, and I'm pretty sure he's in love with a woman named Dorthe."

"Dorthe is his sister," she said.

What a weirdo.

"Don't do it Melanie," I pleaded. "I can change."

"I'm sorry Walt," she said, so gently that it felt as though she'd punched me in my heart. "It's over."

"No…" I said, choking back the tears. "I'm sorry Melanie. I'll make it up to you. Don't go out with him. Please…"

"I'm going to sit at the front now," she said. "Please don't follow me. It'll be awkward otherwise."

She got up without a word, and walked down the aisle. Everyone else was looking at me like a bunch of bloody idiots.

"What are you all looking at?" I shouted (like they do in the films).

Melanie sat down at the front and didn't look back for the rest of the journey. I guess you could say that our relationship was "off again". I felt like I was going to be sick but then I wasn't sick, so I curled up into the foetal position and updated The Facebook.

FOUR

BLOODY HELLESDON

After Melanie and I broke up I had a lot of trouble sleeping, so I contacted my boss on The Facebook saying I would be available to do some night shifts at the sandwich shop if he needed me. Unfortunately, the letter F on my keyboard was broken, which led to an embarrassing mix up that threatened to ruin my interweb-based reputation (e-street cred).

Walton Cumberfield ▸ Glenn Johnson
Would you like me to do some night shits some time this week?
Like · Comment · See Friendship · 2 hours ago ·
Aaron Michaels
Ha ha ha! You fucking TWAT!
about an hour ago via mobile · Like

My life was falling apart before my very eyes. My dog was gone, my relationship was "off again" and everyone at work had started making jokes about my Facebook gaff. I was banned from Rodney Rooney's retirement home after the incident at Bannatyne's, so I couldn't visit Mrs F or put on any more toy theatre productions. I wished that I could go back in time and start again. I wished that the world would swallow me up like a lump of sausage and spit me out far away from all of the bastards (like Aaron Michaels). I wished I wasn't Walton Cumberfield anymore.

But little did I know that this was only the beginning, and one night the following week something very disturbing was about to happen to me. Something very disturbing indeed…

I can vividly remember the dream I was having that night. I was in the bath with David Dimbleby, washing his back with an unconscious duck. Then the water turned into strawberry Ribena and we clapped our hands for some time in celebration. Then David Dimbleby did a dance (with his pants on) and suddenly we were at the Royal Albert Hall. Postman Pat and Father Christmas followed our act with a very serious play entitled *Bleed*, and then Roger (my lodger) did some sword-swallowing while dressed as his drag queen alter-ego "Mrs Livingstone".

Something fell to the floor, and I was running again. *Here we go*, I thought as the man in the hooded cloak appeared and brandished his breakfast sword. And suddenly I knew I was dreaming. I knew I was dreaming but I couldn't wake up.

"You're an idiot!" he shouted. "You're an idiot, and everyone thinks you're an idiot and you'll always be an idiot and I hate you!" I kept running, and he kept shouting; "You'll never amount to anything! You bloody berk!"

I rounded a corner and jumped over a couple of copulating terrapins, just in time to see Keith Matthews run off in the other direction.

"Keith Matthews!" I shouted. "Here boy!"

I ran towards him but the floor was getting gradually steeper and Keith was getting faster and faster. Then Tintin stepped out in front of me and blocked my path.

"You can go no further," he said, while his little bastard dog growled at me and nibbled at my ankles. "Ay, ay, ay! Take it easy Snowy."

I shook my fist at his perfectly round face. "Get out of my way Tintin, you Belgian twat!" I screamed. "I hate you! You're so bloody boring and Belgian!"

Then the man in the hooded cloak came up behind me and stabbed me in the back with his breakfast sword.

And then I woke up.

It was raining outside, and the wind was whistling like an impressed giant. I looked at the clock and saw that it was three in the morning. *Bloody Tintin*, I thought, as I rolled onto my side and folded my arms up beneath the pillow where it was nice and cool. *Now I'll never get back to sleep*. I pulled the duvet up over my head and yawned quite deliberately to make myself feel really tired. It didn't work. I would never be able to resume my slumbering with all of that crashing about downstairs.

Hold on a minute, I thought. *What is all that crashing about downstairs?* Perhaps Roger had got up to make himself a sandwich? No – that didn't sound like something Roger would do. He was normally out like a light after a hard day's work in the chicken costume. Something wasn't right. In fact something was very very unright (wrong).

I knew I was scared because my whole body was tense and my feet were clammy. Had I locked the front door?

No - I'd left it open in case Keith Matthews came home. *What an idiot*, I thought. *What a stupid, stupid idiot I am.*

I wanted to wake Roger and get him to load his air pistol, but when I tried to move I found that I was completely paralysed with fear. I just lay there on my back, helplessly shaking and covering my face with the duvet. And then I heard it; a loud creaking sound that sent a violent shiver down my spine. I would know that creak anywhere. *The third stair.* Whoever was in my house, they were on their way up…

I closed my eyes and listened hard as the footsteps approached along the landing. They were slow - too slow - like a madman stalking a goose… It couldn't be Roger - I was sure of that now. I closed my eyes and held tightly to the duvet as the intruder reached my door and then…

Nothing.

Those next few agonising seconds felt like days. I peered out over the duvet and stared at the door. Still nothing - nothing but silence…

And then the doorknob turned.

And then he came into the room.

I could feel myself shaking with a mixture of fear and rage. I was a coiled spring – every muscle as tight as a monk's bottom. I wanted to cry out for help but it was as though my jaw were wired shut. My whole life flashed before my eyes, sweat poured from every inch of my skin, I sucked in a desperate gulp of air and held my breath. And then they spoke...

"Are you awake, darling?"

It was a man's voice.

"Darling?" he enquired again.

Darling? Immediately I feared that he might do some sort of rape on me.

"Do you want some of this?" he said. "It's very good…"

I had no idea what he was offering me, and I wouldn't like to have guessed. He was almost certainly a madman – a bloody mad rapist madman. Heck, he was probably naked out there, prancing about my bedroom with his lad flopping about like something out of the Bee Gees. I stayed perfectly still beneath the duvet, hoping that he would assume I was a pile of pillows. God, how I wished I was a pile of pillows…

A few more seconds of agonising silence.

And then I felt the duvet move away from me, and the threat level reached critical. He was getting into my bed!

I couldn't tell what was going to happen next – it was anyone's guess – but I don't think that anyone would have guessed the thing that actually happened next, were they to actually try to guess what was going to happen next (because I certainly wouldn't have).

The coiled spring that was Walton Cumberfield sprung forth like a jug of naughts. I screamed at the top of my voice, lunged away from the intruder, and fell to the floor with a painful *thud*. Without a moment's hesitation, I jumped to my feet and faced him in the darkness. And I knew – somehow I knew that I was about to die. And I wasn't very happy about it.

I grasped at the biggest and heaviest thing in my immediate locale - a large book on my bedside table – and I swung it at the intruder's head. It caught him with a great *thwack* and sent him tumbling to the floor. I jumped over the bed and stood over him, bringing the book down on him again, and again, and again. I couldn't help it. I was so afraid…

And then he stopped moving.

And then I stopped moving.

And then Roger (my lodger) came into my room and turned on the light.

"Walton?" he said. "What the hell have you done?"

I was still standing over the intruder, grasping *The Guinness Book of Records 2008* in my hand. There was blood on the carpet, and on the book, and on the bald head of my attacker…

"Oh God," I said, turning to Roger in disbelief. "I think I've done a manslaughter."

"Have you-" Roger began, edging closer to the scene of the crime. "Have you just beaten a man to death with *The Guinness Book of Records*?"

"Yes," I replied. "I am 99 percent sure that *that* is what I have done."

We stood there for a moment. I dropped the book. Roger looked at me in amazement.

"Why?" he asked.

"He was coming to get me!" I shouted. "I had to defend myself!"

"He's an old man!"

I looked at the intruder. Roger was right. This man was old - very old. His body looked frail and his clothes were very unfashionable. He was wearing a loose-fitting, woollen jumper, some bright yellow corduroy trouserpants, dirty old work boots, thick socks and a pair of black leather gloves.

"What was he doing here?" I asked.

"How should I know?" said Roger.

"Do you think he was lost?"

"Well you didn't *invite* him, did you? Of course he was lost!"

I sat on the bed and put my face in my hands. "I should call the police."

"Are you mad?" said Roger. "You've just murdered an old man with *The Guinness Book of Records*."

"I've just *manslaughtered* an old man with *The Guinness Book of Records*," I corrected him.

"You'll go to prison!" he shouted.

"Not necessarily."

"Yes necessarily. Definitely necessarily."

"What are we going to do?" I asked him.

"What's with this 'we'? I haven't done anything."

"You're an accessory," I pointed out.

"How's that?"

"You lent me that *Guinness Book of Records*. You supplied the murder weapon."

Roger folded his arms. "I thought you said it was manslaughter."

"Manslaughter weapon then!" I snapped.

He was starting to get on my nerves. To be honest I had half a mind to take *The Guinness Book of Records* to him too, but *that* would be murder, and I do like Roger most of the time.

"We have to hide the body," he said, after a while.

"How do we do that?" I asked.

"We'll bury him."

Now it was my turn to stare in disbelief. "Bury him? Bury him where?"

"In the woods. We'll wrap him in a duvet, pop him in the back of the Corsa and drive him down to the woods in Fletcher's Park."

"Out of the question," I said. "Besides, the Corsa's still at Bannatyne's. It was clamped because my mother's blue badge was a fake and I don't have access to my bank account because my wallet was stolen and they haven't sent the new card through yet, so I can't pay the fine and... and…"

I started to hyperventilate. Roger held a paper bag in front of my face for me to breathe into, and put his arm around me (in a purely heterosexual manner).

I took a few deep breaths and felt my heart rate slowing. Roger patted me on the back reassuringly. Gradually my senses became clearer, and I could taste a pungent odour as it filled my mouth and nostrils.

"Argh! This bag smells like feet!" I shouted. "Where did you get it from?"

"It was down there," said Roger. "On the floor, by the dead chap."

I quickly recoiled. "Don't shove a dead man's bag in my face, Roger! Never shove a dead man's bag in my face!"

Looking down into the bag I saw the offending article – a small hunk of cheese in a white wrapper. The situation was becoming more bizarre by the minute. Why was this old man bringing me cheese? I pulled it out of the bag and showed it to Roger.

"What is it?" he asked.

"It's cheese," I said. "I think..."

"It stinks!" Throw it away."

I looked at the wrapper. It was completely plain, except for a small red stamped address which read as follows:

The Old Dog and Bottle
Aylesbeare
Exeter
Devon
EX5 2JP

"Sounds like a pub," I said.

Roger was getting agitated. "What does that matter? There's a cadaver in your bedroom!"

"It's all the way from Devon," I said.

"I don't care if it's all the way from *Christ the Redeemer*'s bottom! We've got a dead body on our hands, Walt! Do you know how serious this is? Now what the hell are we going to do?"

I set the cheese down on my bedside table, and scratched my head to help me think. Roger paced around with his head in his hands. I think he needed a sherry, but I didn't offer him one on account of his life-shattering alcoholism.

"What are you thinking?" asked Roger.

I shook my head and sighed.

"I'm thinking it's about time we locked the front door."

*

When Roger first moved in with me in 2009, he brought with him all manner of useless rubbish that he had accumulated during his nervous breakdown (which I am not really allowed to talk about). You see, when his wife walked out on him, Roger spent the majority of his weekends at various auctions and house clearances attempting to alleviate his mental anguish with retail therapy. He bought seven boxes of old books (including the offending *Guinness Book of Records*), some patio furniture, a stuffed fox, a dinghy, some golf clubs, a snowboard, Mark Knopfler's underpants and a very, very large ride-on lawnmower. These possessions were just about all that he was awarded in the divorce settlement, and they now sat out in my garden shed, dusting away and gathering rust.

On an unrelated (but largely relevant) note, my Great Auntie Boris once told me that she thought everything in life happened "for a reason", and that fate had a way of shaping our fortunes with tiny, seemingly insignificant events. Everyone thought she was a nutcase of course, including me – that is until that fateful night in February, when I suddenly started to see what she was talking about...

"Are you sure about this?" asked Roger, as we folded the old man's corpse into his ride-on lawnmower's high-capacity grass collector.

"Nope, but do you have any better ideas?" I asked, very much aware that this response was a bit of a cliché, but too stressed and exhausted to think up original dialogue.

"We could wait," suggested Roger. "Hide him in the shed until you get your car back."

"What? Just leave his corpse to rot in the shed until my new bank card arrives? That's hardly very dignified, is it?" I folded his neck back to fit his head inside the compartment and then bounced on the lid for a bit until it clicked shut. "We need to get him buried as soon as possible!"

"You're right," said Roger. "Better he be in the ground before the Police start looking for him."

I jammed a screwdriver into the mower's ignition and twisted it with considerable difficulty. "Damn you Roger!" I whispered (loudly). "Damn you and your bloody card games!"

I should explain... During the first few weeks of his alcohol-free lifestyle, Roger started spending a considerable amount of time at the bookmakers around the corner and playing cards in the cellar of The King's Arms. After a while it became abundantly clear that he had developed a gambling addiction (which is another thing that I'm not really allowed to talk about). The only reason that I mention it now is by way of explaining the difficulty I was having with the mower's ignition switch. You see, late one night during a poker session at the pub, Roger bought his way back into a game by throwing in the keys to his ride-on mower. When he eventually lost said game, his opponent, a contemporary Neanderthal named "Big Sid", bizarrely assumed that the keys represented a right to ownership of the mower itself (which was neither stated nor agreed). Needless to say, a stink was very much kicked up at this point, and from the sounds of it, Roger was quite lucky to get out of that cellar alive. Regardless, he no longer owned the keys to the ignition, and we certainly weren't going to be paying a visit to "Big Sid" at half past three in the morning! Hence the screwdriver...

"There," I said as the mower's engine roared into life. "Now let's get going."

As a clean licence holder (Roger's had jam on it), I elected to drive the mower south of Hellesdon, while Roger jogged alongside with some shovels and kept a look out for any potential witnesses. Fortunately the streets of Hellesdon are very sparsely populated at half past three in the morning, but just in case we were overheard by any late night Hellesdon hedge-dwellers or nosey Norfolk nymphs, we perpetuated a charade to divert any possible suspicion that may have been aroused. Every now and then we would shout things like "bloody Mr Norman - making us cut the grass in the middle of the night..." and "damn these new nocturnal gardening and hole-digging strategies! I hate working for the council!"

Although Roger's acting skills couldn't hold a candle to my own, I was confident that our theatrics held up to the scrutiny of any onlookers, and we managed to reach the park without incident (except one incident when Roger stepped in some cat feculence and said a bad word).

When we arrived at the park entrance, Roger picked some large leaves from a bush and used them to wipe the sole of his shoe. I killed the lights on the mower, and anxiously drove through the gates into the darkness beyond. Contained within the park was a labyrinth of pathways that negotiated their way around ponds, tennis courts and several small pockets of woodland. It was much larger than the park opposite my house, and I would often take Keith Matthews there for some extra exercise when he was getting fat from too much post-breakfast post eating (which was most of the time). I was sure that the old man wouldn't have minded being buried in such a lovely place. In fact, it is exactly where I wish to be buried, or to have my ashes scattered should I die in a house fire or similar…

When we reached the largest and densest section of trees in the centre, I dismounted the mower and popped open the grass collector. As I stared in at the man's body, packed into the chamber like a geriatric contortionist, I was filled with a deep sense of regret. *Perhaps I should go to the Police*, I thought. *If I tell them I'm sorry, maybe they'll let me go, like Anthony Worrall Thompson.*

"Penny for your thoughts," said Roger.

I sighed and continued to stare at the body. "I'm thinking that if I tell the police I'm sorry, maybe they'll let me go. Like Anthony Worrall Thompson…"

"Anthony Worrall Thompson never killed anyone," said Roger.

"Not yet," I pointed out. "But it's only a matter of time."

"What are you talking about?" he said. "Look, just close that up – we need to keep him hidden until we've dug the hole."

Roger handed me a penny (for my thoughts) and I slipped it into my back pocket. So far I have made a total of £22.78 by selling my thoughts to Roger. In fact, treating the phrase "penny for your thoughts" as a verbal contract has proven to be my second most lucrative business idea - the most lucrative being when I decided to purchase *Marie Curie Cancer Care* from a charity shop, and opened a subsidiary which focused exclusively on the sale and manufacture of mittens. Of course, that's another story, for another time…

A sudden gust of icy wind caught my face with a chill that resonated throughout my whole body. I closed the grass collector, stuck a torch in my pocket and set off into the trees with Roger. I was unable to think of any bogus conversations to provide a caveat for our movements at this point in time, so we decided to venture forth in silence. Besides, Roger assured me that the only people about at that hour would be drunks and cottagers. I just hoped that the drunks were already out for the count and the cottagers were at home in bed (in their cottages). We were pretty sure that no one would be out in the park at that hour – not with the moonlight so faint and the weather so cold. We were sure we could go about our business unnoticed. We were sure that we were alone.

But we were wrong.

Somewhere nearby, hidden in the dark lattice of trees, a disgruntled jackdaw manically flapped out of the undergrowth, as though startled by something. *Or someone!* Then we heard a sneeze. And then we heard somebody say "Shhhh!" And it wasn't me. And it wasn't Roger.

"Did you hear that?" asked Roger.

I stopped and looked around, straining my eyes to see through the thick blanket of darkness. "Yes. Yes I did."

Roger raised his spade defencively, and we crept slowly away from the source of the noise. *It was probably just a badger*, I thought. Either that or my mind was playing tricks on me again. My mind was always playing tricks on me - like the time it made me think I had seen Edward Miliband in Marks and Spencer's, when on closer inspection it was merely a squashed quiche.

No – it wasn't a badger, and that tricksy mind of mine couldn't be held responsible either. Before long we could clearly hear the shuffling of footsteps, and the rustling of leaves. There was definitely somebody else in the woods with us – and they were getting closer.

"Perhaps we should go back," Roger whispered.

"It's too late for that," I said. "If we can hear them, then they can hear us. They already know that we're here."

"Think of something," hissed Roger.

I turned to him. "I beg your pardon?"

"Think of something. Some sort of excuse. Why are we out here so late?"

I could hear the murmur of hushed voices on the wind. There was more than one of them, and they were close now. Very close.

"I've no idea," I admitted. "I can't think of anything."

Roger clicked his fingers. "We could say we're cruising for sex."

"Bloody hell, Roger!" I shouted. "That's the exact same excuse you used when we got lost in the John Lewis furniture department! It didn't work then and it's not going to work now. What is it with you and cruising for sex?"

"It's an easy way out," he explained. "We just say we're a couple of trolls."

I shook my head in disbelief. "Don't be stupid, Roger. Trolls live under bridges. There isn't a bridge around here for miles!"

We heard a cough from behind us. Very close behind us – somewhere behind a nearby thicket…

"They're everywhere," said Roger, quivering. "We have to get out of here."

"No," I said, being characteristically courageous. "We should stand our ground. I will not be intimidated."

Someone else scurried across the path in front of us - though nothing more than a blur of shadow in the darkness.

"Who's there?" I shouted, gallantly. "Show yourselves!"

Nothing happened for a moment. Even the wind seemed to stop, and the world around us came to an abrupt halt. We stood in silence, waiting… I was sick of silences. Silences always seemed to end badly for me - like the silence before Melanie Bogg dumped me on the bus, and the silence before I manslaughtered a man with *The Guinness Book of Records* in my bedroom, not to mention the silence before Doctor Fenton put his hand up my bottom (without permission) and fuddled about. No - I wasn't enduring another bloody silence. *Not today…*

"Who's there?" I shouted again. "What are you doing out here at this hour? Are you from the cottages?"

"We could ask you the same question," came a voice from the thicket.

"We're cruising for sex!" shouted Roger.

I hit him on his arm with medium force.

"No we're not," I clarified. "Now, where are you? Show yourselves!"

Roger tapped me on the shoulder and whispered; "Use your torch!"

"Good thinking," I replied.

I pulled out my torch, raised my arm back and hurled it in the direction of the voice. It was a fairly heavy torch, so I knew it would give them a pretty good lump if it made contact. Unfortunately I think it just bounced off a tree and landed in a hedge.

"You!" someone shouted. "What are you doing here?"

They sounded surprised. Had they recognised me? Surely they couldn't see me in the dark – unless of course they had some of those trendy green binoculars like out of *The Jurassic Theme Park.*

"Get him!" shouted another voice from the thicket.

They *did* have trendy green binoculars like out of *The Jurassic Theme Park*. They must have done - and now they were shuffling about very quickly – presumably in our direction. I took Roger's arm (being careful to avoid his hand should the gesture be misconstrued) and pulled him away from the assailants into a thick clump of what I soon discovered were stinging nettles. We lay there in silence (and agony) for a moment, and listened to the grunts and groans that surrounded us. I could tell that we were listening to a particularly violent exchange, but for some reason it did not involve us at all. There were three or four of them - fighting between themselves.

"What's going on?" asked Roger. "Who are they fighting?"

I shushed him - which I know he hates, but it was an emergency. Whoever they were, we couldn't let them find us. Someone was pummelling the living heck out of someone else. I could hear the dull, repeated thud of a person being battered within an inch of their life. *Jiminy Christmas*, I thought. *I wouldn't want to be that guy!* Then the battering stopped, and a few angry cries descended into the sound of laughter. *Laughter?* Who the heck were these people? Maybe they had gathered for a light-hearted beating like the people in that film *The Fight Club*… No. No such luck. A thunderous war cry heralded the immediate initiation of another battle. I closed my eyes and tried to think of some of my favourite things to take my mind off it, like they do in that song… Well, not exactly like they do in that song, you understand. After all, what kind of boring old codger likes mittens and brown paper packages? Julie Andrews clearly hasn't ever played on the Xbox…

The struggle ended as suddenly as it had begun, and once again we were suffocated by the cold, merciless pillow of silence. Stupid bloody silence! I held my breath and clenched my fists, being careful not to make the slightest noise – to be at one with the silence – to let it enshroud me and allow myself to become a part of it. I was the silence. The silence was me. I didn't exist. Then my tummy made a horrible gurgling sound because I attempted to stifle a trump, and it seemed immediately obvious that I had given away our position. I closed my eyes as tightly as I could and waited for them to find us. But they didn't find us. They didn't even look for us!

Roger rolled onto his front and was about to get up, but I grabbed his arm and told him to wait (I did this silently by squeezing his arm using Morse code). We lay there for a while, saying nothing and keeping perfectly still. And then, after a few minutes had passed, something else happened that I had not planned.

I was running again – running down the greasy corridors in the land of my dreams. And there, behind me, was the man with the breakfast sword. Like a complete bloody idiot, I had gone and fallen asleep in the bush. To be fair, it was the middle of the night, and I had not had an easy evening, but still, I was considerably annoyed with myself.

"Come on then!" I shouted to the hooded man. "Come and stab me with your breakfast sword!"

I knew he had to stab me, because I knew I was dreaming, and I knew I had to wake up again. I presented myself to him, arms outstretched, ready for the final thrust, but the man just stopped and sheathed his weapon.

"Come on!" I shouted. "What are you waiting for?"

I ran towards him as quickly as I could, but then he melted and I was in the John Lewis furniture department, wearing a space suit, sitting on a black leather sofa next to Roger, who was fast asleep. And I was surrounded by people. Melanie was there, and Rodney Rooney and Aaron Michaels and Lizo from Newsround and Hilda McIntyre and Gort and that bloody Belgian bastard Tintin with his little bastard dog. And they were all shouting at me – all at once, as one communal voice. They were pointing at me and shouting;

"You're an idiot! You're an idiot, and everyone thinks you're an idiot and you'll always be an idiot and I hate you! You'll never amount to anything! You bloody berk!"

And then the walls turned to cheese and we all melted away into the lines of a distant poem, which was the most abstract thing that had ever happened to me in one of my dreams.

And then I woke up.

The sun was rising through the trees, and as I pulled myself to my feet I immediately realised the imminent threat that it posed to myself and Roger, who was also coming to. The night was over, and the corpse was still in the back of Roger's mower, which remained at the edge of the tree line, exposed to the scrutiny of daylight. I shook Roger awake and searched the area for our spades, but there was no sign of them.

"What happened?" asked Roger.

"We fell asleep!" I explained. "We fell asleep like a couple of bloody nincompoops!"

Roger looked around. "Where are the spades?"

"I don't know! Whoever was here last night must have taken them."

"Why?"

"I DON'T KNOW!" My voice echoed around the trees and a few more jackdaws took off into the day. Can you take off into the day? You can definitely take off into the night, but why not the day? Yes, I don't see why not. They took off into the day...

"What are you thinking?" asked Roger. I did not reply, since no financial offer was attached to his request, and my thoughts are a valuable commodity.

The ground was churned up and covered with various footprints. That was the only sign of the previous night's scuffle - a few footprints, and some spatters of blood on a nearby tree. The perpetrators had long since vanished, and we were the only ones left. *And there was still a cadaver in the back of our mower!*

"What if somebody's found him?" I asked.

"Who?" asked Roger.

I raised my arms in disbelief. "Who do you think? The man in the grass collector! The man I m-" I lowered my voice; "The man I manslaughtered with *The Guinness Book of Records*."

"Oh," said Roger. "Him."

We looked at each other, and without another word we were dashing through the trees back to the open park where we had left the mower. *What a bloody mess this is*, I thought. *How could one man have such rotten luck?* If luck was indeed a lady, then Lady Luck had not only broken up with me and kept my Aqua CD, but she'd started going out with Aaron Johnson almost immediately and posted pictures of them kissing on The Facebook. Essentially, Lady Luck was exactly like Bertha Harrison.

The mower was right where we left it, and no one was around. I looked at Roger and we both sighed heavily as a surge of relief passed over us. Even though the sun was coming up, it was still quite early, and no one was likely to be walking around there at such a time – not even the cottagers. As we walked over to the mower I smiled at Roger.

"It's fine," I said. "I mean, even if someone has been past – it's a ride-on lawnmower for goodness' sake. It belongs in a park."

"You're right," said Roger. "No one's going to mess about with the grass collector, at any rate..."

"No sir," I agreed. I don't know why I called Roger 'sir', but I think he liked it. He used to be called 'sir', in the days before he was an alcoholic chicken.

"We'll get the body back into the woods and do our best to hide it by hand," he suggested.

"Cool beans," I said, feeling bizarrely upbeat.

"Cool beans," Roger echoed.

We reached the mower and took one more look around. There was no one in sight, and we were right up next to the tree line. Within seconds we could have the body in the woods and out of sight. Then we could go back home, put our feet up, and have a nice cup of hot squash / tea for Roger.

"Here goes nothing," I said, which again I knew was a cliché, but you must understand that I was very tired by this point.

I pressed down the catch on the grass collector and the lid sprung open. I took a deep breath and looked inside. Then I looked at Roger. Then Roger looked inside. Then Roger looked at me. Then I looked inside again, just to be sure. Then I think Roger looked inside again, but I couldn't tell because I wasn't looking at him. I was still looking inside. Then we looked at each other. Then we definitely both looked inside...

The body was gone.

FIVE

MOUSE POO AND ATTIC DUST

The attic was full of memory and loft insulation, which made me feel warmly nostalgic. I pulled myself through the little hatch and crawled up onto the floorboards, carefully avoiding the loose nails and rodent droppings as I did so. The air was thick with the potent stench of rotten leather, which I believed was emanating from a pile of old shoes I had stacked up in the corner next to my old train set. There wasn't much else up there – just an old TV and the fire extinguisher I had stored away because it ruined the aesthetic of my kitchen. At the far end of the attic, behind the TV aerial, was a stack of old boxes and suitcases, covered in dust and cobwebs. In the light black case at the bottom of that stack was the primary objective of my latest attic excursion...

Many people like to save their spare money in a bank such as The Bank of England or HBSC, but such people are not progressive thinkers. Hypothetically speaking, if I were a rotten robber with a view to stealing someone's fortune, a bank is the first place that I would look. The last place that I would look is at the back of the attic in number 42 East Park Avenue, Hellesdon, behind the TV aerial, at the bottom of a pile of boxes and suitcases, inside a small woman's purse. Coincidentally enough, that is EXACTLY where I keep my life savings.

As I approached the pile I was careful not to knock the TV aerial as Roger was downstairs watching *Come Dine With Me.* I had told him to watch the "News" in case there was any word of our missing cadaver, but I knew that he had switched over again as soon as I left the room. Roger was such a fan of *Come Dine With Me* that he had started referring to it as "*Come Dine*" and had applied to be on the show at least eight times.

I pulled away the cobwebs, assuring that there were no spiders still living on them, and moved the boxes and cases to one side so that I was able to pop open the bottom one with the combination 7371 – the same as my PIN number (which is a secret). Inside the case was a very small, pink leather purse, fastened shut with silver clasps. It had once belonged to my late Aunt Penelope, who had been too late to stop me stealing it from her kitchen table. I took out the purse and popped it open. Inside was a small clump of bank notes and coins amounting to £234.57 (after I added the penny Roger had recently given me for one of my thoughts). I stared at the money – my nest egg – my rainy day fund – all that I had saved in this world, and all that I was worth... Had it really come to this?

Yes, was the answer. Yes, it had.

I stuffed the cash into my pocket and climbed down the ladder, knocking a few chunks of mouse poo and attic dust onto the carpet below. I then spent 34 minutes folding the ladder up and sliding it into the loft, having never quite got to grips with the various clips and catches that facilitate its operation. When the ordeal was finally over I sighed three times and went to fetch the vacuum cleaner from my bedroom.

The Cillit Bang I had used to clean up the intruder's blood had made a hole in the general film of dirt that covered my bedroom carpet, and now a shiny stain of cleanliness was staring up at me like an accusatory eye. It penetrated my soul and spoke directly to my blackened heart – softly, like the gentle voice of a cold, calm killer; "Look at yourself, Walton. Look at what you've become... Barry Scott would be ashamed."

My heart was beating so hard that I could hear it, ceaselessly invading my senses like the incessant bass-line of a proletariat neighbour's music. I began to tremble as the cynical eye of Cillit Bang continued to fix its gaze upon me. *It wasn't my fault. He was going to hurt me.* But the eye didn't listen… The eye just kept staring, mercilessly – probing into my core and casting judgment upon me.

Please. I didn't mean to do it. I was defending myself!

My eyes filled with tears, but the eye of Cillit Bang was a callous creature, and I knew that it would not forgive me. I couldn't take it back. The foul deed was done, and I would have to live with it forever.

I'm sorry.

Something touched my shoulder, which startled me so much that I jumped into the air, let out a cry of anguish and released a small amount of wee. It was only Roger of course, who had come upstairs to see what I was up to.

"What are you up to?" he asked. "What were you doing in the attic?"

I caught my breath and showed him the roll of cash. "I was fetching this."

"Your life savings?" he exclaimed. "Whatever do you need them for?"

"I'm going to get the hell out of Hellesdon," I said. "It's only a matter of time before they discover what I've done, and I can't go to prison. I won't survive in prison."

Roger sat down next to me and put his arm around me, his dressing gown falling open for a moment and revealing a flash of something I didn't care to see, like a repulsive version of *Basic Instincts.*

"Can you really live like that?" he asked. "Wouldn't it be best to face up to your crimes? Maybe prison isn't as bad as they say."

I shook my head. "No. A man called Perks once told me all about it. They send you there for life and that's exactly what they take. Prison is no fairytale."

We sat in silence for a while, the kind of silence that gradually allows the tiny sounds of life to fade into perception, like the ticking of a watch or the passing of a distant car. I began to feel very cold all of a sudden, and every sense was heightened by the tension of the moment. I noticed cracks in the wall that had not been there before and I could taste my own saliva. The hairs on my back began to tingle and itch, and my nose was filled with the pong of pungent cheddar. *Cheddar? Oh yes…*

The cheese was still sat on my bedside table.

"Where will you go?" asked Roger, quietly.

I reached out and picked up the cheese, twisting the wrapper in my hand to reveal the red writing.

"Walton?" said Roger. "Where are you going to go?"

I thought about it for seven seconds. Somehow it seemed like the only option. "The Old Dog and Bottle," I said. "The Old Dog and Bottle in Aylesbeare, Exeter, Devon."

Roger scoffed. "Why on earth would you go there?"

"Because," I said. "It's the only place I *can* go. Don't you see?" And just like that, I was back in detective mode…

"Don't I see… what?"

"Everything! Keith Matthews, Shed Seven, the old man with the cheese, the men in the woods," I stared Roger right in the eyes. "What does it all mean?"

"I don't know."

"Exactly!" I stood up and paced the room. "We don't know. And the only real lead we have is *this* address."

"But what has the cheese got to do with your dog and the men in the woods?"

"I don't know - yet. But they must be connected – they have to be!"

Roger stood up, shrugging. "This is crazy."

"Crazy - yes," I said. "It's all crazy. My dog going missing from a locked house – that's crazy. A nonsensical message from a homeless man in the park – crazy. An old man breaking into our house with some cheese – pretty crazy! It's all crazy, Roger. It's all as mad as that TV show *Mad Men*." (I had never seen that TV show *Mad Men*).

Roger frowned. "So what's your point?"

"My point is that life *isn't* crazy. Not really. Not *that* crazy. So what are the chances of so many crazy things happening to me in the space of a few weeks? It can't be a coincidence!"

Roger rested his chin in his palm. "So everything's linked?"

"Everything's linked," I said. "And I'm going to find out how..."

I grabbed the rug from the end of my bed and hurled it over the eye of Cillit Bang. This was no time for remorse. This was a time for action! I threw open the doors to my wardrobe and tossed some of my favourite clothes into a suitcase.

"First thing tomorrow I'll be on a train to the South West," I declared valiantly.

Roger leant back on my dressing table and thoughtfully fondled a bottle of vinaigrette. "Are you sure that's a good idea?"

"It's the best idea I've ever had," I informed him. "The very best." This was mere hyperbole of course, as I've had several ideas that were notably of a higher quality than this one – for example my range of Russell Crowe-themed Tamagotchi cases, and the speculative application I sent to J.K. Rowling to be the ghost writer for the eighth Harry Potters book – but that's another story, for another time...

Roger paced across the room, his dressing gown flapping away and revealing his appendage in split second intervals like some sort of subliminal sausage.

"Will you please tie up your dressing gown?" I said. "Your John Thomas keeps popping out."

"I can't," he explained. "I can't find the cord. I've looked everywhere."

"Well at least put on some pants," I said. "And go and fetch me some Tupperware. I'm taking all the evidence with me. This cheese is going to meet its maker."

Roger politely obliged while I packed the rest of my case with travelling essentials – toothpaste, trouserpants, Pritt Stick, Travel Scrabble™ and plenty of chocolate biscuits. I went through Roger's desk and grabbed his phone charger, a couple of magazines, a stapler and some tissues. The only other thing I knew I would need was an air pistol for protection - but it wasn't in its usual hiding place under his pillow.

"Where's your air pistol?" I asked as Roger came back upstairs.

"Under my pillow," said Roger. "Where it normally is."

"No it isn't," I said. "It definitely isn't."

"That's odd."

"Very odd," I agreed (though to be honest I was getting fairly used to things being 'odd').

"I've just phoned work and left a message," said Roger. "I said that I was ill today, and I won't be in tomorrow."

"Why won't you be in tomorrow?"

Roger smiled and folded his arms. "It's a big case, Walt. You're going to need my help."

I laughed at his naivety. "It's fine Roger. It's got wheels and one of those pull-out handles."

"No," he said. "I'm not talking about your suitcase. I'm talking about the *case*."

By the underlined, italicised nature of his repetition of the word "case", I understood immediately to what he was referring.

"You're coming to Devon?" I asked.

"I'm in too deep to back out now," said Roger. "If you're going to solve this mystery, you're going to need some assistance."

"You might be right there," I admitted.

"You're going to need someone you can count on," he said, putting on his abacus shirt. "And I'm part of this now, whether you like it or not. So, if you'll have me, I'm quite willing to be your Watson."

I thought for a moment. Roger could sometimes be a bit of a liability, what with his depression, cordless dressing gown and the ongoing threat of his latent alcoholism. Then again, at that moment, it seemed as though Roger was the only friend I had left, and I was beginning to admire his balls (not literally, although I had seen them).

"What do you say, Walt?" asked Roger. "Can I be Watson?"

I smiled at my brave lodger, suddenly seeing him in a new light (which we had bought from Maplin a couple of days before).

"You can be Watson," I assured him, patting him on the shoulder. "You can be Watson… and I'll be Francis Crick."

Roger was an oddball sometimes. I decided to let him come along in the end, although to be honest I had no idea what the discovery of the double-helix structure of DNA had to do with anything.

SIX

GAMES, TRAINS AND BOOKMOBILES

As the train pulled into Nottingham station I realised our mistake. In our haste we had boarded the 10:14 to Liverpool Lime Street, rather than the desired 10:16 to London Liverpool Street, and had by this point travelled 122 miles in the wrong direction.

A ticket inspector could easily have alerted us to our mistake at an earlier convenience – but there didn't seem to be any ticket collectors on our service. In my experience, ticket collectors are like David Attenborough; they're never there when you need them and always there when you've lost your ticket somewhere in Winchester on a bird watching expedition. On that particular occasion I attempted to avoid the penalty fare by pretending to be fast asleep (on Attenborough's shoulder) – a charade which backfired somewhat as the on-board staff began to worry that I was dead and phoned for the British Transport Police. By the time I had decided it was safe to "wake up" I was in a hospital in Reading being subjected to numerous medical tests. Fortunately any questions relating to the validity of my train ticket had since been rendered obsolete, so the conclusion of the anecdote is one of bittersweet resolution (and a free chicken korma courtesy of the NHS).

Being very conscious of our limited budget, Roger and I shared a ham panini while waiting for the next train to London. I have since learnt that *technically* speaking we shared one ham panino (singular), and not several panini (plural). Of course some would argue that we have not adopted the singular form in English which means that one "panini" can still be accepted as correct. Whichever way you look at it, it definitely isn't spelt how I spelt it when I updated The Facebook.

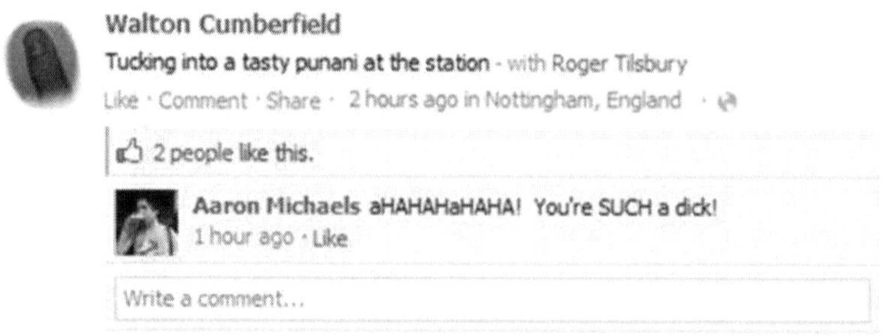

Walton Cumberfield
Tucking into a tasty punani at the station - with Roger Tilsbury
Like · Comment · Share · 2 hours ago in Nottingham, England
2 people like this.
Aaron Michaels aHAHAHaHAHA! You're SUCH a dick!
1 hour ago · Like
Write a comment...

It goes without saying that Nottingham Station is a well-known Wi-Fi hotspot, which meant that I was able to use the extra bandwidth to download some cool new apps to Roger's smartphone. I bought an awesome picture-drawing app called *Freedraw*, a rhyming dictionary called *iRhyme Plus* and a Scottish calculator called *Scottish Calculator.* I was also going to download a free app called *109 Lovely Lady Boobs*, but I was put off by the fact that 109 is an odd number.

We didn't have valid tickets for the train from Nottingham to London, so we both pretended to be asleep when the ticket inspector approached us.

"Tickets please," he said (rudely).

We did not respond.

"Can I see your tickets please gentlemen?" he asked again (really rudely).

I kept my eyes closed.

"I'm going to have to see your tickets, I'm afraid, or I can't let you ride on the train."

He wasn't getting the message, so I started snoring as loudly as possible. I am very good at fake snoring - the trick being a quick, croaky, nasal intake of breath, followed by a long, high-pitched oral exhalation.

"That's not real snoring," said the ticket inspector. "That just sounds like cartoon snoring. No one actually snores like that."

"Actually, my wife used to snore just like that," said Roger.

Damn it, Roger!

"So you're awake then?" said the inspector.

"Ah," said Roger, realising that he had been majorly hoodwinked. "I'm afraid we don't have any tickets."

"We got on the wrong train," I explained, opening my eyes. "We meant to get the train to London Liverpool Street but we boarded the train to Liverpool Lime Street by mistake. Now we need to get back to London – I'm sure you understand."

"A likely story," said the inspector.

Thank goodness, I thought. *He believes us.*

"Now," he said. "I can't let you ride this train without valid tickets. So that's two adult tickets to London. No concessions. That'll be 198 pounds."

Roger and I laughed heartily at the inspector's keen sense of humour.

He stuck out his hand. "Now, please gentlemen."

Bizarrely, the inspector wasn't smiling. After nine seconds I realised that he wasn't joking and our LOLs turned into WTFs!

"One hundred and ninety eight pounds?" I yelled, quietly. "Do you know what we could buy with 198 pounds?"

"Two full price tickets from Nottingham to London," answered the inspector – a self satisfied smirk on his pimply face.

"But we don't have that much money," I said. "My wallet was stolen and my bank hasn't sent a new card through yet, so I've withdrawn my life savings from the stash in my attic."

"A likely story," he said again. I didn't understand why he was still pestering us if he believed everything that we were saying. The man was full of contradictions (and the other thing that people are full of - #lmfao).

"If I may," said Roger. "We're only here because we accidentally got on the wrong train. Perhaps if you could just offer us a concessionary rate…"

"It's 198 pounds," said the inspector, really bloody rudely. "If you can't pay for a ticket then you'll be getting off at the next stop."

"But we don't have that much money!" I cried.

"Then you'll be getting off at the next stop," he said. "And that's my final word on the matter."

But it wasn't his final word on the matter. He proceeded to steal another £28 from each of us to cover the journey as far as Loughborough, and refused to listen when I explained that Roger was mentally handicapped and I was the Mayor of Norwich. I'm pretty sure I could have won him over with the whole "Mayor of Norwich" story, but Roger's impression of a mentally handicapped person leaves a lot to be desired, and it wasn't in keeping with his demeanour at the beginning of our conversation, which presented a flaw in continuity.

When the inspector left I took out Roger's phone and used my new *Freedraw* app to depict him satirically through the medium of art:

"What now?" said Roger, his eyes full with distain. "If we get off now we'll never get to Devon and solve this mystery!"

He was right. I was hoping that the ticket collector would look kindly on our situation and grant us passage without obstruction, but that was not to be. Now I knew I would have to go to Plan B if I wanted to stay ahead of The Game (like the time Ben Drew helped me to beat Jayceon Terrell Taylor in a gardening competition). We did not get off at the next stop as instructed, and deceived the merciless railway professionals by locking ourselves in the toilets until we reached London. Despite the space limitations and the fact that the floor was covered in other people's wee wee, we were determined to enjoy our trip as much as possible. After a few minutes I decided it was high time we broke out the Travel Scrabble™ and a couple of 'tinnies' (of salmon).

I got a 50 point bingo straight away with the word HUNTERS, which Roger subsequently tried to extend into the word HUNTERSFIELD. We then had a brief argument about whether or not proper nouns are allowed in Travel Scrabble™ after which Roger demanded that we should start again as he was not familiar with the rules. He went first this time, and played the word CONCRETE for 74 points. I then pointed out that CONCRETE has eight letters in it, and he should only have started with seven. We went over the rules one more time and drew letters again. The rest of the game went off without incident until Roger attempted to get a triple word scoring bingo with the word JUMENTOUS, connecting the M from his MAGIC with the S from my SYCHO.

"Jumentous is not a word," I said.

"It is a word," he protested. "You're just bitter because you're losing."

I leaned back and folded my arms. "Okay – if it's a real word, use it in a sentence."

"Fair enough. The farmer's coat was quite jumentous."

I scoffed and shook my head. "Right. So it's an adjective, is it?"

"Yes," said Roger. "It means of, relating to or smelling like the urine of a horse or other equine creature."

"Don't be absurd," I said, taking his letters off the grid and passing them back to him. "Have another go."

"It is a real word," said Roger. "Let me have it."

"No."

"This isn't fair!"

"Now listen," I snapped. "If you're going to come on this adventure then you've got to stop being such a moaning Michael! Honestly, do you think Watson ever treated Crick like this?"

"No," he mumbled.

"I can't hear you."

"No," he said, a little louder, and laid the word JETS for 11 points. "But jumentous is a word."

Suddenly we heard somebody knocking on the toilet door and recoiled in silent fear. Wishing not to be rumbled for our deception, I cleverly made some awkward trumping sounds until they went away again. Ironically I did really need to use the toilet at this point, but with Roger locked in there with me I couldn't very readily ameliorate my urges. I knew that I would have to wait until reaching the station in London - where the endeavour carries a 30p price tag and most of the toilet seats are either soiled or broken. I went into one such facility to use the loo and apply my hemorrhoid cream back in 1997 (when I developed hemorrhoids as a side effect of the death of Princess Diana). The toilet wouldn't flush as there was a spanner jammed in the cistern, and as I was struggling to clean the toilet seat with some paper towels, a thoughtless bluebottle flew clumsily into the cubicle and landed in my open pot of Annusol. I then began to wonder if life was one big metaphor, and if I, Walton Cumberfield, was merely a figment of non-literal description in the mind of some great creative consciousness that in itself realised and fashioned the world in which we live. Then I remembered that I was late for my lunch appointment at Nandos, removed the fly from my arse cream and got on with my day. I do not like London one bit…

Here is a poem I once wrote about London:

If you walk down London's streets,
You won't see anyone you know,
And everybody smells of feet,
And no one stops to say 'hello'.

I knew a man whose name was Stan,
Who lived in London for a year.
And now he only eats All-Bran,
And drinks hibiscus flavoured beer.

The smoggy air will make you cry
And every black'ning church appalls
When all the dust gets in your eye,
And you can't even see St Paul's.

But most thro' midnight streets I hear

How the youthful Harlot's curse
Blasts the new born Infant's tear,
And blights with plagues the Marriage hearse.

Coincidentally, the last stanza of my poem is exactly the same as that of the poem "London" by a man named Quentin Blake. As I pointed out to the judges of the Roger Maxwell Poetry Competition in 2003, this was hardly a surprising happenstance, since he and I were drawing inspiration from exactly the same source material (ie the City of London). I also believe it to be the weakest stanza of my poem, and have thought of changing it in the future.

By the time we got to London I realised that our tickets for the second leg of the journey were no longer valid, so I went to the information desk for some advice. Unfortunately the woman on the desk had killed herself with unspecific poison and set fire to the kiosk, which meant that she wasn't in a position to advise anyone about anything. This is the third poorest level of customer service that I have experienced at a London station information desk.

We decided to chance it and travelled to Waterloo using a nifty underground railway system, which Roger showed me how to use. I asked him why it was called an 'oyster' card but he did not know. I then asked a few other people on the underground train the same question but most of them were disinterested and one of them told me to get lost.

I got *Lost* in HMV before boarding the next train, which in retrospect was not a sensible investment, as it set me back another £59 and proved to be a cumbersome addition to my personal baggage. Also, I have seen *Lost* already when it was on the television and I did not understand a single thing about it. Also, I think Roger taped most of the episodes. Also, our DVD player is broken (because of ham).

Roger was dubious about getting on the next train without a valid ticket for the time of travel.

"I'm dubious about getting on the next train without a valid ticket for the time of travel," he said. "And I don't want to be stuck in another toilet with you for the next two hours!"

"Don't worry," I said as we approached our platform. "It's all under control."

Roger shrugged and shook his head, which made me a bit grumpy. He then said something else, but I don't know what it was because I had already popped in my headphones and was kicking back 'old school' with some of my favourite tunes.

When the ticket collector approached us I was listening to the album *Queen* by a band called *A Day at the Races*. *A Day at the Races* are my second or third favourite band because they are excellent. I think that they would be my first favourite, but they lose points when it comes to quantity of work as they have only produced the one album to the best of my knowledge.

The ticket collector frowned at me and gestured (rudely) for me to remove my headphones.

"Can I see your ticket please, sir?" he asked.

"Pah?" I replied (in Danish).

"Your ticket please."

I leant forward and frowned at him, using some of my best acting skills to feign a lack of knowledge of English. I then shrugged and said the following:

"Vaas ting meusal peesen haber ruden Troels Hartmann jonah varen muesh."

"Do you speak English?" asked the inspector, who had clearly been suitably fooled.

"Isk haber runen! Me runen! Me runen!" I shouted, slamming the table for effect.

The inspector sighed and shook his head. "Never mind, then."

It had worked! I couldn't believe it! My acting skill had finally saved the day! I picked up my headphones and was about to switch my music back on when the inspector turned his attention to Roger.

"What about you sir?" he asked him. "Do you speak English?"

"No I don't," said Roger, quite clearly.

Damn it Roger!

"You seemed to understand that question perfectly well," observed the inspector.

"No," said Roger. "I mean, yes… My English is very poor though. The chances are I won't understand the next thing you say. Señor..."

The inspector stared suspiciously at him. "Oh, is that right?"

"There, you see – I didn't understand a word of that."

Roger gave me a "thumbs up" sign, and I palmed my face in disbelief. I then attempted to rectify the situation by shouting "me runen! me runen!" a few more times, but it wasn't enough to divert attention from his terrible acting 'fail'.

"I'm going to have to see your tickets now," said the inspector. "Both of you."

"Vaas tik bakher tack chaer nubbin haar," I said, very seriously.

"That's not a language," he said. "You're just making silly noises but with a sincere tone."

Roger stepped in and produced his ticket. "Look," he said. "We got in a bit of a pickle this morning and ended up on the wrong train. We have tickets, but they're for an earlier train. We couldn't get here in time."

"You need to travel at the time advertised on your ticket, sir," explained the inspector.

"Evidently I am aware of that," said Roger. "But in order to travel on that train, we would first have to travel back in time, which is impossible."

"No it isn't," said the inspector.

Roger and I looked at each other.

"Yes it is," I said. "The concept of backwards time travel introduces too many paradoxes of causality to be entertained as a feasible possibility."

"So you <u>do</u> speak English," said the inspector.

I had been royally <u>hoodwinked</u>. Why were British railway staff so perfectly adept at hoodwinking?

"It has been hypothesised that travelling backwards in time might be possible by travelling faster than the speed of light or using a wormhole," explained the ticket inspector. "Ergo, you could have found a wormhole, travelled back in time and boarded the appropriate service as advertised on your ticket. You chose not to do this, and to disregard our system's rules and regulations with the sort of arrogance and nonchalance I have come to expect of the Great British public these days. Now, if that's everything gentlemen, I'm going to have to ask you to either buy two tickets or get off my train."

"Gosh darn it!" I exclaimed. "Why it so ruddy difficult just to get from one end of the country to the other? Why does it cost 30p to go for a poo in London? Why don't they sell 'Lucky Charms' in England anymore? Why didn't *A Day at the Races* make any more albums? Why did that old man have to come into my room two nights ago? Why, I ask you? Why do all of these terrible things keep happening to me?"

I then started frothing at the mouth and fell to the floor, twitching and moaning so that the whole carriage could hear. I did this quite deliberately of course, as a last ditch attempt to hoodwink the experienced hoodwinker who'd hoodwinked me for the last time.

"Get up sir," he said, very calmly. "If you think I'm falling for the old "seizure on a train" routine then you've got another thing coming. It's the oldest one in the book."

A voice on the carriage speakers announced that we were arriving in Basingstoke.

"I want you off my train," he told us.

"No," I said, grappling at his heels (like they do in the films). "Not Basingstoke! Please! You can't leave us here! Anywhere but Basingstoke!"

I realised at this point that my behaviour was becoming somewhat melodramatic, but I was quite enjoying it, so I decided to carry on in much the same manner as we were escorted from the train.

"You can't do this to me!" I screamed. "You think I'll forget you? I never forget a face! You hear me? Never!"

Roger followed behind without objection, carrying our bags.

"Think hard on this, trainmaster," I continued. "Thou hast made a powerful enemy this day. And it shall be your undoing. I will curse you, and your children, and your children's children's children! And you will rue the day that you ever crossed me! Oh yes. You will curse the day you made an enemy of Walton Cumberfield! Do you hear me?"

In hindsight, he probably could not hear me as the train was already pulling out of the station by the time I reached the end of my tirade. Thick, grey clouds were gathering in the sky above us, and a faint rumbling suggested the onset of the most pathetic fallacy I have ever experienced. I stared helplessly as the train pulled away from us, abandoning us, forgetting us. It felt as though the entire world had some sort of vendetta against me. A solitary bead of lacrimal fluid dribbled down my left check as I settled myself down and turned to Roger.

"Let's get some crisps," I suggested.

*

Forgetting that I am mildly allergic to beef, I chomped away on some Monster's Munch while Roger tucked into a blueberry muffin. I needed to take a break before planning our next move, so we sat in the station lounge for a while and listened to the rain as it pelted the windows like the angry tears of a giant wasp.

"I should have gone to work today," said Roger. "This is ridiculous."

I ignored him and popped in my headphones. He was still gesticulating and going on about something, but all I could hear was "*Some people call me the space cowboy, yeah, some people call me the gangster of love...*" I love Steve Miller Band, though I often wonder why he never went into politics like his brothers David and Ed.

The evening was setting in fast and it was already getting dark. If we were going to get to Devon we would have to act quickly. I took out Roger's phone and launched the *FreeDraw* app, which I used to make a hitchhiking sign. I have heard many horror stories about hitchhikers, but I couldn't let my cowardice govern me at such a desperate time...

Roger glanced at my work.

"It's too small," he said. "No one will see that from the road. And what's with the smiley face?"

"The word Aylesbeare," I replied.

Roger frowned a bit. "No, I mean why have you drawn a smiley face at all?"

"So that people know that we're jolly nice chaps and not animal molesters or something," I said. "I would have thought that was obvious."

Roger shook his head. "It's not going to work."

"No it won't," I said. "Not with *that* attitude."

We both had a bit of a strop at that point and didn't speak to each other for a full 45 minutes. I had another packet of Monster's Munch and Roger ordered a whole panino to himself, like a greedy plonker. He took a handful of toothpicks from the catering counter and used them to make "pop art" on the table for a bit. I don't know when we would have started talking again if what happened then didn't happen. But as it happened, it did happen, and I, for one, happen to be pretty happy that it happened when it did (happen).

The hero was short, with casual stubble and playful eyes. He was wearing a bright yellow anorak and wellington boots – not the traditional attire of a hero, but practical given the weather at the time. Bizarrely, he didn't seem to know he was a hero at all, and neither did we, to begin with. He wandered into the lounge unnoticed and looked around. I don't think we even looked up. And then he saw us, and a wide grin broke out across his little face…

"Hello chaps," he said jovially. "How's it going?"

Roger and I both looked at the hero, and then at each other, and then back at the hero (who we didn't yet know was a hero).

"I'm not late am I?" he asked.

I had literally no idea where he was going or what he was doing, so I couldn't answer his question. I just shrugged and smiled politely.

"This weather, eh?" he continued. "Bloody nasty out there tonight." He sat down next to us. "How are you both, anyway? How's your arm, Roger?"

Roger raised his eyebrows. "It's… fine."

"Wonderful," said the hero. "That's good to hear."

Roger looked at me and made a face (out of toothpicks).

"Well, are you going to sit here making toothpick faces all day or are we going to get going?" said the hero.

"Going where?" I asked.

"You tell me," he said. "I'm parked just outside."

I wrote the phrase "DO YOU KNOW THIS MAN?" on Roger's phone and showed it to him discreetly. Roger shook his head.

"Come on guys," said the hero. "It's getting late."

"Sorry, are you offering us a lift?" I asked.

"Of course," said the hero, his eyebrows shaping a frown of confusion. "What do you think I'm doing here?"

Roger piped up. "Can you drive us to Aylesbeare in Devon?"

"Sounds like a plan," said the hero with a grin. "Let's get going."

I wasn't sure who the hero was, why he thought that he knew us, or why he was willing to act as our personal chauffeur. The fact of the matter was, however, that we were stranded in Basingstoke and this stranger was the only way out of that situation.

"We're jolly nice chaps by the way," I said as we walked briskly through the rain. "We're not animal molesters or anything."

"I know," said the hero, approaching a large white bus.

"Whoa," said Roger. "This is yours?"

"Well remembered," said the hero, opening the back door. "Do hop in."

The bus was covered in brightly coloured writing and pictures of giant books. It looked like something out of a children's televisual show – with sunshine, clouds and rainbows bordering the image. In the bottom left hand corner was a picture of a shark, for some reason. It was either a mobile library, or the vehicle of a madman. I hoped it was a mobile library.

"This chap thinks he knows us," I whispered to Roger.

"It's a free lift," said Roger. "Just go with it."

I boarded the bus and smiled at the hero. "Thanks very much, old friend."

"You're quite welcome," he said, and removed his anorak. Underneath he was wearing a fleece jacket with the phrase "*Bringing the library to you*" printed on the back.

"Thanks very much, Gus," said Roger as he climbed aboard.

"Gus?" I whispered. "How do you know his name is Gus?"

"It's on his name badge," explained Roger.

I nodded and patted him on the back to commend him for his keen detective skills. Turning into the bus (as in rotating, not transmorphing), we were greeted by a vibrant trove of alphabetised literature on bright yellow shelves. I had never been in a mobile library before, and I have to say it was quite wonderful. The floor was even covered in a nice blue carpet, and there were a couple of comfy-looking seats built into the back, which would be perfect for Roger and I to "kick back" on for the next couple of hours.

"Take a seat, chaps," said Gus as he stepped up and made his way to the desk at the far end. "Feel free to grab a book if you'd like."

"Thanks very much," said Roger. "You really are a hero, you know that? We'd be stranded here if it wasn't for you."

Gus lifted the flap of the desk and went behind it, clambering through to the driver's seat.

"You're the hero," he said, very sincerely. "Don't you forget that. I won't let you forget that." (I had no idea what he was talking about).

As the bookmobile's engine roared into life, I sat back on the comfy chair, next to Roger, who gave me a quick smile and a raise of his unkempt eyebrows, exemplifying, quite reassuringly, the reparation of our friendship. There was a black book on the floor by my feet, with an orange picture of a bird on the front cover. I picked it up to replace it on a shelf, but when I saw its title, which was all too familiar, I was halted by a crushing sensation in my chest (which admittedly might have been something to do with the Monster's Munch).

The book was *To Kill a Mockingbird* by Lee Harper. Melanie had told me that it was her favourite book, and explained to me what it was about. I couldn't remember much about it of course, as when she was telling me I was just staring into her eyes (which are really lovely and twinkly). In that moment I realised how much I missed her, and it suddenly spawned on me that she wasn't my girlfriend any more. She wasn't even my "off-again" girlfriend. She was somebody else's girlfriend, and we'd never be able to talk about nice things like books and classical music ever again. Melanie was always inspiring me to try new things and better myself. She was the one who got me into wearing proper trouserpants and introduced me to the band *Grieg*, who did a fantastic piano concert in A minor. Now she would be doing all that for somebody else - somebody who was, by all accounts, a bit of a bastard.

I choked back a few secret tears and decided that even though I would probably never use any of the skills explained in the book, I would read Lee Harper's *To Kill a Mockingbird* from cover to cover. There wasn't much opportunity for conversation anyway, as Roger seemed to be engrossed in a German book about tents entitled *Mein Kampf*.

As the literature wagon thundered through the mist and rain that consumed the M3, I lost myself in a turbulent interrogation of rape and racial inequality. It was a really, <u>really</u> good book and I could see why it was Melanie's favourite. I thought perhaps that I would make it my favourite book, since the events of the previous few days necessitated a replacement for the top spot once held by *The Guinness*

Book of Records 2008. Of course, apart from anything else, it was just nice to escape reality and let my mind wander for a bit.

After a couple of hours I could feel the bookmobile slowing down and thus assumed that we were entering a more rural environment.

"Whereabouts in Aylesbeare, lads?" asked Gus. *Good old Gus…*

"The Old Dog and Bottle," said Roger, putting down his book.

Gus turned back to us for a moment. "The Old Dog? Are you sure?"

"Quite sure," I confirmed.

"Rather you than me," he said, and thankfully turned back to face the road (what a nutter!).

"What do you mean?" asked Roger, looking worried.

"Just wouldn't fancy it myself," said Gus. "Weird sort of a place. Some of the locals say it's haunted."

Roger laughed and shot me a nervous look. I scoffed and went back to *Mockingbird.* I had been reading very quickly and was already on chapter eight. The only criticism I had so far was the lack of poetry or status updates on The Facebook, which I feel are a very original and compelling way to punctuate a longer piece of fiction. Nevertheless I was still very engrossed, and didn't even notice when the bookmobile came to a standstill and Gus shut off the engine.

"We're here," he said.

I didn't want to stop reading mid-chapter, so I carried on for another couple of pages. It was very good.

"Are you coming, Walt?" said Roger. "I'm sure Gus will let you borrow the book."

"Actually," said Gus. "You need to be a member of the library before I can let you borrow anything. But you can carry on reading it the next time we see each other. Drop me a line on Facebook when you're next about."

I looked up for a second. "But we're not friends on The Facebook."

"Yes we are," said Gus. "I'm sure I added you."

I gave Roger a confused smirk and carried on reading.

"Are you coming in, Gus?" asked Roger. "You must let us buy you a drink for your troubles."

Gus opened the flap of the desk and walked through into the back, munching on a scotch egg. "Oh no," he said. "I don't drink in The Dog. It's a rule to live by around these parts."

I remember wishing that they would shut up until I'd got to the end of chapter eight. It was very hard to concentrate with the two of them gassing away.

"Well, thank you very much," said Roger. "You really are a hero."

The two of them shook hands.

"Not at all," said Gus. "You two are *my* heroes. It was great to see you again."

"Yes," said Roger, trying to mask his confusion. "You too…"

I turned to the last page. Jem and Scout were chatting away to Miss Maudie, who seemed to be a bit head-mental. They offered to help her out, but she declined their offer. They had a task of their own to do. Then I noticed someone had stuck a handwritten footnote at the end of the page.

"You take care now," said Gus. "Whatever business you have in there, I suggest you get it done and get the hell out."

"Right," said Roger. "Thanks for the advice."

I read the footnote. Then I read it again. Then I blinked and shook my head and pinched myself. And then I checked it again and again, because I couldn't understand how it said what it said. But that *is* what it said. It definitely said it.

Walt – don't worry. Everything's going to be all right ☺

I looked at Gus. Had he written it? Who the hell was Gus anyway? Roger was heading out of the door by this point, so I closed the book and popped it down on the seat.

"Are you coming or what?" snapped Roger.

"Yes," I said. "Keep your hair on."

Roger scowled at me. He didn't really have any hair.

The rain was still cascading violently around us, and the thickness of the air indicated the approach of an impending storm. Penetrating the numbing chill of the icy wind was a stale stench that assaulted the senses and conjured images of great foulness and degradation.

"What the heck is that smell?" I shouted over the noise of the rain.

"Smells like horse wee," said Roger.

"Yes," agreed Gus, who was standing in the door behind us. "It is a bit jumentous. It often gets a bit jumentous around here."

Roger looked at me, widened his eyes, and tightened his lips.

"Not now, Roger," I said. "This isn't the time."

A faint, threatening rumble filled the sky, and without warning the winds picked up, hurling the rain sideways into our faces.

"Whoa," shouted Gus. "It's really coming down. You folks better get inside – you don't want to be struck by a lightning bolt! I'm sure Roger's been hit by enough bolts, eh Roger?" He chuckled.

What was he talking about? Roger had never been hit by a lightning bolt. Had he?

"No indeed," chuckled Roger, throwing me a look. "Thanks for everything, Gus."

Gus smiled and gave us a cheeky salute. "Any time fellas. And hey - don't worry about the money."

And with that he closed the door, leaving us alone in the elements (hydrogen [x2] and oxygen).

"What money?" I shouted. "Who the heck was that guy?"

"I haven't got a clue," said Roger. "But he seemed jolly nice."

"There was something in that book," I said.

Roger craned his neck and held a hand to his ear. "What did you say?"

"There was something in *To Kill A Mockingbird*!"

"You want me to kill who?"

A flash of bright light filled the sky and Gus switched on the Bookmobile's engine.

"I can't hear you," said Roger. "There's too much-"

His words were interrupted by a clash of thunder that sent us running for the front porch of the Old Dog and Bottle. By the time it had faded, the bookmobile had pulled away and left us.

Roger turned to me and wiped the rain from his face. "So what do we do now?"

I brushed my soggy fringe out of my eyes and spluttered out an answer which I was loathed to state explicitly.

"We go to a haunted pub," I replied. "In the middle of a thunderstorm."

And I pushed open the door…

SEVEN

THE OLD DOG AND BOTTLE

The wind caught the door behind us and slammed it shut as we entered the hallway – a squalid little chamber with damp stone walls and a matted carpet that teemed with the stench of smoke and ale. A battered plastic stand stood tentatively against the wall, overflowing with pamphlets for local events and attractions such as *Parish Praise* and *Digger Land.* We both took off our coats and brushed the loose water from our jumpers and trouserpants.

"Try to blend in," I said. "We're just a couple of cheese enthusiasts from Norfolk following up on some research. My name is Dr Henry Poindexter, and you can be my assistant, Captain Livingstone."

"Why don't we just use our real names?" asked Roger naively.

"Because we're undercover," I explained. "We don't know who to trust around here – and more importantly, I'm not planning to pay for our room."

Roger became suddenly agitated. "We're going to *stay* here?"

"Of course," I said. "Where did you think we were going to sleep?"

"Well…" he stuttered. "Somewhere less… haunted."

I grinned affectionately at his cowardice. "Oh, come on Roger… You're not going to listen to that sort of nonsense are you? It's just a nice old pub in the countryside. There's nothing to worry about!"

The next door opened into a bar area with a slate floor covered in skin rugs and old oak furniture. The expressionless faces of the three patrons therein were illuminated by the flicker of an open fire, which the proprietor was aggressively stoking as we entered. When I closed the door behind us he looked up and brushed the cinders from his abundant moustache.

"Mildred?" he enquired.

"No," I informed him. "My name is Dr Henry Poindexter and this is my associate, Captain Livingstone."

The rest of the patrons considered us with vague interest for a moment, before returning to their drinks. They were all sitting alone, in separate corners of the room, wallowing in solitude like antisocial crabs. The proprietor collected a couple of empty glasses from one of them as he circled back towards the bar.

"What d'ya want?" he asked.

"Just a rest from the road," I explained. "We're after a couple of drinks and a room for the night, if there's one available."

"Ay, thars one free," he said. "Seventy-five."

"Blimey," I said. "How many rooms do you have here?"

"Seventy-five *pound*," he clarified.

I decided it prudent to clarify at this point that we were after a twin room, and not a double, lest the locals turned out to be homophones.

"Tha's what I assumed," said the proprietor, really closed-mindedly. He placed a key on the bar in front of me. "Yer in room one."

"Thank you kindly," I said. "Incidentally, how many rooms *do* you have here?"

"One," he replied.

A torrent of wind rapped against the windows and some roof tiles fell to the ground outside with a *crash*.

"Mildred?" exclaimed the proprietor, his eyes wide with anticipation.

"Who's Mildred?" I asked.

"Yes," he replied, and poured himself a brandy.

I looked at Roger, who was counting out change for the cigarette machine. Classic Roger...

"Want a drink?" asked the proprietor.

"That'd be nice," I replied, politely.

"Just an orange juice for me," said Roger, walking towards the machine.

The other three customers turned and gawped at him, their beards drenched in froth and crumbs of unspecific meat. Clearly soft drinks were an unfamiliar convention to them.

I edged up behind him as subtly as possible and whispered in his ear; "Try to blend in, man. They're all drinking alcohol."

"But I don't drink," he replied quietly through gritted teeth.

"No you don't," I agreed. "But Captain Livingstone does. Captain Livingstone drinks to forget the horrors he witnessed in the Second World War. Commit to the role, man. Commit!"

Roger sighed and nodded. I patted him on the shoulder and turned to the proprietor.

"I'll have a sherry," I said. "And some salted nuts. Captain Livingstone will be joining me shortly."

Roger's cigarettes fell into the dispenser tray with a thud and his coins clattered as they dropped down inside the machine. The proprietor fixed me with a hard stare. He was very good at it – much better than I was, anyway… I had once tried to fix my boiler with a hard stare, but after four hours I gave up and fell asleep in the airing cupboard.

"Do you have a smoking area?" asked Roger.

The proprietor took a long puff of his calabash pipe and indicated the other patrons, who were all enjoying the pleasures of tobacco without restraint. "Yer standin' in it," he explained.

"Right," said Roger. "Yes – I suppose… It's just that they banned smoking indoors a few years ago."

The proprietor frowned as he placed my sherry in front of me. "Who's they?"

"You know – they… them… the government and such."

I elbowed Roger in the ribs, which proved to be a mistake, as he let out a high-pitched squeal that made him sound like a little girl / homosexual. Clearly these people were not concerned with government legislation. They probably hunted with more than two dogs at a time and regularly fiddled their taxes / children.

"Will ya have a drink er not?" snapped the proprietor.

Roger leaned across the bar and browsed the selection. "Can I see the wine list?" he asked.

One of the other patrons erupted briefly with what was either a very happy cough or a particularly phlegmy laugh. I tried to relax and took a sip of my sherry, which was bloody lovely, but not quite sufficient to quell my nerves. Perhaps another would do the trick…

The proprietor slid a small scrap of paper across the bar to Roger.

"What's this?" he asked.

The proprietor scowled. "The wine list."

Roger flipped the paper over to reveal the selection. It was written in comic sans MS, which is something I cannot stand…

Wine List

- RED
- WHITE

"I see," said Roger. "I think I'll try the white one. Is it dry?"

"No," said the proprietor. "It's a liquid."

I took out Roger's phone and checked for a signal. Impressively, it immediately connected with the pub's WiFi and asked me for a password, which the proprietor informed me was MILDRED. I typed in the name and the World Wide Web was at my fingertips once again. Some luck at last!

"I think I'll just have a whiskey," Roger decided. "Straight, with a dash of water."

The proprietor nodded with approval. "S'more like it," he said, and grabbed a tumbler from the shelf behind him.

"Killer!" I yelled as I noticed a new notification on The Facebook. It was a friend request from my old PE teacher Mr Pritchard, who had a thick ginger beard and never wore trouserpants (even when it snowed). I should point out that my celebratory explanation was entirely figurative. Mr Pritchard is not a killer. For this and many other reasons, I accepted his friend request immediately.

Meanwhile Roger was busy accepting his single malt with a nostalgic sigh. He loved alcohol, bless his britches, and hadn't had a drink in over three years. Now he looked upon the golden liquid with tentative titillation, perhaps as one might look upon an old girlfriend, like Hilda McIntyre (who is a liar). He slowly wrapped his fingers around the glass and raised it to his lips.

As I accepted Mr Pritchard's friend request I took a moment to consider the other prospective e-companions on my list. Was it really worth the risk that Great Auntie Boris would soil my public wall with constant references to the healing power of crystals? Did I really want to start a relationship with an interweb greetings card retailer? Was Kevin Donahue one of my old school friends, or just someone pretending to be one of my old school friends? Perhaps I could see if he was friends with Mr Pritchard in order to validate his identity… This line of enquiry would have to wait however, as I was suddenly halted by a mind-boggling epiphany:

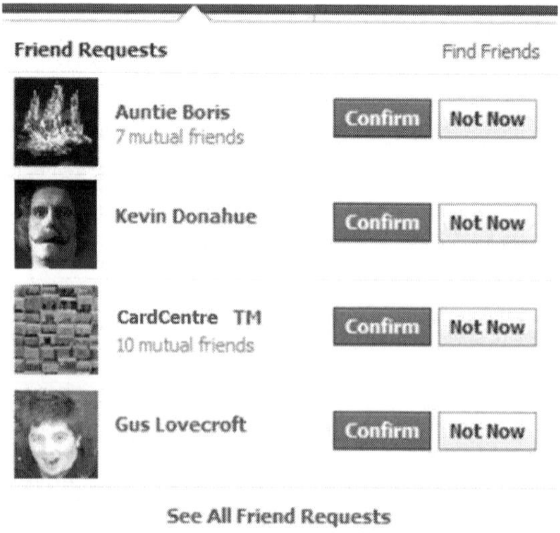

Gus Lovecroft was <u>Gus</u>! I recognised his face now – grinning up at me like a cheeky hero on The Facebook. Perhaps we knew each other after all, and I had just forgotten his face due to some kind of mental brain disease. Maybe the incident in the steam room had erased the part of my mind responsible for remembering new faces… Maybe I was tricked into forgetting him by a mischievous hypnotist like Darren Brown, trawling the streets looking for people to annoy with magic (and suggestion, psychology, misdirection and showmanship to boot). I took another sip of sherry and hit the CONFIRM button as another clash of thunder prompted the proprietor to turn around with excitement.

"Mildred?" he said again.

"Who is Mildred?" I demanded.

"No," he stated firmly. "You do *not* talk a' Mildred. Not to me. Not to no-body. That clear?"

Another man was standing in the corridor behind him, straight-backed, arms crossed, shaking his head and staring in my direction. He was wearing a scruffy-looking apron and green-check woollen trouserpants held up with red braces. His thick-rimmed glasses had been hastily fixed in the centre with sticky tape and rested on a somewhat bulbous nose, complete with a neatly trimmed pencil moustache. Something about him seemed peculiar. Something about him didn't belong. Something about him held my attention for a very long time, until Roger slammed his tumbler onto the bar and demanded another shot of whiskey.

"That's some fine scotch," he declared. "Fill me up again, good sir."

The proprietor obliged, his friend still looming in the corridor and staring at us. When the clock struck half past the hour of 10, one of the patrons put down his half-finished pint of beer, got up, pulled on his jacket, and left without saying a word. Roger flipped a cigarette into his mouth and lit it with a grin. He was in his elephant. I was getting nervous.

"Will ya take another one?" asked the proprietor, picking up the sherry bottle.

"I might," I admitted. "But first I'd like to use the toilet."

"Round back," was the proprietor's detailed and informative response, coupled with a half-hearted nod to his right.

"Good then," I said, dismounting my bar stool. "That sherry's gone right to my bladder."

The man in the corridor walked slowly away from us and opened an old door by the stairs. For some reason it entranced me. He took one last look back at Roger and I, a faint smile crawling across his peculiar face, and then he disappeared (not literally – he went through the door).

The gentlemen's toilets were situated around the corner, next to a battered old pool table and a bust of "Busta Rhymes". They were relatively clean but not without some minor imperfections which put a damper on the general experience. One such imperfection was the inclusion of an overly aggressive flush on the cubicle toilet, which I had elected to use in preference to the urinal. I always use cubicles where possible as I have a shy bladder and usually enjoy a nice sit down. On this occasion I regretted the decision to sit down however, as pulling the chain led to a ball-battering tsunami that left me with a saturated crotch and a sour temperament. And as I stood there in that toilet cubicle, hundreds of miles from home, dabbing at my testicles with clumps of cheap toilet tissue, I found myself asking the most obvious question… *How has it come to this?* As I recall, the answer involved something about a lost dog, a manslaughter, a missing body and a lump of cheese. As such, I decided to treat said question as rhetorical and continued with my review of the pub lavatory…

One particular imperfection which hampered my enjoyment of the facility was the fact that the hand dryer was broken and there didn't seem to be any substitute towels / old jumpers to use in its place. I looked around quite thoroughly but found nothing resembling an alternative drying method and was about to give up hope entirely when the window above me flew open and a large tabby cat jumped in over my head and onto the sink. I stumbled back in surprise and banged my head on the door, my heart skipping several beats (about five, I think) as I did so. When I found my feet again (they were in the usual place) I resourcefully picked up the offending animal and used it to dry my hands, which was surprisingly effective considering the cat must have been out in the rain for some time.

"Thanks little buddy," I said to the cat (for some reason). "You're a useful little thing aren't you?"

The cat purred affectionately in my arms and stared up into my eyes. It wore a bright red collar with a shiny brass nametag dangling from the buckle. I turned the tag over in my hand and asked the cat another rhetorical question:

"What's your name then, little fellow?"

The tag read "Mildred". So *this* was Mildred. Mildred was the *cat.* I popped her down and let her scurry through the door as I headed back into the bar. *Well, that's one mystery solved*, I thought. *Now on to the next one…*

Roger was sitting by the fire and enjoying what appeared to be his third glass of scotch. A grumpy-looking man with a curly black beard was nursing a pint by the door – now the only other customer in the pub. He looked up at me briefly as I came back in, then mumbled something and took a giant swig from his glass. I got another sherry and sat down next to Roger, who seemed to be in good spirits (Pun intended! #LOL).

"It's nice here," said Roger. "You know something, Walt? I think I could get used to this."

"Shhhh!" I snapped. "My name is Dr Henry Poindexter. Remember?"

"Ah yes," said Roger. "Sorry about that."

"That's alright", I said, sipping my sherry. "Just keep it together."

I threw a cautious glance at the man in the corner, but it was okay - he wasn't listening. I took out Roger's Smartphone and had a fiddle on *FreeDraw* for a bit, finding out how to use the tone palette and practicing with it by sketching our immediate surroundings. I was getting better at the *Freedraw...*

By the time I had finished Roger was on his <u>fourth</u> shot of whiskey and I had another sherry sat in front of me. It was nice to kick back 'old school' for a bit, and it turns out that Roger is quite a good person to kick back 'old school' with. He started telling me all about his ex-wife Abby and his eight-year-old son Billy who is good at Olympics. He told me about the trout farm his Dad used to own, and his sister Margaret who has a disorder called myalgic encephalomyelitis which makes her very tired for no reason. I wondered (out loud) if trout ever suffered from ME, and Roger said that he didn't know if they did but that I should write a poem about it anyway, which I did...

Harold the fish had only one wish;
To be friends with the whole of the sea.
But his aspiration saw no cultivation,
Since Harold had chronic ME.

One day he would say he would head to the bay
And perhaps meet a mollusc or two.
But despite all these plans he would soon understand
That sleeping was all he could do.

He enjoyed some discourses with friendly seahorses
And sometimes made many a friend.
But soon made an enemy of an anemone
Who wanted his sad life to end.

So said his new foe; "why don't you just go?
Your snoring is rather distracting.
It's rather immoral to sleep in the coral,
When we're all having fun interacting."

But Harold just slept, while the other fish wept,
For they all thought his lifestyle was dreadful.
Til one day a boatman dropped into the ocean,
A three-quarter full can of Red Bull.

Now Harold is quick, though often quite sick,
One might say he's out of his head.
But he still has an enemy in the anemone
Who wants him to go back to bed.

I read the poem to Roger and he gave it 8/10, applauding its rhythm and structure, but criticising the reference to *Red Bull* as this seems to suggest that energy drinks can be used as a form of treatment for ME (which is <u>not</u> true). I gave the poem to Roger to give to his sister, but he thought that she probably couldn't be bothered to read it. Then I ordered another sherry and we continued to kick back for a while, trading stories and brainstorming ways to be less offensive to people with epilepsy.

I have always enjoyed telling stories as I am an excellent raconteur and have very good <u>diction</u>. Roger sat and laughed / cried at the appropriate moments as I took him through some of my favourite tales of misadventure. I started with the time I went to Bognor Regis and saw a Greater Crested Seabird that was trained to mimic the dancing style of Geri Halliwell. It made me laugh so much that I threw up and had to sit down for a very long time. This story is <u>very</u> cleverly entitled *The Funny Tern* (even though in reality it was a Yellow-Legged Gull).

When we had finished telling stories I sold Roger nine of my thoughts and we began to ponder some of the great questions of the universe such as; *what is Greater Manchester greater than? What does Leanne rhyme with?* And *how is the artist formally known as Prince informally known?* Roger asked me what my favourite question was, which I enjoyed very much as that question *is* my favourite question. Then I told him one more story about the time I was badly burnt on a Bunsen burner on Burn's night in Burnley and decided it was probably time for bed.

I finished my sherry and wrapped up some bacon crisps which I thought would probably do for my breakfast. Roger finished his scotch with one big manly gulp and tapped out the last of his cigarette. Then just as we were ready to make our way upstairs, the proprietor appeared (not literally – he walked over) and sat a couple more drinks down in front of us.

"So yer inta yer cheese then?" he asked, pulling up a chair and sitting by the fire.

"Very much so," I replied. "Captain Livingstone and I have been cheese enthusiasts for many years. We travel the country researching the source of various cheeses that take our fancy."

I suddenly realised that this was a good time to commence a line of investigative questioning with our host, but I was slightly sozzled and couldn't think of anything useful to say.

After a few minutes of silence the proprietor turned to Roger. "So – you a military man, Captain Livingstone?"

Roger was an inexperienced actor and improvisation was certainly not one of his strong points. Putting him in this position was very much akin to casting a rabbit in a show by a long established Cambridge University amateur dramatics club – at least I am 98 percent confident that this is the origin of the phrase "rabbit in the footlights" – which is definitely what he resembled. Luckily Walton "Olivier" Cumberfield was there to lend a theatrical hand (this is not my real middle name).

"Captain Livingstone does not like to talk about his time in the service," I explained, cleverly. "His experiences at the massacre of Dunkirk have left him somewhat traumatised."

"Dunkirk were an evacuation," said the proprietor. "I thought…"

"Yes," I retorted, desperately attempting to recall my fourth form history class. "But it was all those boats, you see… The Captain gets very seasick. He's not a sea captain, after all."

"How old are ya, Captain?" asked the proprietor.

"Believe it or not, I'm 79," said Roger.

Damn it Roger.

"So you was at Dunkirk when you was… nine year old?" deduced the proprietor, like a wise old haddock.

"Yes…" said Roger. "Well, no… What I mean to say is…"

"What you mean to say is that you aint no military man at all. And you aint 79. You look about… 40. Did you think I were born yesterday?"

"No," I insisted. "You also look about 40."

"That's kind," said the proprietor. "But I'm actually 60."

"Incredible," I said.

The proprietor smiled. "Ta. I look after meself."

For a moment I seemed to have distracted him from his line of suspicious enquiry, but it wasn't long before Roger chipped in with another ill-advised nugget of hammy nonsense.

"I am 46," he declared. "But sometimes I pretend to be older than I am to protect my true identity."

"Which is?" asked the proprietor.

Roger sighed, having exhausted the potential of his imagination. "Roger Tilsbury."

I clapped very slowly and sarcastically. The proprietor considered us for a moment.

"This has got t' be the most jumentous story I've ever laid ears on! Now you tell me straight – what are you really doing around these parts?"

We did not reply.

"Well?"

The jig was up. I had no choice now but to confide in our host and pray that he was kind of spirit.

"What are you doing?" he asked.

"I am praying that you are kind of spirit," I replied, explaining my sudden move to a kneeling position with my hands clasped in front of my chest.

"Look," he said. "We aint had strangers in this bar for going on four years to the day. Now you two show up actin' all peculiar and tellin' all sortsa' tall stories. What am I s'posed to make of that?"

I swivelled, still kneeling, and pulled my suitcase towards me across the floor. It was time to show my hand, or rather, show my cheese, which I removed from the Tupperware box in my case and placed in front of the proprietor.

"What's your name, by the way?" I asked him.

"Cedric," he replied. "Why d'you ask?"

"Well," I explained, "I was just thinking that if ever I were to novelise this encounter, it might be helpful if I could refer to you by name. Otherwise I would have to refer to you simply as 'the proprietor', which I imagine would get a little wearing after a few pages."

"A fair point," said Cedric, leaning back in his chair and examining the cheese. "Now this be a most peculiar thing. Where'd ya get it?"

"We found it," said Roger suddenly. "Somebody left it at our house."

"What can you tell us about it?" I asked.

"Well," he said. "I can tell you the same thing what I tell everyone else, but I'm sure you've heard all about that."

"All about what?" I asked.

"The cheese murders."

Roger sat up in his chair and set his glass down with a thump. I zipped up my case and climbed back into my seat. *Cheese murders? Where was this going?*

"What are the cheese murders?" I asked.

Cedric afforded himself a wry smile. "Do you like ghost stories?"

"Yes," I replied, lying (I really hate ghost stories).

"Then this might be of interest," he said, plonking the cheese back in its Tupperware box. "Years ago this pub were owned by a very prestigious cheesemaker. He weren't always prestigious, mind, but we'll come to that in a moment. Anyway, he sets up a little creamery down in the cellar – keeps a few cows out back… It's only an amateur operation, but the stuff he makes is good and he sells it at the bar. Starts making a tidy profit, would you believe it? So he starts expandin' – getting' in some staff to help him out, makin' more cheese, makin' more money…"

Cedric took a moment to light his calabash pipe.

"Go on," said Roger.

"Right," continued Cedric. "Well it were all going swimminly, until one day the staff turn up for work and find everythin' locked up. Now word is, the cheese-maker's discovered a new kind of cheese, but he don't want to share it with no one."

"So he does want to share it with *someone*?" I clarified, misunderstanding his rural use of a double-negative.

"No, no. He's shut himself off, you see. No one gets a taste of the new cheese. No one ever sees him. And the pub don't open again until… well… until he…"

"What?" I asked.

"They say that someone were after his secret. I don't know, could have just been a couple of young thieves in the night – no one can say for sure."

"Say what?" I said, getting slightly agitated that he was dragging out the conclusion like it was something from *Alfred Hancock Presents*.

"They found him in the cellar," said Cedric. "Murdered by a knife to the gut. The stock were all cleared out - no trace of this new cheese of his. Just a corpse."

A short silence was followed by the customary unspecific bang that seems to follow every ghost story. In this case it was more of the roof tiles falling to the ground outside…

"Mildred?" he blurted out, yet again.

"Who else was murdered?" asked Roger.

Cedric frowned at him. "What's that now?"

"Who else was murdered? You said you were going to tell us about the cheese murders - plural. So who else was murdered?"

"Oh right," he said. "It's one of them misnomers. People refer to it as the cheese "murders", but there was only the one actual murder."

"I see," said Roger, getting uncharacteristically cocky because of the whiskey. "And how can you call it a ghost story if there are no ghosts in it?"

"I'm getting to that!" snapped Cedric. "You see, no one goes down into that cellar these days. They say it still be haunted by the cheese-maker's ghost – well, I don't know much about that, but I've heard and seen some strange things since I've been livin' here. Last landlord sealed it off, you see… No one's been down there in many a year. I don't know if there's sense in it, but if you put your ear to the door by the stairs and listen very close-"

"Okay," I interrupted him. "That's enough of this codswallop."

It was all getting a bit far-fetched for my tastes. I didn't believe in ghosts and ghouls any more than I believed in Father Christmas or global warming. I'd heard it all before – the whole "and if you listen very closely…" or "some say on a winter's night" gobbledygook. Now it was getting late and I was quite ready to hit the hay.

"I'm just tellin' you what I've been told meself," said Cedric, shrugging innocently. "They says I've got a haunted cellar. I don't know. I don't go down there."

"But your friend does," I retorted sharply, clicking my fingers to emphasise the sharpness.

"What friend?" asked Cedric, while Roger offered me an equally puzzled look, and a pork scratching.

"Your colleague," I explained. "The man in the apron, with the green-check woollen trouserpants."

"I'm sorry," said Cedric. "But it's just me who works here, and I don't know nothing about no trouserpants."

"What do you mean it's just you?" I laughed. "I saw him with my own two eyes. He stood in that corridor, staring at us - then he opened the door to the cellar and went inside. He was right there, behind you..."

Cedric laughed into his pipe, spraying ash across the table.

"I don't think so, lad," he chuckled. "Aint nobody goin' into that cellar. That door's locked in four different places. I don't even know which is the right key."

I looked at Roger, who shook his head in hopeless bewilderment. But Roger *must* have seen the man in the apron. He was *right there*!

"Somebody went into that cellar," I said. "If what you say is true and you do indeed work alone then there's an intruder in your mist."

I meant to say "in your midst" but I was very tired.

"I think you've had one too many, my friend," said Cedric with a grin. "Go and sleep it off, eh?"

"It has been a long day," agreed Roger.

"I know what I saw," I said – getting very angry at the pair of them for being so dismissive. "Now you can't expect me to sleep tonight knowing that there's someone poking around the place who shouldn't be here."

"Take a look at that door as you pass," said Cedric. "Try to open it if you like. It's locked up tight."

He was right. It was locked tight. As I shuffled along the corridor to the stairs I leant on the door in question and gave it a good hard push. It was definitely locked. There was even a bolt on the outside secured with a very visible padlock. Was I finally going mad? Had it all gotten too much? I knew what I had seen, and yet – it was impossible. I must have been seeing things. I left "Captain Livingstone" joking with Cedric and lugged my suitcase up the stairs to room one. Roger was right. It had been a very long day.

*

Outside the storm was still raging like a confused ox and I was glad to be tucked up in the plump, soft duvet of my single bed. The room was dimly lit and sparsely decorated, with old, faded wallpaper peeling from the walls, and an antique clock standing against a battered old wardrobe in the corner. It had ticked its last tock, and was ugly to boot, but the quality of the décor mattered little as I burrowed down beneath the bedclothes and closed my eyes in a cozy little shroud of darkness. My dreams would be more than decorative enough to make up for the aesthetic shortcomings of the room, and nothing could overshadow the simple reward of a well-earned rest at the end of a difficult day. A *very* difficult day…

At first I could still hear the two of them chatting away downstairs, but it wasn't long before the warm veil of slumber enraptured me and my waking thoughts descended into the sweet nonsense of unconsciousness. The sound of their voices turned to bees on the wind and the rattle of the rain became the rustle of grass in the soft breeze of a summer's day.

And I was running through the field – running naked like the mad kings of old – at one with nature, with a heart full of joyful celebration. Suddenly, Melanie was there – nude as the day God made her, running towards me, her considerable bosoms bouncing up and down, bathed in sunlight, glowing like orbs of naughtiness. And she was calling to me…

As she drew nearer my heart surged with excitement and I let out a cry of joy – but that cry turned into a lightning bolt which struck the ground between us and opened it up into a deep chasm. The chasm ran for eternity in all directions and began to consume everything around it. I told her to run but she wouldn't run. She just stood there and waited as the world swallowed her up. Then it swallowed me up. Then I was in Dixons in Birmingham, trying to buy some virus protection for a second hand laptop (which was referenced in the dream but never seen). The salesman was Cedric, but then he was Gus and then he was Ian Hislop (a possible indicator of my own subconscious preoccupations). Then he said that he would NOT sell me protection, and asked me to leave. I obliged, of course, and soon found myself wandering down greasy corridors and slippery stairwells, waiting for the man with the breakfast sword. But he did not come. He did not come and something was ticking (and tocking) incredibly loudly all around me – echoing through the halls from an indiscernible location.

"Be this thy doing, Tintin, thou Belgian bastard?" I cried. But my words solidified in the air and fell to the ground as a kind of rain that formed a thick layer of cheese at my feet.

And for a split second I saw the face of the man with the green-check woollen trouserpants. Then he was gone. Then I was gone.

I opened my eyes and sat up in bed, dripping with sweat, yet shivering against an icy draft. The room was pitch-black, save a crack of moonlight shining on the ugly clock in the corner. In my troubled rest I had kicked off the covers and was now very much naked in the darkness… Naked and alone…

And the clock was ticking louder and louder and louder.

Tick… Tock…. Tick…. Tock…

I slid off the bed and approached the clock, looking for a way to silence it. Then I noticed that the hands on the clock were moving the wrong way, and time was going backwards. I tried to say something but it came out backwards too, making it sound very much like Danish.

A flash of lightening illuminated the room and the door flew open with a bang.

"Lleh gnikcuf!" I shouted, backwards, thinking once again, for a second, that I had seen the man in the green-check woollen trouserpants. Then everything went quiet for a moment and I trembled in the cold silence of the room, squatting helplessly on the hardwood floor. The clock had stopped ticking, and the hands had disappeared from its mangled old face.

The first whisper was light – so light in fact that I could have mistaken it for the wind, were I not sure that it was sounding out my name. The second was much deeper, and louder, and unmistakably articulated the word *Walton* in what seemed to me to be the second most sinister invitation I had ever received (the first being that of Brian and Linda Guppy's golden wedding anniversary). The whispers continued to echo along the landing as I stepped out without thought and bumbled down the stairs in nothing but my socks and underpants.

"Walton" said the whisper again, reverberating down the stairwell – curling around the banister like an intelligent wind or living trump. I was compelled to follow it – down into the depths – down to the bolted door below, where the man in the green woollen trouserpants had gone before. But the door was not bolted – it swung gently in an invisible breeze – and the living wind was seeping into its dark abyss.

"Walton" said the voice again. *"You must eat of the cheese."*

I heard more voices, and peered around the corner to see Roger and Cedric, still chatting and laughing by the fire. Roger was slapping his thigh and telling the wondrous tales of old, while Cedric told many a joke, some of which were, to be honest, a little bit racist. A hand gripped the top of my shoulder, but when I turned around there was no one there. And the door to the cellar was open wide, calling out to me and daring me to enter.

I reached into my pocket and pulled out Roger's smartphone to update The Facebook, but it was not Roger's smartphone. It was the end of a dog's lead, which led from my hand all the way through the door to the cellar and beyond. Somewhere inside came the gentle ring of a tambourine. I wrapped the lead around my arm as I followed it through the dark door and into the shadows behind.

"Walton" called the whispers again. *"You must eat of the cheese."*

I walked down the derelict oak stairs into the depths of the pub, and held my breath as the darkness consumed me. The man in the green-check woollen trouserpants was sat on the floor in the corner of the darkness, propped against the wall with his legs splayed out in front of him, illuminated by the flicker of a lone candle. His face was sad at first, but relaxed into a kind of contentment as he turned to receive me.

"This is where they killed me," he said, very softly. His voice was not sad, just very matter-of-fact. I reached the bottom of the stairs and tripped on what looked like the remains of a broken wooden stool, next to a picture of a sword (which was not made out of breakfast).

"You are the cheesemaker," I said, stopping short of his immediate proximity. It was more of a realisation than a question.

"I was," he said. "I *was* the cheesemaker."

"Are you real?" I asked.

He returned the question, like an unwanted blouse. "Are you?"

"Yes," I assured him. "My name is Walton Cumberfield. What is yours?"

"My name is Oscar Crouch," he said. "And I have been dead for many a year."

I closed my eyes and struggled to decide whether I was still dreaming. Then I pinched the fleshy part of my thumb in an attempt to induce pain, but I could not decide whether I felt it or not.

"Your friend is gone," he said. "But you <u>will</u> see him again."

"I beg your pardon?" I asked.

He looked me straight in the eye. "You must eat of the cheese."

Mildred the cat crawled suddenly and gracefully into the light and nuzzled at his feet. I suddenly realised that the lead was gone from my hand, and I could no longer hear the soft jangling of a tambourine.

"What do you mean my friend is gone? Do you speak of Keith Matthews?" I was trying to articulate myself in a way befitting of both the energy and formal intensity of the situation.

"Poor Mildred," whispered Oscar, as he tickled her whiskery chin. "You too share the burden of death – 'Tis a small recompense for me, of course. I am glad of the company."

I shook my brain about a bit trying to make some sense of the circumstances, but it simply rattled like a maraca.

"Mildred the cat isn't dead," I informed him. "I saw her just yesterday."

"As you saw me," he pointed out.

"I don't believe in ghost stories," I said.

"You'd best start believing in ghost stories, Mr Cumberfield," he stated plainly, leaning forward into the light. "You're in one."

I cleared my throat. "Sorry," I said. "That was an exact quote from the film *Pirates of the Caribbean: The Curse of the Black Pearl*."

"What's that?" he asked.

"It's the first film of the *Pirates of the Caribbean* franchise," I explained. "Released in 2003. It's very famous."

"Oh," he said. "I haven't seen it. I died in 1954."

I shuffled about awkwardly, slightly regretting my criticism. Oscar had seemed proud of his linguistic skills. Now he was just embarrassed.

"2003," he said (to himself, I think). "Has it really been that long?"

"Actually it's 2010 now," I informed him. "They've made two more films, and there's another on the way."

"Good gracious," he said, rising to his feet. "I have very little idea what you are talking about."

As he stood I noticed the ivory handle of a pocket knife sticking out of his torso. The blade was completely buried in his flesh, but there was no blood.

"Don't worry," he said, noticing that I had noticed. "It doesn't hurt anymore."

"Why do you haunt this place?" I asked. "Shouldn't you move on into the light or something? Can you not see a light?"

"I can see it now," he said, smiling. "I am almost ready."

I didn't understand at the time. But I would, sometime later, or earlier, whichever way you look at it... Perhaps as you are reading this you are as confused now as I was then. If so then my methods have been most effective at conveying the tone and content of this exchange. Top marks for me.

"Why could you not move on before?" I asked.

"I have been waiting," he said, picking up Mildred and stroking her gently in his arms.

"Waiting for what?" I asked.

"Waiting for you, Mr Cumberfield."

The door to the cellar opened with a bang and a bright light shone in from above. The wind coiled around us, carrying the manic cries of the dead and accursed (I think).

"What do you want with me?" I cried over the noise.

"Your friend is gone," he shouted. "But you will see him again."

"You said that already!" I yelled. *Stupid cryptic ghost.*

He smiled and opened his arms as the winds churned up the dust in a cyclone at his feet. "You must eat of the cheese," he said, nodding.

"What are you talking about?" I screamed.

"Your friend is gone. But you will see him again."

"Is this a dream?" I asked.

"I don't know," he replied. "Is it?"

The noise turned to silence in that way that sort of makes you jump in a kind of illogical, paradoxical inversion of expectation. You know how when loud noise becomes the norm and it suddenly stops - and then it's the same as if you were sitting in silence and somebody made a loud noise like dropping a monkey or something? Well it was like that, anyway. And I was conscious again, sitting bolt upright in bed, dripping in sweat, like they do in the films. This time I really *was* awake.

The windows were clouded with yesterday's rain, but it was no longer falling outside. In fact, the room was quite pleasantly bathed in the morning sunlight, and I could even hear the distant sound of Birdsong – a radio play adaptation of the novel by Sebastian Faulks. I tried to relax, lying back against the headboard, when suddenly someone knocked on my door.

"You in there?" said Cedric, his voice muffled somewhat by the thick wood.

"Yes," I replied. "What is it, Cedric?"

"Yer friend is gone," he said.

I did not reply.

"You hear me? Can I come in? Hallo? You decent in there?"

I found myself thinking so intensely that the words forced themselves quietly from between my lips.

"Roger... He was talking about Roger."

Cedric called to me again. "Did you hear what I said? Your friend is gone."

"But I will see him again," I replied.

I will see him again…

EIGHT

A MOST UNPLEASANT BREAKFAST

"Roger is my lodger. He's a tough old codger. He's very nice, and smells of spice, with a face like a Jammie dodger."

Cedric turned to me in confusion. "What's that got to do with anythin'?"

"Well," I explained. "It's a poem I wrote about Roger, my lodger – who is now missing."

"Yeh, I got that," said Cedric. "But how's it relevant?"

"Well, because it's Roger…"

Cedric was getting on my wick. It occurred to me that he didn't understand the poem, so I explained my use of simile to allude to Roger's alcoholism.

"Yeh, no – I get that," he said. "But how's it gonna help us find your friend?"

"Well it's not going to help us find him," I scoffed. "It's just a poem."

"Then why are you mentionin' it now?"

I flapped a dismissive hand at Cedric and turned into the kitchen. Clearly Cedric was a little on the slow side, and not too fond of poetry (not that it is possible to be *too* fond of poetry, I hasten to add).

"So you say he came in here?" I asked, surveying the mess Roger had left in his wake. This is just a turn of phrase of course, as a funeral at this stage would have been somewhat premature.

"He were rather the worse for wear," said Cedric, following me through. "Stopped making sense sometime around four o'clock, I remember. Then he stopped drinkin' and demanded I make him some food. When I refused to cook for him he stood up and stumbled in here mumbling something about toast."

I paced the room, expressionless, like an emotionally-stunted detective from one of the films. The next time Cedric spoke I held up a hand to silence him, not for any real reason – I was just bored of his input, and wanted to see if it would work. It did.

Roger's toast was badly burnt and lying topping-side down on the dusty floor by the oven. I peeled it off the floor and placed it back on the work surface. It was covered in cheese, and he had only taken one bite.

"He just disappeared," said Cedric. "One minute he were here and the next-"

"It doesn't make any sense," I said, itching my invisible beard like a pensive policeman. "Why would he leave?"

"Oh no, no, no," gabbled Cedric. "I don't think you understand. There's only one way outta this room, and I were waiting outside that door from the moment he walked in to the moment he were gone. He didn't leave, mate. He disappeared."

Cedric was right - there didn't seem to be any other way out of the room. Then again, Roger was resourceful, and his favourite film was *The Greatest Cape* which was all about breaking out of prison (in a cape, I assume… I haven't seen it). He may have found a secret passageway and tunnelled away like Steven the Queen. I immediately started tapping the walls to check their structural integrity.

"What you doing now?" asked Cedric.

"I'm looking for a secret passageway," I informed him.

Cedric ran his hands through his tufty hair. "This is all very queer."

"I would have thought you'd be used to a bit of queer," I said shrewdly. "You live in a haunted pub."

"Oh, I've seen strange things," he said. "But none so queer as this. I've had things move about in the night, things going astray, even heard voices – but not never has nobody vanished into thin air before."

"People don't simply vanish into the air," I said, frowning very cynically like a proper detective. "Roger is gone – but we're going to find him."

"I wouldn't be so sure, friend. Like you said – the place is haunted."

"It isn't haunted anymore," I said, opening the oven and looking inside. (Roger wasn't in there).

I remembered that Roger and I would often play hide and seek at the weekends, so I considered that this could just be an elaborate instigation of a spontaneous game. Then I remembered that Roger always did the seeking, and he wasn't very good at it. One Sunday I spent four hours beneath the sofa cushions and almost died of cramp and boredom before he found me. If hide and seek was an Olympic sport I would surely take home the gold. As it stands, it is not an Olympic sport, and my proposal to the IOC has been rejected on seven separate occasions.

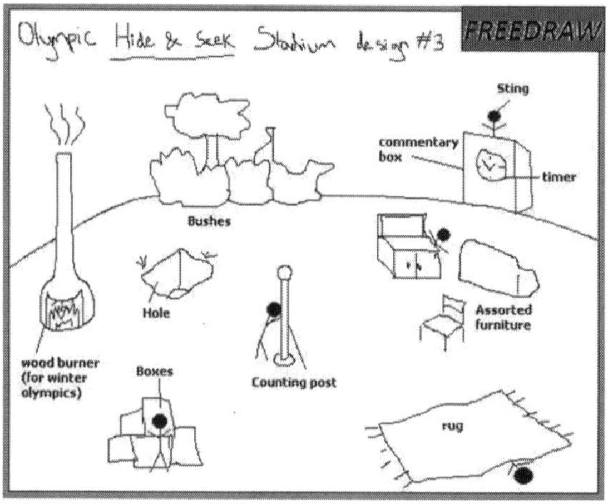

"I must act fast," I said. "Wherever he is, Roger could be in trouble."

Cedric turned to me in confusion. "Then why have you spent the last 15 minutes designin' a hide and seek stadium for the Olympics?"

Cedric was right. I had to stop letting myself get so distracted by the tangential nature of my inner monologue – like when I took my 11 plus and composed a short piece of musical theatre instead of answering most of the questions. Incidentally, that piece of musical theatre eventually developed into the smash hit *Who's Stolen Cheryl Cole's Pyjamas*, so in retrospect the failing of my 11 plus yielded a very positive outcome. I should point out of course that back then Cheryl Cole was not so much in the public eye, being only two years old and having intercourse with far fewer footballers. Thus the title and character specifics were very different, and only changed at a later date to make the piece more "relevant".

"You see," said Cedric. "You're doin' it again. You've been stood there in silence for over a minute. What are you thinkin' about?"

I cleared my throat and pretended I was focused on the task in hand. Perhaps Roger had trapped himself in the fridge like a proper wally… I tried to open the door, but it wouldn't budge.

"Fridge is locked overnight," said Cedric. "Got a lot of steak in there. A *lot* of steak. Can't have no one half-inchin' my wares."

"So how did Roger get to your cheese?" I asked. "Surely you keep that in the fridge?"

"I do," confirmed Cedric. "But it weren't my cheese he were eating. It were yours."

Damn it Roger.

I picked up the empty Tupperware container and immediately recognised it as my own. Bits of the wrapper remained stuck to the bottom, but there was no trace of the cheese itself.

"I threw the rest away," said Cedric. "It were kickin' off a right pong."

"I'm sure it was," I agreed. "God only knows how old it was."

I sat on the worktop and buried my head in my hands. There I was, in the middle of nowhere, without a clue, without a friend, and without the foggiest idea what to do next. Suddenly I realised that I'd never felt so alone. Then I almost immediately remembered that this wasn't true, and I had in fact felt more alone the year that I forgot it was Christmas and went to work at Staples for the day.

"Why don't you give your friend a ring?" asked Cedric. "Does he have one of them portable phones?"

"He does," I replied, clicking my fingers and rummaging through my pockets. "I suppose it's worth a try."

I took out the smartphone and dialled Roger's number. Holding the phone to my ear I immediately remembered that the phone I was using *was* Roger's phone, and I had just asked it to call itself. Cedric shrugged and went off to get on with some pub-related business.

"I'm off to muck out the ducks," he said. This came as a surprise to me as I didn't know that a) Cedric kept ducks and b) ducks require mucking out. Then something very unexpected happened…

The phone had connected and I was getting a ringing tone. Then the tone was interrupted by a click and the sound of someone's voice on the other end.

"Hello?"

"Roger?" I said. "Is that you?"

"No, this is Walton Cumberfield," said the voice. *"Roger is my lodger. Would you like me to get him for you?"*

"I beg your pardon?" I asked, assuming that I must have misheard him. The line was very crackly and I was getting a lot of feedback.

"This is Walton Cumberfield." he repeated. *"Who is this?"*

"This is Walton Cumberfield." I stated plainly.

The voice said nothing for a few moments, and then *"Could you repeat that please? The line is very crackly and I'm getting a lot of feedback."*

"This is Walton James Cumberfield," I said. "Who am I speaking with?"

"You are Walton James Cumberfield?"

"Yes," I said, plugging my other ear with my finger in an attempt to hear him better.

"Oh yes," said the voice. *"I remember. Sorry about the line – I think it's because you're phoning the phone that you're using to phone with. Never mind. Can you hear me alright?"*

"Just about," I said.

"Yes, of course," said the voice. *"Listen, I know it's a bit unpleasant but you're going to have to-"*

The line crackled and his voice faded to a distant murmur.

"Hello?" I said. "Are you still there?"

"-and throw the rest away."

"No," I said. "I didn't get any of that. You're breaking up."

"Oh right," he said. *"Sorry about that. I was just saying you're going to have to-"*

A burst of static interrupted him and a surge of feedback forced me to remove the phone from my ear.

"-and throw the rest away."

"Again," I said. "I'm getting a lot of feedback. What are you saying?"

"I'm saying that I know it's a bit unpleasant but what you need to do is-"

This time the line went completely dead for a few seconds, followed by a burst of electrical interference. The unharmonious mess of noise coming out of the phone's speaker reminded me of when EDF put me on hold back in August and I had to listen to someone called Jester J for 20 minutes. All I had wanted to do was sell them some of the meter readings I had collected that morning in Swaffham. On that occasion I eventually hung up. On this occasion I did not, and before long the voice started to come back through again, though it was only vaguely discernible…

"-just do what he – and then everything – okay. You met him last night in the cellar. Just do as he says. Okay, sorry, I have to go – my toaster is on fire."

And he hung up. I sat there for a moment and stared at the phone in utter silence.

You met him last night in the cellar.

Could the man have been talking about the ghost of Oscar Crouch? How could he have possibly known? It was just a dream… Surely, it was just a dream, wasn't it?

Just do as he says.

I mouthed his words to myself as I tried to make sense of them.

My toaster is on fire.

That bit was largely irrelevant. I racked my brains and desperately tried to remember what Oscar had said to me. I couldn't very well "do as he says" without knowing what it was that he had said to do. "You're friend is gone," he had said – "but you will see him again."

Over and over, that was all that he had said. That, and something else.

You must eat of the cheese.

Why was everything always coming back to this cheese? What was so special about it? The questions were driving me madder than Mad Max in a madhouse (on Madison Avenue). Why on earth would I want to eat some festering old cheese? That would be most-

-*unpleasant but what you need to do is…*

…Eat of the cheese! Somehow in the haze of my sherry-addled mind I was able to piece together the bite-size chunks of mystery that had been imparted upon me from various sources. For some reason, all evidence seemed to indicate that I should eat some of the festering cheese that we had brought down from Hellesdon - just like Roger did... But why? How could the consumption of old cheese possibly help to alleviate the abundance of burdens I had found myself shouldering? As I considered the possibility of obliging the demands of the ghost in my nightmare I suspected with greater conviction than ever that I had developed a mental brain disease like my cousin Po Jackson. Was I really about to eat a hunk of cheese that was presented to me by a stranger in the night on the wishes of an apparition who I had met in a dream? No, I most certainly wasn't! And besides, that plonker Cedric had gone and thrown it all away.

Well, not all of it.

The man on the phone was right. As I picked up the stale, stinky remains of Roger's toast the word "unpleasant" seemed like a bit of an understatement. There were bits of grit and fluff caked in with the rubbery yellow mess that clung to the bread like bird feces on a hot bonnet. In my head I ran through a few phrases that I felt would more aptly describe the endeavour. "Ultra-unpleasant" was my first development, which soon evolved into "super-rubbish". For a while I considered "hyper-bollocks", but I realised that this might have been hyperbolic. Eventually I just settled for "gross".

Walton Cumberfield
This is gross
Like · Comment · Share · 2 hours ago in Aylesbeare, England ·

When I couldn't think of anything else to do or think about in order to delay the ingestion of putrid old cheese, I closed my eyes, held my nostrils tightly shut and raised the toast to my mouth. Then I had to open my eyes again because without them I was unable to quite get the toast into my mouth and was poking myself in the face with it. I sunk my teeth into the cloying, sweaty puddle of cheese, and bit down through the hard, dry toast. I thought I was going to be sick but then I wasn't sick. And then all of the saliva in my mouth disappeared into the foulness of the food and I couldn't get my brain to tell my glands to produce any more. My mouth was dry, and the stinking blob of bread and hardened animal lactate was sitting on my tongue like a beached manatee with personal hygiene problems.

Come on Walton, I thought. *You can do it. You can do it for Roger. You've come this far…*

I closed my eyes and swallowed hard. The first time it came straight back up again. The second time I think I was a little bit sick in my mouth. The third time I couldn't do it. It was too disgusting. I had to spit it out.

You're an idiot, I thought to myself. *You're an idiot, and everyone thinks you're an idiot and you'll always be an idiot and I hate you! You'll never amount to anything! You bloody berk! Just swallow it, man!*

I took a deep, cheesy breath through my nose and used my tongue to push the slop to the back of my mouth. With one big heave of the throat muscles I forced the ball of food down into my stomach and let out a gentle burp as it disappeared into my digestive system. What happened next is difficult to express. I felt suddenly unbalanced, and my head was filled with what can only be described as a burst of deafening silence. It felt as though something in my brain had exploded, and I was falling, for hundreds of miles, over days and weeks, and years, and yet only for a split second. And then everything stopped, and I was left with a dull ache in my head and a ringing in my ears.

And then I opened my eyes.

I reached out to steady myself on the worktop behind me, but it was no longer there, and I fell back against the wall, my head bashing into a few hanging utensils and knocking some onto the floor with a *clang.* The room was darker now, with just a little sunlight pouring in through the small windows at the back, and as such it was hard to get a handle on my immediate surroundings. Needless to say, something wasn't right. I was sure the windows had been larger just a few seconds ago - and who had turned off the lights? *Perhaps it was a power cut*, I thought. My mouth was still rife with the pungent stench of old cheese as I made my way through the darkness to where I presumed the light switch would be. The air smelt different somehow, and I could no longer hear Cedric tinkering about in the bar.

"Cedric?" I said, so quietly that he probably wouldn't have heard me even if he *had* been there… "What's going on?"

Before I could reach the door I heard the handle turn and it swung open, bathing the room in soft light from the corridor behind. The shadowy figure of a man was framed in the doorway and I froze as it came towards me. He reached out to his left and tapped the light switch, causing the room to flicker like a dying candle before reaching a fully illuminated state. The kitchen was *not* as I remembered it. Many of the fixtures were in different places, and all were of an older style - yet somehow newer in appearance. The brilliant white of the walls had changed to a dirty yellow, and the floor at my feet was covered with a chequerboard vinyl finish. Perhaps most perplexing of all though, was the identity of the man who stood in front of me. His face was familiar, though we had never officially met in person before. His unbroken glasses sat atop his bulbous nose and he wore a loose-fitting apron that appeared to be stained with milk and rennet. He was even wearing the same green-check woollen trouserpants that he had become so synonymous with. It appeared, unlikely as it seemed at the time, that I was looking upon the living form of one Oscar Crouch.

"Tell me your name is Walton Cumberfield," he said, smiling.

"My name is Walton Cumberfield," I said. "And it actually is. I'm not just doing as you've instructed."

At that moment I felt as though I were going to pass out, but I feared that this would be too much of a cliché given the circumstances, so I dashed to the nearest sink to splash my face with water and wash the stench of cheese from my mouth.

"I imagine you don't feel at all well," he said, offering me a tea towel. "I can remember how bad I felt the first time I travelled."

"Travelled where?" I asked, rubbing my face with the towel.

"Through time," said Oscar.

"Through time?" I asked, like an inquisitive parrot. "What are you talking about?"

"The year is 1954," he said. "You have come a long way, my friend – I suppose I should thank you for trusting me."

"Trusting you?" I said, still a bit like a parrot. "What do you mean?"

"You've come back to help me," he said. "You ate of the cheese."

"I did," I confirmed. "I did eat of the cheese. But what am I doing here?"

"All in good time, my friend." He took the towel from me and slung it over his shoulder. "Come with me, let's get you a drink…"

We walked out of the kitchen and into the corridor behind the bar. There was the cellar door, next to the stairs – open just a crack – no longer covered in bolts and locks. Everything seemed vaguely familiar, and yet so very different. It was most peculiar. The bar was situated in exactly the same place, and the layout of the room had not really changed. I sat down on a barstool in almost exactly the same place I had done the night before, or rather, approximately 46 years later…

"I'm glad you're here," said Oscar, patting me on the back and grinning affectionately. "Roger will be delighted."

NINE

THE OLDER DOG AND BOTTLE

Roger sat with his back to the fire, sipping loudly from a steaming cup of tea. It must have been the middle of winter, as I was struggling to stay warm beneath a couple of thick blankets that Oscar had kindly bestowed upon me.

"Three weeks," Roger replied. (I had just asked him a question, you see, but chose not to include that in the text in order to invoke a sense of immediacy).

"So you've just been here waiting for me?" I asked. "For three weeks? How did you know I was going to show up?"

Roger took another sip of tea. "It's something to do with 'the inevitability of convicted decisions within the realm of what is possible'. Oscar will explain – I don't fully understand it myself."

"Are you sure this isn't all just an elaborate hoax?" I asked, taking out Roger's smartphone. I had got wise to elaborate hoaxes during my vegan phase, when my mother would trick me into wearing leather shoes and beeswax necklaces by lying about their derivation. One Christmas she forced me to wear a big, bright red, itchy jumper which she said she had knitted herself from "synthetic fibres". She had literally pulled the wool over my eyes, and I wasn't going to let it happen again in a hurry (in a metaphorical sense at least). I am no longer a vegan now, of course, and am happy to receive woollen gifts…

"Well if it's a hoax, it would have to be pretty elaborate," said Roger. "I've been out and about in the village. This is definitely the 1950s."

I looked at the phone and confirmed that I did not have a single bar of reception. Roger was right – either we were in the past or I'd somehow ended up in King's Lynn again.

"So what are we doing here?" I asked.

"Well," said Roger. "I think Oscar just wants to know some information regarding the circumstances of his death, in order to prevent it from happening."

Already this was making no sense to me. How had I travelled through time? How did Oscar know that he was going to die? I put this question to Roger, who sheepishly hid behind his cup and answered softly;

"Because I told him."

"Damn it Roger!" I said (out loud this time). "Why would you tell him a thing like that? Were you drunk again? You got drunk again didn't you?"

"No," he insisted. "And that was *your* fault! You were the one who said I had to drink alcohol in order to 'blend in' with the other customers!"

"Drink alcohol, yes," I shouted. "But don't get so 'Bodger and Badgered' that you start travelling through time! Honestly Roger, sometimes I wonder why I made you my lodger in the first place."

Then I remembered that it was because he was a good subject for poetry and because I couldn't afford to pay my mortgage after losing my job as a taxidermist's assistant when I stuffed the wrong squirrel… but then again, that's another story, for another time.

"I'm sorry," he said. "We were just chatting and it sort of came up. He asked what the pub was like in the future, and I said it was haunted by the ghost of a cheesemaker. I didn't know it was him, did I? He hadn't told me that he was a cheesemaker at that point."

The back door opened and Oscar came in, struggling with a couple of milk churns under his arms.

"Hello gentlemen," he said jovially, quickly slamming the door behind him to keep out the draft. "Would anybody like some fish fingers?"

"Again with the fish fingers," sighed Roger. "It's pretty much all he eats. He brought some back from the future and now he's obsessed with them."

Oscar skipped merrily behind the bar towards the kitchen. "I think I'll just fire up a batch."

Roger leant back in his chair and popped a cigarette in his mouth. "I hate the fifties," he said as he lit it. "Everything's different. And these cigarettes are horrible."

"I just wish he'd sit down and explain to me what the hell is going on," I said. "Do you think he'll be long?"

"Probably," said Roger. "He'll be hours in that kitchen. Sure, he'll pop in some fish fingers, but then he'll find something else to do. He's quite mad, you see. I don't know if it's the isolation, or the travelling through time, but he's really off his rocker. I don't understand what he's going on about half the time."

"Brilliant," I said. "So I suppose there's little hope of him returning us to the present day?"

"I don't know. Every time I ask him about it he just gets distracted by something else. I don't know if he's doing it on purpose or what. Last week he went to fetch some time cheese from the cellar and then just disappeared. I found him hours later tending to his herbs in the back garden."

"Herbs, eh?" I said, nodding. "He obviously has far too much thyme on his hands."

Roger did not laugh because the pun only really works when it is written down. Okay, I didn't actually say the joke at all, but I wish that I had. Spontaneous wit has always been my Achilles' heel. That and my heel, interestingly enough, which has a calcaneal spur. What I actually said was:

"Herbs, eh? Perhaps he can give us some sage advice."

Roger did not laugh at that joke either, because it was not as funny as the thyme one I thought of much later. I had never had much luck with herbs – ever since I tried to pitch a bake at home herb-infused French stick product to the leading supermarkets. Although the pitch was strong (due, in part, to my excellent diction), they turned down my idea because they decided that the brand was not family friendly. To this day I have no idea what they meant, and am very sad to say that shoppers nationwide will never be able to experience the beautiful union of flavours that comes with every bite of bread cooked with my *DillDough*™.

"Szechuan lousy pun you just made there," said Roger, smiling.

"Don't be stupid, Roger. Szechuan is a spice, you idiot!"

We heard the kitchen door swing open and Oscar came back through into the bar, clutching a notebook and a pencil. He poured himself a pint of ale and joined us by the fire, halted from saying whatever he was going to say by the vision of Roger's smartphone.

"Whoah," he said. "What sort of fancy thingamajig is that?"

I picked up the phone and started demonstrating its features for some reason – showing it off like I was working in *Phones 4 U* or something...

"It's a smartphone," I said. "It's got apps and interweb access and a camera and all sorts of funky features. I'm surprised you haven't seen one in your travels to the future."

"I haven't been that far to the future," he explained. "I haven't yet made any cheese that's strong enough. But I will, of course... because that's how you got here! That's how you came back this far! It's all very exciting..."

"So you make cheese that allows you to travel through time if you eat it?"

"That's right," he said.

"How?"

"All in good time," he replied, really bloody annoyingly. "Now, concerning the nature of my death..."

He took out the notepad and prepared to jot down everything I said, holding my gays like a homophobic jailer.

"I really don't know much about it," I said. "I just know that you were stabbed in the guts by some people who were after your cheese. And you died in 1954."

He began to scribble down my words.

"You died in the cellar, sat against the wall."

"Of course," he said. "That would make sense. That's where I keep the cheese."

"Yes," I agreed. "But that's really all I know."

"I must have told you what date it was – what time of year – anything – anything like that?"

"No," I said. "And how do you know that the ghost of your dead self spoke to me in the future? That doesn't make sense."

"I know that it will happen," he explained. "Because I have *resolved* to do it."

Roger tapped me on the arm. "This is it," he said. "This is the bit I don't get. The law of the inevitability of convicted decisions…"

"What's that?" I asked, turning to Oscar. I picked up the smartphone and prepared to take some notes of my own. It reminded me of being at school, except that no one was throwing doughnuts at me and calling me a faggot. Sorry, no – I think they used to throw faggots at me and call me a doughnut. It doesn't really matter...

Oscar sat back and took a large swig of ale. "Do you know how I discovered time travel, Mr Cumberfield?"

I shook my head. "No. Obviously I do not."

"It was very simple in the end," he said. "You see, I read a book a few months ago by H.G. Wells entitled *The Time Machine* – and while I was reading it, I began to think how wonderful it would be to visit the worlds of the past and future. There are so many fascinating questions to answer – about history, about the future of technology and politics – about everything. And then of course there are the two biggest questions of all… where did we come from? And where are we going to end? These are my favourite questions."

"That's interesting," I said. "My favourite question is the question 'what is your favourite question,' as it is coincidentally also my answer to that question."

"How nice," said Oscar. "But if I might continue…"

"By all means," I said.

Oscar put down his ale and leant forward as he continued his tale with genuine enthusiasm. He was a fairly good raconteur, even by my standards…

"You see, I just became obsessed with the notion of answering all of these questions! Albert Einstein once said that 'Intelligence is not the ability to store information, but to know where to find it.' If I had the ability to travel through time, then I would have access to all of the information – the answer to every question – no matter how huge – thus making me, undeniably, the greatest genius in the history of the world."

"But you invented time travel," said Roger. "That alone makes you the greatest genius."

"I *discovered* time travel," said Oscar. "But that was the easy part. Now I have to hone the recipe in order to travel further! The stronger the cheese, the further you travel. I have to say I am fascinated by *your* time – what wonderful inventions you have come up with, the situation of global politics, the literature, the music… It's all very interesting... Roger tells me, for instance, that in the early 21st century the country is run by the working classes."

"Not exactly," I said. "Roger was just being sociologically facetious."

Roger sulked and lit another cigarette. I turned back to Oscar and asked him to continue.

"Well…" he said. "When I decided that I was going to learn the secret of time travel, I realised that this could be a painstaking and time consuming process. So, in order to speed things up a bit, I resolved to discover the secret of time travel, then to travel back through time to tell myself the secret of time travel, in order to save myself the effort. Sure enough, the next morning, the future version of me walked into my room and explained the secret of time travel, which I immediately set about implementing. And do you know the first thing I did when I discovered how to travel through time?"

I shook my head.

"The first thing I did when I discovered how to travel through time," he explained. "Was to travel back in time and explain to myself how to travel through time. And why did I do this? Why?

Because it was inevitable! I had already seen it happen.... This is what I have discerned about time travel! I've started calling it the law of the inevitability of convicted decisions. What do you think? Too long-winded?"

I looked at Roger, who simply shrugged and rolled his eyes.

"I have a question," I said.

"Good!" exclaimed Oscar, chuckling. "I love questions."

"Why didn't you just *not* go back in time to tell yourself how to travel through time? You had the secret of time travel already - that was never going to change."

"You mean why didn't I try to fool the universe by creating a paradox? Just to see what would happen?"

"Exactly," I said.

"The universe is very, very big," he explained. "And I'm slightly afraid of things that are very, very big. Besides, I felt uncontrollably compelled to do it! You see, once something has happened – and this is quite interesting too – you can't undo it… The universe simply won't let you! For example, if I decided that I wanted to go back in time to yesterday and give myself the result of a horse race, I wouldn't be able to, because the future me didn't show up yesterday to give myself the result of a horse race. It didn't happen! If I tried to do it, the universe would find a way to stop me… However, if I decided today, with absolute conviction, that tomorrow I would watch a horse race and then go back in time to today to tell myself the result, then I would most probably appear to myself with the result of that horse race! And then the universe would force me to follow through with that conviction… Do you see? The law of the inevitability of convicted decisions..."

"My brain hurts," said Roger, rubbing his brow.

"Where are you going with this, cheesemaker?" I asked. "I wanted to know how you knew about my conversation with your ghost."

"And I'm trying to explain it," he said. "If you'd just listen, you'd see that it all comes back to the law of convicted decisions. When Roger told me about you, and the cheese, and the fact that I was haunting this pub, I resolved to haunt this pub until such a time that

I was able to communicate with you, and ask you to eat of the cheese in order to come back through time and explain to me the circumstances of my own death. I resolved to do it, and it came true. Do you see?"

"No," I said. "You said that if something has happened, or will happen, then it is inevitable, and the universe won't let us change anything."

"Correct," said Oscar. "That is why when I decided I would send you back here, you ended up here, and I can never change that."

"Then surely the universe won't let you prevent your death. Because if you don't die, then you don't haunt the pub, you don't meet me, I don't warn you and… there you go – paradox."

"Ah yes," said Oscar, leaning forward even more. "But that's the brilliant part! That's the really clever bit! You see, I have resolved to spread false rumours of my fatal stabbing throughout the village, such that the legend of my murder will still come to fruition and be related in your time without it actually having to be true! Then, upon the event of my actual death, I shall haunt this pub until such a time that I run into you, whereby I shall lie to you about the circumstances of my demise."

"Why?" I asked.

"Because then you would still come back here to warn me of the murder which I am now going to prevent from happening."

"I'm right with you," I said.

"I know," said Oscar. "Fantastic, isn't it?"

"No," I said. "I was talking to Roger. My brain is hurting too."

Fortunately I had represented Oscar's explanation in a handy diagram on *Freedraw*, which I decided to study at length until I got to grips with the logic of his story…

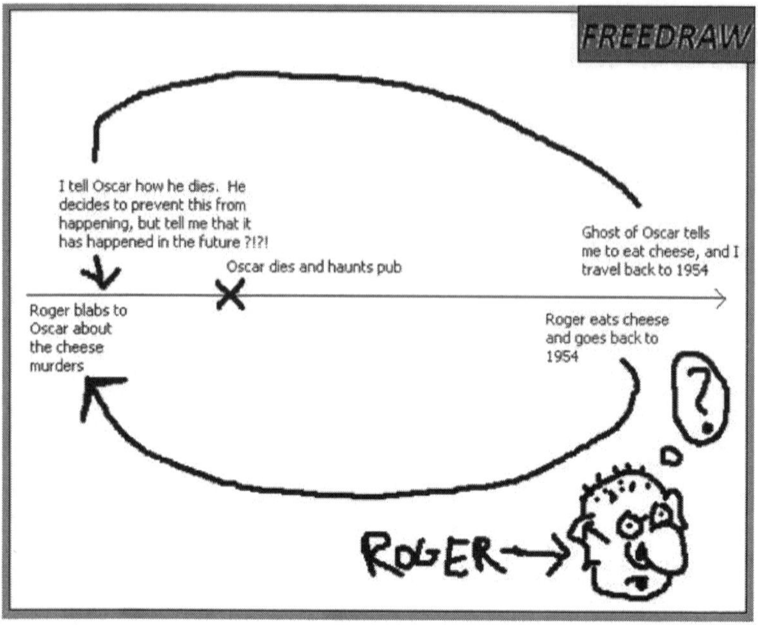
FREEDRAW
I tell Oscar how he dies. He decides to prevent this from happening, but tell me that it has happened in the future ?!?!
Ghost of Oscar tells me to eat cheese, and I travel back to 1954
Oscar dies and haunts pub
Roger blabs to Oscar about the cheese murders
Roger eats cheese and goes back to 1954
ROGER

TEN

THE GIRL WITH THE DRAGON KAZOO

When Oscar Crouch woke up on the morning of September 17th, 1954, he was standing at the end of his bed. That is to say, of course, that upon waking that morning, he found himself confronted by another version of himself (from the future) who was standing, facing him, at the end of the bed in which he lay. And it was at this moment, while still in his pyjamas, that the first homosapien discovered the secrets of travelling through time (after his morning coffee and dunky biscuits, that is).

That morning, future Oscar had explained to present Oscar (now past Oscar) the unlikely concept that enabled men (and women, presumably) to travel through the fourth dimension to a different instance within the spectrum of time. That concept is based on one equally unlikely truth, which has gone without detection for millions of years, most probably due to that very lack of probability (i.e. it is bonkers).

There is a cow in Budleigh Salterton that is independent of the space-time continuum. It was never created and can never be destroyed. It was known in ancient times, and has always been known since as the *Bossintempore* (from the Latin – literally meaning "cow without time"). Oscar told us this, and then he told us some more interesting things: it is very important to understand that the *Bossintempore* has always existed, standing there in the same spot, for the eternity of time. Time itself, you must understand, does not govern it. It does not age and it has no memory. It does not eat, sleep, holiday in the summer or feel any sense of tension during the last five seconds of a round of *Countdown*. It exists in only three dimensions, and is unaffected by the fourth. It is truly timeless. That is not to say, of course, that one cannot interact with the cow, to the reasonable extent that one could interact with any cow. If you slapped it on the rump it would moo and maybe kick you. If you poked it in the eye it would flinch and… well… maybe kick you. And of course, if you milked it, it would lactate (and maybe kick you).

It is said that the ancient people feared the cow, and disapproved of its assertion to disobey the common logic of normality. As such it was despised by scientists and philosophers alike, who agreed that it would be mutually beneficial to hide the cow from the population and allow its memory to fade into legend (like John Major). Unable to move the cow, they built a structure around it to shield it from view. This structure became known as the cow bunker.

At this time an order of protectors was established to protect and conceal the existence of the time cow. This order has survived over many ages, passing on their secret duties from one generation to the next. Now pay attention to this next part as this is the bit which I found the most interesting: occasionally the order would be forced to defend their secret with physical violence, and many battles broke out between the order and the groups who sought to expose the legend of the cow. When entering such bouts, the members of the order would scream words of encouragement to one another, effectively a battle cry, which went something along the lines of "defend the cow bunker!" This was subsequently shortened to "For the cow bunker!" which eventually just became "Cow bunker!" which somehow became "cowbunga" which in turn, for some reason, developed into the word "cowabunga". This is largely irrelevant information, but I thought I'd include it here as etymology is one of my favourite "ologies". I realise that this extraneous waffle may have distracted from the fast-developing and utterly compelling plot that has been unfolding thus far in my story, and for that I make my apology (my second favourite "ology").

There is another simple truth that I must convey before moving on. It is a truth that became known to Oscar Crouch that same amazing morning while he was still in his pyjamas – and that truth is that if you milk the cow, then proceed to ingest the fruits of its timeless teats, you will in fact become temporarily displaced from the space-time continuum yourself. Unfortunately, drinking the milk in its pure form has very little effect, and only displaces you from space time over the matter of a couple of seconds. That is to say that if you drink of the milk, you will only ever travel a few seconds into the past or future. In the ancient times anyone who drank of the milk attributed this disorientation to food poisoning or lactose intolerance. The truth now acknowledged by Oscar, imparted onto him by future Oscar, and shared exclusively with Roger and I, is that if this milk is coagulated and used to make cheese, its effects are intensified considerably… And I mean *considerably*!

"I have a question," I said, putting up my hand.

"Yes Walton," said Oscar, pointing at me and shovelling another vast helping of fish fingers into his mouth.

"When you eat some cheese and travel through time, how do know which way you're going to travel?"

Oscar paused and finished his mouthful. "Well, it depends which way you're thinking. If you want to travel forwards, you have to think forwards, and if you want to travel backwards, you have to think backwards."

"Okay," I said. "So how did you know that I was going to be thinking backwards when I ate the cheese? How did you know I was going to end up back here and not somewhere in the future?"

"Because you were eating some dirty cheese with stale toast based on the wishes of a ghost you had met in a nightmare. That seems like a fairly backwards thought process to me."

"I suppose you're right," I said.

"And as for Roger," he continued. "He was very drunk - and the thoughts of any intoxicated person are always pretty backwards."

"Well, I think you'll find that Roger's thoughts are pretty backwards at the best of times," I said jovially.

Oscar and I pointed and laughed at Roger for some time. He didn't realise this of course as he had fallen asleep during Oscar's long and involved explanation of the Bossintempore. Poor old Roger had been bobbing his head up and down continuously in order to express his understanding, and had quite literally nodded off.

"So how come Roger ended up here three weeks before I did?" I asked.

"It's not an exact science," said Oscar. "I think it's somewhat dependent on how much of the cheese you eat and how backwards your thinking is. Generally speaking though, it's the strength of the cheese that dictates how far you travel. I think my next batch should be pongy enough to get you back to 2010, providing that you're thinking forwards, that is."

"How exactly does it work?" I asked.

"I'm not entirely sure," said Oscar. "But if I were forced to posit a hypothesis, it would be that the cheese reacts with the acid in your stomach and creates a wormhole large enough to transport you and anything on your person to a different point in time. I've always wondered why my clothes always go with me, and anything I have in my pockets."

"Like Roger's smartphone," I said, taking out Roger's smartphone.

"Exactly," said Oscar, gazing lovingly at his last fish finger. "And these fish fingers."

*

We stayed with Oscar for many days waiting for his cheese to mature. It was a bit like a holiday, except that we only ate fish fingers and couldn't watch *Eastenders* or update The Facebook. In the evenings Oscar would regale us with stories of his experiments, which we traded for stories of the future such as the moon-landings and "The Beatles". Roger even taught Oscar to play *Ellen Arigby* on the acoustic guitar, and suggested that he release it as a single in about 1964, before Joe McCarthy and Vladimir Lenin had even thought of it. Oscar laughed at the suggestion, and insisted that the universe would not allow it. He was always going on about that pesky universe.

One very pleasant Friday evening Oscar took us out in his motorcar (of which he was very proud). We drove to a cinema nearby and watched a very boring black and white film that was not as good as the last black and white film that Roger had taken me to called *Sim City*. It didn't matter however, as I ended up spending the whole film sat next to an incredibly pretty lady who shared her popcorn with me. I thanked her for this kindness, explaining that I would have paid for my share if I had any 1950s money, but I only had future pounds. I think this confused her somewhat, so I just pretended to watch the film for a bit and smiled at her intermittently. She had that sort of face that makes you go a bit squishy on the inside, with huge green eyes, long eyelashes, and perfectly white teeth, framed in a smile of blood red lips. She also had nice bosoms, which I tried not to look at.

When the film was over, I helped her to put on her coat (because someone swarve had done that in the film we were watching).

"Thanks very much," she said, with a beautifully soft voice like Marilyn Manson (who was in the film). "What's your name?"

"Walton," I replied. "Walton Cumberfield."

Roger and Oscar were heading out of our row at the other end by this point.

"Come on Walt," Roger shouted. "We're going back to the Dog for a pint."

"Just a second!" I shouted.

"Well it was nice to meet you, Walton Cumberfield," said the pretty lady. "Maybe we'll run into one another again sometime." I liked it when she said my name. I found it bizarrely comforting.

"Maybe we will," I said, smoothly. Unfortunately I didn't know what to say after that, so I put the popcorn box over my head and said; "this'll keep off the rain." In my head it was a hilarious jape, but I immediately regretted doing it, especially since it wasn't raining outside, to the best of my knowledge. I couldn't see her reaction, but then I thought I heard her giggling, so I lifted the box to see if she was smiling.

"You're funny," she said, melting me with her eyes (not literally, as that would have been horrific).

"Thank you," I said. "You're very pretty."

I wasn't very good at the whole 'swarve' thing, so I just opted for sincere flattery (and tomfoolery). I suspected that it was working, as it made her face go almost as red as Roger's rosy red nose. Incidentally, Roger was now standing at the exit, waving his arms about and tapping his watch. The pretty stranger noticed this little routine and pointed him out to me.

"You'd better go," she said, looking at the floor. "Your friend is waiting."

Damn it Roger.

I gave her one of my warmest smiles and politely shook her hand. The world seemed to disappear when I looked into her eyes.

"I was wondering-" I said.

"Yes?" she said, with a big smile, still holding onto my hand.

As I lost myself in her stare, I was forced to recall a brief romance I had enjoyed while visiting Bognor Regis on a family holiday (this is a place, not a person – you're thinking of Borgon Regis). The girl in Bognor Regis was named Penny. I was seven years old (so was she, I hasten to add) and when I had to leave it felt as though I had been slapped in the soul with a fish (possibly a sole). I didn't want to be slapped in the soul with a sole again. I knew I would be gone in a matter of days - back to my own time – and I would probably never be returning…

"Never mind," I said, releasing my hand from hers. "You take care now…"

When I got outside the building it *was* raining, but fortunately I still had my popcorn box hat, which I wore all the way to the car. I slid into the back seat and didn't look back at the cinema once, afraid that if I saw her smiling face again it would intensify my sense of regret. It's funny the things that you remember after a while. I can still remember that moment like it was yesterday. I can't remember the name of the film we saw (yawn!), but I *can* remember how hopelessly sad I felt as Oscar turned on the ignition. I remember the smell of my wet clothes on the leather seats. I remember the exact pitch and volume of the sound it made when she tapped on the window. That's right! She tapped on the window…

"Wait," I shouted to Oscar as he began to pull away. I tried to wind down said window, but it would only open a crack. "What's wrong with this?" I demanded.

"That's as far as it goes," said Oscar.

I looked out at her through the glass and saw that she was still smiling, despite the fact that she was soaking wet from head to toe. Again, I was trying very hard not to look at her bosoms (I noticed that Roger was trying considerably less hard). She took out a small piece of paper and posted it to me through the gap. It fell into my lap and I unfolded it, then she kissed the window and gave me a tiny wave.

"Christ," said Oscar, finally pulling away. "You're cleaning that lipstick off the window when we get back."

I ignored his grouchy temperament and lay back on the seat, reading the little bit of paper. It was just letters followed by numbers, and they didn't make any sense to me.

"What's this?" I said. "Why has she given me her national insurance number?"

Oscar held out his hand and I passed him the slip of paper.

"It's her telephone number," he explained. "All telephone numbers start with letters- it's the name of the exchange."

"Wow," I said. "The 1950s is bloody complicated. Just you wait until you get to the future. It's much easier in our time. You're going to love The Facebook. We can be Facebook friends."

"I'm sure we can," said Oscar, taking a swig of whiskey from his hip flask, which I had already explained to him was a very bad idea. The drink of the road, as everyone knows, is sherry. "So what's her name – this new girl of yours?"

I thought for a moment. "She didn't tell me."

"Well, what are you going to say to her when you phone her up tomorrow?" asked Oscar, grinning and handing me back the slip of paper.

"How do you know I'm going to phone her up tomorrow?" I asked.

"Don't you remember, Walt?" He took another swig of whiskey. "I'm a time traveller…"

He leant back in his seat, turned to me, and tipped me a cheeky wink. I was beginning to like Oscar. He was much more fun than Roger, who was sat there in the seat next to him, puffing away on a cigarette and sulking like a constipated moose. Then suddenly something very unusual happened..

(Here we go again, "change the bloody record" etcs).

"Look out!" I shouted, as a car pulled into the road in front of us. None of us were expecting it, since it was late at night and we were out in the bum-end of no place. Oscar was too busy winking at the time to make a controlled stop, so he slammed on the brakes and we all shot forwards without warning. Roger bashed his head on the dashboard, I caught the side of my face on the seat in front, and Oscar shot head first into the steering wheel with a loud *crunch*, snapping his glasses in half.

The car in front of us stopped too. We hadn't noticed its approach because it had no lights on. Now it sat there in the road – a brown Morris Minor – illuminated in the glow of our headlights.

"Is everyone alright?" asked Oscar, fumbling around for his glasses. "Jesus Christ. What kind of an idiot drives around without any lights on?"

I leant forwards and stared at the other car through the gap in the seats. It was too dark to make out the driver, but I could just about see that there were two figures within. Roger was moaning like a little girl because his forehead was bleeding a bit. Oscar found the two halves of his glasses and held them up to the light.

"Ah brilliant," he said, sarcastically (I assume). "I can barely see without these things! Walton – can you look in the boot for me? I think I might have some sticky tape in there."

I continued to scrutinise the Morris Minor. Why was it just sat there in the road?

"Walt!" said Oscar again. "Can I get a bit of help here please?"

I opened my door and climbed out of the car. As soon as I stood up outside, the Morris Minor darted backwards, turned around and shot off down the road at an inappropriately high speed. I heard

Oscar yelling obscenities from within the car as I opened the boot and rummaged around for some sticky tape. Something didn't feel right. Something about that Morris Minor had made a sinister impression on me, and I was experiencing the early stages of the 'heebie-jeebies'.

"Again," said Oscar, taking a swig of whiskey as I climbed back into the car. "What sort of an idiot drives around at night without any lights on?"

"The sort that doesn't want to be noticed," I said astutely as I handed him the tape.

"Morons," he scoffed, winding the tape around his glasses. "They shouldn't be allowed on the road."

As I watched Oscar making his hasty reparations I realised that there was something more than a little ominous about the scene unfolding before me.

"Oscar," I said. "I don't want to alarm you, but your ghost…"

Oscar spun around in his seat and tried his best to look at me through his unassisted eyes. "What about it?"

"Well, when I saw you, in the future, in the Old Dog and Bottle, you were dead…"

"Yes," said Oscar. "I know that. We've been through this."

"You were dead," I continued. "And you were wearing a pair of broken glasses. *Those* broken glasses - bound together with *that* sticky tape."

As the words left my lips Oscar rolled the last coil of tape around the centre of the broken frame. Nobody said anything after that. Nothing seemed appropriate. Eventually Oscar took another sip of whiskey, shook himself off, placed the glasses on the end of his nose and started the engine.

We all went straight to bed that night. (Well… I think Roger did a poo first).

*

Roger and I went to the village fête on Sunday afternoon to have a bit of fun and unwind from the stresses of time travel, but mainly to get away from Oscar, who was becoming unbearably depressed about his impending death and refusing to wear his glasses except when brushing his teeth or doing crosswords. This meant that he was always either crying or bumping into things, which, although hilarious at first, soon became fairly tiresome and repetitive, like having Rolf Harris at a family barbeque. On the plus side, he probably didn't realise that we were gone, or that we had borrowed his 'motorcar' for the day. It was a fairly nice little thing, but it was certainly no Corsa. Lord, how I missed my Corsa…

I have to confess that I had an interior motive for attending the fête that day, which I did not tell Roger because he'd been sulking like a camel with a hump full of hornets. My *exterior* motive was simply to have a good old knees-up with my friend, but the real reason that I suggested the excursion was that I had arranged to meet my new fancy-lady from the cinema ;-). Her name, as it turned out, was Wendy Turner, and she was very nice to me when I spoke to her on the telephone. Now, if you take into account our respective birth dates, then technically Wendy is at least 50 years older than me, which is why I chose not to tell Roger what I was up to. Roger is not a romantic like me, and I was 88 percent sure that he wouldn't understand. I also suspected that he might be jealous, since he has barely spoken to a real-life offline woman since his divorce.

I get the impression that Roger has never been much of a romantic, since he got married in an office or something with just his brother Michael and some of his close aunts (and his wife, Abby, obviously). Also, I think he proposed to Abby via his work email, and made her choose her own ring from Elizabeth Duke's. Roger told me that his work was very involved and stressful back then, and when it came to relationships he had decided long ago that life was complicated enough... This may go some way to explaining why he married a lady named Abby National.

"I don't understand," I said as we approached the unmanned entrance. "Do we get in for free?"

"No," said Roger, quite plainly. "We do not get in *for* free. We get in "free of charge" or "for no money". *Free* is an abbreviation of the phrase *free of charge*. You wouldn't say "do we get in *for* free of charge", therefore you cannot say "do we get in *for* free". But in answer to your question – I don't think we have to pay to get in."

I could always tell that Roger was in a bad mood when he started criticising my grammar. Often I would counter his intellectual attacks by criticising his grandma, who is 100 years old and votes for the BNP. I decided on this occasion to let sleeping dogs lie.

"Cheer up Roger," I said, giving him one of my second warmest smiles. "We're going to have a lovely time. You and me – the old team – taking on the world…" I didn't really know what I meant by that, but it certainly sounded encouraging.

Roger sighed and looked at the sky. "It's going to rain," he mumbled. "Why have they held a fête in the middle of winter?"

"Because people need cheering up, is why," I said. "People like you and me! Now let's go and win you a goldfish or something…"

I spotted Wendy from across the field, chatting with an elderly man at the jam stall. I remember thinking that she must be a very kind lady, as she was smiling enthusiastically at whatever the old man was saying, which was probably really boring and jam-related. When she spotted me she smiled and gave me a wave. Luckily Roger didn't see, and I was able to disguise my own wave as a mosquito-swatting motion.

"Damn bugs," I said, for authenticity. "Do you want to go on the Ferris wheel or something?"

Roger shrugged. "I guess so."

"Okay," I said, "I'll wait for you over there by the candy floss seller. Have a good time!"

The queue for the Ferris wheel was about 20 minutes long by my reckoning, which would afford me a good opportunity to spend some time with Wendy and share one of those 69s that people often have. This was not compulsory of course – she had every right to choose whatever ice cream she wanted.

"Why aren't you coming?" asked Roger.

"I'm afraid of heights," I explained.

Roger threw me a cynical look. "You're not afraid of heights."

"I am," I insisted. "Ever since I read that book *Wuthering Heights*. It was terrifying. I've never been the same since." (I have never actually read that book *Wuthering Heights*, but I don't think Roger has either, so he was none the wiser).

"I don't particularly want to go on the wheel by myself," said Roger. "It's a bit pathetic."

"No it isn't," I insisted. "Being by yourself is cool, like The Lone Ranger… or Celine Dion."

"If you say so," said Roger. "Do you want to stand in the queue with me at least?"

I pretended I hadn't heard that last part, and skipped off merrily humming my favourite rap song by Example. Unfortunately, if you hum a rap song there is no melody, and it sounds like there's something a bit wrong with you. For this reason I immediately regretted doing it when I reached Wendy at the jam stall.

"Excuse me?" I said to the boring old jam vendor. "I was wondering if I might trouble you for a moment of this young lady's time?"

I decided to be very formal and polite, since it was the 1950s and everyone was very formal and polite in the 1950s (except Ronnie Biggs). The jam vendor was equally polite, but less formal.

"Be my guest," he said, and continued to stir a large vat of marmalade.

I offered my elbow to Wendy and she slid her arm into mine, looking into my eyes and smiling the smile of a thousand angels. As we walked away from the jam vendor, I gestured back to him and made a really good joke.

"Who was that jammy old git?" I asked.

"That was my grandfather," replied Wendy. "He's my absolute hero. He fought in the first world war."

Wendy did not find my first joke very funny, so I tried to rescue the mood with an impression of Charlie Chaplin. Unfortunately she and many of the surrounding public mistook this for an impression of Adolph Hitler, which was widely regarded as both alarming and inappropriate. I therefore redefined the strategy of my charm offensive (more charm, less offense) and bought Wendy a strawberry flavoured ice cream with chocolate bits.

"Thanks very much for this, Walton," she said as we sat down on a little bench at the edge of the field. "Strawberry is my favourite flavour, and it was very nice of you to buy it for me. You're very sweet."

"Actually I got it free with *my* ice cream," I explained. "That ice cream salesman had a two for one offer – I must say, I find his sales and marketing techniques very progressive for the 1950s, but also patently unnecessary. He is the only ice cream salesman here, after all."

"Yes," agreed Wendy. "It's not often you get anything for free in this life."

"No," I said. "You never get anything *for* free. You might get something "free of charge" or "for no money", but never "*for* free". *Free* is an abbreviation of the phrase *free of charge.* You wouldn't say "It's not often you get anything *for* free of charge", therefore you can't say "It's not often you get anything *for* free". Do you see?"

"Wow," said Wendy. "You're very clever."

As Wendy slipped her spare hand into mine, I realised that I had just learnt a valuable truth about women; they *love* it when you correct their grammar... Incidentally, when I say "spare" hand, I mean the hand with which she was not holding her ice cream, and not some sort of bizarre prosthetic third appendage she carried around in case of unexpected amputation or decapitation. That, of course, would have been horrific.

Wendy was charmingly perfect and perfectly charming. She was wearing a white dress with red polka-dots, tied at the midriff with a red sash. It was summer attire, which suggested to me that her desire to look pretty that day had taken precedence over the practicalities of dressing for the weather. This made me feel very guilty, and when I noticed that her arms were shaking I took off my jacket and draped it around her shoulders. Then I started to shiver loads too so she gave it back. We probably shouldn't have been eating so much ice cream.

"So how come I haven't seen you much around here before?" she asked.

"Well, I don't know," I said. "Perhaps you have. Do you remember every face you see?"

She looked straight into my eyes, tilted her head slightly, and brushed a lock of golden hair away from her face. "I'd remember yours," she said, quietly. "I think you're very handsome."

I nearly died. My ice cream had macadamia nuts in it, which I am severely allergic to, and they were causing my throat to tighten so much that I was finding it very difficult to breathe.

"Are you alright?" she asked.

I nodded, which was painful. "Yes I'm fine. Would you like the rest of my ice cream?"

"Oh no, thank you very much," she said. "I mustn't be a pig. I'd never get out of this dress."

"That would be a shame," I said, looking at her perfectly-shaped body. Then I realised that I had just been a bloody massive pervert like Roger Moore, so I distracted her by gently plopping my ice cream onto the end of her nose and saying "oops."

"Hey," she said playfully, wiping her nose with her handkerchief. "What's the big idea?"

"I have many big ideas," I said, my voice becoming ever more croaky due to the onset of anaphylaxis. "Like this one idea I have for social change, where everyone is treated equally regardless of the colour of their skin."

"That's a really good idea," she said. "You are very wise."

"And gay people aren't persecuted for what is a perfectly natural and morally acceptable lifestyle," I continued.

"That's great," she said. "But I don't know anyone who persecutes people just because they're happy."

"And then there's this one other idea I have, which is like a toaster with a radio on it," I explained.

"That's brilliant," she exclaimed. "Then you wouldn't need to buy a toaster and a radio, you could just buy the one unit and save lots of money."

Wendy and I were on exactly the same wavelength. Okay, so I stole two out of three of those ideas from Martin Luther King and Harvey Milk, but I still endorsed them wholeheartedly, and the toaster idea was 100 percent original.

"I think you have very lovely eyes," I said to her.

"Me too," she said, and then giggled. "I mean that I think *you* have lovely eyes too - not that I agree my eyes are lovely."

"Well you should," I said. "Because they are lovely."

For a moment we just looked at each other's lovely eyes and held hands. I thought that we were going to kiss, but then we didn't kiss. Then she sighed a happy sigh and stood up from the bench.

"Let's go on the Ferris wheel," she said.

The Ferris wheel! Suddenly I remembered Roger… What was I going to do? I didn't want him to know about Wendy in case he didn't approve, and I didn't want Wendy to know about his possible lack of approval, as she probably wouldn't approve of that. It was all a bit of a mess.

"Could I just go to the toilet first?" I asked. "Where are the Port-a-Loos?"

"I've no idea what one of those is," she said.

Of course, I thought. *Port-a-Loos weren't invented until the 1960s.* How could I have been so stupid?

"Where does one go to the lavatory?" I asked.

"At the school," she said. "Around the corner. I'll show you."

She grabbed my hand and pulled me up off the bench enthusiastically. She was brilliant. I wanted to spend the rest of the day with her. In fact, if I'm completely honest, right at that moment I wanted to spend the rest of my *life* with her. I held both of her hands for a second and we smiled at each other. I thought that we were going to kiss but then we didn't kiss. Then I clocked Roger wandering about looking lost and scratching himself, so I decided it best to get out of there as soon as possible.

Of course, the whole 'needing the toilet' thing was simply a ruse. I had hoped to slip away from Wendy in order to spend a bit of time with Roger, but this was proving to be more difficult than I had first thought it would be. I told her to go and have a look around - perhaps chat to her interesting war-hero jam-making grandfather again for a bit or have a go on the whack-a-rat - but instead she insisted on taking me to the men's toilets and waiting by the door for me. She *insisted.* I must have made a very good impression (not the Chaplin one) and her enthusiasm was very encouraging – but I simply had to get away from her for a bit lest Roger get suspicious.... My choices at this point were very limited and I was eventually forced to tell her that it "might be big jobs," warning that I "could be some time". This didn't seem to convince her however, and she patted my hand sympathetically.

"It's fine," she said. "You do what you have to do."

I can't spend too much time with Roger, I thought, as I secretly clambered out of the toilet window. *If I keep her waiting too long, she's going to become concerned for the health of my bowels - which is no foundation for a relationship (according to my old neighbour Frank Jefferson).*

I stealthily made my way back to the fête and found Roger in the beer tent, sitting on his own, nursing a pint of bitter.

"What the hell happened to you?" he asked, when he saw my swollen neck.

"I ate a macadamia nut ice cream," I explained. "It's caused me to go somewhat into anaphylactic shock."

"Christ," said Roger. "What do we do now?"

"Never mind that," I said. "What are you doing in here? You're not supposed to drink on account of your life-shattering alcoholism which cost you your job and your marriage."

"I know, I know," said Roger. "But I'm on holiday – and you disappeared!"

"I was just walking around," I insisted.

"No you weren't," said Roger. "That girl from the cinema is here, isn't she? I saw her when we came in…"

"I don't know what you're talking about you old codger," I said. "Now come on, let's go have a look around together – win you that goldfish..."

I almost held his hand by accident but stopped myself just in time. I immediately wished I was still with Wendy. I liked it when people held my hand…

Fortunately we found some epinephrine on one of the bric-a-brak stalls, which soon put paid to my nut-induced respiratory predicament. I also bought a yo-yo and a trendy little kazoo shaped like a dragon, which I thought Wendy would like <u>loads</u>. After that we went to have a go on the splat-the-rat game, but were very much taken aback when we discovered that the rat in question was a *real* rat. I don't know if this was the norm back in the 1950s, or if this was a feature specific to that particular village fête. What I do know is that rat gut-stained trouserpants are a very difficult thing to explain to a potential girlfriend when emerging from a public lavatory after 29 minutes.

"I bought you a present," I said.

"What on earth happened to you?" she gasped. "Are you alright?"

"I'm fine," I said. "Look, I found this and I thought you'd like it."

I handed her the dragon kazoo.

"In the toilet?" she asked, stepping back from me slightly.

"No, no," I said. "Well… You see…"

I heard the voice of my old neighbour Frank Jefferson in my head again (I really must see a psychologist about that)…

Dishonesty is no foundation for a relationship, Walton – neither is a concern for the health of your partner's bowels. Remember this, Walton. Remember this…

I remembered.

"I'm sorry Wendy," I said. "It's just that I don't think my friend Roger will approve of our courting, so I haven't told him that you're here. I'm worried that if he finds out he'll try to talk me out of it."

"Out of what?" she asked, stepping towards me.

"Out of being… your boyfriend or some such," I said. "That is to say, I would… very much… *like* to be your boyfriend - if you're not too busy." As I blurted it out I must have blushed like a vicar who had accidentally clicked onto YouTube, but I was glad to have said it. She looked at the dragon kazoo and took it in her delicate hands.

"Thank you," she said. "It's beautiful."

Our eyes met once again, and she stepped a little closer in my direction. I gulped and took a breath as she fluttered her long eyelashes at me. I thought we were going to kiss but then we didn't kiss. And then I went to say something else - and then we did kiss! We kissed like a couple of cheeky teenagers from that show

Hollyfolks… she tilted up towards me on her tippy-toes, craned her neck gently to one side, and laid a smacker right in the middle of my face! Our lips met like a couple of old friends at a ceilidh in Keighley. I was in my elephant. I was finally in my elephant!

Well done Walton, said my old neighbour, Frank Jefferson, in my head. *You've made the right choice.*

I really *must* see someone about that…

It started to rain very suddenly, so I took Wendy by the hand and led her inside. We spent a while kissing in the corridor by the toilets, but soon realised that this was a bit weird – especially when we got caught by Mrs Glick and her husband Barnaby, who Wendy told me was a staunch Catholic. Soon after that, in order to escape the stench of urinal cakes and shame, Wendy led me through the school to a sheltered patio area by the playground. No one else was around, so we were free to watch the rain and indulge in some more of that lovely kissing. Wendy was a very good kisser, and I think she thought that *I* was a good kisser too, as every time she came up for air she had a huge smile on her face. The rain didn't stop. I didn't want it to stop. That moment was perfect, and I hoped beyond all hope that it would never have to end.

"What's that poking me?" she asked, after we'd been kissing for a while.

"I'm not sure," I said, as she rummaged through her pockets.

It was the dragon kazoo.

"I'm sorry," she said. "I'm not normally like this, you know."

"Like what?" I asked, brushing her hair out of her face like they do in the films.

"You know," she said, blushing. "I'm not normally so… forward."

"Neither am I," I said. "As a matter of fact, a lot of people say I'm a bit backwards."

That made her laugh loads. She had a wonderful laugh, and it made me ache with joy to hear it. I didn't know how or why I was so captivated by her – why I had fallen for her so instantly and helplessly – but it just seemed *right.* She was a beautiful stranger, and yet somehow I felt a connection to her. I barely knew her, and yet being with her was just like being with an old friend. We had the same sense of humour – the same joie de vivre – the same opinions and philosophies... It really did feel like we *belonged* together. When her chuckling subsided she leant in and kissed me again, but this time she held me tighter and pushed her body into mine. I ran my hands down her slender back and held her at the waist. Then, rather cheekily, I kept on going, and felt her lovely bottom. She didn't mind. She just kept on kissing me!

"Is that the dragon kazoo again?" she asked, her eyes sparkling with delight.

"No," I said, winking. "No it isn't."

I was so cool. I was cooler than Cool Hand Luke drinking Cool Aid with L.L. Cool J in 'Cool'chester. I had never felt so cool before. It felt good. It felt *damn* good…

Maybe I don't have to go back, I thought. *Maybe I can stay in the 1950s forever, and marry Wendy, and live the good life, and go dancing on a Friday evening and start a family of little Waltons and Wendys who won't have to worry about the recession or terrorism or Michael Barrymore…*

She tilted her head back and considered me for a moment.

"Penny for your thoughts?" she asked.

I didn't charge her.

I could do it, I told myself. *I could just stay here and never think about the 21st century ever again. I could stay here and never have to worry about lecherous Scandinavians or bastards like Aaron Michaels – never have to work in that stupid sandwich shop or deal with my Auntie Boris and her new-age hippie nonsense.*

"I was just thinking about you," I said. "And this - all of this… I like it here."

"At the school?" she asked.

"No," I said. "Here in this moment. This… perfect moment."

It was all very romantic, and I think that's why Wendy started kissing me again, and hugging me tighter than I'd ever been hugged before – even by Melanie Bogg. Then, for some reason, I started thinking about Melanie again. I don't know why – it shouldn't have mattered to me – not then – not in that moment – but for a split second I felt the sting of her betrayal in my heart once more. And I knew at once that if I stayed where I was I would never see her again, or any of my good friends like Rodney Rooney and Lizo from Newsround – and I'd never get to the bottom of what happened to Keith Matthews, or the old man who I manslaughtered with *The Guinness Book of Records 2008*, or what happened out there in the park that night, or the significance of Shed 7, or that note someone wrote in *To Kill A Mockingbird*. I was still an amateur detective, and I still had a mystery to solve. I didn't have all of the answers - not yet – but I was going to get them, because that's what detectives do… Besides, I wasn't sure if I could really commit to living in a world without the interweb and I certainly wasn't willing to put myself through the monotony of dial-up again before the invention of broadband.

I stopped kissing Wendy. I hated it, but I suddenly knew that I couldn't go through with it all. It was a dream. Just a silly dream.

"What's wrong?" she asked, stroking my face with her soft hand. I looked into her beautiful eyes – so full of life and joy. I didn't mind if my heart got broken, but I wasn't willing to break hers. I knew I had to put a stop to it before things got out of hand. I had been a fool, and I had to make amends.

"I can't do this," I said. "I'm sorry. Where I'm going, you can't follow. What I've got to do, you can't be any part of. Wendy, I'm no good at being noble, but it doesn't take much to see that the problems of two little people don't amount to a hill of beans in this crazy world. Someday you'll understand that."

Okay, that's not exactly what I said, but what I actually said was much less sophisticated and probably made me sound like a commitment-shy bastard. She didn't cry or anything – she just looked very confused and begrudgingly let go of my hands. I cried a few secret tears, but she wouldn't have been able to see them as I walked out into the rain – out of her life – out of her world – forever. She just stood there, turning the dragon kazoo over in her hands, most probably wondering if it had all been a dream.

That was the fourth saddest day of my life.

ELEVEN

THE TIME TRAVELLER'S STRIFE

Roger handed me a cigarette. I don't normally smoke cigarettes of course, but I was feeling down and I needed something to 'take the edge off' – so to speak. Besides, I try to have a couple of cigarettes now and again to elevate my social status, since my doctor told me that smoking reduces something called the 'sperm count' which leads to importance.

"Penny for your thoughts," said Roger, handing me a penny.

I sighed and paused for dramatic emphasis. "Her name was Wendy."

"Who?" asked Roger.

"You know who," I said. "That girl from the cinema."

Roger shook his head in disapproval. "That was never a good idea, Walton. There's so many things wrong with that idea I'm not even going to start-"

"You think I don't know that?" I snapped, slamming my hands on the steering wheel. "You think maybe that's why I'm so glum, perhaps? Hmmm? You think maybe that's why I'm so bloody miserable, you old codger?"

"Sorry," said Roger. "I'm sorry. What happened?"

I took a long drag on my cigarette to make me feel better. It didn't work.

"We went our separate ways," I told him. "It's over. It was over before it had even started."

Neither of us said anything for a little while, and then Roger patted me gently on the back.

"You did the right thing," he said. "You know that."

"I know," I said. "But it still hurts. It hurts like John Hurt working out sine wave frequencies in a rental car."

It was a VERY clever analogy, but I don't think Roger got it. He lit himself a cigarette.

"We don't belong here," he said. "We have to get back to our own time – our own lives."

I hated that. I didn't want to go back to my life – not really. My life was miserable. My relationship was 'off again' and my dog was missing. Was there really any point in going back? Had I really made the right decision?

"We'll get back to 2010," said Roger. "And then we'll get ourselves back on track. You're going to find Keith Matthews and patch things up with Melanie. I'm going to get a better job and put my life back together. We'll forget about all of this. Trust me. Everything's going to be alright."

Roger was a good lodger. I remember the day I first put a 'To Let' sign up on my spare bedroom window. Nobody responded for a few days, and my life was subsequently thrown into disarray when people started letting themselves into my house at all hours to use my lavatory. I soon realised that a dead slug between the O and the L had made said sign look like an advertisement for a public facility, so I rectified the problem using my neighbour Stephen's ice scraper and two days later Roger was at my door, pouting like a scorned duck. He was as nice as a French city and humble as Kate Humble. I liked him immediately, and so did Keith Matthews.

Roger excelled in his interview and did very well in all three of the challenges I set out for him as part of the application process; cleaning the living room, walking Keith Matthews and cooking me a full English breakfast. He answered 49 of his 50 general knowledge questions correctly (he didn't know who Ike Turner was) and was able to demonstrate a clean criminal record, which we listened to that evening while drinking some of his favourite tea. Nowadays he was more than a lodger – he was a friend. A good friend.

"You're a good friend, Roger," I said, smiling at him. "Perhaps I don't tell you that enough."

"It's alright Walt," he said. "You're a good friend to me too. I know we don't always see eye to eye – but you're always there for me when I need you. I can talk to you, because I know you're always going to listen to what I have to say. You know, when I first broke up with Abby I didn't have the foggiest idea what I was going to do next. My head was a mess. I couldn't think. But you listened to me – you helped me reason it through – helped me work out where it all went wrong. I've never thanked you properly for that."

I'm not sure if that was *exactly* what Roger said, as I wasn't really listening. You see, we were pulling up close to the pub and something wasn't right. I leant on the brake and slowed the car to a crawl.

"What's wrong?" said Roger, looking around in confusion.

"There," I said, pulling the car over to the opposite side of the road. "Look over there."

Just by the front entrance to the pub, in the small customer parking area, was a brown Morris Minor.

Roger gasped. "Is that the same-"

"Shhh!" I said. "Keep it down. We don't want them to spot us."

He lowered his voice to a whisper. "We don't want *who* to spot us?"

I climbed through to the back seat and peered out, obscured from view by the conveniently dusty rear windscreen.

"Them," I said, ducking down behind the headrest.

Two young men emerged from behind the pub, both carrying large wooden boxes which they loaded into the back of the Morris. They wore long, white embroidered robes and had strange, plaited beards dangling from their overtly somber faces. One was very broad-shouldered and had those kind of tree-trunk arms that looked as though they could strangle a bear. The other was tall and slender, but equally intimidating with his pointed, rat-like face and large, pulsating eyes. They walked with mechanical purpose and precision – cold and unfeeling like the staff at Tesco Metro in Swaffham. I could feel my heart beating in my throat as they slammed shut their boot and slipped robotically into the front seats.

"Friends of Oscar?" Roger asked with irresolute optimism.

I exhaled slowly and rested my hand on the door handle. "I wouldn't count on it."

The men in the Morris Minor must have been talking about something very serious indeed, as they kept stroking their silly beards and frowning.

"Who are they?" whispered Roger.

I thought for a moment. "Oscar mentioned an ancient order whose job it is to protect the time cow, remember?"

Roger's eyes widened. "You don't think-"

"I don't know," I said. "But those robes make them look like they're from some sort of cult, and if they've found out that Oscar's been milking their cow to make cheese, I don't imagine they're going to be very happy about it!"

The thinner man turned on the engine and pulled out of the pub car park. Roger and I ducked down as they passed us by with the unnerving slowness of an evil slug. For a moment I was worried that they'd recognise the car, but then I remembered how dark it was at the time of our last encounter. Sure enough, they drove past without incident, and we were safe to disembark.

The back door to the pub was left swaying open in the breeze, and beyond it laid a sight that filled our hearts with dread; glasses were smashed all over the floor, cupboards had been turned out, tables upturned, and pictures torn from the walls. The whole place had been ransacked. Somebody had been looking for something. Or someone…

"Oscar?" I called out.

There was no reply.

"Oscar?" cried Roger. "Where are you?"

Still nothing… Roger picked up a broken bottle and brandished it like a mace.

"It's alright," I said. "They've gone. We saw them leave."

Roger held tight to his weapon. "I'm not taking any chances."

In my heart I knew by then exactly where we were going to find our friend. It was inevitable. I had foreseen it. Worse than that – I had experienced it... I knew where Oscar was, and Roger knew it too. Now we just had to face up to the reality of it. Not a word was spoken as we made our way to the cellar door. It was swinging wide open behind a mess of broken locks – gaping like a wound.

"Oscar?" I called again as we stumbled down the stairs into the darkness. "Are you down here?"

Nothing. The cellar was a murky, vapid pit of silence. I reached the bottom step and stopped, unable to go any further for fear of bumping into cheese-related paraphernalia.

"Can you hear me?" I said. "Are you down here?"

We stood in silence for a moment. Still nothing.

"What do we do now?" asked Roger.

I sighed to myself. "I don't know. I can't see anything."

And then we heard his voice.

It was faint and croaky – barely discernible at first – mumbling something about a light.

"Oscar?" exclaimed Roger. "Is that you?"

"The light," he said. "Turn on the light… There's a cord – at the top of the stairs…"

Quick as The Flash I ran back up those rickety steps and fumbled around until I found the pull cord. As the light flickered on I was met with a startling sense of déjà vu. Roger dropped his bottle and ran over to Oscar, who was sitting propped up against the wall, just as he had been in the dream. It was exactly the same scene, you understand, but with more blood – a lot more blood... I shot down the stairs and rushed to Oscar's side, taking his hand in mine and offering him miscellaneous words of comfort and encouragement. And then I saw it – the ivory handle of a knife, sticking out of his gut, a ruby puddle gushing forth onto a pair of green-check woollen trouserpants.

"They took it all," he said, flinching against the pain. "Every last bit."

I looked around. The cellar had been ransacked too, and there was nothing left – not a crumb.

"Who were they?" I asked. "What did they want?"

"They called my work a blasphemy," he said. "A crime against God and science combined."

"We should phone for an ambulance," said Roger, moving to leave.

"No!" shouted Oscar. "It's too late for that. You have to leave! It isn't safe here. Those men were asking about you too. They'll be looking for you." He coughed hard, and blood surged from his wound like jam from the back of a doughnut.

"Where should we go?" I asked. "Where will we be safe?"

Oscar looked at me with dying eyes, his breath deteriorating.

"Back to your time," he said. "You have to go back to 2010. They won't stop looking for you here."

"But we can't go back!" said Roger. "They've taken all the bloody time cheese."

Oscar's voice was barely audible now. I leant in close so as not to miss anything.

"Over there," he said. "On the table. There's a little black book. They didn't take it. Thank God they didn't take it."

I gestured for Roger to bring us the book, and he kindly obliged.

"What's in it?" I asked as Oscar started flicking through the pages.

"Everything," he said. "Everything I told myself about time travel. All of the details. All of the secrets."

It was fortunate for the sake of exposition at this point that Oscar had temporarily regained the power of coherent speech. He coughed again, and this time some blood came out of his mouth, which I think made Roger feel a bit woozy, as he sat down on the bottom step and put his head between his legs.

"I can't see," said Oscar. "I can't see what I'm looking for."

"Is there another light?" I asked. "I could get you a torch."

Oscar struggled to laugh and looked at me with helpless sorrow. "It isn't the light," he said, and removed his glasses from his pocket. As he slid them onto his nose he instantly became the perfect tragic image of his own ghost. He was ready to die.

"How long do I have to haunt this place?" he asked, desperately. "How long until we meet again?"

"Don't think about that," I said. "Don't think about that just now. You've got to hold on."

He choked back more blood and tears and pointed to a page in his little book.

"Here," he said. "This is where you'll find it. This is where they've hidden it."

"Hidden what?" I asked.

"You'll have to start again," continued Oscar. "You'll have to make the cheese yourself. Go to Budleigh Salterton." He indicated the address in his book. "There's an abandoned garden centre on the outskirts of town - a huge derelict cluster of outbuildings swamped in a mess of dead, overgrown foliage. Nobody goes there. People say it's haunted, but it isn't. That's where you'll find the cow… You'll find it-"

He seethed in pain and his eyes rolled back inside his head.

"Oscar!" I shouted, like they do in the films. "Stay with me."

"You'll find the cow…" he continued. "Write this down, because it's important and it's not in the book…"

"Just tell me," I said. "Just tell me what I need to know."

"You'll find the cow in… in-"

"Stop speaking in full sentences!" I yelled. "Just say the key words!"

"It's in…. in-"

And he just stopped moving. His head tilted to one side and his mouth fell slightly ajar, his tongue lolling out to the side. Though his eyes remained open, there was no longer any sparkle of life behind them. Oscar had departed our world – just like he told me he would – and there was nothing we could do to stop it…

You can't change the past.

It seemed appropriate to wait a few minutes before saying anything, or to even think about leaving. The cellar fell into a mournful silence and I spent a moment recalling my fondest memories of Oscar. I believe that Roger did the same, though I can't be sure, as I am not omnivorous. I thought of how he much he loved fish fingers, and how he loved to tell us about his time travelling adventures. Then there was the time that we all went to the cinema together. That was about it, to be honest, as I'd only really known him for a few days. Roger was the first to speak after that, but what he said was largely unexpected:

"We're going to die."

I took Oscar's notebook and placed it in my pocket. "We're not going to die," I said. "Why are you saying that, you negative Norris?"

"Cedric said they called them the cheese murders. *Murders.* Plural. That's us Walt. We're the other cheese murders."

"Cedric said it was a misnomer," I assured him.

"So what do you think is going to happen?" he asked. "We're stuck here in the wrong time with no means of defence and barely any money. Our only connection to this time – literally our only ally on the planet at this moment – has died. And there are two robe-wearing cow-worshipping fanatics who are out for our blood. Please tell me Walt, given those circumstances, how do you fancy our chances?"

A wooden stool suddenly slid noisily across the floor on the other side of the cellar.

"What was that?" said Roger, jumping out of his skin (not literally, as that would have been horrific).

"It's Oscar," I said. "This place is haunted now. It's about time we were leaving."

"We're not just going to leave him here," said Roger.

"Yes we are," I said. "Remember what Cedric said; they found him in the cellar with a knife to the gut. That's how they find him. We don't move him. We don't bury him. Whatever we want to do, that's not what we're going to do. The universe won't let us."

Roger stared at me for a few seconds, rolled up his sleeves, and marched over to Oscar's body.

"The hell it won't," he said, and reached down to pick him up.

I wondered what the universe would do to correct the potential paradox that Roger now seemed determined to elicit. Maybe it would give him a cramp in his leg, or make him need the toilet.

Maybe it would simply give him a thought to change his intentions. None of those things happened. They didn't need to happen. The door to the cellar swung open and smashed into the wall with a *crash*, startling me to the extent that I let out a small trump, and scaring Roger enough to make him say a bad word.

A shadow stood in the doorway at the top of the stairs, , staring down at us like a snooty vulture. My first, somewhat optimistic guess was that this was Oscar's ghost engaging in a bit of poltergeistic tomfoolery – that is until I considered the shape of the shadow's garments. The figure was wearing a dress and moved with feminine elegance – yet somehow I couldn't believe it was a lady. Very slowly the figure took a few steps down the stairs into the cellar, and as the light displaced the shadow it exposed the true nature of the garments; not a dress at all, but a robe – a long, white embroidered robe. It was one of the murderers – the thinner one, with the bulbous eyes – and he was descending upon us.

Roger kicked the leg off a nearby table and raised it behind his head like a baseball bat. I did another trump, which sounded like a guilty frog. The man on the stairs drew his sword.

"This is my sword," he said, showing me the picture he had just drawn. "I'm embarrassed to say that I left it in the car, but this is what it looks like. If you do not do exactly what I tell you, I will go and fetch it, and run you both through with it. Is that clear?"

"What do you want with us, vile villain?" I asked, using biting alliteration to make clear my distaste. "You have no quarrel with us. Let us go free."

The man was now standing at the bottom of the stairs, still pointing at the picture of his sword menacingly. "You are associates of the blasphemer. How much of his ill-accumulated knowledge hath he passed on to you? Speak quickly."

"Hedidn'ttellusanythingsoleaveusaloneandwewon'tgiveyouanybother." I said.

He shook his head. "No, no, no – that was too quick. I didn't catch a word of that. Now look, the cheesemaker had a notebook – we forgot to pick it up. It was over there on the table. Where is it now?"

"One step closer," said Roger. "One step closer and I'll knock your block off, do you hear me?"

Roger was angry. Next he was going to start correcting people's grammar and moaning about the working class again. I could sense things were going to get out of hand.

"You know who I am," said the man in the robe. "You do not stand a chance against us. We represent an ancient and powerful order – and we… and we…" He paused and frowned as his nostrils twitched. "I'm sorry, has one of you broken wind?"

"Sorry," I said. "I was startled on multiple occasions. I have very poor bowel control when I'm startled, or thoroughly entertained, or using a microwave..."

"That is a truly foul and potent aroma," he said. "What have you been eating?"

"Mainly fish fingers," I admitted. "And some ice cream this afternoon."

The wooden stool slid a little further across the floor, startling the man in the robe (who did not trump).

"What was that?" he said. "How are you doing that?"

Roger grinned at me. I think he was thinking what I was thinking, which was that he was thinking what I was thinking, but also that Oscar was still there, and he was most probably a *very angry ghost.*

"You're coming with me," said the man in the robe. "My associate and I will escort you back to our temple for further interrogation. You will be blindfolded, of course, and I should warn you that the more you struggle, the less conscientious we will beco-"

Thwack.

The stool flew through the air and caught him on the side of the head with such force that it broke apart and landed in pieces on the floor. The skinny man fell back into the corner and screamed in pain. That was our cue to exit. We shot across the room and bounded up the stairs as fast as we could, hopping over our enemy as he winced on the floor, cradling his head and struggling to get up again. When we reached the door we slammed it shut behind us, hoping to imprison the man in the darkness of the cellar.

"This way!" I shouted, running past the kitchen towards the back entrance. "Come on, Roger!"

"Hang on!" said Roger as he grabbed a chair and carefully wedged it against the handle of the cellar door.

"That won't work," I said. "The cellar door opens inwards."

Roger nodded enthusiastically. "I know."

Suddenly the door flew open and the chair fell backwards, sending the skinny man tumbling back into the cellar and crashing down the stairs. Roger did one of those "fist pump" things that people do to celebrate their achievements, and we continued to make good our escape.

Outside the pub, the second, shorter, more muscular order member was sitting on the bonnet of his brown Morris Minor, twizzling his silly beard and reading a *Playboy* magazine. When he saw us darting across the car park he threw the magazine onto the ground and immediately gave chase, raising his fist in the air and shouting "Cowabunga!" at the top of his voice. Fortunately we had a good lead on him already, and by the time he caught up with us we were back in the safety of Oscar's car with the doors locked. I turned on the ignition and reversed back into the road as the heavy-set man grappled at the door handles in vain. Then Roger did another one of his 'fist pumps' as we sped off up the road, sending the man spinning onto the ground in a cloud of our dust.

"Yes!" shouted Roger – his eyes alight with glee. "In your mother-chuffing face!" He wound down the window and leant out, sticking his middle finger in the air.

"Are you alright, Roger?" I asked. "You seem to have gone a bit mad."

"Hell yes," said Roger. "I'm the king of the world! Did you see that? Did you see what I did? Wow- what a rush!"

I shook my head in disbelief. "I think you need to calm down."

"Calm down?" he cried. "Calm down? Did you see what just happened to us? Ain't no one taking us down! No sir – not today! We's a pair of bad-ass time-travelling butt-kicking mother chuffers!"

"Why are you talking like that?" I asked.

"I don't know!" he yelled. "My heart's beating really fast. Can you hear it? I think I can hear it. What's my name? I can't remember my name."

"Roger," I told him. "Your name is Roger, and you need to relax."

"Okay," he said, slowing his breathing. "Okay I'll relax. You drive – drive the car – drive to the place with the cow for the milking. Let's milk that sucker dry."

"No," I said. "We need to take stock before we do anything else."

"Good plan," he said. "There's an Oxo factory two towns over. Let's tear the place apart!" He then laughed at this notion for a full three and a half minutes before passing out on the dashboard.

I later learnt that an over-indulgence in TV's *The Sweeney* back in '76 had caused one of Roger's adrenal glands to explode. Some radical new advances in medicine led to the offending gland being replaced with that of a bull, which synthesises far too much adrenaline for his mind and body to cope with. Nowadays, as I would eventually learn, it is not a good idea to put Roger under too much pressure, lest he have an episode such as the one I had just witnessed.

I eased off the pedal slightly, now a mile or two away from the pub, having taken as many random turns as possible to impede the chances of a successful pursuit. Melanie Bogg had an older brother called Simon who had always said that sooner or later the men in white coats would be after me. I never understood what he had meant until now. I checked the wing mirrors and breathed a sigh of relief as my eyes fell upon an empty road. We were safe… for the time being, at least.

I didn't really know where I was going, but I knew that I had to *keep* going if I wanted to stay alive. Roger was right – our eventual objective would have to be Poppyfield Garden Centre in Budleigh Salterton, but I didn't want to rush into anything – not then – not until we had taken some time to recuperate and figure things out sensibly (or at least until Roger had stopped dribbling on the dashboard and regained consciousness). My first thought was to find a hotel, until I remembered I had spent nearly all of our 1950s coinage on tat like dragon kazoos and ice cream. My second idea was to park up somewhere secluded and spend the night in the car, but I was soon put off by flashbacks to the time I had attempted such a compromise near Hampstead Heath with my friend Percy Trent Derby. I don't want to go into too much detail about what happened that night, but it was not a relaxing experience and I would not be making the same mistake again. On the upside, I learnt a lot about late night 'urban' culture, and I did get to meet Michael Portillo.

I have to admit, I was still at a loss about what to do by the time Roger woke up. He opened the window and revived himself in the cold night air as I continued to drive around aimlessly, desperately trying to hatch some sort of plan.

"Let's just head to Budleigh Salterton," said Roger. "At least let's head in that direction. Otherwise we'll just be tootling about until we run out of petrol."

He was right – I hadn't thought of that. We didn't have much petrol left, and now I was cold, hungry, and struggling to stay awake.

"Do you want me to drive for a bit?" he asked.

"No thanks," I replied. "I'll be alright. Besides, you don't have a clean licence."

"Neither do you," he pointed out. "Not in 1954."

I hadn't thought of that either. There I was, driving around in the gathering dark of the evening – hungry, penniless, without a destination – and I didn't even have the law on my side. I hated not having the law on my side.

"There's a sign," Roger said as I eased off the accelerator. "What does it say?"

I brought the car to a standstill at a crossroads, directing the front end such that it illuminated the sign, which Roger read aloud.

"There's a place called Otterton to the left," he said. "And somewhere called Newton Poppleford to the right. I suggest we go straight on – that's signposted to East Budleigh. Sounds about right, doesn't it?"

Roger turned to me, but I was deep in thought, drumming the steering wheel and chewing on my tongue. In the midst of all the madness, something was coming back to me – something from my recent past –and although it hadn't made any sense to me at the time, it was suddenly beginning to…

"What do you say then, Walt?" he said. "Which way are we going?"

I sighed and buried my face in my hands, trying desperately to do some mental arithmetic. I never really understood the term 'mental arithmetic', as the way I saw it, all arithmetic was pretty bloody mental. Maths used to be my second least favourite subject at primary school after Latin, which I didn't see the point of learning, especially at the age of six. I can remember standing up in class and being forced to recite the seven times table by that silly old sod Mr Jameson who smelt like chips. I could never do it. The seven times table has always been one of my buggerbears. Fortunately the maths I was now attempting was a whole lot simpler, and well within my range of capability. It was 1954, so how old would she have been?

"Alright Walt," said Roger, after a while. "Penny for your thoughts."

"Oh no, Roger," I said with a grin. "These thoughts are worth more than just pennies. A lot more!"

As I shifted the car into first gear and pulled off to the right I had a feeling that everything was going to work out after all.

"What are you doing?" asked Roger.

"Going to check in on an old friend," I said, still grinning. I was a genius.

"Okay, I'm confused," he confessed. "Are we going to Newton Poppleford?"

"Yes we are," I confirmed. "We're going to Newton Poppleford. 79 Primrose Avenue, Newton Poppleford."

TWELVE

SEX EDUCATION

"One seven is seven," I said. I could do that bit – that was the easy part.

"Good," said Mr Jameson. "Now, carry on…"

"Two sevens are 14," I said, a little slower, looking at him for approval.

"Yes Walton," he said. "And the next bit…"

"Three sevens are… 21."

Some of the other kids were sniggering at me – notably Matt Beasley and Aaron Michaels. I don't much care for sniggering, as it is an anagram of 'nigger's gin', which is what my racist Uncle Ken used to call white rum.

"And four sevens?" asked Mr Jameson.

I always went into the pot at that point, and the rest of the class knew it. Their sniggering intensified as I puffed up my chest and readied myself for the ensuing embarrassment.

Then there was a knock at the classroom door.

"Come in," said Mr Jameson.

Mr Danforth strode into the room like a bumptious peacock, followed immediately by an older lady, whose gait was more akin to that of a hen. She had bright, curly white hair and wore a floral dress with a purple cardigan wrapped around her shoulders. I noticed that she had large twinkling eyes and many wrinkles around her mouth – the kind you get from a lifetime of smiles. I think it's fair to say that I liked her from the start.

"Sorry to interrupt, Mr Jameson," said the headmaster. "This is Mrs Fupplecock. I mentioned her to you last week."

"Oh yes," said Mr Jameson. "Very nice to meet you, Mrs Fupplecock. I understand you'll be taking on some of our more... 'special' pupils."

"That's right," said the lady, taking out a little piece of paper. "If you don't mind, I have a list of names."

I had sat down by this point, hoping that the interruption would make Mr J forget about the seven times table. Some of the other children were getting on with their work, but my stationery remained stationary as I stared at this new lady – fixated by her presence – immediately desperate to be one of the selected few to progress to her 'special' class. I knew that I wouldn't be, of course. It was bound to be someone like Paul Grossman or Borgon Regis (the person, not the place – you're thinking of Bognor Regis). They were selected to do *everything*. They were the 'special' ones. Nobody had ever said that I was special.

The nice new lady walked to the front of the class and spoke to us. Her voice was sweet and soft like a cream éclair: "Sorry to interrupt you, children," she said. "I'm here to take a few of you off to a special class for the afternoon. Don't worry – it's nothing to worry about. In fact, it's going to be a lot of fun. We're going to learn about lots of interesting things over the next few months."

"Like what sort of things?" said Aaron Michaels (the dick). "Like times tables and stuff?"

"That's right," she said. "But not just times tables. We're going to learn about words and pictures, kings and queens, shapes and sums..." Her eyes met with mine and her smile seemed to widen. "And dinosaurs and prime numbers."

I smiled back at her. That sounded *fantastic*. I remember feeling incredibly jealous of Paul and Borgon – they were going to have so much fun.

"So if it's alright with the rest of you," she said. "I'd like the following pupils to come with me."

She held up the list and read out the names. *Here we go*, I thought, looking at Paul and Borgon, who were beaming with confidence.

"Dennis Potts, Sally Scroggins and Oliver Postlethwaite."

That was a bit of a shocker. Borgon Regis scoffed and went back to writing his novel. Paul Grossman spun around on his chair and sulked quite openly. I just sighed an inaudible sigh and shook my little head as I accepted the inevitable. I wasn't special. I would never be special. Still, I didn't see what was so special about Dennis, Sally and Oliver. As far as I knew they weren't even in the school play, and Oliver was always wearing trousers from the lost property box…

The nice lady put away her list and walked towards the door. That was that, then – no special class for me (Walton Cumberfield). Now where was I? Oh yes… The seven times table. I knew it wouldn't be long before Mr J had me up in front of the class again, trying to remember what four times seven was. What was it? If I could only figure it out before I stood up again then I could pretend that I knew it all along. *One seven is seven. Two sevens are 14. Three sevens are 21. Four sevens are… twenty… why am I so stupid? What is four times seven?*

"Twenty eight," whispered a voice in my ear.

I turned around to see the nice lady, crouching next to me and grinning. How did she know what I was thinking? Was I thinking out loud again? I often did that.

"Was I thinking out loud again?" I asked her. "I often do that."

"No sweetheart," she said. "Now – would you like to come with us?"

She held out her hand and nodded to the door, where Sally, Oliver and Dennis were now gathered (Dennis was trying to eat his buttons as usual).

"Can I really?" I asked. "No fooling?"

"No fooling," she chuckled, and took my hand in hers.

In case you are confused, I should point out at this stage that these events do not follow on chronologically from the events of the previous chapter. You might be wondering how I went from driving to Newton Poppleford with Roger to sitting in a primary school classroom and reciting my seven times table. I should explain: I am currently using a literary device known as a "flashback" to inform the events which are currently unfolding in the main plot, several years later (or before, whichever way you look at it). Mrs Fupplecock had told me that she lived at 79 Primrose Avenue in Newton Poppleford when she was training to be a teacher. I didn't know why she had suddenly told me that, but it now made a lot more sense. In 1954 she would be in her early twenties, and therefore living at that address. She told me where to find her because she knew that I would need to know. She knew I was going to visit her in the past, because in her memory, I already *had*. Do you see? It's all very complicated…

79 Primrose Avenue was a charming little bungalow with a pale blue door and a well-tended garden. Clusters of colourful flowers lined the edges of a neatly-trimmed lawn, bathed in the evening moonlight like something by Monet. It looked like the perfect place for a young Mrs Fupplecock to live – elegant yet quirky, with a few tastefully placed garden gnomes thrown in for good measure. A chorus of invisible crickets heralded our arrival as we walked up the path and knocked on the wooden door. A light was still glowing through one of the curtains, which suggested, quite reassuringly, that she was still awake.

"What's your friend's name?" said Roger.

"Mrs Fupplecock," I replied.

"No," said Roger. "I mean her first name."

I shrugged. "I have no idea. I just call her Mrs Fupplecock."

Roger sighed. "Well what if she's not married yet? You don't even know the name of the person we're looking for!"

The door opened just a crack – a thin glow of warm light pouring out on us through the opening. Two little eyes appeared in the gap and stared at us tentatively, and as the door opened ever so slightly more it was evident that these eyes belonged to a pretty young lady with pale skin and long blonde hair.

"Can I help you?" she said, somewhat nervously.

I considered her for a moment. "Mrs Fupplecock?"

"No," she said. "You must have the wrong house. Good evening."

She went to close the door, but Roger put his hand on the frame.

"Wait," he said. "That might not be your name."

"It isn't my name," she confirmed.

"Yes," he said. "But that doesn't mean that you're not the person we're looking for."

She frowned at us. "I don't understand."

I tried to give her one of my warmest smiles and asked if we could come in for a minute.

"Absolutely not."

"It's alright," I said. "We're jolly nice chaps. We're not animal molesters or anything."

"Animal what?"

"Are you training to be a teacher?" Roger asked.

"I… well… yes I am."

"Then it *is* you," I said. "You're Mrs Fupplecock. Wow! I can't believe it."

"I am *not* Mrs Fupplecock," she hissed. "I don't know any Mrs Fupplecock. My name is Ruth. Ruth Routhorn."

Roger chuckled. "What a beautiful name," he said, somewhat insincerely.

Ruth Routhorn scowled at him. I don't think she liked people laughing at her name.

"Please," I said. "You're the only person who can help us. One day your name is going to be Mrs Fupplecock, and you're going to be a teacher – a really good teacher, at that."

"What are you talking about?"

"Please, just listen," I pleaded. "My name is Walton Cumberfield and we're friends. We're very good friends."

Ruth Routhorn narrowed her eyes and afforded me a cynical little laugh. "I've never seen you before in my life."

"But you will," I said. "You will. My friend and I have travelled back here from the future. When I last saw you – in the future – you told me your address. *This* address. You were telling me to come here and find you."

"I'm phoning the police," she said.

"How else would I know that you're training to be a teacher?" I asked.

She shrugged. "Lots of people are teachers."

It wasn't going very well at all, and Roger wasn't helping. He was definitely staring at Ruth's bosoms and making her feel uncomfortable. But it *had* to be Mrs Fupplecock. I knew it. It just *had* to be. If only I could somehow convince her of our authenticity. What did I know about her that only she and I would know? Then it hit me like a lorry full of lollies.

"Mr Nibbles!" I shouted. "Your cat's name was Mr Nibbles!"

She scowled at me. "I beg your pardon?"

"When you were five you had a cat named Mr Nibbles and you used to write stories about him."

Bingo. If anything was going to seal the deal, that was it. I looked optimistically into her eyes and waited for her to let us in.

"I have never owned a cat," she said, quite plainly. "And I have never written a story. Now get off our property or I'm going to phone the police!"

Roger's hand was still resting on the frame when she slammed the door shut, and he recoiled in a fit of pain, bouncing around like a cracked-up Zebedee.

"Son of a bloody buggering bitch!" he shouted. "I think she's broken my thumb!"

"Pull yourself together man," I snapped. "Don't go ranting and raging in the streets like that – people will get offended."

"Look at my thumbnail!" he screamed. "It's blue. It's fucking blue!"

"But that doesn't mean that *you* have to be!" I said (quite cleverly). "Now stop your swearing. This is the 1950s, remember – these people aren't used to hearing such profanity. They haven't even seen *The South Parks*."

Thankfully, Roger managed to calm himself down, and I remembered that there was still some sticky tape in the boot of Oscar's car, which we used to make a makeshift plaster.

"Fine idea this was," he said as we stood against the car. "I suppose we'd better get out of here. Next thing you know we'll both be arrested and everything will go to hell again."

"I don't understand," I said. "She definitely told me she lived at 79 Primrose Avenue. She definitely said that she had a cat called Mr Nibbles. Why would she lie?"

"Oh, I don't know, Walt – maybe because she's a senile old lady talking a bunch of bloody nonsense!"

I don't think Roger was expecting me to do what I did then. To be honest, I didn't really expect me to do what I did then – but I did it, and at the time I was glad that I did. My fist caught the centre of his nose with a loud *crunch* that seemed to echo down the street. I'm not particularly strong, so he didn't fall to the floor, but he did let out a yelp and double over, cradling his face in his hands. His nose didn't bleed, of course. I really must get my health club ban revoked so that I can work out more…

"What the hell?" he screamed. "What did you do that for?"

"You do not talk about Mrs Fupplecock like that," I told him. "I won't stand for it."

"Jesus Christ, Walt!" he said. "That was a bit over-sensitive, don't you think?"

"She's a very good friend," I said. "And she's not senile! I won't have you saying libelous things about my friends, you hear me?"

Roger stood up straight and steadied himself against the car. "I didn't say a libelous thing," he said. "Nobody can *say* a libelous thing. Libel is written defamation. What you are referring to is slander."

"Well your grandmother's a racist old fuddy-duddy who smells like beef flavoured crisps!" I shouted.

"Oh yeah? Well at least my grandmother's still alive!"

"Ha!" I shouted. "My grandmother *is* alive. It's 1954."

"Well why don't we go and see *her* then?"

"Because she lives in Switzerland you bottom-head!"

A few lights came on in the surrounding houses. If ASBOs had been invented back then, I'm sure one would have been coming our way pretty sharpish. Roger's face was even redder than usual, and I felt angrier than a bird being hurled at a pig.

"This is all your fault, Walt!" said Roger, slamming his hand on the roof of Oscar's car.

"My fault?" I said. "You're the one who wanted to play James Watson to my Francis Crick. I didn't force you to come along!"

"It's John Watson, you moron!" he shouted. "We're trying to solve a mystery, here! I was referring to Watson and Holmes, not Watson and Crick! You're such an idiot!"

That was something else that suddenly made a lot more sense. I didn't admit it, of course. And I am NOT an idiot.

"I'm an idiot?" came my retort. "What about you? Who was the one who got drunk and ate a hunk of cheese that made him travel through time?"

"Oh so it's my fault is it? You're the one who said I had to get drunk to blend in with the locals!"

He gave me an accusatory poke, right in the centre of my chest. I cannot stand it when people poke me (unless it's on The Facebook) so I poked him back, right in the eye.

"Ow!" he screamed. "Not in the eye! Never in the eye!"

He lunged towards me, spouting incomprehensible noises of anger like a furious führer and reaching out to me with clawed hands. During his nervous breakdown (which I am not really allowed to talk about) Roger had taken some amateur wrestling classes in Hellesdon Community Hall. I had never seen him in action before, so the undignified display of aggression unfolding at this point was as intriguing as it was embarrassing. I deflected his attacks pretty well at first, but since Roger had the weight advantage, it was not long before he had me on the floor in half a Nelson, grunting and groaning, strongly advising me to 'submit'. I did not submit, of course, and freed myself by telling him to 'look over there' like they do in the films. I didn't get far before he was on me again, so I took off my shoe and started whacking him with it. I'm not sure how long we would have carried on like this were we not interrupted, but the fact is we *were* interrupted – by one of the last people I had expected to see, I might add…

"Walton?" she said. "What are you doing here?"

When I heard her voice I immediately stopped fighting, allowing Roger to land a cheap shot in my ribs.

"Cut it out!" I spluttered as I clambered to my feet, wobbly and bewildered like Shakin' Stevens. I propped myself up on the bonnet and looked at her, not fully trusting what my eyes were telling me – not at first.

She was now wrapped in a sensible yet elegant winter coat – her face still made-up and radiant – her green eyes sparkling in the glow of the night sky. Somehow she was even more beautiful than she had been when I left her that afternoon. Even in my idealistic memory she could never be as perfect as she was in the flesh. Instantly I remembered how it felt to hold her – the feel of her soft skin – the taste of her lipstick. Needless to say, I was thoroughly unprepared for this encounter and found myself gaping like a guppy until somebody else decided to break the silence. It was Roger, incidentally.

"Hey," he said. "That's your girl from the cinema."

I laughed and shook my head with a mixture of confusion and secret delight. "Her name is Wendy."

"How did you find me?" she asked.

"Yes Walt," said Roger suspiciously. "How *did* we find her?"

Of all the street fights in all the world, she had to walk into mine. It occurred to me that some things in life were far too unlikely, too magical, too miraculous to be defined as mere coincidence. This was destiny. This was fate. Fate had brought us together, the fête had torn us apart, and now fate was forcing us back together again. At least, it certainly seemed that way.

"Wendy! Don't talk to those men! They're peculiar!"

Ruth Routhorn was now leaning out of the window in her nightgown, the cold wind playing roughly with her hair and bosoms. I noticed that Roger had noticed the latter…

"It's alright, Ruth," replied Wendy. "I know these people."

Ruth held out her arms as if to say 'what the fudge?' I don't think that she liked us very much at that point.

"Somebody's peanut smuggling," chuckled Roger, completely inappropriately.

"You *know* these people?" shouted Ruth. "They're a couple of madmen!"

"We're not!" I shouted. "We're thoroughly nice chaps, aren't we Roger?"

Roger did not reply, I suspect because he was still entranced by Ruth's ample bosom.

"Walton, will you please tell me what's going on?" demanded Wendy. She didn't look angry – just hurt – hurt like when I'd left her that afternoon and ran off into the rain with only a flimsy explanation and a dragon kazoo by way of compensation. I felt like a cup. No. A mug. I felt like a mug.

"Wendy," I said. "Believe me when I tell you that you wouldn't believe me if I told you."

She sighed, crossed her arms, tilted her head to one side and looked upon me with a cynicism that I couldn't help but find disarmingly sexy.

"How did you know where I lived?" she asked.

"I didn't," I said. "That is to say that I'm not looking for *you.* But I am glad that you're here. I mean, I know I shouldn't be but-"

"But what?" she snapped, tightening her scarlet lips and narrowing her beautiful green eyes.

"It's so hard to explain," I said. "I don't know where to-"

Those green eyes. I froze with the shock of my own realisation. I had seen those green eyes before – I just hadn't recognised them until now – they were out of context, like a Womble out of Wimbledon.

"It's you," I said, very quietly. "You live here with Ruth at number 79."

"Of course I do," she said. "But what are *you* doing here?"

I moved slowly towards her. "You live here at number 79 and you're training to be a teacher."

"You're scaring me," she said, backing away.

"Don't be scared," I said. "Please – just listen to me. I know this is going to sound crazy but I'm from the future."

She laughed. I knew she would laugh. Of course she would laugh.

"I'm being serious," I assured her. "Roger and I are from the year 2010. Let me explain; there is a cow in Budleigh Salterton that is independent of the space-time continuum…"

She took out her keys and moved towards the bungalow. I probably shouldn't have led my explanation with the 'time-cow' stuff. I looked to Roger for some support, but he just shrugged.

"I'm going inside now," she said, nervously. "I want you to go away."

The front door swung open and Ruth Routhorn appeared, now wearing a coat (much to Roger's disappointment, I'm sure) and brandishing a frying pan.

"Please," I said, taking out Roger's smartphone. "Look at this! Have you ever seen anything like this before?"

Wendy stopped for a moment and looked at the phone. "So what?" she said. "You've got yourself some sort of film prop."

"No – it works!" I said. "Look – it's touch-screen and everything."

Fortunately, during one of my summers off from University I was briefly employed at a shop called *Phones 4 U*, which meant that I was quite accomplished at giving people demonstrations of smartphone handsets. I had never known how invaluable that skill would be until now.

"How are you doing this?" she said as I browsed through the music library, flipped through some eBooks and took a few pictures with the five megapixel camera. "This is madness."

"No," I said, flicking through Roger's music to select *Baggy Trousers*. "This is Madness. They're a ska band from the 1970s and 80s."

I don't think Wendy could believe what she was seeing or hearing. Her face was a striking mixture of intrigue, fear and confusion.

"We're friends, Wendy," I said. "In my time, where I come from, we're very good friends. You told me in the future that *this* was your address."

I think she wanted to believe me from the start – I think she wanted to trust me – but it was all too much, too soon. "This is stupid. How can you expect me to believe-"

"When you were five years old you had a cat," I said. "A cat named Mr Nibbles. You used to write stories about him."

Her mouth dropped open. "How do you know that?"

I smiled my absolute most warmest of smiles, quivering slightly with excitement. "Because you told me!"

"When?"

"From my perspective, about a fortnight ago," I said. "But from yours, not for another 55 years or so."

She seemed unsteady on her feet so I leant in and held onto her. She didn't push me away, but she didn't hug me either. I quite wanted her to hug me, if I'm honest.

"Listen," I said. "We're in a lot of trouble. Please let us in. I'll explain it all – the whole story."

"None of this makes any sense," she said.

"No but it does," I said. "It does make sense! If you concentrate it actually makes a whole bunch of sense."

"Then tell me," she said, leaning into me slightly. I could smell her hair again. I loved the smell of her hair.

I looked at Roger, who gave me a look that seemed to say 'you're on your own, buddy.' Then he gave Ruth a look that seemed to say 'put down that frying pan and kiss me you crazy lady.' I could tell that he fancied her, the dirty old codger.

"Let's go inside," I said. "Trust me, it's a long, long story. You'll want to be sitting down."

"How long?" she asked.

"Very long," I explained. "So long that if I were to document this exchange in the form of narrative prose I would most likely substitute my explanation for one of those mid-chapter dividers that marks the passing of an unspecific passage of time."

*

Wendy and Ruth's bungalow was humble yet pleasant, tastefully decorated with subtle patterns and pale pastel colours. We were in their living room drinking coca-cola and laying out our tale as succinctly as possible. They didn't own a television, so the furniture wasn't really pointed at anything in particular. Roger and Ruth sat together on a small sofa, bonding over the fact that they both smoked cigarettes. Wendy and I sat on some old yet stylish armchairs on the opposite side. It was certainly nice to relax again after what we'd been through that evening.

Two of the four walls were lined with books – more books than I had ever seen before in one home – and I noticed that they had been carefully arranged in alphabetical order. I eagerly scanned the H section for Lee Harper's *To Kill A Mockingbird*, but alas they did not seem to have it.

When we concluded our story, Ruth was the first to speak, stubbing out her cigarette and leaning back casually, her naked foot brushing 'accidentally' on Roger's shin.

"This is the most ridiculous thing I've ever heard," she said.

"I know," I said. "It's pretty ridiculous, alright. Still, I don't know if it's the *most* ridiculous thing I've ever heard."

The *most* ridiculous thing I've ever heard is the sound of Bruce Forsyth attempting to impersonate Lenny Kravitz in order to gain entry to an exclusive nightclub while dressed as a lady and harbouring a stolen poodle. Still, that's Afghanistan for you (big LOLs).

"What happened to Keith Matthews?" asked Wendy. "You never found him?"

"Not yet," I said. "But I will – just as soon as we get back home again."

Ruth stretched her arms up and yawned, pulling her nightgown taut around her chest and demonstrating the shape of her breasts until I thought Roger's eyebrows were going to shoot through the roof.

"So what's the plan?" she asked. "You're going to go and find this cow?"

"I suppose we have no other choice," I said.

Wendy looked at the floor and spoke very softly. "You could just stay here."

Our eyes met, but only for a second. Roger pretended he hadn't heard, and Ruth lit another cigarette. I couldn't stop considering that option – to stay in the 1950s and make a life for myself – to live out my years in the blissful peace of a world without BBC Three or speed cameras, where 'going out dancing' doesn't mean that you have to stand in a darkened room which smells like feet, listening to 'Jester J' or 'I am Will' until somebody throws up on your shoes. But it was no good. I knew that even if I *did* stay in the 50s, my relationship with Wendy wouldn't last. It couldn't last. Sooner or later she would become Mrs Fupplecock, not Mrs Cumberfield. I knew that for certain. The universe wouldn't let me change it. The universe was a bit of an arsehole like that.

"We just need to get some rest for now," I said. "We have to lie low for a couple of days and give those fanatical nutcases a chance to cool off a bit."

"You can stay here," said Wendy. "That's not a problem. Stay here as long as you like. I can sleep in with Ruth and you boys can share my bed."

Roger and I looked at each other for a moment. Roger shook his head.

"That's alright," I said. "Roger will be fine on the sofa, won't you Roger?"

He scowled at me briefly. "Absolutely. That will be just fine. I love sleeping on sofas."

"Thank you," I said, looking at Wendy, and then at Ruth. "Thank you both."

*

"Okay," said Mrs Fupplecock. "Let's start by getting to know one another shall we? My name is Mrs Fupplecock."

We were sat upstairs in the library, gathered around a small table filled with paper, pens and crayons. In the centre of the table was a plate full of biscuits and sweets. This is another flashback, by the way.

"Now let's go around the table, and I want you all to tell me your names and one interesting thing about yourself. Let's start with you, young man."

She gestured to Oliver Postlethwaite, who was trying to lick his own elbow, because I had told him to.

"My name is Oliver," he said, quietly.

"Hello Oliver," she said. "It's nice to meet you. And what can you tell me about yourself?"

"I like pineapples."

What a knob!

"Do you indeed?" she said enthusiastically. "Well that's very good. It's good to eat a lot of fruit."

"No it isn't," I said. "My uncle Ken says that it gives you the 'shits'. My name is Walton Cumberfield, by the way."

Mrs Fupplecock cleared her throat. "Yes, it's lovely to meet you Walton, but I must tell you that it isn't very nice to say words like that. That's what we call a *swear* word and you're not supposed to say swear words. They're very naughty."

At the time I didn't know what she meant, or indeed which word she was referring to, so I just bowed my head 'sheepishly' and apologised. Well, I don't know exactly how 'sheepish' I looked but at least I said sorry. I have never understood what people think is so sheep-like about looking guilty or embarrassed anyway. I mean, have you ever looked into a sheep's eyes and thought 'oh dear - what's he gone and done now?' I certainly haven't. To be honest, if I had to pick an animal to be the symbol of guilt-induced embarrassment, I think it would more likely be a stinky skunk or one of those shaved cats. What does a sheep have to be so embarrassed about? Nothing, is what. Irregardless, my skunky apology seemed to get me off the hook very quickly indeed. Mrs F possessed a lenient quality that set her apart from all of the other teachers I had met. She made me feel at ease.

After we had all introduced ourselves, Mrs F explained that she would be taking us every Monday, Wednesday and Friday afternoon to learn about interesting things and work on special projects together. I can remember thinking that this sounded absolutely brilliant. And it *was* brilliant. Looking back now, I can appreciate that Mrs F's great skill was in coupling the interesting subjects with the boring ones. When we were putting together a project on frogs and toads, we also learnt a bit about multiplication. When she was mainly teaching us about castles, she also slipped in some stuff about spelling and grammar, and when we learnt about dinosaurs, she threw in some stuff about prime numbers. Prime numbers are whole numbers with only two divisors (no more, no less). Some people (like Roger), think that the number one is a prime number. They are wrong. The number one does not have two divisors, it has *one* divisor, which is one. This means that it cannot be defined as a prime number. I actually found that quite interesting, but not as interesting as drawing a tyrannosaurus, which is what I did for the rest of that particular afternoon.

"That's a very good drawing Walton," I remember her saying.

"Thanks Mrs F," I replied, beaming with pride.

"My name is Mrs Fupplecock, dear. You should call me Mrs Fupplecock. Mrs F is a bit too… flippant."

"Sure thing, Mrs Fupplecock."

She smiled and ruffled my hair. "There's a good boy."

She let me call her Mrs F in the end, I hasten to add. But for now, I was calling her Wendy.

*

I had never felt bedclothes as soft and delicate as the sheets I curled up in that night in Wendy's bedroom. They caressed my bare skin like a soft satin lover as I closed my eyes and gently slipped once again into the inescapable world of my dreams.

This time I was walking slowly through the middle of an eternal field, basking in the glow of a giant sun, breathing in the scent of spring flowers and freshly cut grass. I closed my eyes and allowed myself to be saturated in serenity – soaking up the peace like a sponge in a vat of lightly perfumed milk. I didn't feel alive any more – not exactly. I was floating somewhere outside my own life, existing only now as a faint and silent memory. I was just a thought – just an idea – just a whispered word lost somewhere on the wisps of a gentle breeze. And I was free…

Somebody took me by the hand and I opened my eyes. Wendy was with me – dressed in her finest summer dress – her hair gently dancing in the cool morning wind. Her lips parted into a smile for a moment, but only for a moment. She closed her eyes and pursed her lips towards me. I ran the back of my hand over her soft cheek and wrapped my other arm around her waist. A nearby orchestra erupted with a heavenly fanfare as our mouths met – there in that moment – that most perfect of moments.

Two or three or five or seven dinosaurs were grazing on a cluster of luscious trees in the distance. We sat and watched them for a moment, cuddled up on the grass, as utterly content as two human beings ever could be.

"You know this is a dream?" I whispered after a moment. "It isn't real."

"I know," she said. "But let's pretend it is. Let's pretend all of this is real, if only for a little while."

The invisible orchestra continued to play when we kissed again, our very own love theme surging all around us as we fell back onto the grass, rolling around laughing and crying secret tears of joy.

"I love you," she whispered in my ear.

I wanted to say it back, but I couldn't. I couldn't speak. And my ears were filled with a blood-curdling roar as a crudely-drawn tyrannosaurus-rex burst over the horizon and chased away the other dinosaurs, biting one of them on the bottom and roaring manically like a cretaceous cretin. The sun dropped out of the sky like a falling stone and we plunged into darkness – no more birds, no more sunshine, no more orchestra. No more Wendy. I called her name but she was gone – consumed by the prevalence of my own subconscious misery. I wandered through the darkness, blind and alone, stumbling over the jagged rocks and soggy marshes that had replaced the luscious grass.

My hands made contact with an unknown obstacle, bringing an involuntary intermission to my journey. I could feel something in front of me; something large, warm and hairy. Something *alive.* I could feel its abdomen rising and falling as it breathed, grunting and snorting as it shuffled about on the grass.

Hello, I thought. *What's this?*

I took out Roger's smartphone and used the screen to light up my surroundings, exposing the creature with a faint blue glow. This cow had seen better days – probably because, I suspected, it had existed for an eternity…

"You poor bugger," I said, gently patting it on the back. "I bet it's not easy living forever." It tilted its head towards me and mooed affectionately.

Suddenly a bolt of forked lightning shot into the ground beside us and lit up the whole field. It was at this point that I noted that I was encircled by numerous men in white robes, glaring menacingly in my direction.

"Please," I shouted. "Leave me alone! I have no quarrel with you. I just want to get home!"

The men looked to one another and shrugged. They raised their swords in front of their faces and slowly advanced, expressionless, robotic – yet somehow furious and feral like the storm.

"Oh for flip's sake," I said. "Bugger off, will you?"

They continued to approach.

"This isn't fair!" I cried. "I haven't done anything wrong! Please! Let me go!"

Suddenly the cow had gone, and in her place stood the hooded man with the sword made out of breakfast. I closed my eyes as he stabbed me through the heart with his streaky blade.

"No!" I cried.

I was sat up in bed, wide-eyed and breathless, gripping tightly to the sheets by my sides. As I remained in that perplexing state between sleep and awake for a moment, a soft hand settled tenderly upon my own, and someone whispered gently in my ear. I loosened my grip and gently exhaled as the room came back into focus. Wendy was there, sitting by my side, offering to give me a supportive cuddle. For a second I thought that I was dreaming again.

I must only have been asleep for a matter of minutes, as Wendy had not yet readied herself for bed and was still fully clothed.

"It's alright," she said, holding me close to her. "You were having a bad dream."

"I'm sorry," I said. "I have these awful nightmares."

She brushed my fringe away from my face and brought one leg up over my lap, exposing the rim of her stocking.

"Would it help to talk about it?" she asked.

"I'd rather not," I said. "Once I'm awake I just like to forget about them."

She smiled as I kissed her hand. "Do you want me to stay a while?"

"I'd like that," I said. "If you wouldn't mind."

She leaned closer, her lips just an inch or two from my own.

"How long would you like me to stay?"

I inhaled her wonderful smell and almost winced with pleasure as she gently thrust her body into mine.

"As long as you want to," I said. "As long as you can."

This time when she kissed me I began to feel dizzy, and I could feel my hands starting to shake as I wrapped them around her – one behind her head, the other on the small of her back. I think it was that tantalising yet terrifying anticipation of where our actions might lead now that we were alone, in private, in her bedroom. Suddenly I became very aware of myself, and the fact that I was only wearing underpants as I had no pyjamas. Suddenly I felt so ashamed, elated, nervous, excited, self-conscious and yet confident – a cocktail of emotions I had never really experienced before all at once like that.

When we finished what must have been the longest kiss in history, she pulled her face back from mine and smiled the best smile I'd ever seen in my life – her top teeth biting down mischievously on her bottom lip – her eyes glowing with excitement. It was at that moment that I knew what was going to happen next.

We were going to have the sex.

I can't really put into words how nervous I was about what we were about to do – but I can put it into <u>context</u>. Before this time I had not been a party to a great deal of sexual activity, largely due to the fact that I was absent with the mumps during our school's sex-education sessions. As a result of this, my early sexual encounters were very much a case of trial and error (but mainly error). The first girl was called Tina, and I met her in the Student Union bar when I was at University. We went out 'clubbing' and did a bit of kissing, which in retrospect was nowhere near as pleasant as it was when I did it with Wendy. Then later in the evening my friend Percy Trent Derby suggested that I purchase some 'protection' for the night ahead. As I marched into the gents, change in hand, gallantly approaching the prophylactic vending machine like a soldier climbing out of the trenches, I suddenly realised that I didn't have the first idea what I was doing. I had never seen anyone having the sex before, and no one had ever explained how it was all supposed to work. I was almost on the point of giving up when I noticed that the good people at *Durex* had posted some concise yet helpful intercourse instructions on the front of their machine:

INSERT A £1 COIN INTO BOTH SLOTS AND TWIST KNOB.

What followed was a most unpleasant, confusing and ultimately anticlimactic night of embarrassment and broken dreams. The next morning I wrote a strongly-worded letter to the people at *Durex* and am still awaiting some sort of compensation for their mistake.

One year later I courted a nice lady called Rebecca who eventually became a lesbian and moved to Scunthorpe for some reason. I am not entirely sure how one goes about becoming a lesbian, but apparently I did not qualify and as such it was deemed inappropriate to continue our relationship. However, we did do 'it' a couple of times in her Renault Clio, and once in the bathroom section of MFI, so all was not a total loss. Further to this, I have got to the second base with Melanie Bogg during one of our longer "on-again" periods.

Suffice to say, as Wendy flipped the lock on her bedroom door and stood at the foot of her bed with a wicked smile playing across her crimson lips, I was more anxious than a bat with diarrhoea. I sat up and tried to look as sexy as possible, pushing my shoulders apart and tensing the muscles in my chest. She reached slowly around the back of her dress and unbuttoned it with effortless grace. When it fell to the floor she casually stepped out of it and sat on the side of the bed, so beautiful that she looked more like a page of a magazine than a real woman.

But she *was* a real woman, and she was right there, in her undergarments, crawling up the bed towards me. Ian Hislop was standing to attention like a bold, satirical soldier. *Once more unto the breach, dear friends, once more...* I had never been so scared and yet so happy at the same time.

One thing I noticed immediately was that women in the 1950s wore much more underwear than the naughty women of the naughties. Wendy's bra came down much further than the bottom of her bosoms, laced up at the front like a kind of mini-corset, and her frilly knickers were absolutely ginormous! In my limited experience I had never seen anyone with pants that big. Melanie Bogg liked to wear thongs that were so thin you could hardly even tell she was wearing them. In fact, although I'm probably not really allowed to tell you this, on one occasion even *she* couldn't tell she was wearing one, and then got very confused as to why she had gone to the toilet and done two half-poos.

I pulled myself out from beneath the duvet and rolled onto the bed beside her, tentatively curling my hand around her soft, bare waist.

"You're trembling," she said, moving closer to me. "Are you okay?"

"I've never been better," I said, quite honestly. "I'm just a bit nervous, that's all."

She smoothly slid her arms and legs around me as I rolled on top of her.

"You're the sweetest man," she said, fiddling with the rim of my underwear. "Now make love to me until the sun comes up again."

Suddenly my nerves dissipated and I locked my lips around hers, caressing her back and bum and bosoms and any part of her I hadn't felt before. I wanted to feel it all – every inch of her body – so wonderfully warm and soft to the touch. She pulled herself out of her undergarments and tossed them aside, still locked in my embrace, still kissing me, still somehow grabbing at my naked skin. Women are very good at multi-tasking like that.

She ran a gentle hand over my shoulder and slid it down onto my chest, then biting my lip she pushed me to one side, rolling me over and lying on top of me, sliding my underpants down and…

And then…

Then…

Then there was a knock on the door.

"Walton," came Roger's muffled voice. "Do you have a minute?"

DAMN IT ROGER!

"Shhh," whispered Wendy. "Pretend to be asleep."

I held her hands in mine as she relaxed beside me. "Should I do some fake snoring?" I asked.

"No," she replied. "Just stay quiet."

"Walton," said Roger again, "I just wanted to apologise for earlier. Are you awake? I think we should talk."

I said nothing and rolled my eyes at Wendy, who quietly giggled and nuzzled my chest.

"Okay," said Roger. "I'm coming in."

There was a slight thud as he tried to open the bolted door.

"Oh," he said. "You seem to have locked yourself in. Okay, well… I'll see you in the morning then. Good night."

We listened as his footsteps retreated down the hall and immediately set about rekindling the mood from a few seconds before. It did not work. Wendy slid on top of me and kneed me in the thigh. I tried to kiss her passionately but ended up head-butting her slightly and recoiling to check that she was okay. She *was* okay, but the moment had clearly passed, and I was no longer rising to the occasion.

"I'm sorry," I said. "There's something about Roger's voice that makes me feel very un-sexy."

"I know what you mean," she agreed, lying by my side and snuggling up to me.

As I wrapped my arms around her and kissed her on the forehead I realised all of a sudden that I wasn't in the slightest bit disappointed. I was quite content just lying there, cuddled up together, and enjoying the moment. In fact, I had never felt so wonderfully at peace.

"Why didn't you tell me you were a teacher?" I asked, after a while.

"You didn't ask," she said. "And besides, I'm not a teacher. Not yet."

"Well yes," I said. "But why didn't you tell me that you were in training? I mean – that's a huge part of your life, isn't it?"

"Some men find it intimidating," she said. "They don't tend to go for the career woman."

"Well I think you'll find my thinking quite progressive," I pointed out.

"I don't know," she said. "I guess I just don't like telling people about it in case I fail. I don't know that I'm really cut out for being a teacher. I like children but they don't seem to warm to me very much."

"They will," I said. "And you'll be the best teacher the world has ever seen – not just because you're kind and sweet but because you're wise – and you know about lots of different things, like dinosaurs and prime numbers."

She smiled and kissed my hand. "Tell me about the future," she said.

"Well, what do you want to know? Televisions are much bigger. Cars are much faster. Children are much ruder. We're at war with the middle of the East and the President of the USA is a black chap named Osama."

"Mmmm," she said, closing her eyes. "And are all the men as wonderful and charming as you?"

I thought for a moment. "No. There are a lot of bastards about, like Aaron Michaels."

"What a bastard," she mumbled, rubbing her face into my neck. I don't think she was listening to me anymore. She was very quickly drifting off in my arms and it was as perfect a moment as I could ever have imagined. I kissed her on the head and ran my fingers through her soft hair. Then I just sat there for a while and stared at her beautiful face. I wanted to draw a picture of her. I wanted to challenge myself to see if I could recreate that beauty through my own artistic interpretation. There was only one thing for it. I took out Roger's smartphone and drew a picture of her on the *Freedraw*…

I was getting very good at the *Freedraw*…

THIRTEEN

THE SECRET GARDEN CENTRE

"You're very chirpy this morning," said Roger as we pulled out of Primrose Avenue and headed south along the main road.

"Am I?" I said, grinning like a cat that got creamed. "I hadn't noticed."

The back of the car was packed with supplies in case of any unexpected plot twists. We had a picnic hamper full of food and drink, some cash, a map, a couple of rolled-up blankets and an assortment of pointy utensils to be used, if necessary, for self-defence…

"So what's the plan?" he asked.

"Simple," I said, taking out the black book Oscar had given to us. "We head to the address in that book. Poppyfield garden centre – that's where we'll find the cow."

Roger frowned and shook his head. "But if the cow is here in Budleigh Salterton, then you can bet those dreadful men won't be too far away."

"Perhaps," I said. "But they're most likely out looking for us as we speak, and if you think about it – this is the *last* place they'd expect to find us!"

I was teeming with courage as we tootled along on our merry way, rejuvenated with a belly-full of breakfast and a heart full of hope. I just had a feeling – a feeling that everything was going to be alright, no matter what… I don't know if it was because I'd had a good night's sleep or because we finally had a good idea of what we were doing, but either way, nothing could dampen my spirits. Plus, I'd had the sex three times already that morning.

"Do you even know how to milk a cow?" grumbled Roger, flicking through the book.

"No," I admitted. "But I milked a gorilla once when I was working for Woburn safari park."

"Hmmm," he said. "I didn't know you worked at Woburn Safari park."

I shrugged. "There's a lot you don't know about me, my friend. Besides, I was only employed there briefly."

"So what happened there, then?" he asked, suddenly interested. "Why did they ask you to milk a gorilla?"

"They didn't," I replied. "As I said, I was only employed there briefly."

We passed a sign welcoming us to Budleigh Salterton as Roger spread the map out on his lap. I wound down the window to breathe in some of that much sought-after 'sea air' that people are always talking about. To be quite honest, it just tasted like ordinary air. We first headed to the town centre to scope out a good place for lunch and settled upon a little place called Rick's Café (they didn't have a McDonald's). After that, following 10-15 minutes of sloppy navigation from Roger, we found ourselves on the outskirts of town again, parked up at the address in Oscar's book.

Poppyfield garden centre was exactly as Oscar had described it – 'a huge, derelict cluster of outbuildings swamped in a mess of dead, overgrown foliage.' The large iron gates were chained together, secured with a rusty padlock, and the 'welcome' sign was obscured by unattended weeds and the slow decay of time. On first impression, it seemed as though nobody had been there in years. Of course, we both knew that this wasn't the case.

"How did Oscar get in here?" I asked. "He came fairly regularly, didn't he? There must be an easy way through."

Roger flicked through Oscar's notes in search of an explanation. "There's nothing in here – just the address and… an erotic poem."

"Ah," I said, snatching the book from him. "That was me, actually. I couldn't find anything else to write on this morning and I was struck by a moment of inspiration."

"Yes, yes, I'm well aware of that," he grumbled. "The walls in that bungalow are pretty thin, you know. We could all hear your 'moments of inspiration', thank you very much."

"We?" I asked.

"Well *I* could. I wouldn't know about Ruth, of course – she was sleeping in a different room."

I grinned slyly. "Was she now?"

Roger huffed and started rummaging around in the boot of the car. I noticed that he chose to ignore my pointed comment rather than deny the implied accusation. It was fun winding Roger up, except when he overloaded on adrenaline, of course. I sat on the bonnet and had another look at the poem I had written earlier. It was very good.

My dearest, darling Wendy,
I think you're very trendy.
I like your soft brown hair,
And the lovely clothes you wear.

I like it very much, see,
When you kiss me and you clutch me,
And I like it when you touch me,
When we're in that kind of mood.

I like to be around you
Cause it's you that I am bound to.
I'm so glad that I have found you
And I like it when we're rude.

The poem got much less 12A after that, so I will leave the closing stanzas to your imagination.

"What are you looking for?" I asked Roger, who was still fussing about in the car, going through our supplies.

"Something to break the chain with," he replied. "You could help, you know."

"Surely we don't need to break the chain," I said. "If Oscar came here regularly then how did *he* get through the gate?"

"Maybe he unlocked it."

Roger stood up and held out a rusty old key, just about the right size for the padlock in question. *Of course*, I thought. *It was Oscar who locked up the gate.* I hopped off the bonnet and skipped merrily to Roger's side as he slipped the key into the hole and twisted it with a click.

"Yes!" I shouted, punching the sea air and wiggling my hips in celebration. "Everything's coming up Walton! Come on!" I really was in a terrific mood that morning…

Roger pulled the chain away and heaved the gate forwards just enough for us to squeeze through. With a degree of trepidation we crept into the little car park and looked around. It was littered with overturned bins, wooden pallets and the remains of long-dead pot plants. Ahead of us was a small brick building with broken windows and half a front door hanging limply from its hinges. The whole place smelt rotten.

"What do you suppose happened here?" I asked.

Roger thought for a moment. "They probably went out of business."

"Or they never even had a business," I observed astutely.

"What do you mean?"

"Well, think about it – this whole place is just one big front to protect a secret. I think they *built* it this way. I don't think they ever wanted anyone coming in here."

"Maybe you're right," said Roger. "So what should we do? Split up and look for this thing?"

That garden centre gave me the heebie jeebies, so I was hardly crazy about the idea of splitting up. That's always when bad stuff happens in the films.

"Let's stick together," I said, pushing aside some brambles and walking past the old shop building. "This place can't be *that* big."

I was wrong. It was *incredibly* big. When we rounded the old shop we were able to see the whole centre – various run down greenhouses and outbuildings stretching for several acres in every direction. There must have been at least a hundred of them, sloping down a gradual hill to a row of tall oak trees that shielded the whole place from the road.

"Incredible," said Roger. "Why is there so much of it?"

I shook my head. "You want to hide a needle – best place is a haystack."

I thought that was a very clever thing to say, so I looked at Roger for approval, but he didn't seem to have noticed. He just sighed and looked at his watch.

"We don't have time for this," he said. "It'll take all day to search this place. Those men will find us."

I patted him on the back reassuringly. "We'll find it," I said. "We have to. It's your ticket home."

"And yours," he said.

"Yes," I muttered. "And mine."

I think he could see the look in my eye, but he didn't say anything. He must have known that if he queried my reaction the resulting conversation would not have been a short one, and we were in a hurry after all. But he knew – he must have known – it was written all over my face. There was no way I was returning to the future now. I didn't care what the universe had planned or how it wanted to play things – I was staying with Wendy. I could change my name to Walton Fupplecock, marry Wendy, live out my years with her, and eventually die peacefully on the Squirrel Nutty ride at Alton Towers. That would fit with what I'd been told – the things I'd seen and learnt. That wouldn't create a paradox, would it? Surely the universe would let me do that? Oh yes – I had it all worked out…

"Come on then," said Roger. "Let's split up and search the place. How are we going to do this?"

Swamped by an unkempt thicket to the right of us was a large ground plan with numbered squares representing the buildings. Roger pulled back some of the brambles so that we could see it more clearly.

"We'll start with these rows," he said, pointing to the top of the plan. "Chances are they'll have hidden this thing as far from the gates as possible."

"Chances are," I said. "But, in fact, that's not what they've done."

Roger sighed. "What are you talking about now?"

I grinned at him. "Roger. I think I know where this cow is."

"How could you possibly know where the cow is?" he snorted. "That's ridiculous."

"No it isn't," I said. "It's all falling into place."

"For God's sake Walt, we don't have time for your detective act now. What's going on? Where's the cow?"

I pointed to the plan and smiled nonchalantly.

"It's in shed seven."

*

Over the years, many people have asked me if I believe in God, and the truth is, well, I'm not entirely sure. My mother (Raquel Stenington) wasn't really into anything spiritual unless it came out of a gin bottle (big LOLs), so I didn't have any knowledge of religion until we started talking about it at school. As far as I understand it, some people think that the world was created in seven days by a giant man who had an illegitimate son and sometimes threw frogs at people. I'm not entirely sure that I get that – but I do like all the stuff about Noah and his magic boat. I learnt about other religions, of course, like Hinduism and Sikhism, but being a very progressive liberal thinker I've never really approved of "isms". I did look into Buddhism a bit, but the only life lesson I gleamed from that religion was that if you spend all of your time sitting under a tree and thinking about stuff, you're more than likely going to become obese – even if you are a vegetarian.

When I went to University I shared a flat with my friend Percy Trent Derby who is a born-again Christian. He tried to get me into it several times but I was never very enthusiastic about the idea. It sounded very messy. Then I read a book called *The God Illusion* by Richard Dawkins who was troubled by the idea of religion as a younger man and so set off on a quest to find the answers to life, the universe and everything. As I recall, he walked out into an enchanted forest and prayed directly to science. Then science appeared before him and said that there definitely *isn't* a God, there is no such thing as a soul and religious people are 'dickheads'. I didn't get to the end of the book, because I left it in Bradford and never went back to fetch it. Anyway, the crux of the story is that after speaking to science, Dawkins began to harbour a strong distaste for organised religion, which is, as far as I can tell, when a group of people with similar beliefs get together and celebrate that belief while attempting to communicate their ideals to the rest of society. In fact, he harbours such a strong distaste for this concept that he became Vice President of something called the British Humanist Association, which is, as far as I can tell, a group of people with similar beliefs who get together and celebrate that belief while attempting to communicate their ideals to the rest of society. I never really understood it properly, and as I said, I left it in Bradford. Incidentally, if you are ever in Bradford, do keep an eye out for it. I wrote my name (Walton Cumberfield) on the inside cover…

The point is, I never really made up my mind about the whole God thing, but I *do* know that in that moment, opening the door to shed seven and looking upon that immortal cow for the first time, something inside me started to *believe*. I didn't know what or who exactly I was starting to believe in, but I knew at once that there was more to life than I had previously suspected, and it was an altogether humbling experience that left me in a very solemn mood. A very solemn mood indeed…

"Incredible," said Roger. "Do you think that the tramp in the park knew about this place?"

"How could he?" I said. "He said he was just passing on a message. He didn't know what it meant."

"A message from who?" asked Roger.

"From God?" I suggested.

Roger rolled his eyes and turned away. He had never really gone in for the whole 'God' thing either.

"This is amazing," I continued. "This cow has been here since… well… since forever."

I walked up beside it, just as I had done in my dream. The cow remained still, unconcerned with our presence, peaceful as a piece of peace lily.

"What are you waiting for?" asked Roger. "Get on with it!"

I held up a hand to silence him. "Don't be a fool, Roger. You can't just charge in willy-nilly and start milking something. First you have to earn its trust. I mean, would you let me touch your nipples if we'd only just met? I rather think not."

Roger frowned. "I wouldn't let you touch my nipples, period."

I shot him a look. I hated it when he called me a period. I found it vulgar and sexist.

"Just be quiet for a minute," I said, gently patting the cow on the back. She mooed affectionately, again – just like in my dream.

Roger sat on a crate in the corner of the shed and sulkily rested his head in his hands while I rolled up my sleeves and grabbed a bucket that someone had left on the side. Crouching down on the floor and whispering soothing words to the cow, I gently edged my hands towards her udder. Timing was everything. I had to be calm and slow. I had to concentrate…

Then Roger started sniffing the air and coughing noisily like a massive wally.

"What's that smell?" he erupted.

"Will you shut up!" I hissed.

"Seriously," he said. "There's a really funky stink over here!"

I think I made an unspecific joke about flatulence, but I can't quite remember. That's not important anyway. What is important is the actual source of the smell, which we were about to determine…

"It smells like feet," he said, standing up from the crate. "Seriously, can you not smell that? It's really something else. I'm surprised that thing can stomach it."

"Don't be stupid, Roger. A cow can stomach anything. They have four of them."

Roger raised his eyebrows, clearly impressed, as usual, by the depth and diversity of my knowledge. I don't know why I know so much about so many things – I suppose it's just because I read a lot. I had learnt *that* particular fact from a book about bovine digestive habits entitled *Graze Anatomy.*

I reached in again and managed to get a firm but gentle hand around one of her teats. She grunted and shuffled about somewhat, but didn't object as much as I thought she would. We seemed to have developed a good rapport.

"Erm, Walton…"

"Not now, Roger!" I snapped.

I wasn't sure which of the three remaining teats to go for next, so I started reciting *Eeny, meeny, miny moe* in my head while Roger fussed about behind me.

"Walt," he said again. "Look at this!"

"Not now, Roger!" I said again, through gritted teeth. His interruption had caused me to lose my place in the poem, so I had to start again.

"Walton," he said, yet again. "Stop what you're doing and come over here."

"For Pete's sake," I said. "What is it, man?" I don't know who Pete is, by the way, but I like to think that it's a reference to my favourite film actor of all time, Pete Postlethwaite.

"Recognise this?" he asked, and chucked a lump of something in my direction. I was never very good at catching, so it hit me in the face and fell into the bucket.

I looked down and stared at a familiar sight… Could it be? Now, if this book were a film, then this sequence would be shot in such a way that it reflected the moment back in chapter four when I was sat in my bedroom, looking down into that brown paper bag and seeing a lump of time cheese for the first time. It would have the same music and the shot would be aesthetically similar. Also, I would be played by Tom Cruise and Roger would be played by Timothy Spall. It would be directed by one of the greats like Alfred Hancock or Joel Schumacher. The cow would be animatronics (from the Scissor Sisters).

"It's Oscar's cheese," I said. "The stuff that was stolen!"

"Right," said Roger. "The stuff that was taken by the men who killed him."

"Well a hey-nonny-no and a zip-a-dee doo dah!" I cried. "This is fantastic news! Now we don't have to make our own!"

I picked up the cheese and gave it a whiff. It was strong stuff; mature – potent – powerful… and it was wrapped in the same kind of packet as the original piece – the piece that sent us back there in the first place. I turned it over in my hand and sure enough, there it was – Oscar's seal of quality:

```
The Old Dog and Bottle
      Aylesbeare
        Exeter
         Devon
        EX5 2JP
```

Roger was rooting through the cheese crate like a hungry stray, sniffing the different pieces and tossing several chunks into his shoulder bag.

"Whoa, slow down," I said. "You'll give yourself another hernia/nervous breakdown."

Roger leapt to his feet. "Don't you understand what this means? This is Oscar's cheese – the cheese they took from him! They're not going to leave it here unguarded for long, are they? Hell, they probably live here! We have to go… now!"

"Shhh," I said, holding my finger to my mouth.

"Don't shush me," he said. "This is no time for shushing!"

I ran over to him and put my hand over his mouth. "Listen," I said.

We stood in silence for a few seconds. Then I heard it again – the sound of a car door slamming somewhere nearby, and the muffled murmur of voices.

"They're already here…"

We had left the pointed utensils in our car, so it became immediately obvious that our only two feasible courses of action were to run away again or to hide. Roger chucked the scattered hunks of cheese back into the crate and popped the lid back on. Moving quickly but as silently as possible, I grabbed the metal bucket and returned it to its original position. We looked at each other, then at the door, then at each other again. There was only one way in and out of shed seven, and it sounded as though our enemies were very close to it. If we left at that moment we'd surely have had to run away again, and I didn't want Roger going into another one of his adrenaline overloads. I could see very quickly that our best option was to hide.

The doors flew open and our enemies marched in, clad in their trademark white robes, frowning like a couple of petulant pallbearers.

"Do not blame yourself, Gerald," said the heavy-set one. "It is not your fault they escaped. They have some sort of supernatural power we have yet to understand…"

"They can move things with their minds," said 'Gerald'. "They launched a stool at my head, right from the other side of the room."

I have to admit, judging by his demeanour and vocation; I would have guessed that his name was something like 'Azgoth' or 'Denaforth'. Not 'Gerald'! Gerald is such an unthreatening, gentlemanly name. My grandfather's name was Gerald, for Pete Postlethwaite's sake!

"We must destroy this cheese," said Gerald. "It is a blasphemy. What say you, Winston?"

Winston? Seriously?

"Perhaps," said 'Winston'. "But it is not for us to decide, my darling. This cheese must go to the high council as instructed. We must-"

Winston suddenly stopped talking. I held my breath. Why had he stopped? Did I not put the bucket back in the right place? Was the lid not back on the cheese crate as it was before?

"Yes, we can see you," he said. "We can see you there hiding behind the cow. That's a really terrible place to hide, you know. I mean, we can see your legs… quite clearly… and your friend isn't even bending down enough. I can see his head."

Damn it Roger.

We *were* hiding behind the cow, but in my defence, it was the only place we could hide... There wasn't much in shed seven in the way of furniture, and we couldn't very well just *stand* there, now, could we?

"What brings you here?" asked Gerald. "What business do you have in this place? Speak."

"Be careful darling," said Winston. "They may use their psychokinetic abilities."

"Ay sir, 'tis true we might," I declared. I don't know why, but I always seem to get sucked in when other people use archaic speech. I quite enjoy it, being a thespian and having excellent diction, of course. "And you'd do well to retreat, lest we strike you down as we didst before." I puffed up my chest and raised my head, pouting defiantly like a gallant potato. Roger just stood there like a sack of old carrots. He is *such* a terrible actor.

"I will ask again," said Gerald. "Why do you soil this sacred place with your presence?"

They were edging closer to us, a lick of anger and perhaps even anxiety in their otherwise vacant expressions.

"Come no further," I warned. "Or I will use my psychotic powers again."

"You may well try," said Gerald, still advancing. "But I will not be caught out twice by your trickery. You will die for what you did in that cellar, you damned sorcerer."

"Oh for goodness sake," said Roger. "This is just getting silly now! Look, we don't want any trouble. Walton doesn't have psychokinetic abilities, and we're not going to fight you. This cheese allows people to travel through time. We accidentally ate some in the 21st century and we ended up here. We just want to get home, alright?"

Winston scowled at us, one by one. "And where is this home? Is that where you learnt this black magic of yours?"

"We don't have any magical powers!" shouted Roger. "That stool was thrown at you by the unresting spirit of the man you stabbed in the stomach."

Roger had quite literally given up the ghost, and I was furious with him. Their belief in our dark magical powers was the only thing holding back their attack. Now they had reached the other side of the cow and were ready to make their move.

"You go that way, darling" said Winston. "And I'll go this way."

They crept cautiously around the cow – one at the head and one at the bottom – staring intently at the two of us as we stood there helplessly, trapped like worms on a hook. For a moment I really thought that the end was coming – that my short life on the earth was at an end, and I would never see Melanie again. That's right. *Melanie.* For some reason it was Melanie who popped into my head and not Wendy. That was confusing. I thought I loved Wendy more than anyone else in the world, and yet my thoughts turned to Melanie. Why was I thinking about Melanie? Did I love her after all? Was she the one for me all along? Or did I love both of them? Was I torn between two women – doomed to wrestle with bewildering feelings and conflicting loyalties for the rest of my existence? Perhaps I was, but it didn't really bother me much at the time, since I expected my existence was only due to last a couple of seconds longer. That is until Roger redeemed himself with a succinct and helpful suggestion.

"Under?" he whispered, tapping me on the arm and looking beneath the cow.

At first I thought he had said "udder", so I simply nodded to confirm his correct knowledge of bovine anatomy. Then he tapped me on the arm again and made a sweeping gesture directed between the cow's legs. Gerald and Winston were almost on us, and I realised Roger's meaning just in the Nick of time. I don't know who Nick is, incidentally – but I like to think that it's a reference to my favourite unsuccessful crop farmer of all time, Nick Cave…

I nodded vigourously and grabbed the side of the cow for leverage as we slid through its legs and rolled away from our enemies towards the open door. We only had a second's lead on Gerald and Winston this time, but it was enough to see us clear of the shed and rushing like Russians through the maze of garden structures outside. I tried to knock over a few bits and pieces in order to deter our pursuers, but they were fast and strong, with the uncompromisable will of a German gynecologist.

"They're too fast," shouted Roger. "They're going to catch us!"

"Just keep running," I spluttered, already exhausted. I really *must* get my health club ban revoked…

Roger grabbed his side and winced as he leapt over an old gnome and ducked behind a greenhouse. "I've already got the stitch!"

"I know," I shouted. "Me too! Just fight through it!"

I could see that Roger was slowing up, so I sucked up the pain and put on a brief spurt such that I was running by his side.

"Here," he gasped, reaching into his bag. "Take some of this." He pulled out a lump of Oscar's cheese and started to unwrap it.

"What the heck are you doing?"

He broke off two lumps of approximately the same size and handed one to me.

"We'll go where they can't follow," he said. "Just remember to think forwards…"

"I'm not doing this!" I shouted.

Roger popped the cheese into his mouth. "It's our only choice," he garbled as he chewed it up.

I didn't have time to think about it, you must understand. It's not that I wanted to leave – not then – not yet… There was so much left unsaid – so many feelings left lingering and unclarified like standard butter. But Roger was right – It would only have been a matter of seconds before Gerald was close enough to grab me. That man was faster than Usain Bolt, who is a chap I once read about in my favourite athletics magazine, The Daily Thompson.

Think forwards, I thought as Roger began to fade away into thin air. *Just keep thinking forwards.* I tried to remember the things I had read in *Barry Mason's Forward Thinking Business Solutions* (one of the worst Christmas presents I have ever received). I glanced back to see Gerald furiously battling his way through the foliage towards me. He was almost on me. There was nothing else for it. I popped the cheese into my mouth, chewed it up a bit and choked it down as quickly as I could.

As soon as the cheese touched my tongue I knew it was just as strong as the stuff I had eaten before. I felt equally unbalanced and disorientated, tumbling into a pile of brambles and clutching my head as my brain screamed its way out of the past and back to the future. I saw Gerald diving through the air towards me as time slowed to a crawl, and for a moment I watched as he remained suspended in mid air like something out of that *Matrix* film which wasn't about printers… Then he was gone, and the pain made me close my eyes. I couldn't believe it. That old nutter Oscar had actually pulled it off after all – he'd actually made some cheese that was strong enough to send us home. I was going home!

Or was I? When I opened my eyes it soon became apparent that very little had changed. Yes, the plants were sparser and the buildings slightly more wracked with decay, but otherwise things were very much the same as they had been a few seconds before. But then – why wouldn't they be? I mean, if no one but the order was supposed to know about that place, then why would they change anything? Even in half a century…

There was only one surefire way to verify the era. Quick as The Flash I reached into my pocket and took out Roger's smartphone. It was almost out of battery, but seemed to be picking up a couple of bars of signal, allowing me brief access to The Facebook before powering itself off. My latest status was a botched message to my friend Percy Trent-Derby regarding a television programme he had suggested I watch. I remembered the circumstances very well. It was supposed to read "I fancy *You've Been Framed* is a bit too silly for my tastes" but unfortunately I leant on the Enter button before completing the statement.

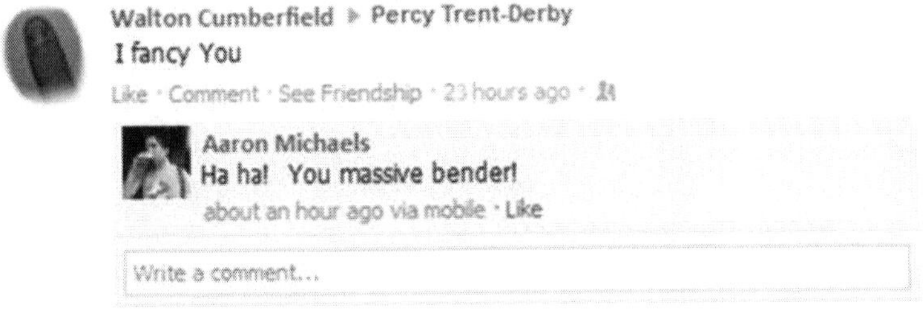
Walton Cumberfield ▸ Percy Trent-Derby
I fancy You
Like · Comment · See Friendship · 23 hours ago ·
Aaron Michaels
Ha ha! You massive bender!
about an hour ago via mobile · Like
Write a comment...

We were back in the future. I thought I was going to be sick but then I wasn't sick. We had evaded our pursuers, but at what cost? I sat up and looked around. Roger was nowhere to be seen. Oscar had mentioned that travelling by cheese is not an 'exact science' so it was likely that Roger would have arrived anything up to three weeks earlier, or later – just like before. Then suddenly I was struck with a spine-chilling realisation – *What if Roger hadn't been thinking forwards at all?* If Roger had been thinking backwards, as he often did, he'd have travelled to the early 1900s – he'd be stuck in a world where everyone drove about in stupid little cars and everything was in black and white. Poor old Roger. I had encouraged his participation in my little adventure, and now he might be lost forever.

What have I done? I asked myself. *Have I lost Roger to the clutches of time? Is this the end of the line for my faithful lodger? Will he be doomed to suffer the monotony of the past for the rest of his days? Oh Roger – will you ever forgive me? If only you'd stayed in Hellesdon… If only I hadn't let you come with me. If only… Oh wait… no… there he is…*

Roger was just around the corner, urinating into a moss-covered old fountain.

"Hi ho, Roger!" I shouted, waving enthusiastically. "Over here!"

Roger was more than a little startled, spinning around and affording me an unwelcome view of his appendage, shaking it frantically as he stumbled towards me. To date, this was the third most undignified image of Roger that circumstances have presented me with.

"Gordon Bennet!" I exclaimed. "I can see your todger, Roger! Put it away, man!"

I noticed that Roger was moving quickly yet carefully, anxiously considering his surroundings.

"What's the matter with you?"

When he was close enough to whisper he hissed at me angrily and said; "Will you shut up! They'll hear you!"

"Who?" I asked.

"Gerald and Winston!"

"Don't be silly," I said. "We've just travelled half a century into the future. We left *them* back in the fifties. We're safe now. Let's go back to Hellesdon."

Roger put his willy away and led me cautiously into the undergrowth. "They're here," he said. "Trust me."

"How long have you been here?" I asked. "A day? A week?"

"Ten minutes or so," he said, crawling under a thick hedge by a dilapidated stone wall. "Long enough to know that we're not alone."

I was very confused. "So what are you saying? That Gerald and Winston travelled here too? Did they eat some of Oscar's cheese?"

"No," said Roger. "They didn't follow us here... They waited."

"Waited?"

The sound of footsteps on the nearby gravel heralded the arrival of our enemies. Roger held his finger to his mouth and shushed me, tucking his legs in and cowering in the foetal position like a cowardly hedgehog. Two voices were mumbling incoherently about something *very* serious indeed. I pulled aside some brambles and peered out at the path through a gap in the stonework. I still couldn't hear what they were saying – the frailty of their voices ensuring that their every word was lost on the gentle whistle of the winter breeze. But I could see them now – crooked and misshapen by the merciless passing of the years, tattered robes hanging from their wasting figures as they croaked at one another like ailing toads. Though both were withered and skeletal in appearance, one seemed to be of a wider natural frame than the other, the shadow of a man who once possessed a far greater physical stature. *Gerald and Winston.* As they turned in my direction their features were unmistakable, even when masked by the wrinkled distortion of old age.

"It's them," I whispered. "Unbelievable. You'd have thought someone would have relieved them from duty by now."

"I heard them talking," said Roger. "They are the last of their order. They have no children of their own, and faced with the cynicism of modern youth they've been unable to recruit anyone from further generations."

I was feeling rather cynical myself. "You learnt all that in 10 minutes?"

"Yes," said Roger. "Fortunately the vast majority of their conversations have been pure exposition."

"That is fortunate," I agreed. "Well, come on then. Let's get going."

"Wait," said Roger. "They'll see us."

"So… we'll run away."

"No," warned Roger. "We can't outrun them, remember?"

I sighed and smiled affectionately at my dim-witted sidekick. "Roger you dopey dingus, they're like… 80 years old."

"Oh," he said. "Yes, I suppose you're right."

I scrambled out of the thicket and casually dusted myself off. Roger stood next to me and stretched himself out, his bones clicking into place in that rather revolting way that some people's do. We made very little attempt to hide ourselves from Gerald and Winston as we headed off down the path towards the exit. I mean, why would we? Part of me was actually curious to see their reaction. Would they even recognise us after half a century? Probably not, the senile old duffers…

Thwack.

A burst of splinters flew from the bark of a tree just a few inches away from my head, and I turned to see an arrow embedded in the trunk, still shuddering from the impact. A few yards behind us, Gerald was desperately trying to reload what appeared to be an antique crossbow, while Winston was hobbling slowly towards us, brandishing a garden hoe of some description. Yes, was the answer. After half a century, they *did* recognise us. And they were packing…

"Bloody hell!" shouted Roger. "What did I tell you?"

"Now's not the time for '*I told you so*'s," I told him. "Now let's get the heck out of here!"

We dashed through a nearby pergola and ducked behind a stack of garden furniture towards the main gate. The good news was that nothing about the centre's layout had changed in over 50 years. The bad news was that the level of security at said garden centre had been significantly upgraded since our last intrusion. In a matter of seconds the whole place was roaring with the sound of an industrial burglar alarm and we were being chased towards the gate by several German shepherds.

"Deine Oma masturbiert im stehen!" they shouted, brandishing their crooks and throwing rocks in our general direction. I am joking, of course. They weren't actually people – they were alsatians (big LOLs)– and they didn't throw anything at us. Nevertheless, they were just as intimidating as their imaginary human counterparts, thundering up the hill towards us, snapping and barking like rabid monsters. Incidentally, the German phrase I used just a moment ago was once uttered to me by an angry Austrian on the number 48 bus, and I have no idea what it means – I just know it was said in anger.

Of course, in the films there is only one course of action a person can take in order to deter an attacking dog or creature of similar ferocity and that is to throw some sort of meat to them as a handy distraction. Unfortunately Roger and I were fresh out of meat as we sprinted towards the gate, dodging the occasional crossbow bolt and producing enough lactic acid to melt a face. We did however have something else which Roger obviously thought might be an adequate substitute. Turns out, his hypothesis was correct…

Were it not for Roger's quick thinking and willingness to act we might have been eaten alive that day, and for all of his stumbles, grumbles and general fumbles (Note to self: new poem about Roger has some legs) he does sometimes come up with the goods – in this case, a couple of chunks of good old-fashioned, home-made "Dog & Bottle" brand time cheese.

Our canine adversaries took to the cheese like hounds to a rabbit, shredding the packaging in seconds and wolfing down its cheesy contents like starving Frenchmen. I took a few moments to congratulate Roger on his resourcefulness, sharing in some fist-pumping and patting him on the back etc, but these pleasantries were soon interrupted by the clang of another crossbow bolt as it ricocheted off the metal gate in front of us. Gerald was a lousy shot, but he was a persistent old fogey.

"Pull, Roger, pull!" I shouted. "We have to get this gate open!" It was no use – a shiny new chain was wrapped around the bars and padlocked in several different places. The last of the German shepherds cocked its head up and snarled at us before disappearing like its friends, but we were still a long way from reaching freedom.

Most of the plant life in that garden centre had expired many years ago, lending the entire place a sort of dead, brown hue. However, just a few yards away from where we were standing, a row of picturesque, flowering mulberries contradicted the overbearing sense of decay with a splash of life and colour. It was behind these handsome mulberries that Gerald took up his post, his withered hands shaking as he attempted to aim his weapon at us.

"Hello gentlemen," he croaked. "How have you been?"

Roger attempted to hurl a rock at him, but the mulberries were providing effective cover.

"I do hope this century finds you well," he continued.

Roger went to throw another rock, but I grabbed his arm. "Don't waste your energy," I said. "He's hiding behind pleasant trees."

"I hope you realise that you won't be leaving here today, darlings," shouted Winston, now hobbling up the hill towards us, using the hoe as a walking aid. "You're not going anywhere – you or your blasphemous cheese."

Our options were fairly limited. We *could* have eaten more cheese, of course, but Zeus only knows when we'd have ended up, and there was a very real chance that we'd have travelled to the same time as those bloodthirsty dogs. Another option would have been to climb the gate, but as inaccurate as Gerald's crossbow skills were, he would probably have hit one of us eventually. Fortunately, Roger stepped up to the plate one more time, and took one for the team...

"Okay, here's the plan," he said, under his breath. "When all of this is over, I'm going to eat some of that time cheese and travel a few years into the past. I'm going to come back here, bring some tools, and make a nice big hole in the wall behind those bushes over there."

"That's great," I said. "But how does that help us now?"

"Don't you see?" he said. "I think I finally understand it now – Oscar's theory of the inevitability of convicted decisions. I've just made a decision to do something, and I *will* follow through on that decision. In the future I *will* travel back to the past and I *will* make a hole in that wall for us. Which means, that if we look behind those-"

Thwack.

Another crossbow bolt shot into the ground by Roger's feet. His reaction to this was very much akin to a clumsy jig, as he recoiled from the point of impact like Michael Flatley on hot coals (or cocaine). I think this must have induced one of his little adrenaline trips, as he shouted some bad words at Gerald and ripped his shirt open like the Incredulous Hulk. He then grabbed me by the arm and ran towards the bushes, waving his middle finger in the air and grunting furiously like a mad pig.

"You can't escape," shouted Winston (as best he could). "There's no way out, darlings."

Roger pulled aside some of the foliage covering the wall and exposed a large hole at the base.

"Wow," I said, as we clambered through it. "This is going to take you ages." Roger wasn't listening, of course. He was panting rapidly, his eyes wide with fury, the hormones of a wild bull coursing through his veins. In fact, he didn't even pause when we reached the other side; he just got to his feet and carried on running. I attempted to give chase but he was too fast for me in his supercharged state, and in seconds I was doubled over with the stitch, watching helplessly as he tore up the road like Wile-E-Coyote or Blade Runner.

"Come back, Roger!" I shouted. "We have to get off the road, like in *Lords of the Ring*!"

Clearly Gerald and Winston weren't expecting to pursue us on foot, and I expected that at any moment their car would come thundering through those gates and I'd immediately fall victim to some sort of horrendous drive-by crossbowing. I *had* to get off the road, but I couldn't leave Roger. A few yards away from me there was a very tempting stile leading into a small field. I could cut through there and follow the footpath back to the village easily enough – but I couldn't be sure that Roger would be safe…

Or could I?

Roger hadn't yet been into the past to dig out that hole in the garden centre wall, which meant that he couldn't die before accomplishing that task. The universe wouldn't let him, as it would create a paradox. So, as far as I understood it, fate was on his side. Somehow, he would be alright. I leapt over the stile and sprinted along by the hedgerow, staying out of sight as Gerald and Winston zoomed past in a clapped-out old hatchback. I don't think they saw me, so I sat down for a moment, caught my thoughts and collected my breath.

The footpath ahead of me led through some woods and down towards the village. I knew at once that my best chance was to head back to civilisation and work out a way to get home. Roger would be heading that way too, and if he had any sense he would stick to our original plan. I held out very little hope that Rick's café would still exist after all this time, but regardless – that's where we had agreed to have our lunch, and lunchtime was upon us. I emptied my pockets to consider my current inventory. Since I never actually paid Cedric for our room at The Old Dog and Bottle, I still had a bit of present-day cash left over, but the majority of my money was now in the useless form of 1950s banknotes. I also had some matches, a yo-yo which I had bought at the fête, and Roger's smartphone (which was out of battery). The final item was Oscar's little black book, which I flicked open to a very special page.

My dearest, darling Wendy,
I think you're very trendy.
I like your soft brown hair,
And the trendy clothes you wear.

The ink smudged with tears as the page filled with the liquid regret of my lacrimal glands. Some things in life are meant to be. Others are but a dream; lost in the changing winds of the choices we make and the pitiless measures of destiny. She had spent her life with somebody else, and I had become no more to her than a silly little boy who didn't know the answer to four times seven.

And yet it could have been so perfect. I could have stayed there in the 1950s and lived out my days with the love of my life. I could have finally been happy. I could have finally been in my elephant. But oh no... Roger had to go and eat more of that bloody time cheese! What a great idea, Roger. Top marks, Roger…

Damn it Roger. God damn it...

FOURTEEN

HIGHWAY TO HELLESDON

Rick's Café was no longer a café – it was a video rental shop with a section at the back dedicated to the retail of fishing rods and general angling supplies (for some reason). Nevertheless, the kind proprietor gave me a pasty and let me watch *Demolition Man* while I waited for Roger to turn up. I sat out in the back, perched on a box of tackle, tucking into my lunch and forgetting all of my woes as I lost myself in the magic of Hollywood. And oh, what magic! I'm not sure if *Demolition Man* has won any Oscars, but I'd be surprised if it hasn't, as it is one of the best films I have *ever* seen.

Roger arrived, believe it or not, just after the film had ended.

"You've just missed a corker of a film," I told him, shaking him by the hand as though we hadn't seen each other for weeks. "I was hoping you'd come here."

"What happened?" he asked. "What did I do? Where did you go?"

"I couldn't catch up with you," I explained. "You spun out on adrenaline again and went off like the clappers. I cut across the fields so they wouldn't be able to chase me by car. You just kept running. How did you lose them?"

"I don't know," he said. "I passed out in a ditch. I don't think they saw me."

I breathed a sigh of relief and sat back down. "Where are they now?"

"I've no idea," he said. "I didn't see them. Maybe they gave up looking."

"That doesn't sound like something they'd do."

The friendly proprietor came through with some forms and asked us if we'd like to join his video club. I thanked him for the offer but politely declined, explaining that we both lived in Hellesdon and couldn't really justify the commute.

"Where's Hellesdon?" he asked, still hopeful of making the sale.

"It's in Norfolk," I said. "About 300 miles from here."

"Norfolk," he repeated, his smile fading. "Well that *is* far away. That's a shame. Still… I don't suppose you want to buy any angling supplies?"

"No, I'm afraid not," I said.

"No, well… that's fair enough, I suppose." He put his hands in his pockets and shifted about awkwardly. "Suppose you young folk get all your angling supplies online these days?"

"No," I explained. "We're just not interested in fishing."

He seemed unable to process that statement and just wittered on as if I hadn't said anything. "Everyone's getting their equipment on that worldwide interweb nowadays. It's the same with the films. People don't want to walk down here to see old Pete anymore. I get a bit of business through the van, but even that's drying up."

"The van?" I asked.

"There's a mobile library goes round these parts. The bloke who drives it rents out a few of my vids for me. Nice chap."

Roger and I looked at each other. We too had known a nice chap who drove a library van.

"Is his name Gus?" I asked.

Old Pete raised his eyebrows enthusiastically. "Oh, you know him then?"

I nodded and looked at Roger. "We're old friends. Good friends! I don't suppose you could tell us where he lives?"

"Not a problem at all," said Old Pete. "Just let me check the database."

Old Pete's "database" was a large lever-arch ring binder with the word "customers" scrawled on the front. He pulled it out from beneath the front desk, blew some dust off the cover (like they do in the films) and began to flick through it.

"Here we are," he said. "Gus Lovecroft. 189 Eight Acre Lane. That's not far from here. I'll draw you a map."

Old Pete was by this point on equal footing with Gus as my joint-favourite bit-part character. We were lucky to keep meeting such helpful and trusting people on our escapades, and though I worried that such encounters would detract from the verisimilitude of our story should I ever recount it in the form of narrative prose, at the time I was just grateful for the luck. We left the video shop with a spring in our step and a song in our hearts. Okay, this might be a bit of an exaggeration, but to say the least, we were bloody chuffed.

"If anyone can help us get back home now, it's Gus," I said with an excited grin.

"Why would he help us?" asked Roger. "I don't understand why people are always so kind to us."

"Well, you know what they say – the road to Hellesdon is paved with good intentions."

"Don't speak too soon," said Roger, suddenly ducking behind a bin. "Look over there."

Three doors down from Old Pete's shop, Gerald and Winston were emerging from the butchers, waving goodbye to the proprietor and politely thanking him for something. They looked up and down the street a few times and then nodded to the next door along. I hid behind a parked car and watched them walk into the Newsagents.

"They're going door to door," said Roger. "They'll be asking if anyone's seen us!"

"Don't worry," I said. "Old Pete won't give us up. He's my joint-favourite bit-part character."

Roger gritted his teeth. "What are you talking about? He was more than happy to tell us where Gus lives, and he doesn't know us from Adam."

"But we're jolly nice chaps," I pointed out. "Gerald and Winston are evil old murderers."

"Yes, but Old Pete doesn't know that does he? To him they're just a couple of innocent-looking elderly chaps going door-to-door."

"You're right," I gasped. "He'll probably just think they're Moomins or something."

"Mormons," said Roger.

I frowned at him, thoughtfully. "What did I say?"

"You said Moomins."

I shrugged. "What's the difference?"

Roger sighed. "A Mormon is an evangelical member of the Church of Jesus Christ of Latter-day Saints. A Moomin is an anthropomorphic Scandinavian hippo-like character from a series of children's books. Why do you always confuse the two?"

"I'm not sure," I admitted. "But there's no time to discuss that now. We need to get to Gus' house before Old Pete gives the game away!"

I snatched the map from Roger (whose navigation skills are famously terrible) and sprinted off in the appropriate direction. Gerald and Winston still had one more business to visit before they reached Old Pete's, which afforded us a bit of a head start. According to the map, Eight Acre Lane was about a quarter of a mile up the main street, over a humpback bridge and down towards the coast. I was looking forward to a nice little walk, but once again we found ourselves running like a couple of infected noses. I was sick of running. Running is for athletes and people who are about to miss a bus. I am neither of those things. The pace of life I had become accustomed to was one of far less haste, enjoying every moment, taking in the scenery, philosophising, creating, drawing pictures and writing poetry. Now suddenly my world had been turned upside down, and my life seemed, at times, more high-octane than *Demolition Man* (which is *really* high-octane).

Gus' bookmobile was parked on the street just outside number 189, its vibrant paintwork lighting up the whole road and instantly reassuring us as we stopped to catch our breath. *Boy will I be glad to see Gus again*, I thought. *This adventure is just becoming one ordeal after another.* When I had caught said breath I articulated these thoughts to Roger.

"Boy will I be glad to see Gus again," I said. "This adventure is just becoming one ordeal after another."

Roger stood up and gasped for air as he stared at Gus' house. "You can say that again."

I chose not to, and instead headed up Gus' garden path to his front door. Roger brought up the rear, remaining vigilant as always, brandishing a large stick that he had pulled out of a bush on the way. Gerald and Winston couldn't be far behind. We knew we would have to act fast.

Ding-a-ling, ling, ling, ding-a-ling, ling ling.

Gus' doorbell was almost as jolly as his disposition. We waited for a few moments, and then tried knocking instead. Nothing happened. There didn't seem to be anyone at home.

"Maybe he's at work," suggested Roger.

"How can he be at work?" I said. "His bookmobile is right there." I tried the doorbell again.

Ding-a-ling, ling, ling, ding-a-ling, ling ling.

What a lovely ditty. But still no sign of Gus. What if he wasn't home? What if he was on holiday? We hadn't thought of that. Who could help us if not Gus? Roger shrugged and sat down on the step.

"What do we do now?" he asked.

"We have to get help from somewhere," I said. "We need to find someone who will take us in and help us get home."

"We could try the church," suggested Roger. "My father used to swear by the church."

I was never too enthusiastic about the opinions of Roger's father. He was a madman who lived in a graveyard and suffered from Tourettes syndrome.

"No," I said. "We need to find Gus. If Gerald and Winston know about him, then he'll be in trouble too-"

Suddenly the front door swung open and, much to our relief, we were greeted by Gus' smiling face.

"Can I help you gentlemen?" he asked, rubbing his hair with a towel.

"It's good to see you, Gus," I said. "We need your help again, I'm afraid."

"I'm sorry? Do I know you?"

"Yes," I said. "We've met before – in Basing-"

"No," interrupted Roger, turning to me. "That hasn't happened yet."

At first I was confused, but being fairly astute, I soon ascertained Roger's meaning. We had arrived in the future a couple of weeks before we had left it. Technically, we hadn't met Gus yet, and he wouldn't have any idea who we were. He only knew who we were in Basingstoke, presumably, because we were meeting him now. My mind was boggling, but I don't think anyone noticed…

Gus looked dumbstruck, so I put a reassuring arm around him and led him down the garden path. He didn't seem too pleased about this, since he wasn't wearing any shoes, but he didn't say anything because he is a really nice man.

"We have to get out of here," I said. "All of us… It's not safe. They probably know where you live."

"Who?" asked Gus. "Who are you? What are you talking about?"

"Can you get us to Hellesdon?" asked Roger. "I know it's a lot to ask but-"

"I don't know you!" exclaimed Gus. "You must have the wrong man!"

"Trust me," I said. "We've got the right man. We just haven't got the right *time*." I grinned at Roger, proud of my stylish articulation of a point that would otherwise have to be made with several minutes of in-depth expositional explanation.

Gus shook his head and stared at the two of us. "This is mad. I have absolutely no idea what you're talking about!" My heart sank as the sinister drone of an approaching car engine brought an immediate close to proceedings. I shot Roger a worried look, and he picked up his stick. This was a quiet little road, and the pitch of the approaching engine suggested that it was advancing at a high speed.

"Back in the house," said Roger. "Now!"

I tried to lead Gus back inside, but he pushed me away in an inconvenient burst of uncharacteristic fury.

"Stop pulling me about!" he said. "Will you just explain-"

"Christ!" shouted Roger, running back to us. "It's them!"

Gerald and Winston came swerving around the corner in their little car, tyres screeching on the tarmac as they skidded up onto the pavement, showing virtually no regard for the residential speed limit. Winston was at the wheel, wide-eyed and white-knuckled, gritting his false teeth in concentration. Gerald was next to him, leaning out of the window, riding 'shotgun'. Well, he didn't actually have a shotgun, fortunately for us, but he *did* still have his crossbow. The first bolt missed us by a mile, though to be fair they were still doing about 30 miles per hour when he launched it. The second one, I am sorry to say, was much more accurate.

"Look out!" cried Roger as he threw himself at Gus, knocking him to the floor. I performed a very slick off-the-shoulder roll (which I had seen in *Demolition Man*) and braced myself against the side of the bookmobile, desperately trying to avoid the line of fire. I heard the car doors open and poked my head around the side to see Gerald and Winston hobbling out, brandishing their weapons like antiquated assassins. Roger rolled onto his back and shouted a bad word. I didn't reproach him on this occasion, of course, since he had a crossbow bolt embedded in his right arm.

"Oh my God!" shouted Gus. "Are you okay? You just saved my life!"

"Bloody hell!" shouted Roger. "This is the worst pain ever!"

We were shitting ducks out there. I've never really understood what that expression means, by the way, but I think it's similar to 'having kittens'. Needless to say, we were definitely having some sort of animal – what with our being out in the open with nowhere to run and nothing with which to defend ourselves. I grabbed Roger and dragged him kicking and screaming towards the back of the bookmobile, frantically trying to get him out of range of Gerald's projectiles. Gus followed, producing a set of keys which he fumbled through as he approached the back door.

"We need weapons," I said. "What have you got in there?"

"Nothing," said Gus. "It's a bookmobile."

I clicked my fingers in order to convey with maximum clarity that I had thought of something. Something brilliant…

"Do you have *The Guinness Book of Records 2008*?"

"I... Well... Yes I do."

He threw the back door open and hopped inside. I could hear Gerald grunting and groaning as he struggled to reload his bow, creeping along the edge of the bookmobile and evoking a sense of mild peril, like a poisonous snail... Roger winced in agony as I lifted him up and tried to help him into the vehicle. Gerald would be on us in seconds, and when that happened, it would all be over. I hoisted Roger up and he just about managed to climb inside, assisted at the other end by Gus, who had returned with my trademark weapon.

Crunch!

As Gerald stepped into view he was instantly met with an onomatopoeic blow to the face from over 280 pages of scintillating, new and fully updated records. His crossbow bolt went flying up into the sky, while the rest of him tumbled to the floor in a heap of defeat. If there's one thing I know about the elderly, it's that they are no match for *The Guinness Book of Records 2008*. Winston was next – sneaking up a few yards behind Gerald with Roger's stick, poised for immediate combat. I launched the book through the air and caught him in the groin, sending him spluttering to the floor.

"Get in!" I shouted, doing another one of Roger's trademark 'fist pumps', which I knew he would have joined in with were it not for the fact that he had a crossbow bolt embedded in his humerous.

"Get in!" echoed Gus, joining in with the celebratory mayhem. "Who's the man?"

"I'm the man!" I declared valiantly, skipping around with delight. I *was* the man. I had taken down two enemies with zero fatalities and minimal collateral damage. Top marks for me (Walton Cumberfield).

"No," said Gus. "I meant 'get in the bookmobile' and 'who's that man with the crossbow?' What does he want?"

"Ah," I said, climbing aboard. "That'd be Gerald. It's a long story, but the crux of it is that he wants to kill us."

Gerald and Winston were still very much incapacitated – though it was unclear how long they would remain that way. Gerald was already sitting up, nursing the bump on his head, while Winston was writhing around on the ground – grumbling, moaning and cupping himself…

"You'll pay for this!" he shouted. "You hear me? I know where you live!"

I declared victory over our enemies by holding out my fingers in the shape of a V. Then I slammed the door and nodded to Gus, who turned on the ignition and pulled away as fast as he could. Roger was lying across the two chairs at the back, gritting his teeth and howling in agony. There was a notice bearing first aid instructions stuck to the inside of one of the windows. Noticing that I had noticed the notice, Gus turned to me and said; "I notice that you've noticed my notice. The first aid kit is under the seat".

Fortunately I had taken three first aid courses prior to this incident – two of which I had passed with flying colours, the other of which I had failed because I sat on the dummy's head while attempting to administer cardiopulmonary resuscitation. Regardless, I knew I had enough experience by this point to deal with the developing situation, and I approached the disaster with unflinching confidence. That is until I opened up the first aid kit and looked inside.

"What the Jiminy Crickets is this?" I shouted as I examined the contents. "This is ridiculous. What am I supposed to do with this?"

The first aid 'kit' consisted of half a tube of *Savlon* antiseptic cream, some extra small plasters and a box of paracetamol.

"I'm sorry," said Gus. "This is a bookmobile. We're only really equipped to deal with paper cuts. I'll drive you to a hospital."

"No!" I exclaimed. "They'll be expecting that! I need you to drive us to a train station. I'll make do with what I've got here."

I undid the strap on Roger's shoulder bag and threw it to one side, spilling five or seven hunks of time cheese all over the floor. I then used some of the children's scissors from 'creative corner' to cut off his sleeve and expose the wound. Since I tend to get nauseous at the sight of blood, I decided to leave the bolt where it was for the time being, and built a dressing around it using 59 extra-small plasters and all that remained of the Savlon cream. Roger was still crying like a massive baby by the time I had finished, so I gave him a couple of paracetamol to cheer him up.

"Water…" he said, mispronouncing my name.

"I'm here," I said. "You're going to be alright. Just sleep it off."

"Sleep it off?" he croaked. "I've got an arrow in my arm…"

"Well observed," I said. "You see – you're already feeling better. Now close your eyes and rest. Gus is going to drive us to the train station."

I patted him gently on the head and ambled over to the shelves, running my thumb along the spines of the H section until I found what I was looking for. Since Roger was taking up both of the comfy chairs at the back of the bus, I decided to settle myself on a beanbag in 'creative corner' – a happy little place that reminded me of my classes with Mrs F, all those years ago. My thoughts turned to Wendy again, and the memory of her radiant smile inevitably induced the onset of a few more secret tears. Peculiarly, I found myself thinking *'she'll be wondering where I've got to – it's been almost seven hours now.'* Then I remembered that to her I'd been gone for 56 years.

No – I wasn't going to let myself get down in the grumps. Not then – not when we were so close to returning home and getting our lives back in order. I choked it all back, took a deep breath, and flipped open Lee Harper's *To Kill A Mockingbird* to where I had left off at the end of chapter eight. I had to keep telling myself that things were going to be alright. I had to have hope. Mr Perks had once told me something about hope – that it is a dangerous thing, and that it can drive a man insane… But Perks was wrong. Hope was the only thing keeping me going that whole time – hope that I would find Keith Matthews again – that I would solve the various baffling mysteries that life had presented me with and that everything was going to be alright. And that hope came to me in many forms; be it a reassuring word from Roger, the kindness of a stranger driving a mobile library, or a message scrawled on the page of a book.

I had to keep telling myself that everything was going to be alright.

And I knew immediately who had written that message at the end of chapter eight.

It was me.

I opened up a little plastic box marked 'pens' and scribbled it down at the end of the page;

Walt – don't worry. Everything's going to be all right ☺

I sat back and smiled at my kind words, happy in the knowledge that they would reassure me at a time of crisis. Plus – I had inadvertently solved another mystery and answered another question, which made me feel jolly super. Roger had either fallen asleep or passed out by this point, so I was blessed with the necessary quiet to lose myself in chapter nine of Lee Harper's masterpiece.

A few chapters later we pulled into Gillingham station and Gus shut off the engine. He sighed and climbed into the back, going straight over to Roger and resting a gentle hand on his forehead. Some people do that for any given ailment, I've noticed, although it is clearly only necessary when you're testing for a fever.

"He saved my life," said Gus (I think).

"Hmmmm?" I said, putting down the book (you see I wasn't really listening to the first thing he said).

"That bolt could have hit me in the chest. He doesn't even know me and he risked his own life to save mine."

"Yeah," I agreed. "Roger's a good egg like that." I walked over to him and dropped the book on the floor. "We'd better wake him up – we have to get out of here."

"You need to get him to a doctor," said Gus. "He's gone a bit blue."

"Roger's always going a bit blue," I chuckled. "You should hear his joke about the man with three-" I stopped myself short; noticing that Gus' expression dictated that this was not a subject for mirth.

"What are you going to do?" he asked.

"We need to get back to Hellesdon ASAP – I know a man there who can help us." I started picking up the scattered hunks of time cheese and replacing them in Roger's shoulder bag. "Only thing is, I don't think we have enough money for the journey. The train fare is a bit expensive. In fact, it's downright extortionate. They should really call it a train 'un-fare'!"

I grinned and looked at Gus, but he had failed to register my hilarious pun. "Don't worry about the money," he said. "I'll cover that. It's the least I can do. Now, what about those old men?"

"Don't worry – they won't bother you again. If I know them, they'll be hot on our tail."

"You think they'll follow you to Hellesdon?"

"I'm certain of it."

Roger began to mumble incoherently and his eyelids started to flicker. "I think he's coming to," Gus observed.

"He *is* coming too," I said. "I'm not going back on my own."

"No, I mean he's waking up."

Roger remained in a hazy stupour as we walked him to the ticket booth and I had to keep poking his tongue back into his mouth with a spoon to stop him looking like a drug addict. Gus very kindly bought us two first-class tickets to Norwich with his debit card and waited with us on the platform for the 17:06. I tried to regale him with some of my favourite stories, but he seemed in too serious a mood to find them amusing. He just kept looking at Roger and saying "thank you" very sincerely.

The bell rang to announce the arrival of our train, so we hoisted Roger to his feet and moved to the edge of the platform. "Here," said Gus, taking a business card from his wallet. "You have to ring me and let me know how he's doing. Promise me."

I took the card and slipped it into the front pocket of my shirt. "I promise."

"Honestly, Walton," he continued. "If it weren't for you two I'd be dead by now. I owe you my life."

Actually, strictly speaking, if it wasn't for the two of us, he wouldn't have been in any way connected to this mess in the first place, but I didn't point that out.

"So if there's anything I can do…"

"Well, there is one thing," I said, as the train came into view around the corner. "On the afternoon of the 19th, we're going to need a lift from Basingstoke station. I know it's a lot to ask, but-"

"Consider it done," he said, without hesitation. "I'll see you then. In the meantime, take care of him, Walton."

Struggling to hold up Roger at the same time, we clumsily shook hands and said our goodbyes. Then, minding the gap as instructed, we boarded the train and set off on what would prove to be a mercifully uneventful journey.

*

When the refreshments trolley arrived, I bought Roger a few mini-bottles of gin (for the pain) and a couple of bottles of mineral water (for minerals). We had no Travel Scrabble™ this time to keep us entertained, so we played a few rounds of 'I Spy' until we reached London. Roger perked up a bit after the gins, and it wasn't long before he was back to his old self, cheating away at every given opportunity… Perhaps unfamiliar with the official rules of 'I Spy', he tried to ask me on more than one occasion for extra clues regarding the object that I had 'spied'. This is <u>not</u> allowed, and I am very strict about enforcing the rules of the game so as to maximise the enjoyment factor. He then proceeded to break with every convention by using his go to 'spy' the abstract concept of loneliness. You <u>cannot</u> do this. Abstract concepts are a definite no-no in the official rules of 'I Spy'. I docked him a couple of points for this blatant foul, but all in all I wasn't too hard on him, since I still managed to guess 'loneliness', and, well… he still had a crossbow bolt impaled in his arm.

Of course, now that we actually *had* a pair of valid tickets for the time and class of our journey, there were no ticket inspectors operating on the service. Outraged by this state of affairs, I forced the refreshments lady to check our tickets instead. Her name was Rita, and she had kind eyes which reminded me of Wendy's. She asked Roger if he knew that he had something impaled in his arm, to which Roger responded; "Well, I don't know much about that, but I do know that you have a lovely smile, young lady." Although I understand this may sound utterly charming on paper, I should point out that the combination of gin and blood-loss was causing Roger to dribble and sweat profusely, which may go some way to explaining why she didn't stop at our table again.

When we arrived in London I went straight to the information desk to present my tickets and log an official complaint about the absence of a ticket inspector. "I mean, what's the point in buying a ticket if nobody's going to check it?" I asked them. They apologised, hole-punched my tickets, and assured me that the service would be fully staffed in the future. I realised about half-way around the circle line that in the future I would *not* have a valid ticket, and as such was quite possibly the agent of my own demise. Still, it wasn't a thought worth dwelling on. The future was all in the past now…

We arrived in Norwich at 'bout tan or summit (local time). I spent a while solidifying the rest of our mineral water in the ice cream freezer at Smith's, ground the frozen contents into tiny rocks of ice, and threw them in the direction of the taxi rank. The drivers just looked confused, and Roger didn't understand what I was trying to achieve, but in fairness, I have never attempted to hail a cab before. I knew that if I took Roger to a hospital they would ask "too many questions" (like in the films), so when we eventually did manage to get his attention, I asked our driver to take us to a small veterinary surgery just a mile up the road from where we live. He did not seem to like it when I addressed him as 'driver' and spent most of the trip attempting to explain, fairly inarticulately, his mildly racist opinions on immigration. This was a shame, as I had previously thought that all drivers were like Parker from *Thunderbirds* or Hoke Colburn from *Driving Miss Daisy*. As it turns out, I was very much mistaken.

Since it was very late, the veterinary surgery in question was locked up for the night and there were no more staff on the premises. This did not matter however, since during a three-week work experience placement in said veterinary surgery back in the summer of 2002, I learnt where they hid the spare key to the back door. At that time I had become addicted to the television show *Animal Hospital* and wanted to follow in Rolf Harris' footsteps working as a professional animal enthusiast. Not a veterinarian, you understand – just someone to look at the animals and pout as they are given the lethal injection, then console the owners. As it turned out, this vocation only exists on television and there is no such thing in the real world, so the whole endeavour was yielded completely pointless… Until now.

I lifted the small, stone-carved frog statue from beneath the bird bath in the street-side flower bed and retrieved the key in question. Roger was clearly very tired by this point, as he had draped himself across the bonnet of a parked Fiesta and had himself a brief siesta. This gave me an idea for a poem, which I decided not to write due to time constraints. I was not too worried about Roger, you understand, as I knew that the universe would not allow him to die until he had gone back in time and made that hole in the garden centre wall. Good old universe… When it comes down to it, it's not all bad. It has its moments…

I opened the back door very quietly so as not to startle any of the 'patients' sleeping in the next room. The lights were all off, but surprisingly we managed to avoid knocking any metal receptacles to the floor as we made our way blindly through the dark (like they *always* do in the films). I laid Roger down in an extra-large dog bed and re-dressed his wounds with some more appropriate materials.

We would be safe there for the time being. Dr Farthing, the head of the surgery, was a very pleasant man who I had known for several years. I had done him many favours in the past, and I was confident that he would be more than keen to reciprocate the gesture. While we were working together back in '02 I assisted him in his search for love by posting his details to several interweb dating forums. This didn't play out very well in the end, of course, as I didn't realise that he wasn't gay until several years later, and accidentally missed the H out of his surname on three separate occasions. Still, it's the thought that counts.

Going home wasn't really an option at this point, anyway, as our house was somewhat occupied... By *us*. Not us, obviously – *we* were camped out in the surgery for the night, snuggled up in the waiting room under a plethora of animal blankets. No – when I say "us" I mean the other "us" – the "us" from the past, who were now living in our present. For them (us) the adventure hadn't even begun.

They (we) would be tucked up in bed, blissfully unaware of the clusterfudge of events that was about to befall them (us).

And they (we) were in for one hell of a ride.

FIFTEEN

THE DOG IN THE NIGHT TIME (A CURIOUS INCIDENT)

"How is Keith Matthews?" asked Dr Farthing.

"He's fine," I said. "Thanks for asking." Technically this wasn't a lie – Keith Matthews wasn't due to go missing until the next day, and as we spoke I was most likely walking him around the park, blissfully unaware of the impending chaos.

"Good, good," he said. "That's good."

Roger was being treated in the consultation room by Dr Farthing's wife, who was also called Dr Farthing. As luck would have it they met each other at a conference back in 2005. I know this because the good doctor contacted me on The Facebook to tell me that he'd met someone and could I please "see my way to removing his profile from those gay dating websites". I could not work out how to do this, but he doesn't know that.

"So how did this happen, Walton?" he asked. "What have you gotten yourself into this time?" I like how he added the phrase 'this time' as if to imply that I often turned up with victims of crossbow shootings (LOLS).

"Trust me," I said, looking him straight in the eye and speaking very seriously. "The less you know, the better." I enjoyed saying that – it made me feel very important and mysterious.

"Suit yourself," he said. "But whatever it is, I hope you know what you're doing."

I sighed and gazed broodingly out of the window. "So do I."

In truth, I think I *did* know what I was doing. I had laid several juicy mind-eggs and was currently in the process of hatching a massive plan. There were many drawbacks to the fact that we had landed back in the future a few weeks early – but there were also considerable benefits. I had lain awake all night realising this, and now I was sure I knew how to get to the bottom of my original question…

Where was Keith Matthews?

At that moment I knew where he was, and where he was going to be. I knew that he was going to disappear from my house at some point between the hours of 11pm and 8am that coming night. Now, the universe wasn't going to let me intervene, but it would let me *observe.* I could stake out my house, stay awake, and finally learn what happened to my dog. Of course, if I was going to stay awake all night, I would need to re-jig my body clock a bit, so I decided to spend the afternoon asleep in the bedroom section of MFI.

Dr Farthing's wife Dr Farthing came out of the operating room and informed us that she had removed the crossbow bolt and treated the wound.

"Is he going to be alright?" I asked.

She told me that he was in a stable condition.

"That doesn't surprise me," I said. "He's always been full of horse shit."

She laughed loads and told me I was a very funny man.

"Thank you very much, Dr Farthing," I said. "Sorry about the swearing just then."

She said that it was no problem and that she enjoyed a bit of swearing now and again.

"Oh well that's alright then," I said. "So where is Roger now?"

She told me that he needed to rest and was sleeping in the staffroom.

"Good stuff," I said. "Well, I have some things I need to attend to in town, so I'll see you both later."

She smiled and said goodbye. You'll notice I have chosen not to quote female Dr Farthing's dialogue directly as she is from Romania and I cannot do her accent.

"We'll see you later, Walton," said male Dr Farthing, shoving a thermometer into a cat. "You take care."

"Will do," I said. "You have a nice day now."

"Ve Vills. Byes four nowj."

You see! That sounded nothing like her…

I left the practice and set off on the five-mile walk to our nearest MFI, feeling incredibly positive as my lungs filled with the icy refreshment of crisp winter air, and a thin layer of frost glistened in the beam of the afternoon sun. Everything suddenly seemed right again in my world, and I was energised by the prospect of locating my missing friend. Also, the bedroom section of MFI was one of my favourite places to be, second only to the playing card museum in Cringleford.

Somebody tapped me on the shoulder and I turned around to see a giant chicken holding a bundle of flyers. In my wistful state I had inadvertently walked right past Apollo's Flame and Grill and was now at the crossroads where Roger liked to peddle his trade.

"Hi Walton," he said, taking off his chicken-head. "What are you doing here?"

At first I didn't say anything, stunned by the bizarre nature of this occurrence. This was the Roger from the past – the Roger who hadn't yet travelled through time or been shot with a crossbow. What the hell was I going to say to him?

"Walt?" he asked. "What's the matter?"

"Nothing," I said. "Nothing, nothing… How are you?"

"I'm fine, thanks. Where are you off to? Shouldn't you be at work?"

"Yes, I should," I admitted. "But they've just sent me out for some… butter."

Roger ruffled his feathers. "Butter? Is that your responsibility? I thought you were the sauce manager?"

"I am," I confirmed. "But butter also comes under my jurisdiction." This was a complete lie, of course, but I knew that Roger would be gullible enough to believe it. As if a sauce manager would have to concern himself with *butter*! The very idea! Everyone knows that butter is an extension of the bread man's responsibility.

"Fair enough," he said. "Well, I won't keep you then. What are you up to later?"

"I have literally no idea," I said, walking away. "I can't remember."

I'm hiding in the park and spying on my own house, mate, that's what I'm doing later. I wasn't going to tell him that in a hurry…

I realised that I had to be more careful about running into people who knew me if I wanted to avoid widespread discombobulation. Were I to be recognised in the street by someone who subsequently spotted me at work, people might have grown suspicious. Fortunately there was a neat little fancy dress shop just around the corner on Brunswick Lane, where I was able to buy myself a false nose, fake eyelashes and a stick-on toothbrush moustache.

"What are you supposed to be? Some sort of gay Hitler?" asked the man in MFI, stopping me on my way to the beds. I ignored him of course, as the alter-ego I had invented to go with the costume was Albanian and deaf in one ear.

The bedroom section of MFI was widely stocked with a variety of beds and mattresses, so it took me a little while to settle upon a favourite. Did I want a single, single double, double, kingsize, *super* kingsize? Open spring, memory foam, latex, pocket spring? Why are there so many different types of everything nowadays? They say, on average, we spend 33 percent of our lives sleeping, but we must spend at least 20 percent *choosing.* No word of a lie – I once spent 33 minutes choosing crisps. *Crisps*! I mean, do they really need to make so many different types of crisp? I ask you…

The winning combination was a rather fun spaceship-shaped bed frame with a single-double memory foam mattress. I asked the stern man at the desk if I could 'take it for a test drive' and he very kindly said that I could 'do as I pleased and leave him alone'. I took off my shoes and placed them neatly under the bed on the right hand side. I then took off my socks, coat, jumper, shirt and trouserpants, folded them neatly and placed them in the bedside cupboard. With a stretch and a yawn I threw back the star-covered duvet and climbed in, sighing a happy sigh as the softness enveloped me.

The last time I had slept in a proper bed, I had been sharing it with Wendy. For a moment I dwelled on this melancholic realisation – but only for a moment… It was not long before I found myself wandering the weird and wonderful dreamscape of my slumbering mind once again.

*

"Get up!" shouted the stern man. "You can't sleep here!" I looked up to see him grimacing at me, surrounded by a crowd of disapproving customers. "This is a shop," he continued. "What do you think you're doing?"

"But I have nowhere else to go," I told him. "Please, you have to let me stay – just for a couple of hours. I need some sleep!"

"No!" he said. "No, no, no. You're an idiot. You're an idiot, and everyone thinks you're an idiot and you'll always be an idiot and I hate you! You'll never amount to anything! You bloody berk!" He pulled me out of the bed and forced me to stand before the gathered crowd in nothing but my week-old, unwashed pants. "Now, get out!"

I shamefully turned and opened the bedside cupboard, finding it to be empty. "Where are my clothes?" I asked.

"We burnt them," he said. "Didn't we, ladies and gentlemen?"

The crowd roared with appreciation. "Now leave this place and never come back, you contemptible cur!"

"Fine," I shouted. "But I'm taking *this* with me!" Fortunately the space-ship shaped bed was an *actual* space ship, and I was able to activate the thrusters and rise up above the crowd. I think it was about at this point that I realised I was dreaming all of this. I flew up and up, crashing through the roof and leaving the stern man helplessly cursing my name and shaking his fists at me. The rest of the crowd were cursing me too – Tintin, Aaron Michaels, Gerald, Winston and Gort. Gort had Melanie on his arm, and she was stroking his huge, Scandinavian chest. But then I noticed another crowd behind them – and this crowd wasn't jeering, it was *cheering*. Wendy was there, and Roger too… I leaned over the side of the bed and spotted the rest of them – Oscar, Cedric, Gus, Old Pete, Ruth

Routhorn, Dr Farthing (male), Dr Farthing (female) – they were all there! And they were cheering me on – willing me to succeed – chanting my name like fanatic fans at a falconry competition. Yes! *Walton! Walton! Walton!*

I flew through the sky and thundered through the atmosphere into the sparkly eternity of space, carefully landing my craft on the dark side of the moon (like that song 'Dark Side of the Moon' by Keith Floyd). I stepped out and looked around, knowing somehow that there was somebody else up there with me. Someone was out there in the darkness, hiding, prowling – watching me. I felt uneasy, like the latter levels of Pacman. Who was it? Where were they? What did they want?

"Show yourself," I shouted, but made no sound (as there is no sound in space).

The hooded man glided out of the shadows, ever so slowly – creeping towards me as the merciless promise of death creeps towards us all. I stepped back and tumbled onto the spaceship bed, falling onto something hard beneath the duvet. I pulled back the covers to reveal a bumper edition of *The Guinness Book of Records 2008*. My weapon…

I picked up the book and invited my foe to advance. He unsheathed his breakfast blade and charged towards me, madly swinging his sword about with both hands. I deflected his first swipe and immediately counter-attacked with a sharp blow to his head. Since there is not much air up in space, blowing on his head didn't have much effect, so I hit him very hard with the book instead. He stumbled back and grabbed his veiled face in shock, cowering for the first time, finally feeling the full force of my not inconsiderable wrath... But that was just the start – I jumped into the air and brought the book down on his head with all my strength, knocking him to the floor. He dropped his sword and rolled to one side, trying to get away. I had him now. This was it. Then, as he desperately clambered to his feet, his hood fell open and I looked upon his face for the first time.

No… Surely not…

I had never given much thought to the identity of the man who haunted my nightmares, but now that I was faced with the answer, I wondered how I had ever avoided the question. It was my own face beneath that hooded cloak. The man with the breakfast sword was *me* (Walton Cumberfield). He got to his feet and armed himself once again. I couldn't move – too surprised by this massive twist to put up any sort of defence. And then he (I) stabbed me right through the chest, and it was all over.

"Get up!" shouted the stern man. "You can't sleep here!" I looked up to see him grimacing at me, surrounded by a crowd of disapproving customers. "This is a shop," he continued. "What do you think you're doing?"

"But I have nowhere else to go," I told him. "Please, you have to let me stay – just for a couple of hours. I need some sleep!"

"No!" he said. "No, no, no. You have to leave."

"Fine," I said, with a grin. "But I'm taking this with me!"

I sat up and braced myself, ready for takeoff. Embarrassingly, it was at this point that I realised this <u>wasn't</u> a dream.

"Sir, please don't make this any more difficult than it has to be."

Several of the other customers were tutting at me and shaking their heads as I hastily dressed myself and re-made the bed. Catching my reflection in the bedside mirror, I was reminded that I was still wearing a disguise that made me look like a Nazi transvestite. *They probably think I'm embarrassed*, I thought. *But this is nothing… They have no idea…*

*

That night I implemented my ingenious plan of reconnaissance and camped out in the park opposite my house. I couldn't afford a tent, so I used the last of my cash to buy a sheet of tarpaulin, which I glued to the climbing frame in the children's play area to create a makeshift shelter. As I sat out there in the cold, shivering and uncomfortable, I found myself feeling very jealous of my past self – tucked up in bed without a care in the world. *Don't get too comfortable,* I thought. *The ship's about to hit the fan.* Keith Matthews was about to go missing, and I was going to find out <u>why</u>.

23.46 – I knew that my past self would be fast asleep in bed, so I ventured out of my den and crept towards the house. The whole place was in darkness, but the faint glow of the streetlight was sufficient to see that Keith Matthews was safe and sound – asleep under the kitchen table where I had left him. I was so pleased to see my friend again that I wanted to let myself in to say hello. And why shouldn't I? After all, why not? It was *my* house. It was *my* dog. I still had my keys in my pocket. Why shouldn't I go in? I crept around to the front door and slid my key into the lock. I twisted it open and gently pushed down on the handle… No – that was a *bad* idea. What if it was *me* who let Keith Matthews out in the first place? What if I opened the door and he ran away? I didn't want to risk it – I didn't want to interfere… I let go of the handle and locked the door again. No harm done.

00.45 – Back in my shelter, I ate a couple of cereal bars and continued to monitor the house. Nothing unusual had happened. Nobody had entered the house and nobody had left it. The whole street was quiet as a prisoner's trump.

02.45 – I crept into the back garden and ensured that the area was secure. All of the windows were closed and the back door was firmly locked. I then crept around to the front again and peered through the window. Keith Matthews was still there, sleeping peacefully. What a good little dog.

03.50 – After enjoying my last cereal bar I suddenly realised that I hadn't been for a poo in over 36 hours. In fact, the last time I went for 'big jobs' was in 1954, but I didn't want to get bogged down with that sort of thinking (no pun intended). My stomach started making some pretty comical noises, but I couldn't let my bowels distract me from my primary objective. I was determined to get to the bottom of the matter (pun very much intended! #biglols).

04.25 – Another trip to the house confirmed that Keith Matthews was still asleep in his bed. As the time drew closer to morning, I found myself getting more and more nervous. *Something* was going to happen, but I had no idea what it was.

05.15 – To my shame, I was forced to abandon my post in order to 'take care of business'. I clambered into the bushes and used my shoes to dig a small latrine, hoping all the while that I would not miss the key event responsible for Keith Matthews' disappearance. I didn't want to do this, you understand, but I was worried that something was going to rupture if I didn't. When I had finished I set fire to my leavings, using the cereal bar wrappers as kindling, and crept back up to the house. There was no need to panic – Keith Matthews was still sleeping peacefully.

06.30 – As the morning approached, the streets began to fill with the early-birds, off to catch the worm. I guessed that I probably had one last chance to check in on Keith without being spotted, but first I thought it prudent to take down my shelter, lest it should garner any unwanted attention. This proved harder than I thought, as the glue I had used to attach the tarpaulin was incredibly strong.

06.45 – I finally managed to remove the tarpaulin after 15 minutes of struggling, and went back to the house to check on Keith Matthews. *Still there.* I couldn't work it out. I suppose I had expected some sort of evil dog-napper to turn up in the middle of the night and throw him into the back of his truck. The answer was not so simple. So what was it? When I returned to the climbing frame there were several birds stuck to the remaining glue. Oops... *So that's what happened there...*

07.00 – It was beginning to snow. I found an old newspaper in one of the park bins, brushed the grease and batter from its pages, and pretended to read it, shielding my face from public view. This was a shrewd move, since I would otherwise have been recognised immediately by the lady who was coming down the road. And not just any lady, I might add. My heart skipped a beat when I clocked her approach in my peripheral vision. Melanie Bogg, the prettiest postwoman this side of Bowthorpe, was making the morning rounds with her usual air of professional elegance. I felt strange when I realised that we were technically "on-again" at the time. That was my girlfriend! *My girlfriend!* It felt good that she wasn't with Gort. She hadn't even met Gort yet! Gort was nothing to her, and *I* was everything... Nevertheless, I remained hidden behind the paper as she popped some post through our front door and went on her merry way.

07.15 – Roger emerged from the house, rubbing his eyes and yawning as he pulled the head of his chicken costume over his face to shield him from the cold. Absent-mindedly he let the door swing shut behind him. But it *didn't* shut. It sprung off the catch and fell open again. *No? Was that the answer? Surely not – not Roger. Not this whole time…* He reached the garden gate and went to open that too. *This is it*, I thought. *This is where Keith Matthews escapes.* And then suddenly, Roger saw the front door swinging open and returned quickly to close it again. *Phew.* It wasn't Roger. As I have said before, Roger is very good with Keith Matthews (except on Wednesdays).

08.30 – Lizo from Newsround came strutting up the road with a self-satisfied smirk on his face. He knocked on the door and inspected his wares as he waited for an answer. Nobody came to the door, so he knocked again. I glanced at my watch. This couldn't be right. This was about the time that I realised Keith was missing. I watched as the door opened and the other me stepped into view shouting "Bloody Nora! For the last time, Lizo from Newsround, I don't want to buy any of your blasted spoons!"

"Just a little one? For old time's sake."

"No. No. No! I don't need any spoons!"

How could this have happened? Nobody came to the house, and Keith Matthews didn't leave. I didn't see anything! After a whole night's reconnaissance I didn't get a single clue! What a complete waste of time this had been… I got up and chucked the newspaper back in the bin, pulled off my fake moustache and eyelashes in a fit of stropiness, and skulked away across the park.

And then I saw him – hobbling along in his tattered old coat, hunched over a fresh cup of soup, Freddy limping loyally at his side. I had been very sad when I saw Freddy die that day, but now that I knew he was Keith Matthews' father, I felt even worse about his impending demise. I knew in my heart that I couldn't prevent it from happening, but I was overcome with a sense of rebellion against that bloody universe. If I couldn't save Keith Matthews, I was going to save Freddy instead. I ran over to the homeless man and wished him a very good morning.

"A very good morning to you, sir," I said. "And how are you on this fine day?"

The old man was somewhat taken aback. "What's it to you?"

"That's a lovely dog you have there," I said, as Freddy hacked up a globule of mucus onto the snow. "You should really keep him on a lead, though."

"Don't tell me how to look after my dog!"

"No, no – I wasn't." I realised I had to be tactful about this. "I'm just concerned for his safety. There are a lot of buses about at this time of day. I think it would be sensible to keep him tied up."

The old man spun around and glared at me. "You think I don't know what's best for my Freddy? What's your problem? Leave us alone!"

"I'm just trying to help," I said. "I didn't wish to offend you."

"Well you have! And you've offended Freddy."

"No I haven't," I said, bending down and patting Freddy on the head. "Have I, boy?"

"Don't touch my dog!" he shouted. "You'll spook him! He's easily spooked. Come on boy!" He turned away and gave Freddy a little whistle. I thought it was a bit silly to give Freddy a little whistle, as dogs cannot use whistles, but I didn't say anything about it, since I was running out of time. I knew that Freddy was going to die, and I had to do something about it…

"Please," I said, skipping up beside him. "Just go somewhere else."

"What's that, now?"

"Don't sit here – not in this park… You shouldn't be here. Go somewhere else."

He turned around and prodded me in the chest with his bony fingers. "You're telling me where I can and can't go? Who do you think you are? Just because I don't dress in your fancy clothes and speak in your posh fancy accent, you think you're better than me?"

"No, no…" I said. "Look, something bad is going to happen. You have to trust me."

"You're mad," he said. "Stay away from me!"

He threatened me with his soup. Nobody had ever threatened me with soup before (except Gordon Ramsay) and it was *very* intimidating.

"You need to do something for me." I said.

The old man laughed. "You want me to do something for *you*?"

"Yes," I said. "Here, I'll pay you." That got his attention… I reached into my pocket and pulled out some change. "Three pounds and… fifty… fifty-five… fifty… seven pence." I counted it out into his hand.

"What do I have to do?" he asked.

"Just leave," I said. "Go to another park. Just for this morning – take Freddy somewhere else."

"Oh, I get it!" he shouted, throwing the money onto the floor. "You don't like homeless people in your park, so you think you can pay us to go elsewhere. You stuck up prick!"

"No," I said, squatting down and picking up the scattered coins. "No, it's not like that at all." I was fighting a losing battle, and I had to think fast. Luckily, I was good at thinking fast… "Okay, okay… You don't need to go to another park. Just tie Freddy up. Tie him to a bench or something. If he runs off he'll-"

"You're something else, you are! You really think you can come out here and make me do whatever you want by giving me a couple of quid? Come on Freddy… We're not sticking around here to be insulted. Don't worry *sir*. We won't taint your precious park with our presence any longer. We're leaving."

"You are?" I said. "That's marvellous!"

"Wanker," he mumbled, spitting on the floor as he turned away. I didn't care about being called names. I had done it! I had saved Freddy. The universe had *nothing* on me! *Nothing*! Take that, universe! The old man was leaving. He was leaving with Freddy, and I was never going to meet him. He was never going to sit on that bench and Freddy was never going to run out under the number 47 bus. I would never see the old man sitting there, I would never go over to him….

…And he would never give me *that* message.

And if he didn't give me the message, then I wouldn't know the right shed in which to find the time-cow! And we'd have spent all day searching that garden centre – and Gerald and Winston would most probably have found us – and we might not have got away – and they could have *killed* us! Now there's a paradox and then there's a *paradox*! I suddenly felt very scared. What had I done?

"Wait!" I shouted, running after the old man again. "I'm sorry – I've made a horrible mistake!" The other me would be walking out of my house at any moment, and if I let events unfold in this contradictory manner, I had no idea what would happen. Would I cease to exist? Would the universe implode? I wanted to save Freddy, but it wasn't worth the risk.

"What do you want, now?" snapped the old man.

"I need you to come back. Come back and sit on that bench. Enjoy your soup."

"Why?" he asked.

"Because I need you to do me a *different* favour."

He rolled his eyes and sighed. "You're three cornflakes short of a breakfast, you are."

"Yes," I agreed. "Yes, I probably am. But you need to help me. Please, take the money – go and sit on that bench."

"Why?"

I threw my house a cautious look. "Any minute now, a man is going to come out of that house," I explained. "He's going to be wearing a black balaclava. I need you to give him a message for me. I know it sounds mad, but trust me – the fate of the universe depends on it!" I handed him the money again.

"Fine," he said, snatching the coins from my hand. "What message?"

"It's very simple," I said, knowing that my past-self would be emerging at any moment. "Just two words – 'shed seven.'"

"Shed seven?"

"Shed seven. Have you got that?"

"Well, yeah, I suppose-"

"Good," I said. "Now, quickly – get to that bench and wait. There isn't much time."

The old man was shaking his head and smiling. "You're doolally, you are… Completely bloody bonkers."

"I know," I said. "And I'm sorry…"

"What are you sorry for?"

For sentencing your dog to death. For robbing you of your only friend in the world. For ruining your life for the sake of the universe.

"Just for being rude earlier," I said. "I'm sorry about that."

"Yeah well…" he said. "I suppose there's no harm done. Come on Freddy."

I couldn't watch. Everything was in place again. Things were back as they should be. I ran off down the road as fast as I could. I didn't want to hear the commotion. I didn't want to know any more about it. It was time to go back to the veterinary surgery before I could do any more damage. Time to go and see how Roger was doing… I cried a few secret tears which froze on my cheeks as I made my way back through the snow.

* * *

"You're kidding?" said Roger, sitting up on the sofa.

"No, I'm serious. That was *me*. I was on my way to MFI for a sleep. I told you I was going to get butter."

"Yeah," said Roger. "I remember. Wow – That's so bizarre. That was you from *now*?"

"Funny old life, eh?"

"You're telling me."

He was right. I was. Roger was looking much better now, his arm neatly bandaged and his face back to a much healthier colour.

"How are you feeling?" I asked.

"Better," he admitted. "Much better. Thanks. God – I'm glad it's all over. When can we go home?"

"Not yet," I explained. "We have to wait a few days, just until our past selves have left for Devon. And it's not over, Roger. Not yet. I camped outside the house last night to find out what happened to Keith Matthews, but I didn't see anything. Nobody went in, and nobody came out. This case isn't closed."

Roger sighed. "It is for me, my friend. I'm afraid you're on your own from now on. When I've rested up a bit I'm going to repay my debt to the universe, and then I'm out. We still have all the time cheese, right?"

"We do," I told him. "I put it in the fridge."

"Good stuff," he said. "Good stuff." He laid back and closed his eyes.

"But for now, you rest." I said. "God knows you deserve it."

"Thanks," said Roger. "I suppose I do. I guess we know now why Gus kept calling us heroes, right?"

Holy buggeration. I'd forgotten all about Gus! He had asked me to phone him to let him know how Roger was, and like a perfect plonker I'd gone and let it slip my mind. I checked my top pocket and found his business card. Thank goodness I hadn't lost it…

> **GUS LOVECROFT**
> **BOOKMOBILE MANAGER / FREELANCE EROTIC DANCER**
>
> **189 Eight Acre Lane, Budleigh Salterton**
>
> **gus@guslovin.com**
> **01395 677544**

I left Roger sleeping and went out into Reception. Dr Farthing's wife Dr Farthing was doing some paperwork or something.

"Would it be alright if I used your phone?" I asked.

She told me that it was fine – not a problem at all, in fact.

I keyed in Gus' number and held the phone to my ear. It only rang a few times and then his chirpy voice came on the other end.

"Hello?"

"Hello Gus, it's Walton," I said. "Walton Cumberfield."

"Hello Walton," he said. *"How's Roger doing?"*

"He's fine," I said. "He's doing really well. Sorry for not phoning before."

"Oh, that's alright. I know you've been under a lot of pressure. Just so long as I know he's alright."

"He's fine, he's fine. I took him to some friends of mine and they sorted him out. Did you get back home okay? Our elderly homicidal friends didn't make a repeat appearance?"

"Oh no, no – no sign of them."

"Good," I said. "No sign of them up here either. Perhaps we've given them the slip after all."

"Well let's hope so," he said. *"But listen – you left something in the bookmobile – some sort of cheese."*

I felt a horrible heaviness in the pit of my stomach as I remembered the contents of Roger's bag spilling all over the floor of the bookmobile. I had to be more careful. If the time cheese ever got into the wrong hands, then who knew what might have happened...

"Oh God," I exclaimed. "I thought I'd picked up all of that. Sorry. Listen, don't touch it. And whatever you do, don't eat any of it. Just get rid of it. Burn it. Throw it away. It's dangerous."

"Dangerous?" he said. *"It's only a bit of cheese."*

"Trust me, Gus, you don't want anything to do with it. Just get rid of it."

"Well, I thought you might want me to send it back to you. I found your address in the phone book."

"Really?" I said. "That was very clever."

"Well, there aren't many Walton Cumberfields living in Hellesdon."

"No, I suppose there aren't."

"Anyway, I sent it first class. Should have got there this morning. I think I got the right address."

"I'm sure you did," I said. "I can't remember what it is off the top of my head."

"You can't remember your own address?"

"Well, no," I admitted. "I never really have cause to use it. I find it much more convenient for people to contact me on The Facebook, and besides, Keith Matthews eats the vast majority of my…"

…post.

SIXTEEN

SAD DOGS AND ENGLISHMEN

It was a cool summer evening in 1999 when Christopher Stephens witnessed an incident that would change his life forever. He was less crusty then, you understand, and walked the Earth with a greater air of confidence and dignity than in his later years. He had been a man of 'no fixed abode' ever since his house was destroyed by The Spice Girls in 1995. Now he travelled aimlessly around the country, moving from place to place like a browning leaf on an autumn gale. You could say that his life was set to 'shuffle' mode, where his every decision, every action and every movement was as random as a box of spider monkeys. Somehow he felt that this unsystematic approach to his existence afforded him less responsibility – bowing out to the authority of God, or fate, or whatever greater power one might happen to believe in. And whatever greater power that may be, that evening in '99 when the sun was setting over the flowering trees of a quaint little park on a peaceful street in the village of Hellesdon, that greater power engineered a twist of fortune that would evoke an encouraging change in Christopher's otherwise empty life.

You'll notice that the narrative has suddenly shifted into the third person. Do not be alarmed. I have not become omnivorous or anything like that. You see, I caught up with Freddy's owner (Christopher Stephens) later that afternoon. We buried Freddy's body in a field on the outskirts of Norwich and held a short ceremony to commemorate his life. We then went back to a little pub called The Bog and Bean where we held a wake and traded stories of the deceased. I told Christopher everything – the whole story – the one you have been reading, from Keith Matthews' disappearance to the phone call with Gus at the end of the previous chapter. When I had finished it was then his turn to take up the narrative mantle. Now, Christopher Stephens is a very nice man with a very interesting story to tell, but he is not the most eloquent of raconteurs and he does not have very good diction. Therefore, I have decided to relate his tale in a more palatable style, using my skills as a writer to decorate his account with an articulate narrative and lots of interesting description. This is why we have suddenly jumped to a third person narrative. Of course, I realise that this approach will lose some of the sense of intimacy and immediacy that a first-person narrative tends to offer, but I was forced to weigh this up against the pros of the prose presented in the upcoming paragraphs. Incidentally, Roger tells me that sometimes books that are really, really good (like this one) are selected to be studied as A-level texts, so this is something that you may wish to discuss in your essays. You may also wish to discuss my use of hyperbole, which is the most interesting form of rhetoric in the entire world (except for bathos, which is probably just as good).

So anyway, back to that cool summer evening in '99. The smell of freshly-cut grass was filling Christopher's overtly hairy nostrils as he sauntered along, looking for a quiet spot to spend the night. He cherished those summer days like a brief romance, a fine meal, or a rental copy of *Titanic*; so very wonderful and yet so very swiftly lost to the merciless resilience of life's ever-ticking clock. He always made a point of appreciating the summer, for as we all know, summer's lease hath all too short a date. See that? That was Shakespeare. Now do you see why I'm telling the story my way? Christopher did *not* use Shakespeare quotes to inform his narrative. This is no slight on him, but really – you're getting a lot more for your money this way, I'm sure you'll agree...

He strolled into the park and took a seat on an empty bench – the very same bench where we first met – and breathed in the warmth of the season like some wonderful drug. Then he took some actual drugs (ketamine, I think) and passed out for a while. He is not on drugs any more, you understand, and has not been for a long time. I feel that I must enforce this point because it is important to note that not all homeless people are on drugs, or addicted to alcohol, or funding their habits by stealing car radios and other stereo types. It's ignorance, is what it is – ignorance and hypocrisy! When I was at university, I was out 'on the town' with a man named Bobby Lee, and on our way into said town we passed a homeless man who was sitting in the doorway of Woolworths (do you remember Woolworths?). Anyway, I gave the homeless man some money and he very politely smiled and said 'thank you very much'. Bobby Lee, on the other hand, not only refused to give the man any money, but reprimanded me for my generosity.

"He's not getting any of my money," said Bobby Lee, like a bit of a dick. "He'd only go and spend it all on drugs and booze."

Bobby Lee then went out and spent *all* of his money on drugs and booze. Explain that. Do you see what I mean? Hypocrisy.

See that? That was social commentary. Again, Christopher Stephens did not include any allegories relating to our collective sense of social morality in his version of events. This is going really well…

It was early in the morning the following day when Christopher Stephens woke up and wondered where he was. This did not worry him, of course, as being a man of 'no fixed abode' he was used to waking up in unfamiliar surroundings. He smoked a cigarette and thought of Rita. *Where had it all gone wrong?* he asked himself. Then he removed his shoes and aired his feet for a while. Rita had given him those shoes. Oh, how he loved those shoes.

Okay, I'm making up the whole 'Rita' thing, but I feel that this is justified since it gives Christopher Stephens a past that is instantly relatable, thus engaging our empathy with the character. I'm using my artistic licence here, which you can order from the WALA (Writers and Artists Licensing Agency) for the price of an envelope and an administration charge of £60. I am ashamed to admit that my licence has three points on it due to a couple of drunken poems I wrote at University which were riddled with spelling mistakes. At risk of cumulating further endorsements, here is one of them:

Some people think I'm bonkers,
But I just think I'm free.
Man, I'm just living my life
There's nothing crazy about me.

I managed to retrieve this stanza from my notes and have corrected the offending spelling mistakes. Unfortunately I no longer have the full poem as it was stolen by my housemate Disney Rascal.

Suddenly, Christopher Stephens heard a shriek and his attention turned to a developing commotion in one of the houses nearby – *My* house, to be precise. Well, to be *more* precise it was the house that I would move into at a future date, which at the time was inhabited by a family called the Johnson-Thompsons.

"Get it out! Get it out!" shouted someone from within. "How did it get in here?"

What on Earth is going on? thought Christopher. *This is most unsettling.* He quickly put his shoes back on and ran over to the house in question, concerned that the residents may be in some sort of trouble and require assistance.

"Oh, it's awful, Dennis. Do something! Do something!"

The front door of the house flew open, and Dennis Johnson-Thompson shouted wildly as he chased a Nova-Scotia duck tolling retriever out into the street with a broom.

"Get out of here you little bastard!" he yelled. "And don't come back!"

Keith Matthews ran out of the gate and sat in the road. He probably thought it was a game. He wasn't used to people shouting at him (except for Roger, on Wednesdays) so he wouldn't understand that he was being reprimanded. Besides, it wasn't his fault. He didn't mean to ingest a vast quantity of time cheese and travel 10 years into the past. He was just trying to enjoy the morning post. Not the Newspaper, you understand. No, no - *The Morning Post* was absorbed into *the Daily Telegraph* in 1937, and Keith Matthews didn't travel back *that* far. In fact, when you consider how far Roger and I travelled on just the strength of a single mouthful, Keith Matthews didn't really travel very far at all. I don't know why this was. Perhaps the cheese affects dogs differently to humans. Perhaps it was some of the milder stuff which doesn't have such a dramatic effect. Perhaps it had something to do with how backwards Keith Matthews was thinking at the time of ingestion. Anyway, I'm not going to let that worry me, and neither should you.

The dog curled up on the tarmac and stared at the house, his ears drooping with disappointment and shame. He had been cast out of his home, and he didn't understand why. As Christopher Stephens looked upon him for the first time, he found himself engaged with an immediate sense of sympathy for the melancholic mutt.

"Come on boy," he said. "You can't lie here in the road. You don't want to get run over now, do you?"

"No," he replied.

Oh no, hang on – sorry, I got confused there. Keith Matthews doesn't talk. I wish he did, but he doesn't. He just got to his feet and scurried over to Christopher, licking his hands enthusiastically. By which I mean that he was licking Christopher's hands, not his own. He doesn't have hands, anyway, he has paws...

"Hello there," said Christopher. "What's your name then?"

He checked the collar for a name tag, but found no evidence of ownership. Besides, it wasn't really a collar, as such. It was a tambourine.

"So you're an outcast too, are you boy?" said Christopher, patting him on the head. "Well, I know how you feel... I suppose you're hungry aren't you? Well, I know a place where we can get some food. It's not far from here." Keith Matthews jumped up at him and licked him right in the face. "Alright, alright... I'll take that as a yes, shall I? Come along..." He walked across the park with Keith trotting by his side, immediately loyal to his newfound master. Dogs are fickle like that, you see; able to adapt and transfer their affections to the nearest source of food and attention. You may think that this upsets me – well, maybe it does a little – but when I hear this story my overarching emotion is not one of sorrow or regret. You see, although I will always miss Keith Matthews and remember him with deep affection; I cannot begrudge the great happiness that this twist of fortune bestowed upon this unfortunate stranger. My loss was Christopher's gain, and may have changed his life forever. And you can't really feel too unhappy about that, now can you?

Two things never happened again after that. Keith Matthews was never called Keith Matthews again, and Christopher Stephens never took ketamine again… or *any* drug for that matter. The dependence of his new friend gave him a new lease on his life, and for the next 10 years or so, they lived happily together.

And he called him 'Freddy'.

Now, it may have already dawned on you, as it dawned on me, that this revelation throws up a mind-boggling truth which it is better not to think about very often, if at all. Philosophically, biologically and logistically, this truth is both unsettling and perplexing in equal measure…

You see, you may recall that when I sat with Mrs Fupplecock in her room at Rodney Rooney's after moving her in, I told her all about Keith Matthew's disappearance, which prompted her to inform me that his father was also a stray Nova Scotia duck tolling retriever with a tambourine collar. His father was Freddy. Which means that…

Keith Matthews is his own father.

So there you have it. Following in the footsteps of Laika the Soviet space dog, Keith Matthews had become a pioneer of modern science. To the best of my knowledge, he was the first and only dog in history to become his own father through the means of involuntary, intrauniversal time travel. I still don't know whether to feel proud or ashamed of this fact, so I just refrain from telling anyone about it if at all possible. As I said before, it is better not to give it too much thought, but I thought I'd better mention it here just to wrap up that thread of the story.

When Christopher finished his account we ordered another couple of tap waters and shared a cigarette which we 'bummed' from a kindly patron at the end of the bar. The air outside was bitterly cold, and casting a crippling chill over the assembled smokers. In the corner of the beer garden, tied to a fencepost, lapping water from a discarded drip-tray, was an elderly Novia-Scotia duck tolling retriever. We both stopped when we saw it – the spitting image of Keith Matthews / Freddy – happily ignoring us and yet haunting our very souls with the bittersweet grief or our memory. It *wasn't* Keith Matthews. It was merely a cruel coincidence.

"What are you going to do now?" I asked Christopher, taking a seat at one of the tables. "You can always come and live in my house with me. I currently have a lodger named Roger but I'm sure he won't mind sharing his room with you. I can build some bunk beds. Honestly, you can start paying rent when you get back on your feet again. It's no problem."

"That's very kind, Mr Cumberfield," he said. "But I don't think I'll be hanging around here for very long. This was our place – me and Freddy."

"Freddy and *I*," I corrected him.

"Sorry?"

"Don't apologise. I make that mistake all the time."

He stared at me blankly. "As I was saying; this is where I lived with Freddy. This place *is* Freddy to me. You'll understand why I can't stay here. Too many bad memories."

"I understand," I told him. "So where will you go to now?"

"I don't know," he said. "I guess I'll just hit the road again and see where it takes me. Maybe I'll find something else worth living for." His eyes dropped as his smile extinguished itself with a gentle sigh. "Then again, maybe I won't. Maybe that's it for me – the end of the road. But hey, a man can dream, I suppose. A man can hope…"

Suddenly we were joined by the cigarette man who had been sat at the end of the bar. As he plonked himself down at our table, I wondered how I hadn't recognised him before – or his dog for that matter. It had been a while admittedly, and since our last encounter he had grown a beard and lost a bit of weight. But it was him, alright…

"Let me tell you something my friend," he said. "Hope is a dangerous thing. Hope can drive a man insane."

"Hello, Mr Perks," I said with a grin, delighted at the sudden reintroduction of this whacky supporting character. "What on Earth are you doing here?" I made the necessary introductions; "Christopher, this is Mr Perks."

"It's nice to meet you," said Christopher, offering his hand. "Any friend of Walton's is a friend of mine."

Perks just smiled and shrugged.

"Mr Perks can only communicate using exact quotations from the film *The Shawshank Redemption*," I explained. "You'll have to forgive him – it tends to render conversation rather difficult."

Christopher leant forwards with interest. "You can only communicate using lines that come directly from *The Shawshank Redemption*? How come? I mean, how does something like that happen?"

"Fuck do you care, new fish?"

Christopher shot me a startled look. I just smiled and rolled my eyes. Classic Perks.

Given the nature of his disorder, it is very hard to establish any information surrounding Mr Perks' background or situation. On this occasion he looked as though he had probably gone to the pub to enjoy a quiet drink after work; a loosened tie hanging from the collar of his smart-looking tailored shirt.

"Have you been working today?" I asked him.

He nodded. "May is one fine month to be working outdoors."

"It is," I agreed. "What a shame that it's February…" He sighed in agreement and set about rolling himself a cigarette. "So what is it that you do exactly?"

"Geology."

"Oh really?" I decided to feign enthusiasm, like when people have the sex with Brian May. "How very fascinating. That must be really interesting. Tell me, what does geology involve?"

"Geology is the study of pressure and time. That's all it takes, really. Pressure and time. That and one big goddamn poster."

I understood exactly what he meant. I learnt the highway code from one big goddamn poster.

Christopher cleared his throat and readied himself for another attempt at communication. "Is that your dog over there, Mr Perks?"

Perks shrugged. "First you hate 'em, then you get used to 'em. Enough time passes, you get so you depend on them."

"Tell me about it," said Christopher. "I depended on old Freddy, that's for sure. Now he's gone and I don't know what to do."

Perks was surprisingly forthcoming in his advice; "Get busy living, or get busy dying."

The barmaid came over to our table, a plump and bubbly sort with a postmodern haircut and several inoffensive tattoos on her right arm. Perks, took out a banknote and slipped it into her hand with a smile.

"All I ask is three beers apiece for each of my co-workers..."

I wasn't sure if he was attempting to refer to us, but I thanked him nonetheless and continued the conversation.

"Mr Perks, this is Christopher Stephens. He's very sad today because he lost his dog. We both are. You see, his dog was your dog's brother... and father."

Perks sat and considered Christopher for several moments. Six moments, to be exact. On the seventh moment, he leant in and said, very seriously; "Mr Stephens has a birth certificate, driver's licence, social security number..."

"No," I said. "Of course not. Mr Stephens is a homeless. Surely, you can tell that? Just look at his shoes."

Perks spat defencively. "How often do you really look at a man's shoes?"

He had a point there. I hardly ever looked at people's shoes, except when they said "hey Walton, take a look at my shoes..." which was hardly ever.

Perks regarded Christopher with an air of sympathy as the barmaid brought us our 'three beers apiece'. I thought that this was a bit excessive, if I'm honest, but I realise that this is most probably the only drinks order that Mr Perks is capable of vocalising. As we sat and drank together I decided to pass the time by recounting my story to Perks, who listened intently and occasionally passed comment when appropriate.

"...so Keith was missing," I remember saying. "Gone without a trace."

Mr Perks shook his head and grinned. "Up and vanished like a fart in the wind."

"Indeed," I said. "Just like that."

Although he had heard the story before, Christopher Stephens sat and listened with equal enthusiasm, literally on the edge of his seat with excitement (and because there was some sort of bird poo on it). You see, that's the thing about this story – it's just as brilliant the second time you experience it – perhaps even better. Honestly, give it a go. When you've finished this novel and recommended it to your friends and family, written a glowing review on The Facebook and leant it to your mother-in-law... why not try reading it again? It's the gift that keeps on giving. I've read it six times already (but that was mainly to check for spelling misstakes).

Incidentally, if this *is* the second time you're reading this book, then good for you. Thanks for taking my advice. Did you enjoy it? Don't answer that, it was a rhetorical question and people will think you're strange. Are you sitting on a bus or a train? Imagine that. Imagine someone sitting on a bus or a train and then going "yes I did enjoy it, thanks very much," to their *book*! People would start freaking out, I'll bet. Ooh, here's fun – If you *are* on a bus or a train then have a look around the carriage. Who do you think would freak out the most? Go on, have a look. Who would it be? That's right. I thought so too. There's something in the eyes, isn't there? Stop looking now, you'll freak them out. Anyway, thanks for reading this novel again. I would recommend that you go back and read it again a third time, but let's be honest; you've got to do something productive with your life at some point.

But I digress... When I had finished recounting my tale for the second time that day, Christopher Stephens gave me a polite round of applause and said the word 'bravo' four times. Perks stared at me, smirking, with eyes as wide as wheelbarrows.

"I have to say that's the most amazing story I've ever heard," he said, almost in disbelief. "I find I'm so excited that I can barely sit still or hold a thought in my head."

He rose from his seat and scurried across the pub garden to where Keith Matthews' sister / daughter was tied up, now snoozing peacefully. We watched him with keen curiosity as he untied her and led her to our table.

"She's beautiful," said Christopher. "What's her name?"

Perks smiled at us and patted her on the head. "Rita Hayworth."

"Hello Rita Hayworth," I said. "That's a lovely name you've got there."

"She's lovely," said Christopher. "Just like her brother." His face dropped at the thought of it. "He was a good dog… A *really* good dog. You know, having him in my life was the best thing that ever happened to me. We had a good thing going. A great thing. Now it's gone."

I patted him on the shoulder reassuringly, but I couldn't think of anything else to say. I had said it all already. Fortunately, in his limited vocabulary, Perks was able to appropriate the ideal response to Christopher's spout of melancholy. He reached across the table and placed the end of Rita's lead in his hand. Then, very sincerely, he told him "no good thing ever dies." I watched in astonishment as he then finished the rest of his beer in one mouthful and made his way towards the street.

"What is this?" asked Christopher. "What are you doing? Are you giving Rita to me?"

Perks nodded. "I've decided not to stay."

"Where are you going?" I asked.

"Zihuatanejo," he replied. "Little place right on the Pacific."

"What, right now?" asked Christopher. "You're going to Zihuatanejo right now?"

"That's a very peculiar thing to do," I added.

Perks smiled and nodded. He took one last look at Rita Hayworth, his eyes glimmering with emotion. Then he looked at me, and then at Christopher. To this day I have no idea who he actually was, where he came from or why he did any of the things that he did. He is not on The Facebook, and I haven't been able to track him down by any other means. It was almost as though he fell out of the sky. An angel, perhaps... Well, probably not an angel. I mean, I've never actually met a real-life angel, but I imagine them to have white robes and halos and wings, and to be able to communicate in words that are not limited to exact quotations from *The Shawshank Redemption.* Then again, who can know for sure? All I know is that with an act of kindness as bizarre and out-of-place as every line of dialogue that came out of his mouth, Mr Perks had done more for Christopher than anyone else he had ever known. It was a touching moment – a heartwrenching conclusion to a day that had been wracked with sorrow, underlined by the near-poetic timing and perfect delivery of Perks' final words.

"I hope the pacific is as blue as it has been in my dreams," he said, turning back to us one final time. "I hope."

*

I felt exhausted as I wandered back through the snowy streets of Hellesdon to the veterinary surgery. It had been a long day, and I was well and truly done for. In fact, I hadn't slept in over 24 hours, which is a feat I had not equalled since accidentally ingesting four ounces of cocaine when I was living in University halls (having mistaken it for a sherbet dip-dab).

Christopher Stephens bade me a fond farewell and left the pub with Rita Hayworth at his side. It was a happy union, and one that filled my heart with a sense of gladness that went some way to displacing the great emptiness I had felt since the loss of Keith Matthews. I couldn't help but think about that morning – that very morning – when I had crouched down beneath that bench to inspect 'Freddy' for the first time. He had recognised me. He had wanted me to pet him and fuss him like in the good old days, but I had recoiled at the sight of his mangy fur and phlegmy mouth. That was the last thing that Keith Matthews ever experienced – being rejected by a man who had once loved him. But I didn't know! I mean, how could I have known? How could I have realised it was him? It was beyond the realm of my consideration. It was impossible.

Impossible. It can't be…

As I turned onto Sweet Briar Road I saw them disembarking the number 29. At first my mind didn't register what my eyes had observed. That could have been disastrous. If I'd carried on walking a moment longer they would have seen me. Fortunately my brain kicked in just in time and I threw myself behind a school to avoid detection. There they were. Clear as day. *It couldn't be... And yet it was.* Perhaps Old Pete had spilled the beans and told them that we lived in Hellesdon. Perhaps they had just followed us there somehow... Perhaps they had been stalking us the whole time, waiting for us to slip up – waiting for us to make a mistake. No... hang on...

Winston had a little map and seemed to be asking a passer-by for some information. Gerald was resting on a bench nearby, tucking into some sort of flan. If they knew where we were hiding out then we would be dead already. So they didn't know – they couldn't know... Most probably all they had to go on was the name of our suburb. Well that wasn't going to get them very far... Even if they did manage to find out where we lived then we wouldn't be there – we'd be at the veterinary surgery. They would never think to look in the veterinary surgery...

But what about our past selves? Of course – I kept forgetting about our past selves. They had no idea what kind of danger they were in. They wouldn't know Gerald and Winston to be a danger if they saw them. They wouldn't try to run, or hide, or defend themselves. They were like rats in a trap.

No. No they weren't. I had forgotten the rules again. Everything that has happened *will* happen. It is inevitable. Gerald and Winston didn't manage to track us down. They didn't find our house. They didn't try to attack us. Our past selves were protected by inevitability. Neither Gerald or Winston was going to get to them. After all, it's not like either of us had any memory of being attacked in the night by some old man...

Suddenly it all fell into place. Who was it? Gerald or Winston? It seemed so long ago now, and I had done my best to block out that memory. I couldn't remember what the old man looked like. I couldn't remember his face. I don't think I ever really *looked* at his face. I didn't want to. I couldn't bear it. But it was one of them. It *had* to be. There was no other explanation. They must have kept some of Oscar's cheese – that would explain how it came to be in our possession in the first place. But what then? The body disappeared! So maybe, whichever one of them it was, they didn't die after all. They are both fairly hardy folk, after all, and both have managed to withstand a blow from *The Guinness Book of Records* on a previous encounter. There was only one thing for it. If they were tracking us, we had to start tracking them. I could feel the answers dangling in front of me like a carrot on a stick. So close – and yet not quite within my reach. But they soon would be. They soon would be…

SEVENTEEN

THE MASTERPLAN

The moon rocks scattered in slow motion beneath my feet as I skidded across the ground beside him, digging *The Guinness Book of Records* into the back of his knee and sending him toppling over, flailing wildly. The man with the breakfast sword wasn't going to get the better of me this time… Not *this* time! This time I had him. I sprung to my feet and held the book in front of me, ready to defend against another tirade of aggression from my demonic doppelganger. He struggled to stand and turned to face me, lifting his sword in the air...

But he did not advance.

Very slowly, the man with the breakfast sword raised his other arm and pointed to something behind me, urging me to turn and look at whatever it was that had caught his attention.

Yeah right. Like I was going to fall for the whole 'look over there' gambit… That was the oldest trick in the book! This is not a reference to *The Guinness Book of Records*, you understand. The oldest trick in *The Guinness Book of Records* is 'that trick where you make it look like you're pulling off your own finger, but you're not really pulling off your own finger.'

He remained still. I stepped back cautiously, vigilantly shielding myself with the book and keeping both eyes fixed upon my enemy. He began to gesticulate slightly, compelling me to turn around and look behind, but I did not comply. I knew that the moment my back was turned he would run me through with his breakfast blade… so I just stood there, watching and waiting. Seconds turned into minutes. Minutes turned into hours. Hours turned around in small circles until they were dizzy and needed a bit of a sit down.

And then Keith Matthews was barking.

And then Keith Matthews wasn't barking.

And then I turned around.

Keith Matthews was snuffling about, clearly searching for some morning eatables. Suddenly I was no longer on the moon. I was in my hallway. The man with the breakfast sword was nowhere to be seen, and the promise of a fresh new day was filling my heart with great merriment.

"Hip, hip, huzzah," I cried, clapping my hands together and jumping around. "Tis truly wonderful to be woken by the sweet and gentle kiss of morning light. Perchance what gaiety shall I indulge in on this fine, fine day?" The well-versed reader will of course recognise this quote as the opening line from *Who's Stolen Cheryl Cole's Pyjamas?* My subconscious was obviously still rife with memories of that fantastic play, and happier times...

Somebody squeezed a package through my letterbox. It fell to the floor with a thud - a neat little brown parcel tied up with string, sitting there on the welcome mat, inviting and delicious-looking. Keith Matthews was on it before you could say *Don't eat that parcel, Keith Matthews*, which is something I tried to say, but couldn't, because my mouth had disappeared and been replaced with a stapler. Helplessly I watched as my dog tore apart the parcel and devoured the entire contents in a matter of seconds. I couldn't move. My feet were glued to the spot. I knew what was coming next.

He disappeared. He disappeared into the very fabric of space – on a path that would ultimately culminate in his death.

Suddenly the room turned very cold, and a frosty wind blew open the front door with a loud bang. The man with the breakfast sword charged through, jumping through the air and launching himself in my direction. I had no way to defend myself – nowhere to hide – nowhere to run.

Time to wake up.

He thrust his sword through my tummy as the equally disconcerting reality of my waking life replaced the world of my dream. I sat up in my makeshift bed on the staffroom floor, panting, covered in sweat, gripping at the sheets in despair and confusion… But Wendy wasn't there to comfort me this time. Roger was gently dozing on the sofa a few feet away, and the rising sun was shining through the frosted glass windows. In my exhausted state I had dozed through the night, the day that followed the night, and then the night after that. Roger, to the best of my knowledge, had done the same. I had been out for so long that my eyes were sore and encrusted with those little eye-bogeys that accumulate as you sleep. I wiped them off and shook myself awake. I was back in the world.

And there was still a mystery to solve.

"Roger," I whispered, crawling over to his side. "Are you awake?"

"No," he mumbled. He was lying. I could always tell when he was lying.

"I need to tell you something," I said. "I wanted to tell you the other night but you were fast asleep when I got in."

"I'm fast asleep now." Another blatant lie…

"Listen," I said. "You remember the old man who I manslaughtered with *The Guinness Book of Records*?"

He mumbled a nondescript sound which suggested the affirmative.

"Well, I know who it was," I continued. "It was Gerald."

Roger sat up, his floppy man-boobs spilling over the covers as he turned to me in sudden alarm. "How do you know?"

"They're here, Roger. Here in Hellesdon. Obviously they're going to find us at home and try to murder us again – it all adds up..."

"Not really," said Roger. "That old man looked nothing like Gerald."

"Well, Winston then," I said. "It doesn't matter. Don't you see? It's all OK now. I really *was* acting in self-defence. I don't need to feel guilty anymore."

"No," said Roger. "As I remember it, he didn't look much like Winston either."

Damn it Roger.

Just when I had it all figured out he had to go and sneeze all over my buffet.

"It was one of them," I insisted. "It had to be."

"And why just one of them?" he asked. "Why not both of them? They tend to stick together, those two – wouldn't you agree?"

"Well perhaps that explains what happened to the body in the grass collector – perhaps the other one took his friend's body away."

"Or perhaps he wasn't dead," suggested Roger. "Which means that in a few days' time they'll both be back on the street and hunting us down again. I don't like it, Walt. I'm tired of all this. We've got to do something about those two."

I wasn't going to kill them. That was the problem. I'm no murderer. I'm a detective, not a mercenary – and a good detective doesn't go around killing people. Just look at the world's greatest detective – Batman. Batman doesn't kill anybody. Batman doesn't even use guns. Well, except when he's driving the Batmobile... There seems to be some sort of loophole in the morality of the concept of Batman which means that he's allowed to use loads of guns when he's driving the Batmobile. I have considered having some armaments installed on the Corsa in the same fashion, but KwikFit refused to quote me for the job. Perhaps it wasn't the best of ideas. Besides, if I'm honest, I'm loathed to place my vehicle in the hands of any organisation who don't know how to spell the word 'quick.' But back to the moral dilemma at hand...

We had to get Gerald and Winston out of our lives without ending theirs. It was a conundrum alright, but one that I felt perfectly capable of solving with a bit of time and a large mug of hot blackcurrant squash. I took a bit of paper and compiled a short list of our opponents' strengths and weaknesses...

STRENGTHS	WEAKNESSES
-Cunning	-Lack of physical strength
-Persistent	-Poor bladder control (possibly)
-Free public transport	-Nobody listens to old people
-Able to manipulate people by appearing as 'nice old gents'	

I showed the list to Roger, who pointed out that we didn't know for sure that they had poor bladder control, which is why I added the caveat 'possibly' in parenthesis. We studied the list together and enjoyed some ham on toast which Dr Farthing (female) made for us. It was a bit dry, but still very much appreciated.

It took me approximately 58 minutes to come up with my masterplan. I realised that I needed to focus on our opponents' weaknesses while being mindful of their strengths. *Nobody listens to old people.* That was the key. That was the weakness we had to exploit, and I knew exactly how we were going to do it… Well, not exactly – not at first – but I was nestling a clutch of mind eggs that was almost ready to hatch.

I turned to Roger. "Do you remember when you developed a gambling addiction when you were trying to overcome your alcoholism which cost you your job and ended your marriage?"

"Yes," said Roger, nodding. "I think I remember that."

"And do you remember the poker games you used to play in the cellar of the King's Arms?"

Roger looked worried. "Where are you going with this?"

"There was a man you used to talk about – someone who could get hold of fake IDs, forged documents, that kind of thing…"

"Dave Pottergate," said Roger, frowning. "What's he got to do with anything?"

"We're going to need his help."

Roger stood up and began pacing the room, frantically. This was the first time I had seen him on his feet since the crossbow incident, and I was glad to note his swift recovery.

"Oh no," he said. "No, no, no. I'm not going back to the Kings. They'll rip me apart in there. Don't you remember what happened with the poker game and the lawnmower keys?"

"I do," I said. "Which is why *you're* not going back there. But *I* am. They don't know me, after all."

"No Walt," said Roger. "This is a terrible plan. This is a really terrible plan."

Okay, to be fair, I had conceived some terrible plans in my time, but this was <u>not</u> one of them. It certainly wasn't as terrible as my plan to reinvent the wheel by attaching an mp3 player to it and painting it yellow. I called it *Wheel 2*, incidentally. At the time I was very excited about it, but it was difficult to elicit the same enthusiasm from anyone in a position to manufacture the product. My neighbour Steven told me about a television show in which contestants pitch ideas to a panel of rich investors who then ask questions and declare themselves 'in' or 'out'. I think it was called *Young, Dumb and Living off Mum.* I applied nine times and was never invited to audition, but that's another story, for another time…

"Here me out, Roger," I demanded, following him as he paced the room, like an unenthusiastic cat chasing a disabled mouse. "Surely this Dave character likes to do business? Well, I have some business for him."

"Do you know how much he charges for work like that?"

"I do not," I admitted. "But I have a very good relationship with the lady at the bank. I'm sure she can arrange a temporary overdraft on my account."

The lady at the bank was named Tiffany, and she had a dog named Bertie who Keith Matthews used to enjoy playing with when we went out for a walk. Sometimes I would then go back to her house for breakfast (like in the film). Please understand that she is <u>not</u> a love interest as she is much older than me and doesn't approve of The Facebook.

"So what's your plan?" asked Roger. "We can't just change our identities and flee – that's not going to solve anything."

"Ah," I said, playing my cards close to my chest, like a tyrannosaurus rex. "Who said anything about changing *our* identities?"

*

I entered the bank at half past one, dressed in one of Dr Farthing's smartest outfits. To be quite honest, it didn't fit me very well, and the ensemble attracted a bit of unwanted attention from the other customers in the queue. In retrospect, I should have asked to borrow some of her husband's clothes instead.

The queue had nine people in it and only two cashiers on duty at the time. Classic bank. For legal reasons I'm not allowed to tell you the name of my bank, but what I will say is this; it *is* one of the proper banks, and not some far-right political party which formed as a splinter group from the national front. I've never understood why my mother insisted on banking with the BNP when we lived in France, but then, I've never understood a lot of things that my mother did.

Since Tiffany wasn't one of the cashiers working that day, I realised that I would have to turn on the charm in order to get what I needed. I glanced at my reflection in the glass and shaped my hair into its trendiest possible shape before being called forwards.

Cashier number three please.

I leant on the counter casually, one leg crossed over the other, smiling coyly like John Travolta. I clocked the cashier's name badge immediately. His name was Billy.

"Hello sir," said Billy. "How can I help you today?"

"Hello Billy," I said with a kind smile. "That's a lovely tie you're wearing. Very snazzy. Where did you get it?"

Billy looked somewhat taken aback. I'd hit him with a sack-load of charm and he didn't know what to do with it – not at first…

"It's standard company issue," he said. "Everyone wears one."

"Well, you pull it off very well, I must say."

"Erm… thank you."

I could tell that Billy was warming to me, so I decided to hit him with my demands. "Okay Bill," I said. "I like you, so I'm going to cut to the chase. I need an overdraft - as much as you can give me. I need that money available in my account and I need it today."

Billy drew breath, clearly still recovering from all of the charm. "That's impossible. It takes a few days to get an overdraft approved."

I placed both hands on the counter and faced him, square on. "Damn it Billy, we don't have time for your corporate bullshoes! I need that money ASAP – capiche?"

My charming Fonzie-esque demeanour had somehow shifted into that of an Italian gangster. I don't know why, but I decided to roll with it…

"Well, if you fill out the forms today, then we can get things moving."

I thought for a moment. "Okay Billy, make with the forms…"

"Right," he said. "If you'd like to take them over to the waiting area and fill them in, I can deal with the next customer."

"Very good Billy," I said. "I like your style."

I thought it prudent to drop another compliment-bomb before concluding proceedings. I then casually picked up a pen from the counter and flipped it into my top pocket. This didn't quite make me seem as cool as I had intended, as it took six attempts to get it in there, and as I walked away it transpired that the pen was connected to the counter with a chain, culminating in a major kerfuffle.

I sat in the corner and filled in the forms, requesting the maximum £2000 limit. Surely this Dave character wasn't going to ask for more than that? No – it would be fine... This was a good plan – an excellent plan – and I was pulling it off with great aplomb.

Before signing the form at the end of the 16 pages of data collection, I ensured that I had read all of the terms and conditions in full. This took over two hours, which meant that by the end of the process Billy had gone and I was forced to try out my charms on a new member of staff. Her name was Ginene, and she had one of those nose piercings that I don't like. Also, she did this annoying thing with her little finger that made it click as she examined her hands with disinterest.

"Yeah?" she asked.

"Good morrow to you madam," I said, charmingly. "I've been conversing with your colleague Billy regarding the possibility of an overdraft on my current account."

"You what?" she said, entranced by her hand. When the news reported a drop in interest rates in the banking sector, I wasn't aware that they were referring to the staff! (LOLs!)

"I'd like to set up an overdraft. Here, I've completed all the relevant paperwork. And may I say what a lovely nose jewel you're wearing…"

She looked up from her hand and stopped clicking her little finger, engaging me with a smile for just a moment. I had charmed my way into her affections, if only for a few seconds… I was like Vince Charming – the principal character in my toy theatre production *Vince Charming: Charmed and Dangerous.*

"Thank you," she said, taking the papers through the slot at the base of her window. "It was a present from my boyfriend. He left it by the bed this morning – the sweetie. Anyway, I'll just need your debit card to process the application."

"Not a problem my dear," I replied, smiling and reaching into my pocket.

Things were going much more smoothly than I had originally suspected they would. I have to admit, it was a bit of an ego boost. You see, it may surprise you to learn that on more than one occasion my skills as an amateur detective have been called into question. For instance, when my friend Percy Trent-Derby had his laptop stolen at university, he hired me to investigate the crime and indentify the culprit. After much deliberation I concluded, in front of a room full of fellow students and several members of the metropolitan police force, gathered around the fireplace of a large Victorian living room (as I had requested), that Percy had in fact broken his laptop by <u>accident</u> and it had not been stolen at all…

I explained to the assembled that it was my firm belief he had lied about the theft in order to claim on the insurance. I also suspected that he had hired me to investigate as a sort of double-bluff to divert suspicion away from his fraudulent activities. As it turned out, his laptop had actually been stolen by a chap named Doug who lived on the Council estate around the corner and sold second hand laptops on a dodgy market stall. What made matters worse was that I had actually bought Percy's old laptop from Doug the day after it was stolen, as my own laptop had been stolen some three months prior to the crime (also, as it turns out, by Doug). It wasn't my finest hour, but now things were different. Now it *was* my finest hour…

I was no longer Walton Cumberfield the bumbling buffoon of Bryn Eithin. I was Walton Cumberfield – the finest detective in the Norfolk area – the perspicacious provocateur of Park Avenue (East). Nobody was getting the better of me! Nobody was foiling me this time! I was leaving no stone unturned, no T uncrossed, no I undotted. Everything was going according to plan.

"Bugger," I shouted, a little too loudly, as I remembered that my wallet had been stolen way back in the early chapters. "I haven't got my bank card. It was stolen way back in the early chapters."

"That's alright," smiled 'Ginene', still thoroughly charmed. "Have you got any other sort of ID on you?"

"No," I said, hanging my head in defeat. "Everything was in my wallet."

"I'm sorry," she said. "But we can't do anything without seeing some proof of identity."

"My name's stitched into my socks," I exclaimed, lifting my foot onto the counter excitedly. "See – it says here, Walton Cumberfield."

"I'm sorry."

"Please," I said. "I really need this money now. I'm a friend of Tiffany. Do you know Tiffany?"

"I'm sorry, sir. There's nothing I can do."

Suddenly Ginene went back to examining her hand.

"Please – you've got to help me."

Cashier number three please.

Ginene had already pressed the button to call up the next customer.

"Please. You don't underst-"

"You'll have to move along, sir."

"PLEASE!"

"Now sir."

Dang fudge it! I was so close!

I left the bank in a slump of depression and trampled along the slushy street to Roger's favourite bakery – a nice little place on the corner of Royston Road where he used to go with his wife in the 'good old days'. We had agreed to meet there after I concluded my business at the bank. It was one of those miserable winter days where the snow had all but melted away and a layer of damp, cold, icy muck covered the once brilliant white ground. Something about it reminded me of miserable times.

I think Roger could tell from my expression what the situation was as soon as I walked in.

"No luck then?" he asked, barely looking up from his doughnut.

I sighed, shook my head, and slumped ungraciously into the chair next to him. The waitress came over with a pot of hot coffee, but I politely declined it. I didn't feel like drinking at the time. I didn't really feel like doing anything. I felt utterly defeated – as though I was destined to fail – as though as soon as I got any sort of grip on the situation, destiny would see to it that my fingers slipped and I tumbled into an escapable pit of underachievement. Back to square one. Start again. The old drawing board…

"How did you afford those cakes?" I eventually asked, barely curious, my head resting in my hands.

"Dr Farthing leant me a tenner," he said. "Pretty nice of him, huh?"

I didn't look up. "I suppose."

"So what was the problem at the bank?"

"I don't have my bank card."

"How come?"

"Because my wallet got stolen!" I snapped. "Don't you remember?"

"Jeez, sorry Walt. A lot's happened since then, you know…"

"Yes, I suppose it has."

We didn't say anything for a little while after that. Roger chomped through a couple more doughnuts and slurped down a cup of black with two sugars. I pouted and fiddled with his smartphone, just because I liked holding it. I would have liked to update The Facebook, but it was still out of battery, and we didn't have access to a charger. Everything was miserable.

Until…

"Why are you eating so many doughnuts, Roger?"

"Because I'm hungry," he said. "I bloody love these doughnuts. Plus, if you buy four doughnuts, you get the fifth one free, and a cookie shaped like a heart – see?"

He held up the cookie. A free cookie shaped like a heart… but why? What was the occasion? Ginene's voice echoed through my mind.

It was a present from my boyfriend. He left it by the bed this morning – the sweetie…

Presents from boyfriends… Heart-shaped cookies... The melting snow had brought back miserable memories…

And just like that, I remembered what day it was.

"Happy Valentine's Day," I said, swinging out of my chair and leaping to my feet. "Now, how much of that tenner do you have left?"

Roger looked puzzled. "About six pounds."

"Give it to me."

"No. Why? What for?"

"Roger, this is no time for games. Give me the money."

Roger begrudgingly reached into his pocket and brought out the rest of his cash. I snatched it, perhaps somewhat rudely, and darted off towards the door. What can I say? I was on a tight schedule. I knew what I had to do and my window of opportunity was closing by the second.

"Where are you going?" he called out as I opened the door.

"I'm catching a bus," I told him.

"Whatever for?"

"Roger… I think I know who stole my wallet."

He grimaced with confusion and wiped some jam from his chin. "What do you mean? Who was it?"

I tipped him a wink and a furtive smile.

"It was me."

*

I *hope they have a McDonald's*, I thought, fondling through my remaining change as I disembarked at the bus stop near Bannatyne's Health Club. *I'm starving.*

As I walked across the car park I saw a man in a high-vis jacket fixing a clamp to the front wheel of my Corsa. The startling sense of déjà-vu instantly reminded me that they did *not* have a McDonald's. They really should get a McDonald's…

It was somewhere between an out-of-body experience and a memory – walking through that reception room again. There was Beth, legs up on the desk, phone tucked between cheek and shoulder, filing her nails like a cartoon secretary. There was the smoothie bar where Melanie had called me a 'smoothie' a few hours before. There was the sunbed where I would soon be hiding to avoid detection by the security team. Ah memories… But this was no time for nostalgia. I had a job to do…

Seeing as Beth was clearly not in a very vigilant frame of mind, I hurried down the corridor towards the male changing area as quickly as I could. She didn't say anything, of course, too preoccupied with her hands to notice. Honestly, why are women so obsessed with their hands? I rarely give mine a second thought. I suppose the concept of knowing something 'like the back of one's hand' carries far more clout when it comes from a woman. I probably couldn't even identify the back of my own hand if I had to select it from a police line-up of several hands. You may think this scenario absurd, but my neighbour Steven would tell you that it is a perfectly valid form of identity confirmation in a criminal investigation. In fact, this was the exact process by which they managed to identify the villain who stole his trousers from beneath the cubicle door when he was having a poo in Sainsbury's.

The changing room appeared to be empty, so I sneaked up to the block of lockers and tried to remember which one was mine. Fortunately, I always stick a small novelty sticker to the bottom right hand corner of my locker when I am using public changing facilities, and this occasion had been no exception. A small sparkly heart was twinkling at me from the edge of door number 12. I remember selecting it from my novelty sticker pack at about the same time that I wrote Melanie's card and planned our excursion. I closed my eyes and tried to remember how it felt to be so hopeful – so happy – so contented with life... But I couldn't. I just couldn't conjure the emotion any more...

Enough. As I said before, this was no time for nostalgia. I emptied my pockets onto the floor and rifled through the contents for something with which to pick the lock. Fortunately, I am one of those people who always has all sorts of bits and bobs in their pockets, torn between my desire not to litter and my lack of commitment to finding a public bin. *I'll just pop it in my pocket and throw it away later,* I always tell myself. But I never do. I never do...

Now, nobody has ever shown me how to break into a locker, so it goes without saying that I didn't really know what I was doing. My Dad once took me to B&Q at the weekend and said he was going to show me how to pick a lock, but it transpired that what he actually meant was he wanted me to help him choose a new padlock for his bicycle. We settled upon an Abus 70IB/45 45mm Brass Marine padlock which, as far as I am aware, continues to serve him well. Sadly the bike in question was stolen while we were in the shop, so he had to buy a new one that afternoon. It wasn't a very positive experience. Neither, I might add, was fumbling through my knick-knacks on the changing room floor at Bannatyne's in search of a safety pin or paperclip. Fortunately I managed to find both, and a bit of broken plastic which I think used to be part of one of those data memory stick things you put in a computer.

I wedged the chunk of plastic into the bottom of the key slot and twisted it slightly to the right. Nothing happened, of course, but I wasn't expecting it to. That's not how it works in the films. In the films they use a kind of long, thin hook thing to unclick something at the top of the lock. I crafted my own sort of long, thin hook thing by bending out the paperclip into the appropriate shape, shoved it into the slot above the broken plastic and started poking around a bit. I could feel the bits inside start to move. Then there was a click. Was it working? It *was* working. I couldn't believe it. I was actually picking a lock! I poked around a bit more. Another click. Yes! I felt like such a bad-arse. I was like one of those bad arses out of *Oceans 11* or *The Great Muppet Caper.* Just a couple more clicks and I'd be in! I pushed my long, thin hook thing further into the lock and gently nudged what I assumed to be the final pin. Almost there…

Bang.

It was only the sound of the door swinging open, but as far as I was concerned it could have been the sound of a thousand bombs, all going off at once. I recoiled in shock and dropped my tools onto the floor, turning to see one of the members of staff who had entered the changing rooms with a mop and bucket.

I spun around and put my ear to the wall, tapping it in several different places.

"Yeah, jus' checkin' the walls, mate," I said in a bizarrely proletarian accent. I panicked, you see. I didn't know what else to do. Why would I be 'checking the walls'? It didn't make any sense! He was never going to believe *that.*

The young man plunged his mop into the bucket and slopped it onto the floor without looking up. He was onto me. I knew he was onto me. I frowned and stuck out my tongue slightly, as if concentrating. *Should I say something else?* I thought. *Will that make the situation more believable?*

"D'ya see the game las' night?" I asked him, keeping my head to the wall. "Bloody ref." I had to stay in character now – I was committed…

"Sorry, are you talking to me?" asked the young lad.

I nodded. "Yeah, mate."

"Oh. Well no, I didn't see it in the end. Too much coursework." He rolled his eyes and sighed a bit. "What was the score?"

I had no idea. To be honest, the fact that there even *was* a game was a turn up for the books. But now he wanted to know the *score*?

Why was he giving me the third degree? I mean, was he testing me? Waiting for me to slip up? *What was the score?* Sure, it's easy to make up a couple of numbers, but I didn't even know which sport I was referring to. Football, would be the most logical assumption, but I have never watched football, because, as I mentioned earlier in the novel, I am not a fan of racism. I have no idea how football is scored. Roger would know. He plays for Manchester City. At least, I think he plays for Manchester City, since when they win he always says "we did really well last night".

I bought some time by listening to the wall again for a bit, but before long I knew that I would have to say something. *Come on Walton, it's not that difficult. Just say two numbers!* "19-7..."

The young chap stopped his mopping and looked at me. "19-7? Are you serious? Who won?"

I thought very quickly, searching for a vague word that could apply to most football teams. "City won, innit. City is well good."

"Wow," he said, leaning on his mop and staring in disbelief. "But 19-7? I mean, that's a record breaking score."

"Yeah," I agreed. "Belter."

"Was that on aggregate?"

"No," I replied. "It was on BBC One."

Swish. I returned to my wall examinations, confident that the boy had bought into my charade. He carried on mopping up for several minutes, and I had no choice but to continue 'checking the walls'. What a stupid thing to say – I mean, what was I checking them *for*? Sometimes I think I'm not as clever as I think I am, which is a paradox, and therefore can't be true. Or can it? Wait… it doesn't matter. The point is that after a while the young man packed up his equipment and left, allowing me to return to my amateur lock-smithing.

As I went about my work, I glanced over to the door of the steam room. Any minute now, someone would be coming in to turn down that temperature dial. Any minute now, my former self would start to recover from heat exhaustion and begin to regain consciousness. Any minute now… My hands began to shake as my anxiety intensified. I *had* to get that wallet. It *had* to be me. Whoever turned down that temperature gauge would be coming through the door at any moment, and I couldn't let them see…

Wait a minute…

As the lock clicked open I was struck by both the locker door and a startling epiphany. When I woke up in the steam room that day, I was alone. Whoever turned down that thermostat didn't want to use the steam room itself. But why? Why would you reduce the temperature unless you wanted to use the facility? It didn't make any sense! The only explanation was that the person who did it was somebody who knew of my predicament and wanted to help me out. Gort perhaps? No. Okay, he was the only person who knew I was in there – but he didn't strike me as the type to have an attack of conscience… It couldn't have been him. Which meant that the only person present who knew of my predicament and had any possible inclination to help me out of said predicament was… well… *me*!

"Sorry about this Walton," I said, slipping my wallet into my pocket. "But I'll make it up to you."

And make it up to me I did. For if it wasn't for me, then who knows how long I would have remained comatose on that steam room floor, pale and incapacitated, sweating away my sanity like a bleached whale…

I crept over to the steam room controls, twisted the dial to the minimum temperature, and exited the changing rooms.

Another job well done.

Well, not quite…

I tried to look nonchalant as I sauntered back through the reception area, not wishing to arouse too much suspicion. I was a thief now, after all, although I'm not sure if it really counts as a crime if the victim in question is yourself. Beth was still there, of course, happily reading a magazine. She didn't even look up as I strode past her towards the door, but I didn't ever think that she was going to be a problem. Oh no – *she* wasn't going to be a problem at all.

When I saw them outside the front door I immediately doubled back inside and hid behind a large pot plant. She was standing in that way that she stands when she wants people to notice her body – cocking her hips to one side and puffing out her chest to exaggerate her ample bosom. Gort appeared to be doing the same, clearly flexing his man-muscles at her as they said goodbye, grinning wickedly and staring at her breasts like a ruthless rutabaga. He said something and she laughed. It wasn't a proper laugh – not like when *I* make her laugh – but the fact that she forced it somehow made it worse. Then she touched his *arm.* I thought I was going to be sick and then I wasn't sick. Then he made a move to leave and she stepped towards him. *Don't kiss*, I thought. *Please don't kiss.* She put her arms around his tree-trunk of a neck and kissed him on the cheek. I saw his big courgette fingers wrap around her tiny waist and give her a little squeeze. Then he looked down at her body again, clearly undressing her with his eyes (not literally, although that would have been very impressive).

I couldn't watch any more. I scurried back across reception and ducked into the cafeteria where I hid behind a *Dennis the Menace* comic and enjoyed a half-eaten fruit scone someone had left underneath it. What a horrible day this was turning out to be! Not only had I been reduced to stealing like a sneaky bandit, but I was being forced to relive the heartbreak of my relationship ending all over again. Now, in case you are wondering, I haven't forgotten about what happened with Wendy back in the 50s. I'd just like to reiterate the fact that Melanie and I were most definitely off-again when *that* happened, and also, if you want to get technical, Melanie hadn't even been born yet. This thing with Gort was different. You can call me hypocritical all you like, but it *was.* And before you say anything, I am <u>not</u> fickle. I loved Wendy and I still love Melanie. Perhaps in the usual circumstances that would be wrong, yes, but when you consider the fact that I was travelling through time... Oh forget it; I don't have to explain myself to you! Haven't you ever seen *Goodnight Sweethearts*? I think the truth is that if I had the chance to be in an actual relationship with either one of them then I would love *only* that person, but as it stood, I couldn't help but pine for the both of them. And when I say that I'm pining for Wendy, I mean the young Wendy from the 1950s– not the Wendy who currently lives at Rodney Rooney's. I mean, I still love that Wendy, in many ways, but… she's in her eighties, for goodness sake! That would just be weird…

I dropped my magazine for a brief moment and saw that Melanie was sitting on a nearby table, looking grumpy and regularly glancing at her watch. *Poor Melanie*, I thought. I wanted to go over to her. I wanted to go over and explain everything – to make everything better again – to win her back and put things straight… but what was the use? She wouldn't believe me. At any rate, the universe wouldn't let me do that. And as if to prove that point, she got up and left the café with a sour look on her face.

And I was alone.

"Alright, what the hell is this?" shouted Dan Prescott, bursting through the door. "This better be good! I was on my break!"

One of the employees abandoned her post at the salad counter and scooted over to Prescott. "I'm so sorry Mr Prescott," she said, timidly. "It's this man – he says he's the new catering manager. I think he's a bit mad…"

Oh no.

You know when you've done something embarrassing, and people say to you "if only you could have seen yourself…" well they're not wrong… It was a terrible thing to behold. There I was, ladling peas out onto imaginary plates, humming the tune to *Uptown Girl* and barking orders at the other caterers. Melanie had missed my performance by mere seconds…

"How's that casserole coming along?" I shouted. "Auntie Margaret will be here at six, and she doesn't take kindly to tardiness. Sunjin, stop talking to that elephant and help the others. Time is against us, friends!"

I couldn't face it. Prescott was storming behind the counter now, gritting his teeth and fuming.

"Now, just who do you think you are?" he shouted.

God knows, I thought, picking up the magazine and concealing my face. *Time to go now, before things really start kicking off…*

I affected an innocent whistle as I strolled out of the cafeteria and back, once again, into the reception area. In a matter of seconds the security team would be searching the building for someone matching my description, and not wishing to be 'roughed up' by a bunch of muscle-bound mercenaries, I decided that a very hasty exit was in order. I dropped the magazine on a chair and picked up the pace, almost breaking into a jog as I headed towards the front door. Nearly there now… so close to freedom…

No! No! No!

I spun around and dived behind a nearby sunbed. A busload of pensioners was heading towards the entrance, led by none other than Rodney Rooney himself. I couldn't let him see me – he would probably want to talk to me about putting on another toy theatre production or helping out at the home. Let's not forget, I hadn't done anything to anger him yet. Behind me, the security team were gathering at the reception desk. I was surrounded. There was no way out…

Or was there? Rodney and his 'crew' marched through reception and gathered for a roll call. At any moment I would be 'made' by either him or the security team. I had to hide – but where? There was only one solution. I lifted the lid of the sun bed and crawled inside.

Safe at last. I laid there and tried to listen – tried to hear if the oldies were dispersing, or if the security team had left the area. It was no good. The buzzing sound of the sun bed was too much. *Why didn't I switch it off before climbing inside?* Because I'm an idiot, that's why. I'm an idiot, and everyone thinks I'm an idiot… well, you get the idea. I don't know if you've ever been in a sunbed fully clothed before, but it's not a very pleasant sensation. Still, at least I was concealed. For now…

A few moments later the lid flew open and a man attempted to crawl inside next to me. I tried to inform him that the booth was occupied, but he wouldn't listen and brought the lid back down on us before I really knew what was going on.

"Hello," he said. "What's your name?"

I said the first name that came into my head. "Dennis. Dennis the Menace."

"It's nice to meet you, Mr the Menace," he said. "My name is Percival Bum-Trumpet."

"No it isn't," I told him. "It's Walton Cumberfield."

"Is it? Oh yes, I remember. What are we doing in here?"

"We're hiding," I told him. "Hiding from the security team."

"Why? What have we done?"

"*I* haven't done anything. It's you who's been causing all the trouble. Which, I suppose, by extension, means that I'm implicated too."

"You're a funny sort of chap," he said. "I'm going to write a poem about you."

"You do that," I said. "I'm getting out of here before I get burnt again."

They say that talking to yourself is the first sign of madness, so I decided to get out of there as soon as possible. I lifted the lid and tumbled out, shutting Past-Walton in behind me.

"There he is!" shouted one of the security team. "Over there!"

A mustachioed middle-aged gentleman with a beer-belly and three chins was waddling over to me as fast as his stumpy little legs could carry him. He was clearly not in good shape, despite the fact that he worked in a health club. The irony was not lost on me, but I didn't have much time to dwell on it, since he was very suddenly joined by several younger, more athletic security guards.

Time to run again. I *really* should have hit the gym while I was there...

*

"So what happened then?" asked Roger, reclining in his favourite spot in the veterinary surgery staff lounge.

"I ran across a busy road and they were too sensible to follow," I said. "It was a daring move, but I didn't have a lot of choice in the matter. As luck would have it, nobody was hurt."

"So you've got your wallet?"

"I have. I'll go to the bank first thing tomorrow and then we'll be cooking on gas, metaphorically speaking. Anyway, what have you been up to?"

"You'll love this," he said, sitting up excitedly. "When I was on my way back from the bakery, you'll never guess who I saw..."

I loved Roger's little games. "David Attenborough," I guessed.

"No," he said. "Come on – who do you think it was?"

"Terry Wogan. It was Wogan wasn't it?"

"No, it wasn't Terry Wogan. Why would I be so excited about seeing Terry Wogan?"

"Why *wouldn't* you be excited about seeing Terry Wogan?" I asked him, suspiciously.

"Look, it wasn't Terry Wogan, alright. It was Gerald and Winston."

"Well, don't tell me!" I snapped. "That completely defeats the point in the game!"

"Did you hear what I said?" he roared. "I've found Gerald and Winston! I followed them. They're staying in a B&B about a mile away from here."

Good old Roger. That was some fine detective work, all right. I didn't tell him this of course, as I still needed him on his A-game and I didn't want him to get complacent.

"What are you after, some sort of medal?" I asked him, cynically.

"Hey – I thought you'd be impressed! I know where they're staying. It's a breakthrough."

"It's a start," I said. "But it's only a start. I need you to keep an eye on them – day and night – we have to know what they're up to."

"Right," he said. "And you're going to do what exactly?"

"I'm going to sort out the money and speak to your friend at the King's Arms. Or did you want to do that? Honestly Roger, sometimes-"

"Alright!" he interjected. "Have it your way. I'll get over there first thing in the morning."

I cleared my throat and crossed my arms. "Day *and* night Roger. No slacking."

"You want me to go over there *now*?"

"Right now. They could be anywhere. Heck, they could be right outside for all we know…"

Roger sighed and laid back down. "I need sleep, Walton. I can't stay awake indefinitely."

As I suspected… He was getting complacent…

"Fine," I said. "Then we'll take it in shifts. But I have to be at the bank first thing, so I'm sleeping now."

"Good night then," said Roger, rolling over and curling up in a tired lump of grump. "See you in the morning."

"Don't worry Roger," I said, shutting my eyes. "It will all be over soon."

EIGHTEEN

MISCELLANEOUS HELLESDON 'HELL' PUN

Dave Pottergate charged me £1800 for his services, which left me just enough money to buy some snacks, some fresh trouserpants and a digital picture frame for Dr Farthing as a token of my gratitude. 'What services?' I hear you ask… Well, we'll get to that. But for now just sit back and enjoy the epic conclusion of my story – the action-packed, white-knuckle, edge-of-your-seat finale to this exhilarating adventure…

Are you ready? Perhaps you'd like to go and fix yourself a drink – maybe a bowl of crisps or nuts? Unplug the phone, log out of your Facebook account… Put the children / elderly relatives to bed. Empty your bladder if you need to. Relax in your favourite chair. Smoke a cigarette, if it is your custom to do so. Don't get ash all over the book though, you'll spoil it for the next person who wants to read it – which could be you… Have you done all that? Good – then here we go…

Thwack!

I landed a right hook on the side of his hooded face, sending him tumbling over into an impressive cartwheel. I lunged for him again, but he doubled over backwards and averted my jab, flipping into a backwards somersault and kicking me in the chest. I fell onto my bottom with a painful crunch. We were surrounded by many characters, both good and bad, cheering and jeering at the appropriate moments.

Suddenly the man in the hooded cloak unsheathed his breakfast sword. He was tiring of this dance. It was time to end things. The crowd gasped as I dodged one, then two, then three of his swipes. The fourth one caught me in the leg, but it was only a flesh wound. I stumbled away from him but he didn't let up. A fifth strike, then a sixth. I kept dodging and he kept on coming. Seven. Eight. The crowd roared with excitement. Nine… 10. I fell down and rolled away. 11. 12. He was towering above me now. Unlucky 13. Once again, as he lifted his weapon, I knew I had been defeated.

Then, out of nowhere, a Nova-Scotia Duck Tolling Retriever flew through the air and knocked my assailant to the floor, nipping at his cloak and growling wildly. Keith Matthews had materialised in my subconscious and leapt to my aid. I turned to see Christopher Stephens and Mr Perks, looking on and smiling. Tintin attempted to counter this development by commanding Snowy to attack, but since Snowy is a really rubbish, tiny little bastard dog, Keith Matthews bit his head off and ran away with it down a nearby crater, leaving Tintin mopping the tears off his perfectly-round, Belgian face.

I rose to my feet and picked up the breakfast sword. Its grip was a fat slimy sausage, its pommel a fried tomato, the cross-guard a slice of fried bread and its scabbard a long, sharp shard of crispy bacon. It was mildly disgusting and greasy to the touch, but it was mine now, and I wasn't giving it up... The man in the cloak stood up and pulled down his hood. Once again, he revealed himself to be myself (Walton Cumberfield).

"You can't kill me," he said. "I am you."

"No you're not," I said, pulling back the sword. "You're an idiot. You're an idiot, and everyone thinks you're an idiot and you'll always be an idiot and I hate you! You'll never amount to anything! You bloody berk!"

I plunged the streaky scabbard deep into his chest, his face exploding in shock as a shard of light beamed from the wound. The crowd went wild. Roger (who was dressed as his drag-queen alter-ego, Mrs Livingstone) took out some maracas and began to party like a Brazilian. Many others followed suit. My enemy faded into forgotten memories and disappeared, his cloak dropping to the floor like a discarded tissue. Melanie let go of Gort's arm and ran towards me, wrapping her arms around me and kissing me. I looked at Wendy, who was standing with the others. She was smiling at me and nodding, a few tears in her eyes. Melanie held my face in her hands and stared at me very seriously.

"Walton," she said. "I can see your testicles."

I cocked an ear towards her. "What did you say?"

"I can see your balls, man! Cover yourself up!"

Dr Farthing was standing in front of me, holding a cup of coffee in one hand and a Cornish pasty in the other. "For goodness sake," he said. "My staff have a right to use their lounge without having to look at your dangly balls all day. Why are you asleep anyway? It's only eight o'clock…"

The moon had faded smoothly into the reality of the surgery lounge. I hastily reached down and popped the offending appendage back into my underpants.

"Sorry, Dr Farthing," I said. "My sleep patterns have been a little disrupted of late."

That was true enough. Roger and I had been sharing the responsibility of watching the 'gruesome twosome' for the last couple of days and I had somehow ended up with the night shifts.

"Well you'd better get up and sort yourself out," he said. "Roger just called. He wants you to meet him – sounds urgent… He's by the climbing frame near your house, for some reason."

That's odd, I thought. *I wonder what he's up to…*

I got up and put on one of the fresh pairs of trouserpants I had bought with the overdraft money. It felt good to be in clean clothes again after all this time. I went to the sink and washed my hands, face and underarms with washing-up liquid. I had a feeling that tonight was going to be a big one, and I needed to be ready for it. Tonight was the night that either Gerald or Winston would break into the house and make an attempt on my life. We *had* to see how it all went down. That must have been what Roger was calling about. I pocketed my wallet, house keys and Roger's smartphone, thanked Dr Farthing for his hospitality, packed up the rest of the time cheese and marched out into the night like a valiant warrior on the eve of some great battle.

When I arrived in the park a few minutes later, the whole place was deserted. A faulty streetlight flickered over the silent road like a dying flame, and the wind turned cold like the icy breath of a giant snowwoman. The hairs on the back of my neck stood on end as I walked over to the climbing frame and sat down on one of the bars. Roger was nowhere to be seen. Across the street the lights in our house were still on. Past Roger would have been watching the telly, and I was probably sulking in my room. I wondered what would happen next as I gripped the cold metal around me. My hands started to shake.

"Pssst."

Either one of the local louts was opening a can of lager nearby, or somebody was trying to get my attention. I listened closely and scanned my surroundings.

"Pssst. Over here."

Someone *was* trying to get my attention. That was reassuring. I was glad it wasn't one of the drunks from St Barnaby's Close. I didn't have time for their shenanigans. A head popped out of one of the bushes nearby. I squinted and allowed my eyes to adjust to the darkness.

"Roger?" I whispered. "Is that you?"

"Walton? Oh, thank God… Get over here!"

Roger was standing in almost exactly the same spot as where I had burnt my leavings a few days before, but I didn't tell him that.

"What is it, Roger?" I asked. "What's the sitch?"

'Sitch' is short for situation. I decided to throw it in because I felt it reflected the urgency of the mood.

"Over there," said Roger, pointing at something. "Outside number 37…"

I glanced over at where he was pointing and immediately saw what he was referring to. A clapped-out old hatchback, parked up at the side of the street, with two shadowy figures inside. I'd recognise that car anywhere (except in Birmingham).

"Gerald and Winston," I said. "I knew it."

"They've found us" said Roger. "What do we do?"

"Well, we know that whichever one of them goes into that house isn't coming out again. I suggest we stay here and keep an eye on the other one – see what he does..."

"Agreed," said Roger. "I thought you might say that, so I brought some beers along. You can't have a stakeout without beers."

"Are you sure? What about your life-shattering alcoholism which cost you your job and your marriage?"

Roger sighed and popped open a bottle. "Pah, I'm in a good place with that."

We sat there in the bush, shared a few beers, smoked a few cigarettes and waited for stuff to start 'going down'. I felt like one of those cool policemen from the American TV shows – dark, gritty and ready for anything. I asked Roger if he wanted to talk about 'birds and that' to make the experience seem even more authentic. He opened the discussion with some observations on the migratory habits of barnacle geese. Roger would never be one of those cool policemen from the American TV shows. If I were a character from television, I would probably be Magnum or Jack Bauer. Roger would be Bungle from *Rainbow*...

When all of the lights went off in our house, we crept forwards a bit to get a closer look at what Gerald and Winston were up to. It wouldn't be long before one of them left the vehicle and made their way inside number 42. The front door was left wide open, after all.

"Any minute now," said Roger, crouching in a state of readiness. "Something's about to kick off."

I was holding an empty beer bottle in my right hand, and I could feel it quivering. Something had been building inside me ever since Oscar had explained the rules of time travel to us. "You can't change the past," he had said. "What has happened has happened. You can't alter the course of events that have already transpired."

The universe won't let you.

It was a bit like when you stand on the edge of a big drop, or the platform of a train station. You know, when a small part of your brain, a tiny, tiny bit, has an urge to jump off – or when you're talking to a really, really important person, like Glenn Johnson, and you find yourself completely preoccupied with the fact that you could punch him in his face. Not that you *want* to punch him, you understand – just that you *could.* It would be possible to do so, if you were so inclined. And that knowledge keeps building and building – getting stronger and stronger and burning a hole in your brain. I suppose that's what was happening to me with the whole 'paradox' thing. If I wanted to, I could hurl the beer bottle at their car – chuck it right through the windscreen – stir things up a bit – stop them from going inside. I could create a paradox. I didn't *want* to, you understand, but…

I couldn't control it. My arm lifted to shoulder height and my wrist flicked the bottle away from me with a great deal of force.

"What the hell are you doing?" hissed Roger.

"I…"

The bottle landed on the roof of their hatchback with a loud thump, causing the shadows inside to recoil and spin about in surprise.

"What did you do that for?"

"I don't know…"

Had I created a paradox? Was the universe going to implode? Of course, it wasn't – you know that – otherwise how would I be able to write this story? How would you be able to read it, for that matter? No – the universe didn't implode, because I hadn't created a paradox. Everything was happening exactly as it should have done. You'll see why in a moment...

Gerald and Winston hobbled out of their car and walked as briskly as they could in our direction.

"It's alright," I said. "They won't see us. It's too dark."

First one torch lit up, then the other.

"They've got torches, you fool!" snapped Roger. "What are we going to do?"

"Maybe we'd better run," I suggested, scrabbling to my feet. "Come on…"

I grabbed Roger by the arm and headed for the road behind us. Gerald and Winston would have been able to see us, I knew that, but

I was confident we could outrun them, and they seemed to have left their crossbow at home, which came as a considerable relief.

"Go after them, darling," shouted Winston. "I'll stay here and take care of business."

Of course! That was it. Winston went in alone because Gerald had to follow *us*. I hadn't created a paradox at all – I was always supposed to throw that bottle!

Universe 1 – 0 Walton Cumberfield.

"Wait!" I said, stopping Roger in his tracks. "This isn't going to work."

"What?" he snapped. "What are you trying to do?"

We could no longer see the house. We could no longer keep track of what was going on. I had to know. I had to be sure…

"Follow me!"

We ducked behind a row of parked cars on an adjoining street and swiftly but silently made our way back to the house from the other side. Gerald was still walking around the park, shining his torch at the trees and hedges. We had given him the slip, for now at least… Winston was sitting back in the hatchback again, putting on a pair of leather gloves. I couldn't see what else he was wearing, but I remembered the gloves…

"Come on," I said. "We'll hide in the garden."

We crossed the road and found ourselves at the side of the house, our bodies pressed flat against the garden wall. I gave Roger a 'leg up' and he attempted to climb over. He failed, I hasten to add. He then offered me a 'leg up' which in hindsight was a much more sensible idea as I am a lot more sprightly and weigh at least two stones less than he does. I climbed to the top and lowered myself down on the other side, crushing some of my favourite roses in the process.

"I'm over," I hissed.

"Great," said Roger. "Now what?"

We hadn't thought it through. If Roger couldn't get over with my help, then how was he going to get over on his own? *Think Walton, Think…* I crept further down the flowerbed to where the garden hose reel was secured to the brickwork.

A light went on inside the house. Roger's bedroom. It was all kicking off.

I unravelled the hose and tossed one end over the wall.

"What's this?" asked Roger.

"Can you reach it?"

"I think so."

"Then climb, man, climb!"

I could hear voices inside the house now – it was Roger and I. It had happened. Winston was dead and we were flapping about, debating how to dispose of the body.

"Come on, Roger. We haven't got a lot of time!"

The hose went taught and I heard Roger's feet shuffling against the bricks on the other side. He was grumbling and groaning, but it sounded like he was making progress.

"You can do it," I said, encouragingly. "Come on Roger. Just a little bit further."

"You can't even see me," he spluttered.

"But I *believe* in you," I said. "I don't have to see it to *believe* it…"

"What are you talking about now?"

He rolled over the top of the wall and almost squashed me as he fell sideways into the flowerbed with a great big 'plop'.

"Fuck!" he screamed. "That was my bad arm!"

"Less of the potty-mouth, Roger," I scolded him. "What *will* the neighbours think?"

Roger gave me 'the finger' and struggled to his feet. He gazed up at the illuminated windows and shot me a look.

"That's right," I said. "Winston's dead." I bowed my head and crossed my chest like they do in church. I don't know why – it just seemed like the most appropriate thing to do.

"What now?" Roger asked.

"Follow me."

For the next few minutes we hid in the hedge behind the garden shed. I didn't like it. It was tight and prickly and full of bugs that crawled about on my face and neck. I hate that sort of thing. Spiders are the worst. My mother always used to say that they were much more scared of me than I was of them. This is utter rubbish of course, as I would never crawl into a spider's bedroom when it was sleeping and hide under its bookcase. I'd be too scared to do that. Clearly this isn't true of the spider when it comes to *me*, *my* bedroom and *my* bookcase... Also, once when I saw a tarantula at Bristol Zoo I screamed and wet myself. The spider did no such thing. My mother suggested that the spider was a lot older than I was, and that's why it didn't do that, but I looked it up in my encyclopaedia and tarantulas don't live to the age of 12. Stupid Mum!

Eventually we heard our own voices approaching the shed. Our past selves opened the doors and began the process of faffing about with Roger's ride-on mower.

"Are you sure about this?" asked Past Roger.

"Nope, but do you have any better ideas?" came my own voice.

"We could wait… Hide him in the shed until you get your car back."

"What? Just leave his corpse to rot in the shed until my new bank card arrives? That's hardly very dignified, is it? We need to get him buried as soon as possible."

"You're right," said Roger. "Better he be in the ground before the Police start looking for him."

I heard myself struggling to lodge a screwdriver into the mower's ignition. "Damn you Roger! Damn you and your bloody card games!"

I shot Roger a look and shook my head. He just shrugged and rearranged himself, pulling a twig out of his lower back. I held up a finger to shush him, even though I know he hates that. Suddenly the mower's engine roared into life.

"There. Now let's get going."

When we were sure that they had gone we tentatively emerged from our hiding place and Roger looked at me expectantly.

"What now, Sherlock?" he asked.

"Now we follow them," I said. "Gerald's going to be hot on their tail, and we need to stop him before anyone else gets hurt. But first we need to collect some supplies…"

I pulled my keys out of my pocket and unlocked the back door. We were in a hurry, certainly, but that didn't stop me from taking a moment to enjoy that wonderful feeling when you first get home after a long time away. I hadn't realised how much I missed that place until I walked through that door again. The warmth of the kitchen greeted me like a gentle cuddle from an old friend. Home… It's true what they say. There's no place like it.

Roger went to the cutlery drawer and started sorting through the sharpest knives we had at our disposal.

"What are you doing?" I asked.

He looked surprised at my enquiry. "I'm looking for a weapon."

"No," I said, firmly. "We need to scare Gerald, maybe even incapacitate him, but we don't want to kill him! Too much blood has already been spilt tonight. Don't worry - I have a plan - we need something to stun him with, and something else to tie him up…"

Roger nodded and trotted up the stairs while I looked in the fridge for something to level my thoughts. That beer had gone straight to my head, and I needed to get myself together before heading out again. I found half a Snickers and a bottle of *Star Wars* themed energy drink (George Lucasade) which I consumed in seconds before Roger returned from whatever he was doing.

"Sorted," he said, presenting me with his air pistol and the cord from his dressing gown. "Will these be alright?"

I smiled and took the goods from him.

"Perfect."

*

By the time we reached the other park, the ride-on lawnmower had already been abandoned at the tree-line. Our plan was to hide in the trees and wait for Gerald to turn up and retrieve his friend's body. I just hoped we weren't too late.

Roger loaded his air pistol as I looked around for a suitable place to conceal ourselves.

"Shouldn't we check that he's still in there?" asked Roger, nodding awkwardly towards the grass collector. I grimaced at the thought of having to see that body again. I'd had enough of bodies in grass collectors to last me a lifetime.

"I suppose you're right," I said. "If he's already been and gone then we're wasting our time here."

We popped open the catch and looked inside. The body was still there. Only…

"That's not Winston," said Roger.

"Of course it's Winston," I said. "Who else could it be?"

"It's not. It's not him. He has more hair than that…"

It was quite difficult to see in the dark, and the cadaver in question was all squashed together like a dead contortionist. Perhaps Roger was on to something stupendously sinister, since something certainly seemed seriously strange, but admittedly that was hard to say…

"We have to know," I said, taking a deep breath. "If that's not Winston, then the two of them could be anywhere."

"Alright," said Roger, turning on the mower's headlights. "Quickly then…"

We had packed the body in tight, so pulling it out again was very tricky – twisting out the various limbs in what seemed to be completely the wrong order, and using them to get some leverage on the rest of the corpse. I thought I was going to be sick but then I wasn't sick. Then Roger pulled at something which came off in his hands, and he was sick.

"Pull yourself together man!" I said. "What are you getting so het up about?"

"I just pulled his bloody hand off!" he yelled. "Oh Christ." He spat up some more.

I looked at the discarded limb lying on the floor by Roger's feet – flat, shiny and black. It wasn't a hand at all…

"That's his glove, you idiot! Pull yourself together."

I turned back to the body and resumed the task at "hand" (LOLs), using the cord from Roger's dressing gown to lasso the rest of the torso and pull it free from the compartment. Then, after a bit of a struggle and a few bile-inducing clicks, snaps and pops, the gentleman's remains spilled onto the grass like a broken scarecrow. I dragged the old man over into the beam of the headlights, and Roger steadied himself on the side of the mower.

"That's not him," he said.

I stared at the body. "You're right. I don't recognise this person at all."

"What's up with that?" said Roger, pointing at the gloveless hand. "He's only got three fingers."

I crouched down and examined his freaky mitts. Actually he only had *two* fingers – two fingers and a thumb, to be precise, but I suspected that this was no time for semantics. For a moment I thought that Roger might have pulled off the other two digits with the glove, but the stumps were healed over, and they had been for a long time. Plus, there's no way Roger is that strong.

"How very curious," I said. "Who is this chap?"

"It doesn't matter," said Roger. "We need to do something about-"

Whoosh!

We cowered like cowards as a jackdaw fluttered out through the trees above us and took off into the night. Gerald and Winston were both still alive, and I had a feeling they weren't too far away. One way or another, they had to be stopped. I could tell Roger was forming the same hypothesis, as he gripped tightly to his weapon, frantically cupping it from below with the other hand. I'm talking about his air pistol, of course – I didn't mean that last sentence to sound nearly as rude as it did. Sorry about that. The unidentified stiff was still lying in plain sight, illuminated by the mower's headlights. I flicked off the switch, took a moment for my eyes to adjust to the darkness, and without another word, I walked into the woods.

"What's afoot?" asked Roger, bringing up the rear.

"It's a weight-bearing anatomical structure on the end of a leg," I replied with a grin.

Roger scoffed. Now was clearly not the time for word-play – I knew that, but heck, what can I say? I was nervous. I thought I'd alleviate the tension with a bit of humour. It's just my way, I suppose. I would say anything to take my mind off the fact that we were walking blindly into a pitch-black forest in search of two hardened killers with nothing but an air pistol and a dressing gown cord.

An ominous breeze disturbed the foliage around us like a whispered warning. My broken breaths seemed to echo through the darkness as my heart pounded the inside of my chest like a desperate drunk at the door of a tavern. *When will it all end?* I thought, wishing with all my soul to be in any other place. *Why did this happen to us?* I tried to slow my breathing – tried to stop myself from shaking, but my bodily functions were beyond the control of my conscious mind. The fear had me now. The fear was in charge.

I had never felt so exposed – so naked in the blackness – creeping helplessly through liquid ebony like a myopic fish in search of a hook. It would be over soon. One way or another, our journey was nearly at an end. A bramble got caught on the zip of my jacket and sprung backwards, catching Roger in the eye with a sharp, whipping sound. He didn't cry out. He was in control. At least, I thought he was in control. I had forgotten about his hay fever.

"Muh… uh…"

"Are you alright?" I whispered.

"Ugh… Murgh… Ah…"

"Those are some very strange noises you're making."

"Ah… Ah… Ah… CHOO!"

Without thinking I leapt at Roger and knocked him to the ground. His sneeze was so loud that even the hardest of hearing would be able to pinpoint our position.

"Shhh!" I hissed (even though he hates that).

I didn't dare move, which was a little awkward as I was lying on top of him. Footsteps were approaching our location, quietly shuffling through the fallen leaves just a few feet away. I looked at Roger. His eyes were wide, his face was red and his teeth were biting down hard on his bottom lip. *Oh no,* I thought. *The fear has him.* And with fear comes adrenaline, and with too much adrenaline comes, well… you know by now how that goes. Then I realised that it wasn't fear on Roger's face at all. My right knee was jammed in his knackers. I rolled away to his side and allowed him to breathe a gentle gasp of relief. Then he gave me 'the finger'. Then we began to hear the hushed murmur of whispering voices. *Our* voices.

"It's us," I said, crawling through the undergrowth in the direction of the noise. "Come on."

Roger climbed awkwardly to his feet, picked up his air pistol, and followed me cautiously through the undergrowth. We could distinguish the content of the whispers now – familiar words from a not-so-distant past that seemed like an eternity ago in my mind.

"…We just say we're a couple of trolls..."

"Don't be stupid. Trolls live under bridges. There isn't a bridge around here for miles!"

Somewhere beyond the voices came the sound of a thick, raspy cough. It wasn't me, it wasn't Roger, and it wasn't Past Walton, and it wasn't Past Roger… The cough belonged to an older voice, somewhere on the other side of the path.

"They're everywhere," said Past Roger. "We have to get out of here."

"No. We should stand our ground. I will <u>not</u> be intimidated."

Perhaps inspired by my own words of courage, I dashed across the path and made my way towards the location of the coughing sound. I skidded to a halt in a pile of soggy soil and looked around. Roger hadn't followed. I had lost him in the dark.

"Who's there?" I heard my own voice cry. "Show yourselves!"

Where was Roger? Had he chickened out and left me to fend for myself? No, that didn't sound like something he'd do. Perhaps he ran into a tree and concussed himself – that sounded far more likely. What a plonker.

"Who's there? What are you doing out here at this hour? Are you from the cottages?"

I sat prone in the dirt as the voice of my past-self echoed around me. I was on my own now, but I had to keep going…

"We could ask you the same question," shouted a familiar voice. Gerald was only a few metres ahead of me. This was it. This was the moment. *Do or die, Walton… Do or die… Or both, of course…*

"We're cruising for sex!"

I'd forgotten about that. *What a bloody wally!*

"No we're not! Now, where are you? Show yourselves!"

I inhaled slowly and silently, my chest quivering. My opponents were old and infirm, but there were two of them, and Roger had disappeared with all of the weapons.

Damn it Roger.

I swung back on my heels and got ready to propel myself forwards. It was too late to back out now. I would have to take them on – unarmed and outnumbered. The last dance of Walton Cumberfield…

Clunk.

Some heavy object ricocheted off a tree above my head and landed in the bush to my right. I jumped back at first, assuming that someone was deliberately launching projectiles in my direction. Then I remembered. I reached into the bracken and wrapped my hands around a cold metallic cylinder. My torch. *Now* I had a weapon. *Now* I was ready.

A shaft of moonlight was cutting through the canopy and exposing my foes as silhouettes against the featureless flora that surrounded them. They were peering through a gap in the greenery, fists clenched, knees slightly bent, watching our past selves and preparing for the attack. Winston brandished a large stick in his right hand, while Gerald held tightly to one of those novelty-sized yard-long packets of Jaffa Cakes. My knuckles whitened as my grip tightened and I knew I was frightened. This gave me an idea for a poem but it *really* wasn't the time. *Where was Roger?* I needed him now more than ever…

Winston took a step back and raised his stick in the air. He looked at Gerald, who nodded in approval. This was it… this was the moment… I had to do something. I was *going* to do something. The universe wouldn't let me *not* do something. What that something was, I had yet to find out.

I cleared my throat.

The two men spun around to face me, holding their weapons in front of them defencively, scowling with bitter resentment.

"You!" shouted Winston. "What are you doing here?"

I didn't reply. I just held tightly to my torch and prepared myself for the inevitable onslaught.

"Get him!" shouted Gerald, suddenly dashing towards me and swinging his yard of Jaffa Cakes like a tangy truncheon. My heart jumped into my throat and suffocated me with dread. I couldn't move. I was completely stiff, my neck taught, my spine a solid plank of pure terror. My right arm jerked against the paralysis, but it was no use. I was done for. Gerald swung the Jaffa Cakes behind his head like a baseball bat and continued to charge, his old eyes burning with hate and some sort of conjunctivitis…

The paralysis released my legs, and only my legs… Before I knew what I was doing, I found myself fleeing back the way I had come, dodging through trees and branches, scratching myself to bits on the thorns and brambles that daggered into my path like the claws of invisible beasts. And then I fell. My foot must have caught on a stump or a vine and sent me toppling into the filth. I rolled onto my back and tried to right myself, but there wasn't enough time. Gerald was on top of me, his crinkled old face pressed hard against mine, gritting his teeth and pouring out all of his malice.

"We told you what would happen if we saw you again." he hissed. "We told you we would kill you."

"No you didn't," I said. "You never said anything of the sort. What are you talking about?"

Winston thundered through the ferns and into the clearing with a wicked smile on his colourless lips. You know – the kind of smile that you only ever see on a cartoon villain or Alan Sugar. A smile of inhumane joy, a smile of purest evil…

Gerald stood up and towered over me like a geriatric giant. He raised the Jaffa Cakes above his head and prepared to deliver the final blow. I closed my eyes and sobbed a single, secret tear. It was over. They say that your whole life flashes before your eyes just before you die, but it doesn't. Or at least, it didn't – which was a shame, because I was quite looking forward to that. What did happen is that time slowed down to an excruciating crawl – forcing me to endure the fear of death for even longer than I would otherwise have had to. I couldn't look, so I tried to close my eyes, but even that was so monstrously gradual that I was made to watch the slow approach of his weapon right up until the climax of his fatal swing.

Okay – well you're not stupid. You already know that the swing wasn't fatal. After all, this is a first-person narrative and if I was killed at this point then how could I be regaling you with this story? Also, Gerald is an 80 year-old man and he was attacking me with a tube of Jaffa Cakes… No, obviously I am not narrating this to you from beyond the grave – that would be mad. Don't worry... This isn't that sort of story. Saying that though, his attack was fairly vicious, and I did wince in agony for some time as he delivered blow after blow to my lovely face, my lovely body and my lovely bones.

It didn't last for long. The thin, card packaging of the Jaffa Cakes split and crumpled under the strain of his assault, a crumbly chocolate mess bursting forth all over my helpless, cowering form. When the beating reached an intermission, I turned up my head to see what was happening. Gerald was out of breath and bending over, wheezing noisily with his hands on his knees. Now it was Winston's turn. He rested his dirty boot on my stomach and raised his stick in the air.

Pop.

He stopped moving – frozen mid-attack like an epic sculpture with a look of pain and surprise on his face. The gentle whine of agony began to escape his mouth like the gradual whistle of a boiling kettle, building to a dull, sobbing moan as he staggered away from me, dropping the stick and clenching his buttocks in a comical display of anguish.

"What's wrong?" asked Gerald. "What are you doing?"

"Somebody…" gasped Winston. "Somebody shot me in the arse!"

I couldn't help it. I started laughing.

"Shut up!" shouted Winston. "You blithering imbecile! I'll get you for this!"

"Now now," I said, amidst an inescapable fit of the giggles. "You really should learn to turn the other cheek!"

Even Gerald laughed a bit at that one. Well, it was an *excellent* piece of improvised comedy on my part, you have to admit... Winston glared at his partner in crime, which only served to intensify his laughter even more. This, in turn, made me laugh hysterically, and then finally the collective mirth even infected Winston – shaking behind his frown as the giggles began to take hold.

We were all laughing – laughing in the forest like the Merry Men of old – chuckling together like a bunch of crazy children. There were tears in my eyes. Winston was roaring with glee. Could this be the common ground that united us after all this time? A simple joke? An effortless lampoon? The shared shedding of happy tears as we basked in the joy of my excellent witticism? Perhaps it could have been... But no... This was only the eye of the storm...

"Geronimo!"

Roger leapt out of the thicket like a mad matador with mad-cow-disease. He had tied the end of his dressing-gown cord around a lump of soggy bark, and was swinging it around his head like a medieval flail. I lunged forwards and tackled Gerald to the ground as Roger's weapon caught Winston in the stomach and knocked him into a nearby tree. I flipped Gerald over, pressing his face down into the dirt and bending his arm behind his back.

"Gerald," I said, with a definite hint of smugness. "I'm placing you under a citizen's arrest. You have the right to remain silent. You do not need to say anything but anything you do say will be taken as evidence and may be held against you in a court of law. No, I'm only kidding. How would we ever explain all this to a judge?"

Big LOLs.

Winston made a move towards Roger, who jumped back and levelled his pistol right at his face. Winston stopped. His expression was a mess of frustration and depression. He knew he had been defeated.

We used Roger's dressing-gown cord to tie Winston's right foot to Gerald's left foot. That would stop them running away, we thought – unless they were experienced veterans of the novelty 'three-legged-race' like my friend Percy-Trent-Derby and his cousin

Rick. Fortunately for us, they were not, and we were able to frog march them out of the forest like a couple of sad old Dads crossing the finish line on sports day after all the other Dads (like Billy Rymell's Dad).

Past Walton and Past Roger were by this point sound asleep in a clump of stinging nettles somewhere nearby. We found their spades lying in the dirt just a few feet away and used them to usher our enemies out of the darkness and into the soft scrutiny of moonlight beyond the trees. Roger sat on the ride-on lawnmower to recuperate. I think at some point back there he had OD'd on adrenaline again.

The stranger's corpse was still lying in front of the mower like an abandoned rag doll.

"Who the hell is that?" asked Winston, stopping in his tracks.

"We have no idea," I said. "We thought maybe you could shed some light on that one."

Winston looked at Gerald, who shrugged and shook his head. Their ignorance appeared to be genuine. They seemed too tired to bother lying about it.

"Where's your car?" I asked, standing over the body.

Gerald spat. "Like we'd tell you…"

I sighed. Why did everything have to be so difficult? We had beaten them. Why couldn't they just cooperate with us?

"Please?" I asked again. "Let's not do this…"

He looked me right in the eye and tensed every muscle in his face. "Go to hell."

Suddenly Roger bounced off the mower like a belligerent basketball and shoved his pistol into Gerald's mouth.

"Tell us where it is, you son of a bitch!" he screamed. "Tell us where it is or I'll pump your cake-hole full of lead." Clearly the adrenaline still hadn't quite worn off…

"Alright, alright," said Winston. "Calm down. It's just around the corner."

Roger stepped off and steadied himself on the mower.

"Is he alright?" asked Winston.

"He's fine," I said. "He has this thing with adrenaline... Isn't that right, Roger?"

Roger shook himself off and holstered his pistol. Well, he didn't actually have a holster, but he shoved it into the front of his trousers and tightened his belt to hold it in position. The barrel poked forwards and shaped a lewd lump in the middle of his crotch. I think I made a joke about that, but I can't quite remember. I was very tired by this point, you understand.

"Alright then," sighed Roger. "You two have to help us put this guy back in the grass collector."

Gerald and Winston looked at us as if we were crazy, which was rich coming from two men who had spent their lives protecting an immortal cow in a garden centre.

"Wait," I said. "We're not putting him back. We're taking him with us."

Roger frowned at me. "Why?"

"Because one way or another, this body is going to be gone by the morning... Remember? So, if we leave it here, then somebody else is going to find it, but if we take it with us now…"

"Then it was *us* who took the body all along," said Roger with a smile of realisation. "Very clever."

"I know," I said. "I am pretty clever, aren't I?"

"Not too clever," said Winston, folding his arms. "What do you plan to do with us? Hand us over to the authorities? You said it yourself – no judge is going to buy into all this madness… So, what? You're just going to keep us hostage forever? How long do you think that can last?"

"He's got a point, Walt," said Roger, picking up the spades. "What are we going to do with them?"

I tapped the end of my nose and tipped Roger a crafty wink.

"Don't worry, Roger. I always have a plan."

*

The funeral was short. None of us knew the deceased, after all, but we felt it appropriate to hold some sort of vigil none the less. Gerald and Winston were less than enthusiastic about the whole affair, but Roger and I said a few words to give the old stranger the best send-off that we could manage under the circumstances.

We buried him in that same field on the outskirts of Norwich right next to where Christopher and I had buried Keith Matthews a few days before. Perhaps, I thought, they would find each other in the afterlife. Of course, I didn't know if the deceased was even remotely fond of dogs, but something about the sentiment filled me with warmth and bittersweet contentment.

I thought about that moment for a long time afterwards. The ordeal was over, but the memories would haunt me forever. That night we all slept in Gerald and Winston's car, and I cried myself to sleep. Roger stayed awake for as long as he could, his gun trained on our prisoners, vigilantly keeping watch as they dozed away in the back seat. They didn't try to escape, of course. They were just as exhausted as we were. In fact, they didn't wake up until we arrived at our next destination. They didn't wake up until we arrived at their new home…

Rodney Rooney greeted me in his usual manner.

"Cumberfield? What the fuck are you doing here? I thought I told you-"

"It's alright Mr Rooney," I interjected. "I'm not staying. I'm just dropping off a couple of new arrivals."

Mr Rooney scowled at me and leant in to get a closer look at the two men in the back.

"What's going on here, Cumberfield?" he asked. "Who are these two?"

"This is my grandfather, Winston, and his friend Gerald."

Rooney scowled again. "Why are they tethered together with a dressing gown cord?"

"I don't know," I said. "They're quite mad, you see… Delusional, in fact." I had rehearsed this speech in my head a few times on the way there. "The thing is, they've been living with me for some years now. At first it was fine. We got along alright, had a laugh, played some canasta, that sort of thing… I mean, sure, they were a bit barmy but who isn't a bit barmy these days? Am I right?"

He didn't reply.

"So anyway, everything was going fine, until their minds started to deteriorate. They both started rambling on about cows and cheese and time travel. They started to see Roger and I as their enemies. Then they became violent…"

I managed to squeeze out a few fake tears. *Thank God I am such an excellent actor*, I thought.

"So you see, I can't face taking care of them anymore. They need professional care, and I can't provide that for them. I'm sure you understand."

Rooney's face softened up just the tiniest little bit.

"You can't just show up here," he said. "It doesn't work like that. It's not like the tip, you know."

"I know," I assured him. "And if you check your records I'm sure you'll find I've made all of the appropriate reservations."

He tightened his lips. "Really?"

"Really."

In the back of the car, Winston opened his eyes and yawned, gradually beginning to take in his surroundings. They yawn must have been one of those infectious yawns, because it made me yawn as well, and then Roger, and then Rodney Rooney, who opened the back passenger door with an apathetic shrug.

"What the hell are you doing?" asked Winston. "Where are we?"

"It's alright, Grandpa," I said, in my kindest possible voice. "We're at that nice place I was telling you about."

A look of horror crept across Winston's face. "Grandpa? I'm not your grandpa! What is this?"

I rolled my eyes at Mr Rooney. "You see what I mean? Completely doolally."

He reached in and placed a gentle hand on Winston's arm. "It's alright, Winston. My name is Rodney. Rodney Rooney. You're going to come and stay with me for a little while."

"No!" screamed Winston. "It's all lies! They're tricking you! They killed a man! They killed a man and buried him in a field!"

Mr Rooney raised his eyebrows. "Did they indeed?"

"You don't understand! Our work is very important! We protect an ancient magic – these two have abused that magic! They have travelled through time-"

"Alright, that's enough," warned Mr Rooney. "If you don't calm down I'll have to get one of the nurses to sedate you."

He looked at me and I shook my head, circling my ear with my index finger to make one of those *'he's bloody mental'* gestures.

"No! Please," shouted Winston. "You have to listen to me…"

Nobody listens to old people.

That was the key. That was the weakness we had to exploit…

Mr Rooney got a firm grip on his arm and hoisted him out of the car. Gerald, who was still tied to Winston's foot, was dragged halfway out with him. He woke up with a start and began to panic, shouting and kicking the air in an attempt to free himself. Several other members of staff came out to see what the commotion was about and immediately began to assist Mr Rooney in subduing the cantankerous old codgers. Gerald managed to slip his foot out of the dressing gown cord and escape through the door on the opposite side of the car. He was caught approximately 10 seconds later by a young man-nurse named Greg who managed to drug him with Ovaltine and secure him in a wheelchair. When Winston saw this, he knew at once that resistance was futile, and relaxed his protestations considerably.

"So, Mr Cumberfield," said Rooney. "How will you be paying for their care?"

"Good question," I said. "But largely irrelevant. You see, I can't afford to pay for any of their care. I'm from what you might call a 'low-income' household. These two old duffers have been receiving benefits from the Council for many years now. The local government have agreed to fund everything."

"I see," said Mr Rooney. "And I suppose you have the paperwork to support all of this?"

"That, I do," I replied, producing an envelope. "That I do…"

I handed the envelope the Mr Rooney and bit the inside of my cheek, hoping beyond all hope that the documents would stand up to professional scrutiny. *They had better do*, I thought.

They cost me nearly £2000...

"Alright Cumberfield," snapped Rooney. "You win this round."

I thought that was a bit of a peculiar thing to say, since I hadn't been aware of any pre-existing competitive circumstances involving myself and Mr Rooney. It seemed to me that his tone was, well, inappropriately hostile, to say the least. Perhaps it was a joke…

"I'll revoke your ban," he said, begrudgingly. "But only because I can't stop you visiting your relative."

"Which relative?" I asked.

Mr Rooney looked puzzled.

"Oh," I said quickly. "You mean Wins-… I mean, Grandpa."

Rooney huffed. "I don't like you Cumberfield. You got that? I don't like you one bit. Just see to it that you stay out of my way while you're here. Understand?"

It was good to see Mr Rooney back to his old self – the whole 'ironic hatred' thing was one of his better gambits…

"So I'm not banned anymore?" I asked.

"No," he said. "You're not banned."

"Well that's fantastic news!" I cried, throwing my arms around his neck. "Just you wait, Mr Rooney. Just you wait… My next toy theatre production will be even bet-"

"No!" he screamed, pushing me away. "No more! No more of that fucking toy theatre bollocks! You hear me? No more! I can't fucking stand it!"

I laughed out loud. Vintage Rooney.

"Well," I said (when my laughter had subsided). "Since I'm no longer banned – perhaps I might pay a visit to an old friend?"

Rooney threw his arms up and stormed away. "Do whatever the hell you like, Cumberfield. I no longer give a shit."

Wow, I thought. *That guy must really love me.*

I left Roger sleeping in the car and made my way up the stairs to room number 42.

NINETEEN

IODINE AND OLD SOCKS

When I arrived at number 42, I noticed that the door was already slightly ajar, so I knocked gently a couple of times and showed myself in. The room was filled with boxes, and they were packed with clothes, books, ornaments, records and various other trinkets. Everything we had unpacked together that day was boxed up again, ready for moving...

How unusual, I thought. *Perhaps she didn't like it here after all? Maybe that wretched son of hers has stepped up to the plate and invited her to move in with him… Maybe…*

And then I saw him. His bulbous bottom was protruding from the cupboard, bursting out of his trousers like a hairy blimp. Nigel Fupplecock. Finally learning how to be a good son…

I cleared my throat. "Nigel, is it?"

I didn't need to check. I knew that was his name, but that's just what people say, isn't it? He turned around to receive me, and I noticed that there was a fairly substantial piece of Battenberg caught in his beard.

"Hello there," he said. "It's Walton, right?"

I smiled politely. "Right you are. Walton Cumberfield, to be exact."

"She said that you might come," he said, nodding morosely. "You're an old friend of hers, right?"

"Right again," I said with a grin.

He lifted a box of old shoes onto the bed and stood over it for a few seconds, recomposing himself as though the box had been incredibly heavy. It hadn't, of course. It was just shoes...

"Is she moving in with you?" I asked.

"I beg your pardon?"

"Well, I presume you're not packing up her things for the sheer amusement of it? Are you moving her into your place? I think she'd like that. I mean, this a nice home, but it's far better to have your family around, isn't it? Plus, the main lounge smells a bit like iodine and old socks."

Nigel took a deep breath and ran his big meaty hands through his unkempt, curly hair. Suddenly he looked at me – I mean, properly looked at me – looked me right in the eye and held my gaze for a good 30 seconds or so. I noticed that his eyes were bloodshot and glazed over. I suspected that he might have an infection or an allergy of some kind, but I didn't say anything. That would have been rude, after all.

"You haven't heard," he said, sitting down on the small armchair beside the bed.

"Heard what?" I asked.

He covered his face with his hands and knocked the lump of Battenberg out of his beard. It fell to the floor by his foot, which I think confused him for a moment. He glanced down at it, a brief suggestion of perplexity flickering across his face. *Where the heck did that come from?* Then the curiosity was gone, and all that was left was the grief. I could see it now – the slow indeterminate movements, the watery eyes… It wasn't the box that was heavy. It was his heart. I knew what had happened before he said the words, but they still pelted me like bullets to the soul.

"She passed away," he murmured. "Two nights ago."

I couldn't move. The saliva seemed to strain from my mouth as though my jaw had suddenly turned into a colander. A strange sort of dizzy sensation started in my nose and drifted up into my head, resting just behind my eyes as the first tears began to form in the corners. Everything was silent. My consciousness had blocked out the rest of the world. I still had my eyes open, but I don't think they were registering anything around me. I was alone in my head, with nothing but this sudden shocking truth for company.

I thought I was going to be sick, but then I wasn't sick.

It was Nigel who broke the silence again. He opened the drawer of Wendy's bedside cabinet and pulled out a small rolled-up piece of paper, which he held in both hands for some time.

"She left this for you," he said. "I didn't read it."

I tried to speak, but I couldn't. I wanted to say "that was good of you, thank you," but when I opened my mouth I felt the pain attempting to escape from my lungs, and I closed it again to stop the onslaught of misery that would otherwise have burst forth all over this poor man, who was clearly already in enough pain as it was. My lips were quivering as I took the paper from him, and I think that he noticed.

"You and my mother were close?" he asked.

I nodded and turned away, squeezing my eyes shut as salty tears slid down my cheeks and into my mouth, allowing me to taste the extent of my own despair. I sat on the end of the bed, facing away from Nigel, and wiped my face on my sleeve. The letter was tied up with a piece of green string. I slowly undid the bow and rolled it open, failing to notice an object concealed in the centre, which slid out and fell onto the floor.

Time had robbed it of its vibrant red shine, and much of the detail on the paintwork had been lost. I picked it up and held it gently, like a delicate, precious jewel.

"What is that?" asked Nigel. "What have you got there?"

I smiled slightly, but I did not reply. I still didn't feel capable of speech, and I was afraid that if I opened my mouth again I would just start bawling uncontrollably. Besides, how on earth was I supposed explain the significance of a 55 year old kazoo shaped like a dragon? I turned it over in my hands for a bit, and then carefully placed it to one side as my attention turned to the accompanying letter. The handwriting was neat and joined-up, just like she wanted my handwriting to be like when I was a boy. It never was, of course. I never quite got to grips with that.

I tried to read her words, but somewhere between the illegibility of her overtly elegant hand and the misty haze that covered my mournful eyes, I couldn't process their meaning.

"How did you know my mother?" asked Nigel.

I took a breath and managed to mumble a response. "We're old friends," I said, choking on the words. "She used to teach me back at school…"

"She was an excellent teacher," said Nigel. "She loved it dearly."

I nodded, but I couldn't look at him.

"Would you like a hot drink?" he asked.

I turned to him, slightly. "I don't suppose you've got any hot blackcurrant squash?"

"No," said Nigel. "I'm sorry."

"Then, no – thank you. I'll be alright."

I didn't know if that was true. It was too early to tell. I wiped the tears out of my eyes and unfolded the letter again. I swear to you, as I read those words, I could really hear her voice inside my head. It was just like in the films.

Walton,

If you are reading this then my dying wish has come true, and you are alive and well and back in the year 2010. When you told me last week that Keith Matthews had gone missing, I knew that it was time… I also knew that there was nothing I could do to stop you from leaving. The universe wouldn't let me, after all.

I don't know if I am writing this letter to a man or a ghost, but in many ways, I suppose that doesn't matter. You did not return to me that day in 1954, and you have not returned to me now. Yet somehow, I still know in my heart that you are alive, and that you will find your way back to me. Alas, I may not be here when you do.

I want to thank you for being who you are, for loving me, and for looking after me. I want to let you know that I do not hold anything against you for the circumstances of our relationship. You are a good man, Walton Cumberfield. The very best of them...

If you are reading this then you are alive, and I am gone. Please do not waste your energy on grief, but take heart in your own mortality. I have lived a long and happy life, and now you can do the same. I hope that you can do the same. I will die with that hope, but I will never know for sure. The world will still have its secrets when I die, and I will still have secrets from the world. I suppose that's just the way it goes.

Give my love to Roger. Tell him Ruth says hello. I think that she is still alive and living in Scotland somewhere if he wants to look her up!!!

I love you, Walton Cumberfield; in every way that a person can love another. Know that, and know that I will be with you forever.

Yours,

Wendy.

x x x

I turned the letter over to stop my tears from smudging the ink. Someone was hoovering in the corridor and it was annoying me, so I got up and slammed the door. Nigel was half-heartedly emptying the rest of her bedside cabinet and sorting through the contents. There were tears on his face now, but I suspected that they were secret tears, so I didn't let him know that I had noticed.

"It's not fair," I said, after a while.

"No," he agreed. "It isn't." He picked up an old clock radio and stared at it as though it were the root of all his suffering. "She shouldn't have died here."

The tears were coming thick and fast now. Perhaps they were still supposed to be secret tears, but there was no way he could keep them to himself any more. He tried to sniff away the sobs and wipe his face on his handkerchief, but it was no use. He was crumbling in front of my eyes. It was a jolly wretched thing to behold.

Nigel was at least 20 or 30 years older than me, and the years had rendered him with a fairly plump build and wrinkled skin. Everything about him seemed so adult – so incredibly man-like – and yet somehow, watching him squatting in the corner of his dead mother's room, bawling his eyes out like a toddler, I felt overwhelmingly paternal towards him.

"It's alright," I said, placing my hand on his shoulder. "She's gone to a better place."

"She should have been at home with me," he sobbed.

I agreed with him there, but it wouldn't have been appropriate to say that out loud.

"Don't punish yourself," I told him. "None of this is your fault."

"I should have been a better son."

I put my arm around his shoulders. "Hey, hey, hey, come on now… I'm sure you were a wonderful son." I didn't really know him very well, so I just had to guess at that one…

"I wasn't there for her when she needed me…"

Again, I suspected that was true, but I didn't say that. I just gripped his shoulder firmly and said; "Come on champ – she wouldn't want to see you like this. You've got to be strong. She'll be looking down on you now and saying, 'come on Nigel, pull yourself together. You're making a scene.'"

He laughed through the tears.

"That's my boy," I said. "Now, come on – I'll help you sort out this mess."

Somehow, pretending to be strong for Nigel made me feel stronger in myself. I stood up and picked up one of the empty boxes.

He managed to stop himself crying, but he still wanted to talk about it. I didn't mind. Clearly, he needed to get things off his chest.

"I left her here," he said. "I left her here alone. She hated to be alone."

"Well, she's not alone now," I told him, firmly. "She's with your father."

Nigel rolled his eyes. "Whoever that is."

"Your father," I repeated. "Mr Fupplecock."

"Albert wasn't my father," he said, shaking his head. "He and my mother met sometime after I was born. I took his surname because, well… it was the best thing to do, under the circumstances."

"So… you never knew your real father?"

"No. Mother said that he left before I was born. She said that it was a complicated situation. He was a good man, apparently, and he couldn't help what happened."

Now, as you are reading this you are probably beginning to get suspicious. I know I was at the time…

"When were you born, Nigel?" I asked.

He looked puzzled. "1955… July 27th, 1955."

I ran the numbers through my brain. 27th July, 1955... Approximately *nine months* after our romantic liaison. I knew what it meant. There was no getting away from it. I thought I was going to be sick, and then I wasn't sick.

"I don't believe it!" I said, out loud.

"Don't believe what?"

"How could she do this to me?"

"Do what?" he asked, looking very confused.

"Don't you see?" I yelled. "Whoever your father was, he conceived you in the winter of 1954! That's when *we* were together… That's when… Christ I just don't believe it!"

"Mr Cumberfield," said Nigel, apprehensively. "You're not making any sense."

"Lies!" I screamed. "It was all lies! The whole time she was with me she was sleeping with some other guy – this 'father' of yours! She was a rotten, two-timing, lying, cheatbag! Damn her! Damn her to hell!"

"Mr Cumber-"

"Don't talk to me!" I shouted. "I have nothing more to say! I am both shocked and appalled in equal measure!" I threw the empty cardboard box onto the floor and kicked it into the cupboard.

"Have you gone completely mad?" he shouted.

"No, sir." I declared. "In fact, for the first time in a long time I am seeing things quite clearly, and I will not stay here to be made a fool out of any longer!"

I screwed up the letter and pitched it across the room. It was all a lie. If she had really loved me then who the heck was this other guy? Who had she slept with to get pregnant with Nigel? I didn't know. I didn't *want* to know. The thought of it made me sick to my stomach.

"I am sorry for your loss," I told him. "But it is no longer *my* loss. I am sorry to say it, but your mother is dead to me now."

"Well, yes – she's dead to me too."

"Really?" I asked. "Why? What did she do?"

"She died."

"Oh right," I said. "Fair enough."

I would realise my mistake in time, of course. I (Walton Cumberfield) was Nigel's biological father. It should have been obvious, shouldn't it? I don't know – perhaps my mind was in too fragile a state to make a sensible analysis of the information I was presented with. Perhaps subconsciously I wanted to believe she was two-timing me so that I could hate her to make her passing that little bit easier. Perhaps I was just too bloody knackered from staying up the night before... I don't know, but the important thing is that I learnt the truth of it all in the end. Actually it was Nigel who set me straight on the matter. As it turns out, he has inherited my enthusiasm for sleuthing and was determined to understand what the bloomin' heck I was going on about that day in his mother's room. He started with the letter I had discarded, which led him to Ruth Routhorn, who filled him in with the truth of his parentage. He told me all this in a card he sent to me the following year (on Father's Day) and we subsequently bonded by building a carnival float together for the Mayday parade… but that's another story, for another time…

For now I didn't know he was my son. I didn't know that Wendy had been true to me all along. I didn't know what a perfect arse I was being.

I shook Nigel by the hand and took one last look around the room. Then I pulled up my trousers and left the area. I really must buy a new belt.

TWENTY

BURN IN HELLESDON

The breakfast snack I like the most,
As I sit there and munch, engrossed,
In reading all the morning post,
Is just a simple piece of toast...

The following morning I popped a couple of slices of bread in the toaster and tried to get myself back into poetry again. The weather was brightening up, Roger's smartphone was fully charged, and things were just about getting back to normal. For the first time in ages, I felt happy and calm. I felt like being creative again…

It puts you in a vibrant mood,
The finest of all breakfast foods…
So raise your glass from coast to coast
And let's all give a toast… to toast.

Perfect. I read the poem over and over again. It was flawless – perhaps the best poem I had written all year. I grabbed Roger's smartphone and set about uploading it to The Facebook. The morning, it seemed, was going from brilliant to fabulous…

Aaron Michaels
Just got back from seeing my doctor. Turns out I have gonorrhoea again. :-(

Like · Comment · 8 hours ago via mobile ·

Walton Cumberfield likes this.

My toast popped up with a 'click' and I skipped over to retrieve it. Unfortunately, it wasn't quite done properly on one side, so I shoved it down for a second go. Mine wasn't the greatest toaster in the world, you see. To the best of my memory, I purchased it from the same chap who sold me a black thermal overcoat (complete with face mask) without informing me of its religious connotations. You'll be pleased to hear that I don't really go to car boot sales any more.

As I returned to the kitchen table to open my letters, the room was suddenly alive with the sound of *Who Let The Dogs Out?* – a catchy little jingle which I downloaded and selected as the ring tone to Roger's phone (the Frank Sinatra version, not the 'Baha Men' version).

Although I was loathed to do it, I silenced the jolly melody by pressing the green button and taking the call.

"Hello?"

"*Roger?*" said the voice on the other end. "*Is that you?*"

"No, this is Walton Cumberfield," I said. "Roger is my lodger. Would you like me to get him for you?"

Roger was asleep upstairs, I think. He hadn't been back to work yet because he said he had a 'nervous stomach' – whatever that means…

"I beg your pardon?" said the voice.

"This is Walton Cumberfield." I repeated. "Who is this?"

The line was very crackly and I was getting a lot of feedback, but the person on the other end seemed to be saying; "*This is Walton Cumberfield.*"

"Could you repeat that please?" I said. "The line is very crackly and I'm getting a lot of feedback."

"This is Walton James Cumberfield," said the voice. *"Who am I speaking with?"*

"You are Walton James Cumberfield?"

"Yes."

Of course. We had left for The Old Dog and Bottle yesterday morning, so by now I would be standing in the kitchen and using this very phone to make a call… to *this* very phone!

"Oh yes," I said. "I remember. Sorry about the line – I think it's because you're phoning the phone that you're using to phone with. Never mind. Can you hear me alright?"

"Just about."

"Yes, of course…"

I tried to recall what I was doing that morning. We had been up late drinking with Cedric the night before, and then… Then I had suffered a restless night dreaming of Oscar's ghost. Then, what was I doing the day after? Where was I when I made the call? Oh yes – I was standing in the pub kitchen, looking for Roger. That's right – I was looking for Roger and I was about to eat some time cheese for the very first time. I remembered now. I remembered the sticky, stale cheese on toast that Roger had left behind. It was all coming back to me, and it made me wretch just thinking about it. "Listen," I said. "I know it's a bit unpleasant but you're going to have to eat some of that time cheese…"

"Hello?" said the other me. *"Are you still there?"*

"Yes I am. Now, you're going to have to eat some of that time cheese. Take a bite from the toast and throw the rest away…"

"No," he said. *"I didn't get any of that. You're breaking up."*

"Oh right," I said. "Sorry about that. I was just saying you're going to have to take a bite of that time cheese – it'll send you back in time to 1954. That's where Roger has gone. So take a bite, and throw the rest away…"

"Again," he said. *"I'm getting a lot of feedback. What are you saying?"*

"I'm saying that I know it's a bit unpleasant but what you need to do is eat some of Roger's cheese on toast and throw the rest away. Do you remember the ghost you met last night in your dream? Well, just do what he told you to do and then everything will turn out okay."

There was no reply – just a faint buzzing.

"Come on, Walt! Remember? You met him last night in the cellar… He told you to eat of the cheese. Just do as he says…"

I could smell burning... My toast should have popped up again by now, but it hadn't. I turned back to the kitchen counter and saw a plume of black smoke billowing from the bread slot.

"Okay, sorry, I have to go," I said. "My toaster is on fire."

I hung up the phone and lunged across the room to quell the emergent inferno. I had never been in that sort of situation before, you understand, so I didn't really know what I was doing. First I tried to cover it with a tablecloth, but that didn't seem to help. In fact, the tablecloth caught on fire as well, and I lost valuable firefighting minutes by taking it upstairs and extinguishing it in the bath. By the time I returned to the toaster, the fire had spread to Roger's collection of old cellulose nitrate film reels, which I had told him on more than one occasion not to leave lying around in the kitchen.

"Damn it Roger!" I shouted, taking my largest coffee mug and filling it with water from the sink. "What did I tell you?"

Boom.

For some reason, when I poured water over the flaming appliance, it caused some sort of horrendous electrical explosion, sending me tumbling to the floor in a heap, shielding my face as sheets of burning metal flew across the room in every direction. Roger must have heard the commotion, because he soon came trotting down the stairs to see what 'the hell' was going on.

"What the hell is going on?" he cried. "What have you done?"

"Me?" I scoffed. "You're the one who insists on keeping your collection of cellulose nitrate film reels on the kitchen worktop!"

The room was filling with smoke now, and it was making me feel nauseous.

"Call the fire brigade!" he shouted, using a tea towel to waft the smoke away from his face.

"No," I said, struggling to my feet. "I don't want strange people in my house. They might steal things."

"It's the fire brigade!" he yelled. "They're not going to steal from you!"

He fought away more of the smoke and dashed over to the freezer on the other side of the room, coughing and spluttering. "Where's the time cheese?"

"Where's the what?"

"The time cheese! Where did you put it?"

I opened the window to let out some of the smoke. "Why does that matter, now?"

"Because we can't let it burn," he said. "I still have to go back in time and make that hole in that wall. Remember? We *need* that cheese!"

"Don't worry about that," I said. "There's a fire extinguisher in the loft. It'll be alright."

I scurried off up the stairs leaving Roger rooting through our frozen goods in the sooty smog like a massive wally. His time would have been better spent quelling the flames, not trying to save the time cheese! The very fact that he had not yet used the cheese to repay his debt to the universe meant that it *couldn't* be destroyed in the fire, but I knew he was too simple to get his head around that. Personally, I didn't want anything more to do with the stuff. I hated time-travel – It made things so extraordinarily complicated. I remember saying to Roger as I packed it away in the freezer *"this bloody time cheese will be the death of me."*

I opened the loft hatch and pulled the ladder towards me. That part always freaked me out. I always thought it was going to hit me in the head. I think that's because this one time, when I was trying to pull it out, it, well, it hit me in the head... So it was a rational concern… Also, as I've said before, I never really got to grips with the various catches and hinges that facilitate its operation. And this day was no exception.

When the ladder was about halfway down to the ground it jammed. The top section refused to slide down to the floor. This had happened to me once before, but I had somehow managed to free it with a bit of fiddling about. On this occasion however, I simply didn't have the time. I could feel the floor getting hotter beneath my feet. I *had* to get to that fire extinguisher… I just *had* to… I reached up and grabbed the ladder, hoisting myself onto it, my legs dangling beneath me like a gangly goon. I was never very good at gymnastics, you see – I didn't have the upper body strength for it. However, I did manage to pull myself up a few rungs and wedge my knees onto the bottom to gain some stability.

That's when it happened.

I heard something slide out of position with a sharp 'ping' as the bottom half of the ladder started falling to the floor. I began to let go, but I wasn't quick enough, and before I knew it the side of my right hand was trapped between the sliding rungs of sharp, rusty metal. An intense pain shot up through my arm and roared inside my head as I dropped onto the carpet, gripping my injury and wailing like a Japanese hunter. The sliding metal had guillotined two of my fingers clean off, and warm blood was pouring down my forearm. The final piece of the puzzle fell into position with an earth-shattering thud as I stared at the mangled stumps where my ring finger and little finger had been severed from the rest of my hand.

"What's up with that?" Roger had said, pointing at the gloveless hand. "He's only got three fingers."

The stumps were healed over, and they had been for a long time…

He had come into my room with a lump of Oscar's time cheese – a doddery old man who didn't know any better.

"Are you awake darling?" he had said.

He didn't even know what had happened. He must have gone senile like Clive Howard's grandfather. He must have forgotten about the cheese…

"Do you want some of this?" he had asked. "It's very good."

That's why we didn't see anyone else going into the house that night. He didn't enter through the front door. He must have materialised in our kitchen – crashing about because the time-travel had left him disorientated. He came back upstairs to his bedroom and tried to speak to his wife, or at least somebody who he referred to as *darling*…

And then I beat him to death with *The Guinness Book of Records.*

He didn't have a clue what was happening. He didn't mean to do me any harm. And the worst part of it all…

He was me.

Effectively speaking, I had accidentally committed suicide.

My head dropped back onto the carpet and I whispered a bad word. I heard the distant sound of sirens as the room began fading to black, and my last thought before passing out was what a perfect bloody idiot I'd turned out to be after all.

*

When I got out of hospital I took all of the time cheese into the living room and lit a roaring fire, thinking, perhaps foolishly, that I could burn it all – every last scrap – thus creating a paradox that rendered my inevitable demise to be impossible. It was a hopeless endeavour, of course. I should have learnt by then that I couldn't outsmart the universe. You see, the universe is very, very big, and I am very, very small. No matter what happens, the universe will always win.

I threw the first piece of cheese into the fire. It bubbled and burst with an awful stink as the flames obliterated it. I picked up the second chunk, and the fire went out. Then there was a power cut. Then a pigeon flew into my window with a *splat* and startled me so much that I let out a very girly scream. It was like the universe was shouting "stop it!"

The fire wouldn't light again after that.

I opened up the freezer and replaced the cheese, tucking it away at the back behind Roger's special ice cream. I couldn't change the past, and I couldn't change my future. My destiny was set, and there was nothing I could do except embrace it. I closed the freezer and tried my best to forget about it for the time being. Roger would still need to use the cheese at some point anyway – he still had to repay his debt to the universe, and dig that hole in Budleigh Salterton. For the next few weeks I kept asking him when he was going to see his way to sorting that out, but he kept changing the subject to *Come Dine With Me* related banter.

In order to take my mind off the failed attempt to destroy the cheese, I went out to the shed and began work on my next brilliant toy theatre production for Rodney Rooney's. It was going to be the best one yet – just as I had promised. I had a great idea for a new story, about a hero named Wilson Cumberbatch and his lodger Robert who set off on an adventure to solve a great mystery involving a murder, a haunted pub and a mysterious piece of cheese. I wanted to call it something peculiar and abstract – some sort of reference to one of the more subtle recurring elements of the story, like *Dinosaurs and Prime Numbers*, but Roger thought that this title was 'a bit gay'. I ended up calling it *A Study In Stilton*, even though the cheese in question wasn't really anything like stilton. Roger gave me the idea from one of his Sherlock Holmes stories, which he let me read.

Now that got me thinking about how easy Sherlock's job would have been if he too had an ample supply of time cheese. After all, he wouldn't have to spend ages solving the crime; he could just eat some of his time cheese, go back in time, see who did it, come back to the present again, and reveal the culprit. "*Not too shabby, Sherlock*," the others would say. "*You truly are the world's greatest detective…*"

And so it was that the next time I opened up my freezer and noticed the stash of cheese hiding behind the ice cream like a silent predator, I wasn't filled with such a foreboding sense of dread. Okay, so one day I would lose my mind, defrost some of that cheese, eat it, travel to the past and end up getting manslaughtered by my former self with *The Guinness Book of Records…* but *heck*, I thought, *there has to be a positive side to all of this.* After all, you never know when a bit of time cheese might come in handy…

…and come in handy it did. But that, dear friends, is another story…

For another time…

THE END

FURTHER READING

Subscribe to Walton's blog at **www.waltoncumberfield.com** for exclusive content and news and from the world of Walton Cumberfield.

You can also follow Walton on Twitter: **@iamwalton**

Tom Moran can be contacted on tom_moran2@hotmail.com

WALTON CUMBERFIELD
WILL RETURN
IN
A DEBT TO THE UNIVERSE
(Autumn 2013)

ACKNOWLEDGEMENTS

Thank you to everyone who made this book possible, for all your help, support, guidance and feedback. Special thanks go to my brother, Bob, for the cover design and general creative encouragement, Rose Tomaszewska, Simon Routhorn, Ant Cule and Joz Norris for reading my drafts and helping me to improve them, and finally to my wife, Jemma, for putting up with all the madness.

No doubt, there will be more to come.

ABOUT THE AUTHOR

Tom Moran is a writer, comedian, actor and husband. He is 0.0012 miles in height, and weighs approximately 0.083 metric tons.

Tom lives in Norwich with his wife and Ford Fiesta. This is his first novel.

4125706R00176

Printed in Great Britain
by Amazon.co.uk, Ltd.,
Marston Gate.